almost

almost

a love story

anne eliot

Butterfly Books, LLC

This book is a work of fiction. Names, characters, places, and incidents are the product of the author's imagination or are used fictitiously. Any resemblance to actual events, places, organizations, or persons living or dead, is a coincidence.

ALMOST, Published by Butterfly Books, LLC

Copyright © Anne MacFarlane 2012, writing as Anne Eliot.

1 3 5 7 9 10 8 6 4 2

ISBN: 978-1-937815-01-1 (Print Version)
Butterfly Books, LLC. First Ed. 2012, Cataloging Information:
Eliot, Anne
Almost / Anne Eliot

Summary: Three years after an attempted rape, Jess wants to trick her parents into believing she's better, so she hires a fake boyfriend who helps her come to terms with the night that changed her forever.

1. Young Adult Romance—Juvenile fiction. 2. High schools—Fiction.

3. Rape—Fiction. 4. PTSD Post Traumatic Stress Disorder—Fiction.

Original Cover Photo — by Kika and Anne MacFarlane.
Book design and cover art— by Peter Freedman
Original Cover Font, *Soymilk* used with permission from creator, Denise Bentulan

Printed in the United States of America

dedication

for a: You got away with broken ribs and everyone saying that you were 'a very lucky girl' when you felt the opposite. Your strength and your reassurance that others might need this story inspired me to keep going. Thanks for teaching me what courage looks like.

I published this and found some courage of my own because of you.

for b: You spent many years hiding behind your beautiful smile and trying to forget. We should have told the police, our parents, anyone. We should have talked about it more. I'm sorry.

I wrote this for you.

for c. d. e. f. g. h. i. j. k. l. m. n. o. p. q. r. s. t. u. v. w. x. y. & z: So many of you have shared personal stories with me since this book was first published as an e-book. Stories about amazing guys who did the right thing. Stories of girls and women who were hurt, scared and sad. Stories about how you're 'okay' and/or still living with being almost, very nearly, and not quite *over it* every single day of your lives.

I'm humbled and grateful for your honesty, your perseverance, strength, and for supporting this story.

thank you.

1

jess

The third Red Bull was a mistake. I should've munched some actual food before parking at the interview. But I didn't. Too nervous.

So now, my stomach is liquid snakes and spinning nails. My bad.

I raise the volume on my iPhone and pull one leg past the steering wheel so I can half-curl up next to the door. Not easy in the driver's seat of a Jeep. But very do-able if you're short. It's also surprisingly comfortable if you have the right blanket.

I have the right blanket. Brown, double plush and fleecy. Mine is a gift from my little sister. She's the only one who knows how often I nap in here. Last February, she thought I'd freeze during my school lunch naps so she bought it for me with her babysitting money. She's always trying to help me catch up on lost sleep.

Unfortunately, thanks to my breakfast of *stupid,* no one can help me today. I won't be catching up on any lost sleep either. Worse, I think I might puke in the parking lot of Geekstuff.com before the interview starts. Maybe during.

Wouldn't that be epic?

Excuse me, Mr. CEO-Guy-I-Want-To-Impress. Could you hold

that question while I BARF BARF BARF?

They'd probably assume I was hung over. Or a drug addict! Which…I suppose, I am. Everyone knows caffeine is a drug, after all. And I'm definitely addicted to it.

My stomach clenches and twists again so hard I want to cry. Instead, I close my eyes and breathe slowly, willing the energy drinks—more importantly that amazing caffeine—to stick. The cool glass against my forehead seems to help and the cramps fade away.

Thank you, God.

I snuggle deeper into the blanket and try to focus on my interview plan. The iPhone is playing classical. Classical works best when I want to visualize end results. Tactics.

Olympic athletes run their moves before they compete too.

I know landing the summer internship at Geekstuff.com is no Olympics. But to me, this interview is the most important competition of my life. Without this job, my future is doomed.

I see myself enter the same room where I beat thirty applicants yesterday.

The CEO asks to see my mock product samples. *He's impressed!* I imagine myself smiling and being all social. I mention that I own most of the 'geek-toys' department. How I can't wait to see the inner workings of an online store.

The social part is hardest. All bluff and faking it. But me, owning the products, is complete truth. I love every geek-gadget, toy and t-shirt they sell here—even the Star Wars stuff. There's no cooler company in the world.

I run through the sales history and the $34.00 price of my favorite product: *The Mood Jelly Fish Lamp.* I imagine saying: *I can't live without this awesome lamp.*

Another truth. I love the lamp. It's my nightlight.

I'm smiling, accepting the internship—handshake and all—when something slams into my Jeep.

Hard.

Not with another car—but with a fist or a body! *I don't know what*—because my eyes were closed! The Jeep rocks. I whack my knees into the steering wheel while my head hits the window with a dull *thunk*. When I look up I'm almost nose-to-nose with a guy. A guy who's peering into the windshield like he wanted to see my reaction to his lame prank!

I recognize him from my school: Gray Porter. Junior—soon to be Senior. Same as me.

And not one of my usual tormentors.

My carefully constructed interview-bun slips. Wisps of curly frizz fall around my shoulders. *Perfect.*

Feeling overexposed like some caged circus act, I manage to paste on one of my defensive sneers. "What was that about— *jerk?*" I shout. I know he heard me.

But the guy doesn't move. He's just staring. Not even blinking.

So I stare back. It's all I can do not to blush like a dork. I haven't been this close to a guy—heck—anyone besides my family, in years. That's when I notice Gray Porter might own the most stunning, crystal-green eyes on the entire planet.

Holy wow…

It takes all my strength to hold the pissed-off expression in place and repeat myself: "I said, what was that about? JERK."

I try to read his expression. I'm really good at that. He seems alarmed. Or does he look…apologetic? Or high?

Weird. And double-WTF?

I take stock of myself. My heart's pounding jacked-up-stereo loud, but he can't hear it through the glass. I check my hands gripped on the steering wheel. Thankfully, they've got no signs of visible trembling.

After three years of practice, I'm a master at keeping all body shakes hidden. Even so, he's got me so rattled I have to work to decide my next move. Why is he still staring? I must need a more scathing expression on my face. I choose *fearless scorn*—one of my best. Took months to perfect this one. I sneer, and twist my lip.

Ba-Bam.

That got his attention, because he just turned all red. He's opened his mouth like he's going to say something.

As if there's anything to say.

I fire out my *dismiss-the-dumbass* blinks as fast as I can.

And bam-ba-bam, bam, bam!

He winces and steps back.

Then, like it never happened—or like he's wised up and is finally afraid of me—the guy executes a 180 to dash across the parking lot. He's making a beeline for Geekstuff.com's massive front door.

I let out a tight breath, uncurl my aching fingers from the steering wheel and jump out with my bag in tow. I can't gain any ground. He's easily over six-feet-huge and that includes some long legs. I'm only five-four. No way I'll catch him unless I order him to stop. Or run him down like a dog.

Not my style.

I'm all about control, fast smack-downs and keeping people at a distance with my ever-expanding repertoire of rock-solid, *back-off* expressions. (Expressions laced with eye-snapping sarcasm and disdain, of course.) It's been a lot of staring-in-the-mirror hard work. But my skills are perfected.

I've recently convinced *the best therapist in town* that I'm well enough to move on to college. I didn't even have to lie. I simply deleted info, kept the expressions in check, hid my messed up sleep schedule, and POOF: Everyone thinks I'm *cured*.

What I think is that I'm tired of talking about the things that will never be fixed.

As in me. How I'm *almost* better. *Almost* back to normal.

After trying things their way for so long, I got tired of waiting. I've made a ton of progress with faking it, that's for sure. And so far, so good. No, I'm not 'better'. I'm the same; but none of my pretending seems to make me worse. So it's kind of working. And there's been one huge change that works for all of us. My parents and little sister have never been happier.

Them, being happy, is about as close to *me* being happy as I'll ever get. It's enough.

If I can make more *progress* (Mom's favorite word) I get to apply to colleges next year. They promised. This means I'll get my life back, head to the dorms and move out from under the parent microscope. Out of sight, out of mind, right?

I'm going to be what they want this whole year: *Just fine. Fine. Fine. Fine.*

I stop to catch my breath, trying to decipher why Gray Porter chose today to join the ranks of people who mess with me. He's never talked to me once—I'd remember. Because I'm sure I'd never forget those amazing green eyes. Who could forget those things?

As I look around the Geekstuff.com parking lot it takes only seconds to realize the visitor side is completely empty—besides my car and his. It must be *me* against *him* for the final interview. I suppose he's trying to start the battle early.

The guy's taking the front steps two at a time, and I swear he's talking to himself. I wonder if he might be more of a freak than me. Just in case he decides to look back, I hold my position and stare holes into his obviously new, package-creased, button-down interview shirt as he disappears inside the building.

Good luck you poser—you bully. That's the only point you're going to get.

I glance at the time on my iPhone. Five minutes to spare. He's probably watching me from inside the lobby—or maybe he's setting up some sort of trip line.

I start forward at an ultra-slow pace. I'm scouring my brain for any school gossip I might be able to use against him. This kid and I run in completely different circles. His circle is popular and cool, and my circle takes me from school to the teacher's lounge. For excitement, I hit the nearest store with a Red Bull aisle. He goes to parties, and football games and all that other stuff. I never even see this guy in the halls.

The only real memory I have of Gray goes back to the day he helped Jenna Shattuck when she broke her arm.

Major broke her arm.

It's one of those mythic school tales. Re-told every year to all incoming students. It happened freshman year, second semester. A few days after I'd come back to school from my 'special months' at home. Months spent munching bottle after bottle of anti-depressants and almost going off the deep end. Forever.

Everyone swears they saw Jenna fall. I really did.

Back then, I'd been hanging in the bleachers *not* participating thanks to a doctor's note. I hadn't worked out how to hide my emotions yet. Not like I do now.

I did a lot of looking down that year. Shoe staring. Counting tiles. Grossing myself out by analyzing dirt in corners. That kind of stuff.

I wouldn't talk to anyone, either. Opening my mouth used to make me cry for no reason. Something about feeling air hit the back of my throat set it off. It was humiliating for me and beyond awkward for anyone who came near me, so no one did. I prefer it that way, anyhow.

Jenna tripped and broke her arm during a volleyball game. She fell right in front of my feet. She was hard to miss. Her hand twisted under her, and there'd been lots of snapping. Like someone walking on sticks. When she sat up, her bones had come through the skin in two places near her wrist. Another jutted out higher—above her elbow.

Total freak show. She'd hit an artery.

Jenna never once made a sound. Just blinked and blinked. Blood spattered the gym floor—tons of it—like it was falling from the fire sprinklers, and the teacher screamed so loudly everyone thought *she'd* been hurt.

No one else moved or made a single sound either. Not for the longest time, including me. Especially me.

Jenna—probably all of us—had been in shock. I know shock. It's when you can't process or do anything properly during a messed up situation. Often—after—you might not recall one bit of what happened. Jenna still swears she doesn't remember falling.

Gray had been the only one to step up. He sort of saved her.

He took Jenna's face in his hands. Very gently...I do remember that. He tilted her chin toward his so she couldn't see her arm or any of the blood. He also blocked her view of the teacher, who by that point, had quieted because she'd vomited under the basketball net.

"Look right here. Right at me," Gray said, signaling someone to run to the office. He wrapped her arm with the sleeve of his hoodie and applied pressure like some sort of first-aid expert.

"Keep your eyes on me, Jenna," he said. "The nurse is coming. She's going to get your parents. Just hold on. Stay with me. Eyes on mine. Right here. You're going to be fine, Jenna. Just *fine*."

I shudder as I remember the sound of his voice. He'd been kind. Confident. Worried. Afraid.

Today, after the close-up view of his green eyes, I now understand why Jenna hadn't moved the whole time.

He'd hypnotized her with those things.

I shake my head and sigh. Gray's not a bully. He's the opposite, which is much, much worse. He's a hero. Hero guys tend to win stuff even if they aren't qualified.

He's probably here at this second interview because he pulled off something impressive and cool-headed yesterday, but what? Kitten rescue? Toddler running in front of a bus? The CEO choking on a mini-solar phone charger?

Let's hope not.

I hadn't even considered the possibility of losing this internship to someone else.

But what if? What if Gray wins it?

I can't let that happen. I can't. I won't.

I take in a few more long breaths and switch my expression to *serene* and *confident* as I hop up the curb leading to the front steps. Confidence beats any other emotion when trying to convince people you've got things handled. I need Geekstuff. com to believe I've got what it takes, and now I need Gray to believe it too.

How hard could it be to return his lame attempt at a shake down with one of my own? All I can do is what I know. Fake it, stay awake, smile, and see what happens.

The Geekstuff.com people can find out *after* they hire me they've picked the lemon.

As for Gray Porter? He can *suck it* on the way out.

The stinging in my forehead intensifies to remind me the guy inside the lobby is already one point ahead. I reach up and find a huge, warm lump above my right eye. It's bad—like a mutant spider bite—and it hurts.

Of course it does. Fine.

He's two points ahead. I'll give him two.

I pull more bangs loose so the lump is covered, and I add Gray Porter to my 'hate list', right between seashells and parties. I feel instantly stronger. My hate list hasn't changed in years.

Total proof of progress! If only I could share this one with my mom. But she doesn't know I like to keep lists. Either way. I'm calling it.

One point for me.

2

gray

Does she remember? Does she remember me?

"I should've left her alone. I can't learn. *I can't learn*," I say, not even trying to whisper as bile settles at the back of my throat—more with every step *Jess Jordan* takes in my direction. I couldn't be happier the lights in the lobby of Geekstuff. com are off. Because it's Sunday, it appears no one is waiting to greet me for the interview.

To greet *us*. Holy shit. *Me and Jess Jordan.*

I cringe, hating the idea of being trapped in this room with her.

I push away the images of the party that changed—no—*ruined*—both of our lives freshman year.

Does she remember? Does she remember me?

"I did the right thing to wake her up," I say even louder. As though noise could drown out my questions, hide my cowardice and undo what I did wrong out there in the parking lot. What I didn't do right at that party years ago...

Goose bumps plaster my arms as I replay the promise I made to this girl's parents three years ago: *Stay out of Jess Jordan's radar and don't go near her. Ever.* A promise I'd kept faithfully for three years—until today.

Of course I'd kept it. Her psycho mom told me if I approached Jess, the girl would suffer a serious setback. Or a flashback, or... something terrible.

I would have promised anything back then. Hell, I'd offered to do way more, but her parents wouldn't let me. They only wanted me to stay away from their daughter. I didn't want to risk Jess suffering any more hurt, so I agreed to never approach her.

Only, crap! I just did *way* more than approach her. I accidentally scared the hell out of her. Then I blinked at her like a gaping dork. And ran. Let's not forget *that* classy move.

My pack's heavy. Full of mock *product ideas* required for the second interview today. Mine are hockey pucks in various duct-taped configurations. And, I'm pretty sure they suck, but I didn't want to show up empty handed. Who knew they'd sound like an exploding bomb when slammed into her Jeep? It's not like I slam my backpack into random vehicles to test the sound it's going to make.

She's stopped walking, and now she's staring at the front door. Probably planning how she's going to kill me.

I swallow and scan the room for exit signs.

"If I'd left her there asleep? If I'd walked away...then what?" I mutter, glancing quickly over my shoulder to make sure I'm still alone. I contemplate leaving again, but this makes me angry with myself and unfairly, at her.

I want this internship. I can't afford to walk away from an $8K payoff and perfect working hours for me.

ME. This is about me! Me. Me. Me.

Not Jess Jordan.

I'd figured Jess had parked behind the dumpsters to pull some sort of surprise attack. At the very least she'd been trying to eye the competition. It's why I'd shown up early. I'll admit that. I'd wanted to call her bluff. Let Jess know her car had been spotted.

But then...*hell.* I saw her. Sleeping away in that Jeep, blanket and all. Acting as though she didn't have a care in the world. I must've been struck with temporary insanity. That, or a giant alien magnet had drawn me straight out of my car and right to the side of hers.

She'd been so far gone, I'd spent three good minutes peeking over her dash watching her breathe. All that time, I tried to convince myself to leave her there. Jess, missing this interview, should've been my personal gift from fate. A gift I well deserved after all the bullshit I've had to eat because of her—that night—that party.

I'd almost had myself talked into bolting, when she'd smiled in her sleep. Held out her hand like she was having a strange dream.

After that, I couldn't leave her there alone. Wouldn't.

What went down at that party years ago wasn't her fault. It wasn't my fault, either.

Not directly.

But I'm not one to repeat my mistakes—that's for sure. Maybe I screwed up by freaking her out; but I wasn't about to leave Jess Jordan needing something from *me* ever again.

I run my hand through my hair and manage to swallow the tight ball of what feels like dry, *scared-shitless-dirt* lodged at the back of my throat. The nagging questions won't stop: *Does she remember? Does she remember me?*

I don't know why I'm worried about that. From what her parents told me—from my careful *non-interactions* with her— Jess has no idea who I am. No memory of the night I stopped her from being raped by a senior asshole at a hockey party. The night I chickened out and ran out on her after she'd asked me to stay. God...I'd been such a loser that year.

I'd done my best to make it right *after.*

After is when the guys on the team beat the shit out of me for blowing the whistle. *After* is when I quit playing competitive ice hockey when the coach wouldn't prosecute the player who tried to hurt Jess. *After* is always too late. I've learned that lesson the hard way.

No such thing as re-plays or penalty points in real life, no matter how valid and real the fouls might be.

I eye the large, over-stuffed bag Jess has brought along for her interview. I can only imagine the perfect product samples she's concocted to win this internship. The girl's loaded, has straight A's, and adults love her. I can guarantee her product samples won't be made out of tape, hope and bullshit like mine.

The people who run this place must have fallen for her big-time. But they'd liked me too! Invited me back—like they'd invited her. Yesterday, the CEO, Mr. Foley, told me I *have the creativity and motivation Geekstuff.com looks for in an intern.*

And hell yes, I do.

Desperation and an empty wallet makes for buckets of *creativity and motivation.*

I stare, knowing she can't see me behind this door. I take in her small frown, fair skin, and determined expression. She's sporting some brown, geek-girl shoes, and her long legs are hidden under the weirdest grey skirt I've ever seen. Her strange pioneer/nerd outfits are always a source of school conversations.

Looking at her now, I remember my stupid freshman crush on this girl. How she'd always had this easy smile and quiet laughter. How she also blew me off every time I came near, and how empty and lost her eyes had seemed after she'd come back to school.

I pull in a ragged breath. I think Jess was the lucky one to have her slate wiped clean. Remembering all this time has been hell. As much as she might *not* know me—as much as I've worked to keep myself away from her radar—I've been tracking this girl out of the corners of my eyes ever since.

Jess makes it to the landing and pauses. For the second time today, glass is the only thing separating her face from mine. It's impossible not to notice how beautiful she still is.

A trickle of sweat drips between my shoulders and my knees start this embarrassing quaking thing. Exploding grenade heartbeats kill my chest, reminding me—*begging me*—to do the right thing. Only, after my backpack move, after staring at her like this, I have no idea what the *right thing* is supposed to be anymore.

I hold my ground and decide to play it out. It's not like this same girl can trash my life twice. I've already broken the promise I made to her parents. I can't erase the fact that she's seen me up close. Way too close. If the girl is going to have some sort of episode or flashback thing—then I suppose I should hang around.

Try to make things right, or call an ambulance—or something.

I step into a darker part of the room, watching as she frowns at her reflection in the door. She pauses to mess with her bangs.

"Besides, I'm staying because I need the money," I mutter, over and over again.

But I can't silence the nagging truth: I'm simply too curious to leave. I wonder...I want to know...

Does she remember me at all?

3

jess

All of my imagined *warrior-princess-bravado* fades when
I'm vanquished by Geekstuff.com's gigantic door. As I push
through, it knocks me forward like a paper doll. It's all I can do
to save myself from tripping flat on my face in the dark lobby.
The contents of my bag create a junk and paper waterfall. I
manage to maintain my mask of composure by keeping my
eyes trained on the
scattering mess.

Make-up containers and my precious iPhone have been
ejected like bullets. They travel the farthest, coming to a rest
at the base of the receptionist's paisley-shaped, and thankfully,
vacated desk.

It's not lost on me in this air-conditioned battlefield that
my breathing sounds embarrassingly erratic next to Gray's very
calm and *employable* steady intakes of breath.

He's somewhere on my right.

I glance through my lashes and find his navy blue Converse
moving toward the epicenter of my mess. I move in the opposite direction. As he bends to scoop up a few of my things, I'm
completely aware that the guy has open access to my interview
secrets.

This makes me feel slightly ill and annoyed at myself for losing control of my things.

And of myself. I never lose control of that.

I panic for a moment and look into my bag, relaxing a little when I realize it's only my makeup and product samples—about twenty bumper-stickers—that have spilled. The résumés and the ridiculous 'How to Be Normal' checklist my ever-helpful sister handed me this morning, must still be at the bottom of my bag.

Safe.

I'm proud of the bumper stickers so…let him look. Maybe they'll intimidate him.

Because I'm not prepared to have any sort of intelligible smack-down session—a session that *must* happen soon, I go after the other stuff.

I scoop up my phone and the *Sunshine Glow Mineral Powder* first. This item has exploded into beige dust-bombs a few times in my bag. I'm happy to find it's intact and not all over the eggplant-colored carpet. I hate the junk, but it's the only product that can wipe out the permanent dark circles I have under my eyes from not sleeping at night.

I pick up the blush compact next. It's necessary because it has the mirror and the *freshening pink tones* my grey-colored cheeks crave. My lip-gloss, then the red-reducing eye drops are last. I shove the items into my skirt pocket and feel slightly comforted by their presence. I'm not vain or anything; it's just that without these products I look like the walking dead.

Once I'm sure my expression is solid and calm, I force myself to turn and look at my opponent. Gray's gathered almost all of my bumper stickers. Instead of looking impressed and floored by my cool product samples, he has the nerve to be sporting a confused expression. He's also shaking his head.

With a lightning quick glance at me first, he reads one

bumper sticker: "Member: BBB. Boys in Books are Better?" He shakes his head again. "I didn't know *you* made these bumper stickers. This one's been on your car since last month."

I gasp before I can stop myself. "How do you know that?"

"I like cars and I love Jeeps."

His eyes flit to my face again and his cheeks go all red. This time he's trying to hold my gaze so I lock onto his for a stare down and don't respond. Silence always freaks people out.

He shrugs as though he hasn't noticed and continues, "Your Jeep is the most tricked out vehicle in the whole school." He waves my bumper sticker in the air. "You slapped this very same chunk of duct tape silliness right onto the *paint*. They're called bumper stickers for a reason. They go on the *bumper*. Although with your chrome package I wouldn't even do that."

I have no idea what he's talking about. What's a chrome package? Amazingly, the guy doesn't break my stare despite the ice bullets I've slammed into him. Maybe he's not wearing his glasses, or it's too dark in here for me to be properly effective. It's all I can do to keep a straight face and the glower from slipping. I think I'm losing control all over again. This is because I've registered two things above and beyond his hypnotic green eyes and rock star hot voice.

1. His perfectly square chin has one of those little divots dead center.

2. He's taller, and wider across the shoulders than I'd thought.

My heart ramps into some sort of a private hailstorm.

My list won't stop.

3. His hair is still shower damp. It's made up of little, ink-black curls—an amazing amount of them.

4. The dumb eyes aren't simply green. They're like an exploded rainbow of greens and gold and browns. On closer inspection, he's…he's simply overall amazing and…I'll just say

it again: *HOLY. HOLY. WOW.*

"So...*Jess Jordan*...cat got your tongue? Do you really believe that bumper sticker? Is that why you put it on your Jeep? That boys in books are truly...better?" He shoots me a small smile.

I have to hide a second gasp of surprise. I can't believe this perfect-looking dude knows my name as well as my Jeep, and what sticker I've put on it!

Whaaat-the-DOUBLE-F?

I shrug. "Yep. I believe it. I'm amazed you can read those. They've got some big words, *Gray Porter*," I cover, tossing his full name right back at him and layering on the sarcasm while I work to control the tremor threatening my voice. I'm about to go into shake and quake mode. I can't believe I've reached this state—not from a nightmare—but because I find a guy to be *stunning*?

Or is it because a guy's said my name?

I need to get myself together enough to make sure Gray understands I'm not here to *chat* or make friends—no matter how pretty he is! I don't have enough energy in me today for conversations like this.

"Mind handing my stuff back?" I say in my meanest voice, lowering my eyebrows into attack mode. I head closer, trying very hard not to blink. I also work to keep my shoulders down and my expression bored. Very bored, plus dripping with utter dislike and contempt.

Once again, the guy doesn't do what I expect.

Instead he meets me in the middle of the room and holds up two more bumper stickers. "I'd rather be in *Forks*? I shop the *HOB*? What do these even mean?!"

Time to end this right now. It's all suddenly too close.

That, or he's just too darn close to me. I never let anyone enter my bubble, but this guy has almost popped it.

Destroyed it.

He's touching all of my stuff and he smells like limes…
or something shampoo-soapy. I raise an eyebrow, working to
achieve the right tone of intellectual superiority. "If you've
never read the *Twilight* books or the *Hunger Games* series you
wouldn't understand. Not. One. Bit. They are complex stories.
Big words. Probably beyond you."

"Hey, no self-respecting dude would read those books, or
admit to reading them." He laughs.

I don't answer. Instead, I drop down to create some needed
distance while I pick up the remaining slew of bumper stickers
still on the floor. I'm horrified to note one of my résumés has
escaped. I glance up to see if he's got any printer paper in his
hands.

He doesn't, *thank God.*

"So…you're not going to tell me what they mean? C'mon.
What's the Hob? Why Forks?"

When I stand, I switch to my *blatantly rude, you're-an-idiot*
tone. This is the one that always pisses off my mom. To be sure
he's not missing my insult this time, I also cross my arms and
speak very slowly like I'm speaking to a toddler. "*The Hob* is
from *The Hunger Games.* It's the underground market where
the characters trade food and information. *Forks* would be the
town in *Twilight.* The setting. In boy-speak, Forks equals the
planet *Tatooine* for *Star Wars.* You know—Anakin Skywalker's
childhood home? Or are you not familiar with *any* global
blockbusters? I suppose I could use Sesame Street or Pokémon
for a reference—if it would help you understand better?"

Bam. That should seal it. I couldn't have sounded more like a
total bitch.

He nods. "No, I've got it. My bedroom was *Tatooine* for all
of third and fourth grade. Boy-speak…that's funny." He laughs
again, and it sounds warm and—and—not at all offended!

Worse, the laugh has disoriented me all over again. "Oh?"

becomes my dorky uncontrolled response. I suddenly have hundreds of questions about how his room might have looked.

"Yeah," he goes on as though he can read my mind. "I draped my walls with these ugly tan sheets to make the desert lands go on forever. It was more of a fire hazard than anything good." His gaze is now glued back on my face as though he's looking for something, waiting for me to do something.

But what?

I glance down and fiddle with the zipper on my bag, hoping he hasn't deciphered that I'm in absolute unfamiliar territory here. By now, even the toughest kids would be running in the other direction. At the very least they'd be pulling the silent treatment on me. Maybe I'll have to take this on the direct. I could try: *There is no reason we need to talk to each other. So let's just stop. As in. Forever. Don't talk to me, I won't talk to you. Deal?*

He clears his throat as though he's signaling my turn, but when I refuse to engage he continues, "Anyhow... *Twilight, The Hunger Games.* Those books were read by thirty million girls and their moms. Guys who admit to being into romance crap are lying or whipped. Major whipped. How's that for boy-speak? And those movies? You have to admit they were lame."

I make the mistake of looking up just then, prepared to blast him for the 'romance crap' comment and he stuns me stupid. He's in the middle of a total—entire face involved—eyes crinkling—happy grin. Grinning and happy at me, I guess?

"Tatooine, huh? So awesome you know Star Wars facts," he adds nodding. "Do you ever watch the animated stuff?"

Grin. Grin. Grin.

I'm seriously at risk of an old-style faint.

Holy-WTHECK?

My neck and cheeks are volcano-hot. My entire chest swarms with an uncontrollable butterfly attack. Butterfly riot.

Butterfly massacre.

Person slaughtered: Me.

Method used: Dimple.

The guy has a dimple. Of course he does. To match the Hollywood chin divot. To make the lump on my forehead pound even harder.

Points for Gray Porter: 3,000,000-bajallion, trillion to the millionth power.

Say something, Jess. Say anything.

And just when I'm about to think of what I *should* say next, my mouth goes into whacked overdrive like I'm possessed. "The graphic art in Clone Wars is my favorite," I say. "I love how they drew the characters. You know—how everything looks so angular and—"

My words tangle and freeze when my brain finally arrives to shut it down.

Say something but NOT THAT, you psycho!

"Clone Wars. Love it, do I? Yesss." He's actually responded in a Yoda voice!

I blink.

His eyes are kind, sparkling with laughter and still, all too green. Yoda green!

Am I losing my touch? Why won't this guy act like everyone else?

I want to giggle and smile back at him. It takes every ounce of my strength to tamp that urge away and revert to glaring. At a loss, I turn away to shove all of my product samples into my bag as a grey-haired, oompa-loompa looking guy stumbles through a door behind the reception area.

"Good, good. You're both here," the man says, pausing to right his glasses. "I was worried you'd have wandered off."

"No sir, Mr. Foley. Not a chance. Nice to see you again." Gray steps forward and shakes the man's hand.

My heart feels like cards have just been shuffled under it.

I recognize my instant disadvantage. How does Gray already *know* Mr. Foley, the CEO!?

I reach up to make sure my bun is holding and take a couple steps in their direction while I staple on a confident smile of my own.

Mr. Foley saves me by speaking first. "You must be Jessica Jordan." He shakes my hand. "I heard you had quite an interview yesterday. My product development manager says you're fantastic. She hasn't been this fired up about new products since we put unbreakable Plexiglas on the Dragon-Fire Sword replicas! Can't wait to get a look at your geek-girl book bumper stickers. I hope you brought them back."

I shoot Gray a smug smile. "Of course. It's an honor to finally meet you, Mr. Foley."

"Yes. Good," Mr. Foley says. He seems to be observing me.

I hope he approves of my carefully chosen Geekstuff.com outfit: the *Ultimate Long-Safari-Skirt. Color: Puce. Sale price: $42.95.*

I've combined it with the *Peter Pan Office Shirt. Color: Bright-White. Price: $34.00.* An item that has never been marked up or down for the past two years. A point I can't wait to bring up during my interview.

Mr. Foley's smile and small nod shows he's recognized that I'm not only an interviewee, but a valued customer, as well.

Let my points roll in. Fifty—zillion for me. *Take that, Porter!*

"Do you two know each other?" Mr. Foley gestures between us.

"Oh *yes*," Gray says in what sounds like a sarcastic tone.

"No." I blast Gray with a look. He better cut the games, *now.*

"So you do, or, you don't?" Mr. Foley asks again, scratching the top of his balding head.

"Sort of," I say.

"Yeah...that's what I meant," Gray says. He breaks my gaze and flushes.

"We're in the same school," I add.

"Good. That makes what I have to tell you less awkward." Mr. Foley smiles.

I have to force myself *not* to roll my eyes.

If this morning gets any more awkward, I could easily self-combust.

Mr. Foley continues, "Our order fulfillment servers went down and I'm helping Q.A. review a temporary hack. It's why I'm so late. Might take awhile before I can get to the interviews. Can you hold here until the fire's out?"

"No problem." I nod, hoping my expression is a perfect mix of concern and absolute *hire-me, NOT HIM,* sparkle.

I risk another glance at Gray and note he seems supremely uncomfortable about the new plan. We've sort of exhausted all bizarre topics possible. I'm guessing he's not looking forward to the next round of being alone with me.

Hanging with him is not at the top of my list either, but I'm not going to let anyone know that with a crappy poker-face. If Mr. Foley notices Gray's reaction, I'll simply gain another point for my side.

I shoot Gray a taunting, deadly smile as I continue, "I have all day, Mr. Foley. Please take your time."

"Yeah, as long as you need," Gray says.

Gray responds to my challenge with a head-shake and an odd half-smile. The guy is whacked, that has to be it.

"Are we the only people expected for the final interview?" Gray asks. He's turned his back on me. I think he's trying to block my view of Mr. Foley with his giant...giant *self!*

"Yes. You two are the best of the bunch. Wish I had the budget to keep you both. This is not going to be an easy decision." Mr. Foley sighs and removes his glasses to polish them on his shirt.

I step around Gray so I can be in Mr. Foley's view, but Gray beats me to the conversation again. "Is there anything we can do to help? Maybe extra hands are needed?" He sounds infuriatingly competent.

"Yes. Can I help too?" I ask, but I know I sound unoriginal—like I'm copying.

Because I am! I can't believe I underestimated Gray this much.

I'm hardly able to hold my placid smile steady through my gritted teeth, but Mr. Foley doesn't seem to notice.

WHY?

Because he's not looking at me! He's busy smiling at Gray as though they shared some sort of private joke at yesterday's interview.

As though Gray Porter had gone home for dinner, met his wife and saved his dog from drowning!

For a consolation prize, my soon to be NOT BOSS tosses me a nod as he directly answers Gray's question, not mine. "Might take you up on that, *son*. Sorry about this. It won't be too long, just hang tight and I'll be back." He gives us one last, apologetic glance and a small wave before darting through the door.

I want to scream.

Mr. Foley just called my only competition for this internship, *son*.

SON!

It's apparent I've lost the job. I eye the tense set of Gray's back and wonder what's bugging him. Can he not tell? He's Mr. Foley's golden boy.

Gray's paced across the room to the farthest point away from me. I've heard him mutter the word "crap" like six times. As if he's the one who needs to freak out right now.

I consider the possibility that he's been pretending to be

relaxed around me but can no longer hide the fact that I've finally broken through. Made him back off and fear me like he should.

Good. Let's hope that's the case.

I can't leave here without this job.

Maybe I can push him harder—convince him to leave. If he's too stupid to know he's *the chosen one,* I'm not going to bring it up. I mean to imply the opposite.

I let out a long, attention-getting sigh and fold my arms to re-muster my smug confidence while swallowing the lump of fear lodged in the back of my throat.

"So...do you want to confess anything to me? Come clean? We seem to have lots of time."

He sucks in a breath as though my comment startled him.

"I—what—d—do you mean?"

Yes. He stuttered!

I'm back on, and I'm kicking off round two. This time, I know all of his tricks: dimples, divots, smiles, and cute eye-crinkle things. Bring it on.

When he turns, I could swear he's gone completely pale and my confidence builds. I go for another sigh—the *dismissive, bored* one. The one that used to make the therapist say, "I think we're done for today, Jessica."

I dig in again. "You know you don't belong here. You aren't even a geek. I think you should tell me *why* you thought it appropriate to fling yourself all over my car. Were you trying to scare me?"

"I didn't think and I—" He flushes, still stuttering, "I—"

"Just say it; you were trying to make me bomb the interview. I'm not an idiot. Scaring me off is the only way you'll get this job, and I think you know it." I stroll to the purple couch, place my bag on the glass oval coffee table, and take a seat as though I own the place. "Decent, but *failed* attempt. You won't be getting any second chances."

"You were the one pulling the park-and-hide trick, not me," he says, all hints of his previous stutter are now erased. "In case you didn't notice, the spot where you chose to park is hidden by dumpsters. Come clean on *that,* because it looked like you were playing your own game out there."

I'm beginning to suspect this guy is as good at hiding his true feelings as I am. I know I had him sweating it just seconds ago, but now he's turned it back on me. I'm not about to admit that I arrive early to *everything* so I can take a nap first. I go for a half-truth. "I parked in the shade to hang out. Behind the dumpsters is the only shady spot in the whole lot. Last I'd heard, parking in the shade is not a game, or a crime. But stalking and attacking innocent people are felonies."

"Christ! I *noticed* your car, and I *noticed* you in it—snoring away. I also *noticed* you weren't going to wake up. You're lucky I took the trouble to give you a little assist. *You owe me.* You could have missed this whole interview."

I move into full-fight mode. "Oh, *I owe you*, do I? FYI. I wasn't asleep, you moron. I was resting. Listening to my iPod. Thanks to you, I've got bruises on my knees and a lump the size of Texas on my forehead. If you're looking for some kind of payback for what you did—well, you caused more damage than a herd of buffalo. *You owe me*—like plastic surgery or something!" I point at the lump.

"I'm sorry, okay? I did not intend to scare you." He stalks toward me so quickly that I don't have time to move or read his expression—as if I could.

He squats low and moves my bangs aside to survey the lump. I'm staring at the way his beige interview pants have tightened over his thighs—the way his shirt stretches over his biceps. Then, I stop breathing altogether.

When I look up I read only sincere concern and apology

in his expression. Not sure what to do with a guy this close to me, I decide to keep holding my breath until I count the gold flecks in each of his irises—five times two is ten total. Slowly, I risk one slow breath through my nose. And then another.

"It's pretty bad—needs ice," he says, jolting me back onto the planet by running his thumb lightly over the lump. I gasp, trying to hide the goose bumps that are running up the back of my neck. "Sorry. Is it really painful?"

"Yes—no, I don't know. Sort of." I blink, annoyed by my epic choice of one syllable words.

"I see lots of head bumps with the kids I coach at the rink. This one looks okay, but if you feel nauseous you might need to visit the ER."

"Not a chance—but again—a nice attempt to get rid of me."

He smiles as his eyes scan my whole face. "You're funny. Anyone ever told you that?"

I feel a strange flutter at the base of my throat and more growing deep inside my chest.

Holy. This has to be more butterflies. Terrible butterflies. My lungs tighten, twisting as if they've imploded. I work to swallow. I'm suddenly afraid rainbow-winged insects are about to shoot out of my mouth and hit him in the nose.

"I didn't mean to scare you in the parking lot. Swear," he goes on, oblivious to the fact that I'm losing my mind. His gaze bores deeper into mine. "I'm sorry. Really, sorry. I messed up. *Jess*...I swear I thought you needed me to wake you up."

I think I love and somehow *hate* the way Gray has just said my name. Like he knows me.

Like we're friends when we're anything but.

I swallow and stare at his chin divot because I'm terrified to look anywhere else. My therapist told me if I was ever surprised by someone—a guy—approaching me—touching me—that *anything* could happen.

Anything as in: *me*—going berserk.

But I didn't. And I'm not going to!

As awkward as this moment is, I'm intrigued with the possibilities of what this could mean. Gray Porter holding up my bangs while I memorize the depth of his chin divot ranks at the top of my *things-that-have-overly-surprised me* list! I don't really have such a list. But when I get home, I'm making one.

I have no urge to scratch out his eyes, or cry or—well—do anything my therapist said I might do.

The only urge I'm resisting right now is the one to stare at his lips—and that is beyond strange. I force myself to meet his gaze again, determined to test this feeling—or lack of feeling— a little more.

When nothing happens after another long examination of his beautiful eyes—not counting my increased heart rate and the half-panicked look crossing *his* face (and who can blame him for that? I'm acting like a freak with all the staring) I have to squelch a smile and twist my expression into what I *hope* has me back to my *rock-solid-annoyed-mask*.

He drops my bangs and sits back on his heels. "So...apology accepted?"

"Mmmh," and a small nod are all I can manage because I don't want to let on that I'm bursting with excitement. I'm way more *cured* than I'd thought. That, or Gray and I are somehow the human personifications of positive and negative forces. Like we are Yin and Yang, or oil and vinegar! Maybe we cancel each other out by default. It's pretty obvious he doesn't react to me like he should. And, not counting the butterfly feeling which seems pretty easy to hide, I don't react to him in a crazy way at all.

Eat that, Dr. Brodie, and hello progress!

I point at his backpack to get his attention off me and back onto the interview. "Show me what products you brought to impress Mr. Foley. You saw mine. It's only fair."

He takes the bag into his lap and holds on tight as he stands and heads back to the receptionist's desk. "It's not my fault that you dropped your stuff. I can't—*won't*—show you what's in this bag. Sorry."

"Always *sorry*, aren't you? Sorry. Sorry. Sorry," I tease, meeting his gaze.

Whatever I've said has made Gray's face turn bright red. He quickly turns away.

This is a good thing because after all this concentrated *progress*, I'm getting hit with a major wave of dizziness. I dig my hands into the couch to hold myself steady and try to evaluate if the feeling is still the butterfly thing—or if it's coming directly from *me, myself*, and *messed up I.*

It only takes a second to realize it's the latter. I've become so dizzy, I feel as though I might faint. The Red Bulls have worn off and it's going to be awhile before I can catch a nap.

Exhaustion and the fog that comes with it settles in, adding to my light-headedness. Gray Porter as my opponent is replaced by the need to win against a bigger villain: my body's endless craving for sleep. A low pounding swells inside my head. Great. Crashing with an audience is never good.

"You look sort of pale." He sounds far away like he's speaking through water.

"Small headache, no thanks to you and the lump," I quip, rubbing my temples and trying to breathe deeply. I don't want him to realize I'm at a weak point so I strive to keep the conversation going. "You're right though…it's not your fault I dropped my stuff…it's mine. Totally my fault."

I hear him pacing the far side of the room. I scan the ceiling, find the air conditioning vent and scoot under it before he can turn back. Cold air always helps. After a few moments I'm freezing, but I can process again. I pinch my sides as hard as I can, a tactic that will work for a while. Unfortunately, even under an icy blast, couches have a way of becoming too comfortable when I feel like this. The sleep demon wants a deposit. There's no way I can beat it much longer.

I close my eyes and pray I can think of a plan.

Pray harder for Mr. Foley to hurry.

4

gray

I lean against the receptionist's desk and take in Jess's closed eyes, crossed arms and drastically changed, pale face. She's doing some sort of strange yoga-type breathing. I wonder if the lump on her head is worse than she says. Maybe she has a full-on concussion?

I'm convinced she doesn't remember me.

Not at all. I would venture a guess that she's better. No nervous breakdown so far. The girl seems perfectly normal. Prickly yes—but she's also smart, funny and, yeah, as normal as I am. She gave no sign that she knew anything about me beyond my name. And *hell*, I was surprised to learn she knew that.

I spot some papers lodged behind the large potted tree near the door. I wander over to investigate if they're hers.

Dead on. It's a pile of school transcripts and some copies of her résumé. I read through her endless list of accomplishments.

"Why are you here for this job?" I ask softly.

"Please. This internship is perfect for me and you know it. I've been on the interview list since junior year." She opens her eyes and hits me with a serious, cold stare. "Did your parents get you a last minute interview? You weren't on the list I saw."

I think she's trying to be mean and make me nervous, but

the sassiness she'd had earlier is missing from her voice. It's like the fight's gone out of her.

The fight's gone out of me too. So I tell her the truth. "My parents are dead. I live with my grandmother. My college advisor made some phone calls and got me in last minute."

Her eyes widen. "Holy. Guess it's my turn for sorry. Truly—I didn't know."

"It happened when I was a baby. I only remember Gran as my mom, so...yeah. It's just...my life, you know? No need to apologize for what's been great." I flop down on the couch beside her. "I need this internship so my grandmother won't have to pay my college tuition. Job pays $8K total for only a few weeks work. I'm also hoping Geekstuff.com will allow me to work during the holidays and weekends next year. I can save a ton if I get started this summer. Plus, they have an amazing scholarship to School of Mines."

"Oh? Cool. My Dad works there," she says, pushing her face toward the vent in the ceiling. "Hmmm. $8K, huh? I forgot about the money. I'd work here for free if they'd let me."

"I'm all about the money. Can't afford to forget that so..." I pause, fascinated with the way the vent's blowing cotton candy looking curls around her temples.

"So—what?" She quirks a brow, shooting me a weird glance.

"So—no matter how great your geeky outfit looks, and despite your Star Wars lore, your awesome bumper stickers, and your flipping *perfect* résumé, I have to roll the dice. Just in case. No hard feelings, okay?"

"You liked the bumper stickers? I thought you hated them." She smiles, and then frowns. "How do you know what's on my résumé?" Her blue eyes widen as she realizes what I'm holding.

I wave the pages. "If I didn't witness your entry, I'd accuse you of planting these babies as an alternate, sneaky way to impress any staff members you didn't meet in person." I hand her the transcripts and one of the résumés, then I move down the length of the couch away from her. "You raised goats for 4-H?" I smile.

"When I was ten." She stuffs the papers into her bag and comes after me. "Stop reading. It's private information."

"You took the time to make copies so you must want someone else to have a look." I hand her another paper and read the next. "I think you should be the one to bow out of this place. Now that you know my poverty stricken, orphaned truth, how can you not let me have this job?" I plead, trying to look pitiful.

She rolls her eyes. "Please. You said it yourself. You aren't suffering one bit."

"Don't you have some sort of beach cottage or mountain condo retreat you need to visit all summer? If your dad works at Mines, you already have a full ride scholarship to at least one top school by default. With your grades, I bet you've already been accepted to a ton of places. If not, you can get in anywhere because of your family's future 'charitable donations'."

"How dare you assume things like that about me?"

"Why not?" I shrug. "Everyone knows your grandfather is *The* Edwin Donovan. His brewery employs half the county. It's clear that your family bank account is doing way better than mine."

"Rude, much? You have no right to bring up my family and our finances."

Her eyes are back to shooting sparks but she's wincing like her headache is worse, so I tone it down. "I'm just trying to list the facts between us." I shrug again. "My need is obviously greater than yours."

"That's bull. My need is just as huge. I want this job because it's going to get me the letters of recommendation I *need* to go Ivy League. Sue me for having goals. Plus, this place will make me look very well rounded." She flushes. "And I'm having trouble with that at school because all my stuff is academic. No teams—no social clubs."

She corners me on the edge of the couch and holds out her hand. Suddenly, all I can notice is how very well rounded she is, and worse, I realize she still smells like cinnamon and sunshine. Just like she did three years ago.

"Give. Those. Back."

I pass off a few more résumés and jet away from her and that cinnamon smell, reserving the last paper in my hand so I can finish reading it. "Whoa—hello. What's this?" I mumble, staring at the paper. "Jess Jordan's *How to be Normal Checklist*, by Kika Jordan? Who's Kika?" I laugh.

The way her face has turned whiter than the ice at the sports complex, I think this paper is no joke.

"Kika's my little sister. Hand that over!"

Do the right thing. Like she said, this is private information. None of my business.

Only, it could possibly be my business.

Indirectly. Not her fault…not mine…

Jess's eyes have turned wild, exposed. "She made the list for me—as a *joke*. It's revenge. Last week I made her one on personal hygiene called, *How NOT to Repel All Mankind*."

I smile as Jess makes a leap for the list, but I sidestep her easily. The top of her head doesn't reach my shoulder. The only way she can get to this paper is if she tries to climb me. I'm confident she's not about to go there.

"Please," she whispers. "Please don't…"

Her anguished tone causes my heart to twist. I almost relent; but suddenly, facing this girl—I feel like I'm no longer myself.

The fact that I didn't drive away when I spotted her car proves it.

The fact that I sought her out and willingly broke the promise I made to her parents proves it again.

The fact that I'm still here when I should probably walk away and never look back solidifies it. This must be what it's like to wake up and discover you've become a drug addict overnight. I'm so high and out of control right now, I can't stop myself.

High on curiosity. On Jess Jordan's voice. My need for more information has become unquenchable, unstoppable.

Now that I'm certain she doesn't remember me, I want to know *her*. The real her.

Not the odd-ball-super-bitch everyone thinks she is, but the girl in front of me now. The one with a headache that takes the color out of her cheeks. The girl who likes Clone Wars art, and defends block-buster romances. The girl who I swear hid a few smiles from me earlier.

The girl whose same '*please*' and haunted blue eyes have tormented me for three years.

Relentlessly, I read on: "Number one: Make at least two friends your own age. Number two: Go places besides your room. Number three: Get boyfriend. Number four: Make sure Mom and Dad notice numbers one through three."

I lower my hand.

"You suck," she says, crumpling the list as she turns her back on me. Her narrow shoulders heave as though she either can't breathe or she might cry—or both.

"Your list—it's real, isn't it?" I press on, "It's why you really need this job."

She's stalked to the coffee table where she left her bag and stuffs the list inside. "So what if the list is real? I'm sick, okay? Not cancer or anything extreme. Sick here." She taps her temple with one finger and meets my gaze dead on. "Permanently messed up." She shrugs. "The parents are tracking my lack of social life. Something you wouldn't understand. This internship is going to get me what I *need* in order to prove to my parents that I can do normal things like survive a summer job. If I can't pull it off, they won't let me move out and go to college. Happy? Now you've seen the proof. I need the job more than you. So—how about you do me a favor and step out like I've been asking all along?"

"Jesus. You're completely serious." I swallow.

"Go ahead. Laugh. I'm sure you can get days of amusement off this info at school." She crosses her arms. Instead of looking brave or comically defensive like she had earlier, I get the feeling she needs to hold herself up. Like she's not okay, and it's got nothing to do with me.

"What do you have—what makes you sick…or whatever?" I ask softly, wondering how far she'll go on details.

"Please. I'm not going to give you more ammunition to hand to your gossipy friends."

"I wouldn't tell. I'm not like that."

She shakes her head and looks away. "Everyone's like that."

"Right." I don't push her again because my conscience has caught up. My friends would have a field day with her list. I've already gone too far. Besides, I know her diagnosis: *Post Traumatic Stress Disorder*. Those are the exact words her mom told me years ago. I'm no expert, but PTSD is what war veterans have after battle—and accident survivors—and crime victims too.

I thought PTSD made people shout, cry and lose it when provoked. Only, I'd been provoking Jess since I'd slammed into her car. If she's admitting she's still sick that means *I do suck*.

My chest tightens. I can't swallow as I take in how her shoulders are still trembling—how she doesn't want me to notice that they are.

Foul on me for being the world's biggest jerk to the one girl who doesn't deserve anything but absolute kindness—especially from a person that knows her real deal. By reading that list I'd torn off her face mask and shot for the goal well after the whistle had been blown.

She turns to face me and I try my best to apologize.

"Whatever you want to do—or say to me right now—*hell*, I deserve it, okay? I'm a complete asshole. You can even punch me, if you want. I'm not going to tell anyone about this conversation—about you—the list—anything. It's a promise."

Taking a deep breath, she notches her chin one inch higher. She shoots me a look that says she's not hurt, or insulted or shaking all over right in front of me. She wants me to think she doesn't care about what I've just done.

The blatant vulnerability I'd seen disappears. The trembling in her arms and hands stops. The girl layers on another one of those ice-blue glowers, and fires out a wall of contempt. If I hadn't been staring directly at her the whole time—if the glower hadn't *exactly* matched the one she gave me from the cab of her Jeep, I might have missed it.

"Want to be my number three?" she asks, and raises both eyebrows up and down in a distracting offensive.

And it works. I'm completely blindsided.

Humbled. Awed.

She's got game face. Major.

This girl's an expert at the cover-up.

After thousands of hockey games against formidable opponents, I realize I've taken Jess Jordan down, but no way is she out. More buckets of guilt and a fresh dose of self-loathing crash around me, almost bringing me to my knees.

She continues on, "What do you say, Porter? If I land the boyfriend on that list, I'm golden." Her voice rings with reckless bravado. "You in?"

"Uh...no...no," is all I can muster because I have no air left in my lungs.

"You don't have to look so disgusted at the idea." She shrugs again, while my mind reels out of control. "I'm sure you have girl standards that I don't meet. Why rub that in with the bitter-lemon face?"

"I'm not making any faces. You're just—" I stop myself because I can't think of anything to say that doesn't sound hurtful. And at all costs, I vow to never willingly hurt her again.

Ever.

"Go on. Just what?" she demands. "Whatever you say won't shock me." Her tone is now so obviously self-condemning I wince as she continues, "There's thousands of ways to finish. You think I haven't heard them? Try these: I'm *too bitchy* to be your girlfriend, *too dorky, too weird, too whacked, too smart?*"

"I didn't mean that *I* wouldn't want you for a girlfriend," I say gently, refusing to rise to her bait. "I meant someone else might. I don't have girlfriends as a rule. They take up way too much time."

She glances sideways through her lashes and I get the sensation she's studying my expressions. "What would my half of this job be worth to you? You said you want money. C'mon. I know there's a deal to be made here."

I feel like I've just entered crazy land.

"There's no *half.* There's *one* job and I mean to get it. Frankly, you turning *normal* this summer seems to be way easier than me winning the lottery."

"Can you be so sure you're going to get the internship?" she asks, leaning closer.

"I'm almost sure," I lie.

"The *whole* of this internship equals eight thousand dollars summer pay." She reaches into her bag to pull out the crumpled *normal list* and hands it back to me. "I offer to work it for free, and you agree to be my fake boyfriend for the duration of the summer. How hard could it be? We'll keep it light. We won't have to use your real name. If you're fictional, then you won't have a family that my parents need to meet. I just need someone to pick me up in a car once in awhile and—"

"No. Stop. Absolutely not."

"*Yes!* It's perfect and you know it. I get the *normal,* you get the money, we both get the letters of recommendation. Plus, Mr. Foley gets two interns for the price of one. Say yes." She blinks.

"Impossible." I blink back. "You—you have no idea what you're asking me. I'm really busy," I beg, hoping she will believe this is all about me—not her. "I work another job—at the sports complex, and I take care of my grandmother. No. Too complicated."

I stand and pace the length of the room re-reading the items on her list. Even if I did agree, how would I be able to hide my identity from her pit-bull parents? If they ever found out, they'd skewer me.

But hell...I have to admit...she's right. It's a good idea. Could we pull it off if she doesn't use my real name? I rake my hands through my hair. "No. No. It's insane. It's impossible."

I look back. She's crossed her arms and is tapping her ugly shoe on the carpet.

"You're doing it again," she says.

"What?"

"You're turning all pasty and greenish. And you're muttering to yourself again. Can't you at least hide your complete aversion to me? A few more minutes in your company and I might as well go tie myself to a train track."

"Don't say that. Don't even joke about it! The idea of ten weeks with a single, locked-down girlfriend—even the fake kind—gives me all over body hives. Sue me for making a face about *that.* I don't think you've thought any of this through. It would involve all of our friends, parents—even if we don't use my real name—text messaging, emails—and a lot of time. Time is something I don't have to burn. Plus, it would kill the variety of…of…yeah…*girl fun* in my summer," I imply, wondering if she'll call my bluff. The only real summer varieties I score are the extra odd jobs I pick up at the rink.

She turns bright red and I have to hide my smile.

"Disgusting," she scoffs and reverts back to rubbing her temples. "But, if I can't convince you, then maybe you could put in a good word with one of your friends? One who isn't such a boy whore like you?"

"What?" I gasp. Amazed. She's hit me in the gut all over again. "If…if I say *no*, you—you—mean to ask *someone else*? Are you completely mental?"

"I thought we'd covered that topic. Are you completely slow? YES. I'm mental. This is why I have a list called 'how to be normal'."

My heart twists because I think she truly believes that. "You'll be destroyed by gossip. Approaching anyone else would be social suicide. You can't tell anyone else this plan!"

She grimaces. "Would you stop yelling? My head split in half five minutes ago. No need to drain out what's left. Besides, I'm way beyond worrying about gossip that's applied to me. I'm sure I could find someone who would take $8K to *pretend date* me this summer."

When I meet her gaze, I can tell she's in major pain but I'm almost sure it's got nothing to do with the bump on her head like she's been swearing.

I take in a deep breath, and slowly return to sit beside her on the couch. "Why don't you just try to get a boyfriend the usual way? You know…meet people. Talk. Be nice? Save your money," I whisper.

"I don't… I can't," she whispers back. Not meeting my gaze she goes on, "I'm not like that. You wouldn't understand."

But I do understand. And I hate that I do.

Before she can say more, Mr. Foley is back in the room. "Okay! Problem solved. Who's first?" He nods at me. "Ready, Mr. Porter? I can't wait to see your product ideas."

"Ready." I hand Jess the list and stand.

I make the mistake of giving her one last glance. I sort of expect to see her about to cry, but she surprises me again. Her expression has turned defiant, challenging. I'm pretty sure she's shooting me a bright blue, F-U with those big, closed-off eyes.

My hockey-puck samples clump against my back when I sling my pack over one shoulder. I can hardly breathe.

I can't walk away from Jess now that she's *asked* me for help directly.

Plus, I'm well aware my bag is full of crap. If it comes down to product samples, she's going to win. She believes I'm about to steal the internship from her, but after seeing those bumper stickers I know *I'm* the long shot. As soon as Mr. Foley compares my half-page résumé boasting a lame assistant-coach job plus snack-bar expertise to what Jess has typed on hers, I'm dead.

As I move to follow Mr. Foley, she pulls out her bumper stickers. She flashes me the top ones: *Boys in Books are Better... Boys in Books are Better.*

Crap! It's partly my fault Jess Jordan believes that damn bumper sticker is true.

"Sir," I call out to Mr. Foley before I can change my mind. "How about you interview us together?"

Jess's mask slips. She meets my gaze and her eyes are so alight with hope, relief and trust that I'm sure I've done the right thing.

But then she shoots out of her seat and stands too close to me. "Do you mean it?" she whispers.

I nod, and she smiles. I'm overcome with thoughts of

cinnamon-sunshine and how much I like this very *real* smile—
so different than the ones she'd been faking all morning.

"Thanks." She latches on to my arm as though she's scared to
let go. "This is going to be awesome. You won't be sorry."

I want to shout: *I'm already sorry. I've been sorry for three
years!*

Instead I smile and say, "Yeah. We'll work out details at
school. Monday."

She nods again. Her small hand trembles against my arm.
Her fingers seem really fragile—with nails that have been
chewed down to nothing.

*Maybe this is absolute wrong thing to do. Crap. Crap. And
Crap! What have I agreed to?*

It's not like I can take it back now. She'd told me she was
going to hire *someone else* if I didn't sign on. I couldn't let that
happen. And dammit! I need this job.

I vow to just watch over her. Make sure she's okay. Make
sure she doesn't get hurt any more, even by herself and her
strange ideas. Hell, I've been watching over Jess Jordan for
three years in secret already. She doesn't remember me, so what
harm can come from trying to be her friend?

"What's the idea?" Mr. Foley asks, retracing his steps down
the hall.

Jess pipes in, "If you agree, Mr. Foley, we have a way you
could hire us both, but only pay one salary."

Mr. Foley raises his salt-and-pepper brows high above his
glasses and smiles. "I'm listening."

5

jess

Footsteps on the hall floorboards bring me fully awake and stop my nightmare. *Thank God.* My heart's racing. I'm covered in sweat, but hopefully I can recover myself in time.

The clock blinks 2AM from the far side of the room as the footsteps draw nearer.

As happy as I am my torture has been derailed, my heart fills with dread. If someone's prowling this side of the house past midnight, I must have just ruined months of hard work by crying out in my sleep.

My fault for risking it, but the bed had looked so comfortable. I'd only meant to stretch out for a minute, but I'd been so tired after the interview I must have drifted off.

I bite my lip and hold quiet. I can tell by the pace that the person lurking is my mom. She's not going to stop until she checks on me. I force my sleep-heavy limbs to move off the bed. Comforter in tow, I make a break for the desk and wipe the tears from my cheeks and eyes while I quickly run a hand over my keyboard. The laptop surges to life just in time, illuminating the far corner of the room as she opens the door without even knocking.

"You okay?" she asks, voice tight. Worried. Waiting for me

to admit to the nightmare.

"All good," I say, using a cheerful tone. I need to play this perfectly or I'm toast. I angle the monitor light away from my body and burrow into the comforter before pretending to type. When Mom doesn't leave, I'm forced to look up. Hopefully my *serene* expression is locked in place, but there are no guarantees. Not after the nightmare.

If she catches on that it's resurfaced, I won't be allowed to start my internship when school lets out next week. Instead, she'll make me head back into therapy.

I layer on a small smile. "I…I'm too excited to sleep so I thought I'd check out some campuses. Forgot to lower the volume before playing a video. Sorry if it woke you."

"Shouldn't you be getting sleep for finals?" she asks, but it isn't until she yawns, tightens the belt on her baby-blue fleece robe and leans on the doorframe to assume her *parent-lecture-stance* that I risk releasing one full breath of air.

"I'm sure your father will agree that it's premature for you to be on college websites. We've reserved the right to pull the plug on our decision at the end of the summer," she says, thankfully not watching me as she yawns again. She's bought in to my lies.

"Dr. Brodie gave me the thumbs up. Why can't you believe it?" I bark out, still trying to hold as much of my breath as possible.

"College is a long way off. One step at a time. The fact that you impressed them into offering you a second, unpaid internship is a great start. You're a *very* lucky girl. And—"

… *You're a very lucky girl. You're a very lucky girl.*

The police officer's words from my nightmare mesh with my mom's speech and explode into painful lightning inside my head. Mom has a talent for saying just the wrong thing at the worst possible time.

And catching me, post nightmare, would qualify as the *worst possible time*. My stomach twists into a ball and my legs tense until they ache from holding back the tremors.

I've never told Mom or anyone the exact words that trigger me into losing it. I know she didn't say them on purpose. The words hit me again.

... *You're a very lucky girl. You're a very lucky girl.*

I try to maintain a calm expression as drops of sweat slide down my neck. My hairline prickles painfully. Soon moisture will roll down my forehead and she'll see it.

... *You're a very lucky girl.*

I force my eyes to stay open and cross my arms over my rolling stomach as the leftover panic from the dream now builds steadily inside me like a giant wave. I bite the insides of my cheeks and train my fuzzed-out gaze in the direction of Mom's still moving lips.

... *Lucky. Lucky girl.*

I steel myself to deflect the strobe light images: a silver belt buckle, purple tipped seashells, a crystal bowl, hands on my skin, and the color white all around me.

... *Very lucky girl.*

I bite harder and concentrate on the metallic taste of blood on my tongue, well aware that I must get my mom out of this room. It's a major feat to check back into the conversation, uncross my arms, and try to switch my expression to *vacant*.

Vacant, in this condition is not easy, but it's the best choice to piss her off.

"...and, summer aside," Mom's blabbing on, "there's still the matter of you surviving *senior year*. You have to also score well on the SAT's *and* the ACT's," she finishes.

I slouch deeper into the laptop monitor and click the mouse. Click. Click. Clickity click.

"Jess, are you listening?" Out of the corner of my eye, I see her fling her arms out in total frustration. Her voice goes up two decibels, right on cue. "Dad and I want you to prove that you can branch out—beyond this room. We want you to—"

"Be normal. I'm on it," I manage to say, bored voice, eyes glued to the computer.

One more mouse click and then: type, type, type, type.

"Prove it, then. Sleep. See if you can make it to school minus your skeleton's face and the under-eye circles."

"That was low, Mom. Even for *you*." I release a long puff of air, hoping to sound offended instead of half-dead from holding my breath. I stage the cold glare and flick it toward the door, but I'm unprepared to meet the absolute anguish I find in her eyes.

Regret and apology flash between us like the sudden glimmer of a butterfly's wing. Shame stings my eyes because of all the lies I'd told so easily during dinner. Lies about the internship. Lies the whole family had bought without question.

I waver, imagining me taking them all back—longing for the soft, lavender-scented warmth of my mom's hug. But how can I tell her my nightmare's been back full-force for a week?

I don't want to push her buttons like this, but the alternative, *the truth*, means the whole family returns to square one.

Good bye *progress*. Good bye future.

I pull my gaze away from hers. My hands have started to shake and my legs will soon get worse. I have to hurry. The shadowy memories push at me, and demand to play themselves out. There is no stopping them once they've started to surge like this.

...

Lucky. Lucky, lucky girl.
Nothing happened.
You're fine. Just fine.
Please. Don't leave me.

...

"Jess…I—"

"*You* go to sleep, Mom," I shout. Shouting always hides the tremors that take over my voice. "Skeleton's face or not, I can stay up all night. Unless you and Dad are going to *pull the plug* on that too!"

"Look, I'm sorry I said—"

"God! Just—get out! GET OUT. GET OUT!"

She reels back like I've slapped her and she slams the door.

Relieved, and in survival mode, I pull my legs up so I can place the weight of my thousand pound head on my knees. The remnants of the nightmare cut into me. Razor sharp stones. Blinding, strobe lit, indecipherable fragments of the memories caught in my head.

...

You're a very lucky girl.

Let's go! Dude, nothing happened.

Nothing really happened.

Wait. Please. Please, don't leave me here.

I'm sorry. I'm so sorry…I can't…

Look at her. She's so hot it's almost worth getting caught.

I'm so sorry…

She lied to us.

It's not her fault.

She's fine. She's fine.

Nothing happened.

I believed him. He said I was beautiful.

It is my fault. All my fault.

...

As the initial violent spinning lessens, I'm able to count. Dr. Brodie taught me counting helps find the end.

It works.

At 100, I move to my next ritual. I turn my attention to

the jellyfish nightlight. I count higher and wait for the light to change from a pulsing white rectangle back into a cute, water-filled, mood lamp with three jellyfish swimming inside.

Like I said. I love this thing. The jellyfish are friends.

Sort of my pets. Witnesses, mostly.

Either way, I can't survive this without them.

When I'm able to see the details of their transparent, paper-thin tentacles, I know it's safe for me to move. That's when I stop counting. If I stop too soon, I end up crying like a freak and sometimes I can't stop. It scares my family. Heck, it scares me too.

Tonight, I don't let myself move until I reach number 459.

Not the worst number, but last month I had made it down to the 20's. I thought it was going to count down to zero and finally be over. I believed what everyone else believed. That I was getting better. Guess not.

I reach for a pen and scratch the number into the column of numbers I've carved into the wood on my desk. My history book is still open on the Final Exam Study Guide. At least the stupid nightmare allowed me six good hours of sleep before surfacing. That's way more than my usual. I'll be feeling good for the first round of finals.

Better, I'll be able to hang around with the family and have breakfast instead of driving off early to nap. We can all sit to-gether and talk about my new job…and how much I really like my new friend. My new friend that is also a guy.

My heart races in a good way as green eyes and a dimple erase all remaining shreds of the nightmare from my mind.

I imagine the proud, happy smiles of Mom, Dad, and Kika when I mention that my new friend is really *cute*. I won't even have to lie about that. It will also kill them when I refuse to tell *his* name.

Not quite yet.

Oh. What Progress!

Glimmers of success and the possibilities ahead replace my last jagged heartbeats with an amazing feeling of hope.

6

gray

It's Monday lunch hour. I've been avoiding talking to Jess all day, mostly because I've been telling myself I need more time to think of exactly what I'm going to say to her. Plus, I have no idea how we're supposed to start this whole rent-a-boyfriend thing. But of course, that's not the direct truth.

I'm simply afraid, as usual. Gray Porter, the chicken-shit-loser is afraid of Jess Jordan, the hundred pound girl.

Again. Still. Always.

At least I can admit it. Besides, she seems to be avoiding me, too.

"Crap," I mutter and step back a little as I spot Jess exit the building.

She never hangs outside at lunch, but nothing's on schedule during finals. Today, everyone's cleaning out lockers and milling around. My friends have also spotted Jess walking across the quad. We usually comment on anything out of the ordinary crossing our vantage point on the high steps leading to the teacher parking lot. Jess Jordan, when sighted, is always an easy target for conversation.

"Look. Jess Jordan's stealing one of the Bunsen burners and some beakers to boot," says my best friend, Corey Nash. He's moved to the edge of the steps to get a better view of the giant pile of stuff she's hauling toward her car. "That girl would *so* be the type to have some sort of secret school supply theft ring. She might be selling stuff on eBay or Craigslist right now. She probably makes millions, and no one's caught on yet!"

"Doubtful. She already has more money than God," Claire Bradford pipes in, trying to catch my eye.

I ignore her. Claire's not part of our usual crowd. She's been hanging around a lot. Corey says she's flirting with *him*, but our friend Michelle says she's into me. I hope not. She's pretty, but she's mean and she talks way too much. Like right now.

"She's not stealing," Claire continues. "She has her very own set of weirdo science junk." Claire smiles, and tosses her super straightened—stiff looking hair around her shoulders.

"How do you know?" Corey asks, sliding closer to her. I almost laugh because he's totally trying to look down her shirt. Claire's so focused on me, she has no clue.

"Jess was my lab partner this entire semester. Mrs. Smith loves that girl. They're constantly chatting about supplies and actual science. I think Jess helps the teacher order the stuff for class...like for *fun*. She's is such a terminal geek."

She flips her hair again, and I can tell she's hoping I'll turn to look at her.

I don't.

"Brutal," says Corey, shooting Claire his sympathetic, 'interested look'. Corey's hoping his focus on Claire will get him some action. But mostly, he wants to make Michelle jealous for rejecting him last month. "How'd you survive working with her?" Corey mock-shudders.

"I got an amazing grade. But, she was just so harsh. If it weren't for the part where she called me stupid with her eyes every single day, I'd beg to be her partner next year," Claire says.

"Come on," I defend Jess. "She's not so bad. She's...nice

actually. If you get to know her."

"*Smoke-crack-much*, Porter? Jess Jordan is like every female super villain I can think of: hot, smart, dangerous and frightening as hell," Corey snickers. "No way is she nice."

Adding a sulky pout, Claire joins in, "I can't believe you'd say she's hot."

I try again. "Jess is anything but a super villain. And yeah, she's amazing hot," I add because I know it will make Claire mad. And because it's true.

Corey blinks at me. His smile fades when he gets I'm serious. Thankfully, he's too stunned to speak. For Corey Nash, this a rare moment.

Michelle finally joins us along with half of her cheerleading squad. The three of us have been best friends forever.

"What's the topic?" Michelle ramps in as she and her friends drop their backpacks and dig into lunches.

"Gray is suddenly convinced Jess Jordan is nice," Corey says, shooting Michelle a look.

Michelle raises one dark eyebrow at me. "Really?"

"I hung out with her at the interview, and *yes,* I think she's nice. So what?"

"Holy crap. The girl must have pummeled your head," Corey adds.

I can tell he's about to burst out laughing. There will be no more moments of silence coming from him.

"Of course she was nice...*to you.* You could make any girl be nice." Claire winks at me and licks her lips. It's all I can do not to cringe.

Michelle pulls a face, fluttering her eyes behind Claire's back. "Who got the job?"

"We both got it. Jess and I are going to share the internship. So...I guess...get used to her hanging around me. Maybe you'll see for yourselves. She's cool."

"I thought they only ever took on one applicant?" Michelle frowns. She was one of the hopeful interviewees, but she got axed immediately.

"Yeah…I know." I stop and scour my brain for something to say that isn't a lie. "They created two spots at the last minute because they liked us both so much. I get paid…so…I'm good with it. Cool…huh?" I shrug. My throat has gone completely dry, and I can't meet Michelle's eyes. She'll be able to tell something's off—if she hasn't already noticed.

"And he gets paid *so* much. It's not fair." Corey laughs, smug with the amount I'd told him last night. "Too bad Gray's going to have to bow down and lick Jess Jordan's feet all summer. If they make that girl your boss on any level—you need to quit. No money is worth being bossed around by *that*." He jerks his head toward Jess.

I can't answer. I only shake my head and curb the impulse I have to punch my best friend. Then I feel bad for that thought. I'm the one who's shifted the balance by acting out of the norm, not Corey. I'm the one about to pretend to fall for Jess Jordan. I can't even imagine what they're going to say when I launch that batch of *madness* in their faces.

Worse, I can't tell them the truth, and we've sworn to never lie to each other. Never. But I need to talk to Jess first. Find out what's okay with her. Figure out boundaries. It's only been one day, but leaving Michelle and Corey out of the loop is going to make this painful. Mostly because I'm a terrible actor.

"Poor girl. She's too loaded down," Michelle adds, watching Jess stop to balance her mountain of stuff. "Should have made two trips, I think. Hey…is that our laboratory equipment?"

"It's hers. Claire knows all about it, don't you?" I say, flicking my first real glance at Claire. She grins and I try to smile back. But now that I think I'm an *actor*, I can't get rid of the idea that I'm trapped on some sort of stage.

Bombing my lines.

I smile wider at Claire and try again. "Isn't that right, Claire Bradford…who got a great grade in science this year."

"What's the deal with you today, Gray? You seem off. Stay up too late studying?" Michelle crosses her arms.

Crap. At least she didn't point out that I just sounded like a freak robot.

I toss another cardboard smile at Claire. She looks startled because I'm finally paying her some real attention. Only her expression is sort of creeped-out.

Who can blame her? I'm creeped-out on myself. Whatever. I already have a girlfriend.

I choke back a laugh at that thought, and toss a glance at a very confused Corey. Michelle is still frowning at me, waiting for me to answer.

I'm waiting for someone to tell me my next lines, or at least scream, "FRAUD!" But no one does. They only blink like they don't recognize me. Perfect. I turn away and stare at Jess. The alien-magnet thing that happened to me yesterday ramps back in—along with one of those odd, painful heart-flips. She's slowed to a snail's pace, looking quite pitiful. And alone.

Suddenly, chasing after Jess Jordan, the girl I have no idea how to talk to, seems way better than hanging here and lying to my best friends.

"I—I'll go. I mean…you're right, Michelle." The robot voice won't die.

"What?" asks Michelle.

My eyes feel wild as they dart from face to face. "Someone should help her, huh?"

"Who? Dude!! Not you. You don't work for her—*yet*! Or do you?" Corey shouts, but I'm already bolting down the steps with a quick glance over my shoulder.

Their mouths have all dropped open. Wide. From the

shocked, pissed-off look on Claire's face, I can tell it won't be long before her gossip train leaves the tracks.

Good.

I'm going to need all the help I can get.

7

jess

I shift the massive pile of year-end locker junk so I can catch my pink hoodie before it slides off my shoulder. With the load rebalanced and the pressure off my aching arms, I contemplate for the zillionth time the insane deal I'd struck yesterday.

I can hardly believe any of it really happened. Since I haven't seen or heard from Gray Porter once today, I'm beginning to suspect he's changed his mind.

Mr. Foley's only requirement had been no slacking off or whining about me not having any funding later on. I'll prove myself to him. The job was my goal, never the cash. He'll see how happy I am. After we'd sealed the deal, Mr. Foley had taken me on a facility tour.

Gray didn't stick around because he'd already had the tour the day before.

It seems he's kept his mouth shut as promised—about me, about the deal, and apparently, everything. So far I've not been the target of any unusual snide remarks in the hallways. Despite the finals schedule, everyone's been treating me the same—ignoring or avoiding me—as usual.

Not counting my family, of course.

They've been beaming at me like a toddler who'd finally

made it to the big girl potty. Mom even chose to ignore my yelling at her like a jerk last night. This morning, when I didn't head off early, she fixed me poached eggs and apologized to *me* for invading *my* privacy!

That's about as twisted as me hiring a boyfriend for the summer.

I'm letting myself hope that Gray hasn't approached me because he doesn't want to start our *relationship* until school is over on Friday. Maybe he thinks it will be easier with fewer witnesses to his shame. I don't blame him. I'll just ignore him too, until the first day of work. Once we're forced to share the tiny intern office Mr. Foley gave us, things should move along just fine. Gray made it pretty clear he needed that money. To get it, he's got to show up, eventually.

Like I've conjured him with my thoughts, Gray Porter is suddenly standing in front of me.

Staring. Again.

Rather than slam into him with my mouth hanging open, I skid to a very ungraceful stop and hold tight to my science kit, my beakers and my Bunsen Burner. The books, papers and other less valuable things fall on his feet.

"Really?" I say, keeping my tone sarcastic to cover my racing heart. "Could you not have given me some warning?"

This time, I don't even try to save my hoodie from falling because I've made the ultimate mistake of looking at his face. Having no other choice, I try to keep myself steady and solidify my bearings. Obviously, I'm allergic to beautiful, green, sparkling things. Like his stupid eyes.

"It's called paying attention," he says, copying my sarcasm. "I thought you'd see me. Good save on the breakables." He laughs and drops down to scoop up my stuff.

I still haven't been able to move. How is it this one person can shake my control so easily? He smiles up at me and tosses me a wink. Of course my legs turn to rubber.

"Is this a habit of yours?" he asks.

"What?"

"Dropping stuff whenever you first see me? It's kind of cute. Flattering," he adds, straightening while easily holding all of my stuff in his giant arms.

I've recovered enough to roll my eyes. "Maybe the habit is connected to your urge to rifle through my private things every time *you* see me?"

"It's possible. Your stuff is so randomly interesting." He eyes my science kit and then scans through the pile of papers in his hands. "You got any other lists that need checking off? College tuition aside, I'm also trying to save for a new car." He laughs.

When I don't answer, his expression changes to genuinely concerned. "Hey. Kidding. I make stupid jokes all the time. You'll get used to me, don't worry...or...I can stop making the jokes, I guess."

"I...I'm not worried," I lie, trying to keep my voice steady because I feel like I've entered another world. A world where Gray Porter is holding my things and telling *me* I'm going to get used to him. "We need to meet and flesh out the details of our...you know...whatever. I don't know what to call it. Our contract."

"I was thinking the same thing. But can we call it our *epic summer romance*? *Contract* sounds so stuffy." He smiles again.

Again, I don't smile back.

"Sorry." His laugh sounds embarrassed. "It's quite possible I won't be able to stop the jokes."

"Try. I'd prefer to keep this—us—all business."

"I'm going to work on it. Promise. What should I do first? For the job, I mean. Besides no more joking."

I let out a long sigh. "You'll need to break up with all your *hopefuls*, or whatever you call the girls sniffing about your ankles. And I mean today." I jerk my head at the gaggle of girls waiting for Gray at the top of the steps that lead down to the parking lot.

He glances behind him and grins. "Wow. We have quite an audience. I'm holding at single status. Waiting only for you. And that's not a joke, by the way. So where should we meet later?"

It's all I can do not to cringe and run away. Instead, I swallow, realizing too late that I've hired the wrong guy. Pretend-dating Gray Porter is going to be like pretend-dating a rainbow. Everyone looks at him all the time. Which means, if I'm near him, everyone's looking at me. Not ideal. I feel like holes are being stared into my back right now. "I help with Coach Williams' after-school music program from two-thirty to four-thirty. How about you meet me in his classroom at 3:45?"

He shakes his head. "Coach Williams' classroom? Hell, no. He's a complete ass. Pick another spot."

"No. I only have a thirty minute break in there. Meaning, I can't leave to meet you anywhere else. Coach Williams heads to the weight room to check on the hockey team. I'm supposed to set up his room for the next group of kids. I'm mostly a sitter to anyone who's dropped off early. After the music program's finished, Coach Williams meets the team over at the Golden sports complex and—"

"I know where he goes." Gray's voice has turned cold. "I work afternoons and nights at the sports complex. I simply don't want to go near that guy's classroom."

"Why? Did he cut you from the hockey team and now you're bitter?" I guess, relieved his bad attitude has nothing to do with me. As much as Coach Williams is a softie for the music kids, everyone knows he's rough on his team.

"Not *even*. I play competitive *inline* hockey. My ice time is spent teaching the little guys at the complex. I'd never play ice for that tool."

"Okay." I shrug. "I don't speak sports. I have no idea what you just said. You're going to have to get over your Coach Williams phobia and meet me in the music room. 3:45. Don't be late."

"Listen to the boss-girl." He sounds really agitated.

"Please," I soften my tone. "I swear he won't be around. Meeting there will be private. No one will see us." I point to the now even larger crowd of people watching us. "Your pride and your popularity will be safe."

He shakes his head. "That's what you think? That I don't want anyone to see me with you? Why do you think I approached you with everyone watching? I did it on purpose."

"Oh...well...next time can you not be so obvious? I'm truly uncomfortable, if you must know."

He sighs. "We're about to be going out. *Us* going out has to start with *us* at least hanging in public and talking, or no one's going to buy it."

I nod, hating that he's right. "I guess I didn't think through the day-to-day mechanics of having a fake boyfriend. Hmm. Public hanging out...seems so extreme. We only have this week of school left. Will anyone really care or notice?"

"It's up to you, but you need to decide. Don't think I'm giving up the money. We shook. Next week we both report to Geekstuff.com. How deeply you want to play the rest of our deal is up to you."

His smile is shameless as he points to the audience at the top of the steps. "If you don't want my services, then it's only fair you cut me loose so I can make another girl or two happy this summer. Or three." He shifts my papers into a neater pile.

"What will they do once I take you off the market?" I ask. "I can only imagine the poor girls wandering around like a lost herd of sheep all summer, wondering where you went." I risk another glance at the staring girls and shudder. "Do they even blink? Baa. Baa. Baa."

He shakes his head and laughs. "Like I said yesterday, you're really funny."

I arch one brow as high as I possibly can, pretending to ignore him and the fact that his compliment almost made me smile. "It's nice to know Michelle Hopkins has some other skill besides chewing gum and tossing pom-poms. She's texting so fast her phone's about to catch fire. And what's up with the tall blonde who's giving me the stink eye?"

"Hey, Michelle's cool. But you're right about the blonde. She's got some sort of crush on me. I'm hoping our budding relationship will kill it, so thanks. My bonus will be *her* moving along."

"Serious?" I glare. "I'll need a list of your most dangerous stalkers. I don't want to end up in a surprise nail scratching event over you."

"Would you please try to muster at least one expression showing you *might* be happy we're talking to each other?" He reaches forward and tucks a stray lock of hair behind my ear.

I'm startled, but then happy because, just like yesterday, I didn't have the urge to flinch!

And then, I'm annoyed. With him and myself.

Those stupid butterflies are back. Wreaking havoc from my stomach to my toes. Does this mean all summer long I'll be dropping stuff, feeling slightly dizzy and unable to breathe?

I'm about to launch one of my scathing comments; but before I can zing one, Gray places his fingertip gently against my lips.

He shakes his head as though he knows my game and jerks his head toward the people behind us. "I'm thinking a smile would work better. We should use the attention to our advantage."

His voice is butter soft as he continues, "Come on, Jess. Just try…or pretend or whatever works to get you through this. It's all for show."

Brutally aware of just how warm his finger is against my lips, I oblige his request. "Like this?" I roll my eyes, pulling my fake, too-many-teeth-showing, camera smile, and I shove my Bunsen Burner between us like a shield.

He grins. "Ridiculous, but it's a start. No more snide comments." He moves his finger to run it down the bridge of my nose, tapping the tip once.

I'm completely undone. Melted, mush.

All I can do is stare at the way his smile makes the corners of his eyes crinkle! Do all cute guys have these things?

And his lips…the guy has amazing lips.

And damn those eyes straight to hell. How is it possible he has lashes that look like they came from a magazine?

I clutch the beakers close when I realize my grip has become dangerously loose. Tearing my gaze away from his face, I feel heat hit my cheeks and burn down to my toes. With two small touches and a smile, he's killed my brain.

Baa, Baa, Baa! I'm just like those other sheep.

Just in case Gray's noticed my complete lapse, I widen my smile and speak through my teeth, trying to make myself look like an obnoxious ventriloquist. "How long do I have to keep up the *happy part*? I'm getting a cramp."

"That's the spirit." He chuckles, leaning forward as though to look deep into my eyes. I figure he's trying to make a show to his friends that we're sharing a private joke. So awkward. Instead of pulling back like I want, I laugh too, and continue to avoid his gaze by darting a glance over my shoulder to check if everyone's still watching us.

Oh, they are. My heart is racing so fast I feel faint.

The way Michelle's holding up her phone, I wonder if this

moment is about to be posted on YouTube.

When I turn back, Gray's moved even closer. As in, double-awkward-closer.

"Jess," he starts, flushing slightly. "I'm assuming we could make the best of this. Us hanging out—it doesn't have to be *terrible*, does it? We could try for some fun? Be friends when it's all over?"

"I—I—uh—possibly," I cover, because his suggestion is a complete impossibility. He has no need to worry about me making any more snide comments, either. The only thing I can think of saying now involves adjectives describing how breathtaking his voice is.

Keyword: Breathtaking. As in, stopped my breath.

Yep. I've stopped breathing.

Baa, baa, BAA-OHMYGOD. I hate myself right now. I think I also just blatantly sniffed him! But, he smells so—fresh.

"Do you want me to help you walk to your car?" he asks, breaking the huge silence I've created.

"No. Absolutely not!" I shout, half-grateful I'm not making any farm animal noises out loud.

"Why?" He steps back, looking slightly surprised.

Should I tell him the truth? That if he takes one more step I might pass out because he's so gorgeous? Maybe I could mention I had this odd idea I wanted to kiss him back when I was staring at his lips? For real! What is wrong with me?

What in the heck would Dr. Brodie and my parents think about that? What would the audience on the steps have done? What would Gray have done? Run screaming, probably.

Is this considered *progress* or do I need to be committed? I don't even know this guy!

"Give. Me. My. Stuff."

"I'll be happy to walk you?"

"No. I'm good. Just hand it over. Now," I order.

"Okay. Whatever you say, *boss*." His grin returns. It's the double-wide one from yesterday. Dimpled, square chinned... *UGH*.

I refuse to look at his dumb smile or his cute eye-crinkles one more time. He gingerly stacks my pile of things onto my newly-adjusted science kit and beakers. This leaves me staring at his strong-looking hands. Of course it does. And of course his hands are also amazingly, perfectly, and annoyingly well made. Like the rest of him.

Without another word, I turn my back and start for my Jeep, wondering if he can hear how loudly he's made my heart pound.

"Okay then, see you after school, *Jess*. It's a *date*. We'll have some *fun*! Good luck on your afternoon final!"

He sounds like a stupid megaphone.

When I don't answer and hunch my shoulders, his low laugh adds a trail of goose bumps coursing down my neck.

The guy is out of control—which causes me to be out of control. That is an unacceptable option! This afternoon, I'm going to pin him down with some solid rules.

I make it to the Jeep, dump my stuff into the back, and scramble ungracefully into the driver's seat. I'd meant to catch a cat-nap during lunch, but now, that's going to be impossible. I decide to drive through Starbucks. I can get a *triple anything* or a snack to boost the two churning Red Bulls that got me through last period.

I start the engine and shoot a glance through the tinted window, figuring if anyone is still watching, they can no longer see past my silhouette. Gray seems to have been waiting for a movement like this. He's waving like a dork and swinging my long forgotten pink hoodie high in the air so I can see it.

He's yelling, "Bye Jess!"

He flips my hoodie onto his shoulders and ties it around his neck until it looks like a ridiculous scarf—as though he means to wear it like that for a long time.

My stomach lurches. I want to laugh, but deep down I should cry. I'm going to be so far behind on sleep that I won't be able to avoid my bed tonight. Finals, plus all that's happened with Gray has me worried my nightmare is going to crash back in again.

I need to come up with a new daytime sleep schedule. Fast. Things should settle down once the new job starts. Once I get used to Gray Porter talking to me as a daily norm. I'll also be able to log almost four hours of sleep each day after dawn, starting next week. I won't have to be at school at 7AM anymore. The internship starts at nine. That's lots of quality car napping. More than I'm used to.

In the meantime, I'm back on high alert. Tonight, I'll even stuff a towel under my door just in case I start making a bunch of uncontrollable noise in my sleep.

But I won't. I'm sure last night was just a one time stress thing. Positively, hopefully, almost sure that I'm going to be fine.

Soon. Next week at the latest. Tonight if I'm lucky.

Please let me be lucky.

8

gray

I stop one of the gangly-looking middle school boys exiting Coach Williams' music room. "Do you know Jess Jordan?"

"She's in there." The kid points over his shoulder.

"Thanks." I head in, surveying the giant room. A room I've avoided like the plague since freshman year. I linger near the door in case I spot Coach Williams. In case I need to make a quick exit. So far, all seems safe enough. Two oak teachers' desks are pushed up next to the far window. Heavy, iron music stands and folding chairs are arranged orchestra style in front of a large wooden podium. Choir risers have been set up in a semi-circle on the miniature stage filling half the room.

"Jess?" I call, when the last kid files out and I still don't see her.

"Back here." Her voice is muffled by the heavy, red and gold velvet curtain.

I hop onto the stage and joke-sing: "*The Phaaaanntom of the Opera is there, innnnnside your mind.*" I attack the curtain with a flourish and sing on, "*Innnnside your mind.*"

Jess is sitting on an ancient, faded couch with her arms crossed over her stomach. Her face is extremely pale, and she's not at all impressed with my song.

"You okay?" I let the curtain drop.

She nods. "I didn't sleep well last night. And I—had a weird…lunch. After I saw you nothing went right."

"Bummer." I walk nearer, taking in the deep shadows under her eyes, and I wonder if she's telling me the whole truth. "What can I do to help?"

"Honestly? Let's just get through this. I want to draw up a real contract. So we both know what to expect. And what *not* to expect." She shoots me a pointed look.

I want to tease her, but I don't have the heart. She looks so darn pitiful. "All right." I sit on the floor near her and look up. I'm instantly sidetracked by the color of her clear blue eyes under the stage light. It doesn't help that her cinnamon-sunshine smell has completely taken over the small space. I concentrate on quieting the unsteady beat of my heart.

"What have you thought up so far?" I ask.

"I have some rough ideas. Like, each weekend we probably need to hang out like you said. You know. Go on sort of… real looking…dates?" She sounds so timid, like she thinks I'm going to laugh.

"I figured. Go on," I encourage quietly, taking note how supremely uncomfortable the word 'dates' made her. I wonder if she's ever been out with anyone.

"We should also hang out a few nights during the week. If that works for you? And then, to keep the whole thing believable, you simply dump me at the end of the summer."

"Hold on there—I—"

She holds up her hand. "Wait. Just listen or I'll lose my train of thought. I don't care how you break up with me, or the reasons you give," she rushes on. "I'm *so* good with the break-up part. Looking forward to it, actually. No offense. I will also need you to call me, and text me. A few times a week. When my parents are home—after 5:30 PM. That, and pretend to like to me…when we're together. Sort of like today on the quad. I'll try not to hate it so much. So, yeah. Can you think of anything else?"

"You hated me talking to you?"

She flushes. "Do you want me to lie?"

"Yes. Yes I do. My feelings—they hurt really bad right about now. Duh." I pull a frown.

"Please." She laughs, finally appearing to relax a bit. "No joking. Where were we? We need to make the hanging out bits *last* longer."

"Check."

"You seem really good at making…things so believable. No fixes on how you're acting, just on my acting. And then…you can ignore me otherwise. I won't bother you during the in-between times. When you're off duty or whatever. So, yeah. I think that's it. Easy. Right?"

"You're serious?" I now feel slightly sick myself. Does she think I can really do what she's asked of me without caring?

She blinks. "What? Am I missing something?"

"Don't say anything else, just let me process." I stand and pace away from her and all that cinnamon air so I can think. So I can keep my freaked expression out of her too observant line of sight.

The girl wants me to ignore her during the 'in-between times' and dump her at the end of the summer?

What excuse could I possibly use to dump Jess that would not simply create more brutal gossip for her life? Does she not get that gossip is forever?

"Let me just say this all out loud because I wonder if it's even going to work," I start.

"What do you mean?" She wrinkles her brow.

"I'm not sure I have the time to do weeknight dates. I work a ton of hours at the TOG complex. Until 9 PM on weeknights and 10PM on weekends. You're asking me to take my one hour of free time, collect you, and *pretend* to take you on dates?"

"You're getting paid a lot," she says and frowns. "I'm sure you can squeeze me in."

"Maybe. But I have a grandmother to take care of and the internship hours are huge. And friends…and…"

Her face crumples. "Right. I didn't figure all that in. I don't have an 'outside life' to consider."

"Look." I sigh, feeling like an ass. "This is not personal."

"It sounds personal."

"This is why I told you during the interview that I don't have girlfriends long term. You think I'm a player, but it's not like that. There's simply no room for you—or *any girl*, to be in the middle of my messy, over-scheduled life. Even if you pay me, there's only 24 hours in a day."

"Do they have tables at the TOG complex? Some place I could just sit and read? I won't bother you, and I'll drive my-self. Happy?"

"You want to sit around and stare at me while I work?"

She nods. Her expression is so earnest. Desperate. "As long as I'm out of my house and I can say that I'm hanging out with you—a *real, live, guy*. Might be easier if I drive myself, anyhow. Then my parents won't try to grill you on our front porch."

"Well, that solves one of my biggest obstacles to this entire contract. I'm not a fan of meeting your parents at all." I cover the fear-twist in my heart with a laugh, remembering all too well the overprotective Pit Bulls Jess Jordan calls *Mom and Dad*. Those people wouldn't just grill me on the porch, they'd shoot me dead like a rabid wolf.

"FYI, I don't want them to meet you, either. I'd just prefer to keep you at a major distance. My mom's so embarrassing, and my dad is really uptight about me dating anyone, so—um, yeah. We're in agreement."

I nod and tap my fingers against my knees. "What to do with a girlfriend while I work my hours at the TOG. Hmm. Can I really do this? Will I be able to pull it off? Will she be able to read at the snack bar tables without losing her mind," I mumble.

"Do you always talk to yourself?"

"Yes. Bad habit. Does it bother you?" I walk back over to her side of the small stage.

"No. It's interesting. I hate people knowing my thoughts. But yours just fall out of your head so easily." She shrugs.

"I never thought of it like that…but you're my girlfriend now…so who cares if you know what I think?"

Her cheeks turn pink, and I laugh.

Suddenly, I'm unable to break my gaze away from hers. I witness what I saw yesterday. She's covered her personal information slip with one of her small glowers. Her eyes darken with her snapping, challenging glare and erase all signs of the vulnerability she'd just exposed.

"We'll need to clarify for the record, that I'm a *pretend girlfriend*. Pretend," she demands. "Got it? If you're giving me that goofy look because you think there are going to be *benefits* as part of this deal, you can just hold it right there! *Pretend girlfriend*. Say it with me."

I shake my head at her outrageous comments. "Please. I've got that understood."

"Good."

She looks so prickly and uncomfortable now, that I can't resist a little dig. "That goes two ways, you know? I'm no piece of meat. Don't expect these lips to be at your beck and call. Not even for eight thousand dollars. But, I am going to have to hold your hand, put my arm around your shoulders, things like that. Let's lay *that* on the contract before you land a couple of punches on my face for doing a 'good job'. I am not nearly as handsome or as marketable with double black eyes."

"Okay. Okay. Don't want to damage the merchandise. I'm all for making this look realistic. But...um." She pauses and looks sort of hunted.

"What?"

"Promise you'll give me the heads up before you try to put your arms on me—or whatever. I'm just—well, at least I think I am—sort of jumpy about being touched without notice."

"I can do that."

I quickly avoid her eyes because I get the sensation that she might be able to see through me so I change the subject. "You don't look as pale as you did before. Are you feeling better?"

"Yeah...a bit. Probably because this conversation has made me turn red too many times."

"Could be. Any more embarrassing topics to cover before the last of your pink fades out again?"

She nods. "One more."

"Shoot."

"I don't think I could stand everyone knowing you were hooking up with girls on the side, and then laughing at me. So...could you not cheat on me?"

My jaw drops open. "Say you're joking. I wouldn't do that. Promise. And I don't break promises." I stop myself, and feel heat sting my own cheeks.

She raises an eyebrow as though she knows I'm full of crap. I play off my pause and try to head near the truth, so I can at least look her in the eye. "I've broken a few promises, okay? God. Who hasn't? But I won't let anyone laugh at you, and I won't cheat on you. I swear." I sit again and mess with one of my laces. I'm sure she can sense the guilt oozing off me.

Am I really so bad to have broken the promise I made to her parents in the past? I think they wouldn't fault my intent if they knew Jess had meant to offer this *pretend boyfriend job* to a bunch of random guys. So why do I feel like such a criminal? I wasn't the one who'd hurt her freshman year. I'd been trying to help. I'm still trying to help. Or I wouldn't be here. She doesn't remember, but I do. Ancient history or not, I feel like I owe her something.

This time, I'm going to do things right.

When I find her gaze again, she hits me with a tentative, almost trusting smile. One that serves to double my guilt and marks me a total bastard.

As if I know how to do right by this beautiful, amazingly strong, but fragile girl. I don't deserve her trust. But I mean to earn it.

"Hello...? Are you with me?" She smiles. "Do you want to write this all down or should I?"

"Sorry. Yeah. I've got it." I flip to a blank page in my note-book and click the pen.

"I'm in charge of all recorded details unless I ask for your input." She's rubbing her temples, and her face has gone all pale again.

"Go for it," I say quietly, and hover my pen over the blank page.

9

jess

The pounding in my head has ramped up to high. A signal that I'm running on empty, and about to hit bottom. Thankfully, Gray had bought my 'bad lunch' excuse for why I look like crap right now.

As if that matters. Do you have to look nice for a guy you're paying to date you? I close my eyes because they've started to hurt.

"I'm waiting, " he asks in this ultra-soft voice. Like he somehow knows I'm about to bottom out on him.

"Okay…well…I officially ask for your input. Give me *your* run-down on the details." I keep my eyes closed. "I have no idea how to proceed with making a contract like this. Just make it fair. Honest."

"Okay." Gray tries to sound like he's clearing his throat, but I can tell he's just swallowed back a laugh. I'm afraid to open my eyes because he's probably doing one of those huge smiles. I cannot take a rush of butterflies right now, so I squeeze my eyes closed tighter.

"Let's talk about phone calls first," he starts. "How many times a week do you expect your pretend boyfriend to call you?"

"Please. I don't even have girlfriends who call me. How would I know? What's the standard?"

"We could start with one per day?" His voice has softened and the laughter is gone from it.

I open my eyes and met his gaze dead on, trying to re-focus. I hate when people feel sorry for me. And I think he's doing that. "Seven calls per week, then. Yes. Seven sounds good. Oh, and texting. We won't start really *fake-hanging-out* until after the internship begins. Is that what you want?"

"I thought we were hanging out right now. I'm all for starting this off today. We had successful exposure at lunch, so let's keep it going. I'll text you tonight." He writes something on the paper. I tilt my head to the side to watch his scrawling handwriting fill up the lines on the page. He looks up at me, waiting for more. I can only blink and stare at the curls just above his forehead. "What's next?"

"How do you normally *start* the girlfriend bit? Is today a good example? You hunt down your prey as they head to their cars, and then you're so cute and charming that it's an automatic *go*?"

He laughs. "It's a 'go' whenever it's a 'go'. There's no time stamp on it. There's lots of talking, flirting, hoping, staring, awkwardness—the usual. You know."

I shrug. I don't know, but I'm not about to tell him that. "Where, besides the long walk to the parking lot, are your best pick-up spots? Just wondering."

"I've done okay whispering to girls in the library. The lunchroom also works well because it's easy to joke around in there. I've never analyzed it." He shrugs back, looking way too calm about this totally messed up conversation.

"Hmm," I cover, acting as though this doesn't bother me either. "Curious information, nonetheless. How do you know it's working—that she's into your moves—or whatever?"

"She gives me her phone number, or I give her mine. Then we…flirt text. When you—um—*we* want things to go public, it goes on Facebook. The *in a relationship* line will get us our best exposure."

"Yeah…uh, about Facebook…all that social networking. I don't have it. My parents check my sister's emails, Facebook, and texts like stalkers. In order to get our cell phones, Kika and I had to agree to the *Jordan Household No Privacy Act*. I do have a school email account. But Facebook and Twitter…if you're *me*…there's no point. You'd be my only 'friend' besides my family."

"Ahh…okay." He nods and looks away.

I want to punch him because I don't need anyone feeling sorry for me, and that is exactly how his expression reads right now. If I didn't feel like my head had turned into a brick I'd so rip him. All I can do instead is swallow the cardboard lump that's taken up residence at the back of my throat, and hate him—or myself.

"I suppose it's a good thing you aren't connected," he says finally, running a hand through his hair. "They—your parents —would see my profile. That would get awkward. Plus they would expect you to *friend* your boyfriend, so yeah…I like that actually. No Facebook…"

While he's writing, I'm unable not to stare at the way he looks so boyish with his curls messed up.

He meets my gaze with a shrug. "How about we go for a major amount of obvious text messaging and talking about each other. That should be enough. Then, we can just go on from there."

"What does *major amount* mean?"

"Enough so when this week is over there's some sort of alert to our…audience."

"Oh. God. Right. Like caution signs. A definite signal that

you've lost your mind?"

"No! Well, yes. Sort of. Without some warning, my friends, especially Corey, won't buy in. It's important they believe this. We have a few days left before school ends. If we do it right, it should be enough."

"How annoying, but I agree. My family would also flip with a zero-warning-boyfriend announcement." I groan and shake my head. "What would be an *appropriate* amount of time for you to...flirt text and then fall for me? We've already done the long hang out in front of the school. We must be half way there, huh?"

"At least that." He laughs. "I'm very good at flirt texting... irresistible, even."

I know he's joking, but when he grins the butterflies I'd been battling flood my aching head, despite my attempts to stop them.

"I can't wait," I say, blasting him with my most unimpressed eye-roll.

He laughs again, but at least this time it doesn't sound so confident. "Once the family and friends are sold, we can lay out the details of our weekend dates during the first week of the internship." He writes quickly then, his eyes intent on the page. "I think I've got it all."

"Please add that I get to make any needed adjustments to this contract at any time."

"God. What a high maintenance girlfriend you're turning out to be. As long as I get paid, you can change anything you want." He scribbles that down. "Anything else?" he asks.

"Friends. I need some, so I'll have to borrow yours. Some-how, you're going to have to include me in your golden circle of popularity."

"What? I have no golden circle. Has anyone ever mentioned how skewed your mind is?"

"Look, you're going to have to get over that part about me. The reality of me, not being normal, has landed you the best paying summer job of your life."

"You really need to stop saying that about yourself. If you're crazy, I'm crazy. Everyone's crazy, Jess. You seem fine enough to me."

"Let's hope you never have to see the real me, then."

"Whatever. Bring her on. I'm sure I wouldn't notice a difference. Or care."

My heart races and I look away. "Well, I care. Write it down. For nine weekends and eight thousand dollars, what's yours is mine including your friends." I throw in a little sarcastic eye flutter. "We're going to be so head-over-heels-in-love. I can't wait to see how *romantic* you are!"

"Oh no. I refuse to be your kind of *bumper-sticker-romantic*. Don't mistake me for Mr. Darcy."

I gasp. "You don't know Hunger Games or Forks, Washington, but you know Mr. Darcy? Start talking."

"My grandmother's a fan. She's tortured me since birth with Mr. Darcy. Thanks to her DVD collection, I can quote Jane Austen faster than the Elmo song."

I laugh, surprised again. "Prove it."

"Elizabeth, daaarling!" He's launched into a breathless English accent. "I *love, love, love* you, and I never want to be parted from you from this day forward. Pardon me, whilst I puke..."

"No way!" I beam. "Let the contract state that I want the Mr. Darcy accent once a week!" I can't help but laugh again because he's shaking his head and laughing back.

"Not happening. No one can know my secrets."

I could swear he finally looks uncomfortable.

"You'll get plenty of revenge when you dump me," I say.

"Oh. About that. I'm not dumping you." He scratches out something and writes above it. "I insist that at the end of the contract, you, Jess Jordan, have to dump me, in public. You're required to create a total scene. I'll make it easy on you by doing…something."

"Something?"

"Yes, something so obviously offensive that everyone will know it's my fault you had to end things."

"That seems like a lot of work. Isn't it easier and more tragic to be on the dumped side?" I ask. "Being dumped will get me points with the parents."

"Not fair." He pushes out his bottom lip into his version of a pout and makes his eyes go round like a basset hound puppy. "When it's over, I want to be like poor old Humpty Dumpty. Smashed to bits. Imagine the ladies who'll feel sorry for me. I'll need lots of help to tape my sad, confused, and broken little pieces back together again."

I shake my head. "God. That's disgusting really, but it's the least I can do if it's what you want. Consider me the dumper. I suppose it fits my reputation." He frowns when I say that, but I'm still beaming. Running with the idea. "Either way, while you're licking your wounds, I'll have a solid excuse to retreat back into my room with my own broken heart. That's all I need."

"Why is that good?" He holds my gaze. "It sounds…"

"Perfect," I finish. "Our sad ending will free me from what my parents call *normal high school social activities* for the entire semester. I can avoid homecoming, and dress shopping, and pep rallies. By the time I come up for air, my college applications will have been sent and hopefully accepted! Right in time for me to start chatting to my mom about how college relationships will be better than my time spent dating immature, terrible YOU!"

I'm filled with blissful relief at that thought; but the guy is still frowning at me like a black cloud. "What?"

He flushes and looks at the paper. "You'll have to meet my grandmother. Is that okay?"

"Why?"

"She's seventy, but totally with it. I'm not going to have her worrying. She's really old fashioned, and I will tell her about you some."

"Oh. Okay. Sure." The idea of meeting his grandmother makes my stomach do a funny spin.

"I'm adding in a line next to the *Zero Parent Contact* bullet that also includes no real names on your side," he says, clicking the pen nervously. "That's the plan, right?"

"Yep. That's the plan. My mom's guerilla telephone spy network will get her the information she needs on any name I give her. In less than three phone calls, she'd be knocking on your front door. Plus she and my sister Kika would know it was all fake if they found out I was into some perfectly chiseled superjock. I'm more of a nerd-lovin' kind of girl."

"I'll try not to be too insulted." He shakes his head. "But you should know—prickly, cute, relentless girls with big blue eyes, geeky clothes, and great grades are completely my type. If this were real, I mean."

"Okay. Touché. Thanks for lying, but you suck at it. You have a lot of work to do to make *that* sound convincing." I laugh, but when I meet his gaze he looks strange. Flustered.

He breaks eye contact with me and taps his pen against the contract. "Look, Jess...I wouldn't be able to sleep tonight if I didn't at least try to convince you not to do this. You've said it yourself. I am the last guy you should date this summer. And it's completely true."

"Spare me. We've been through the shakedown thing. Just keep writing and stop trying to weasel out of this. I'm not going to back out now. You—we—already got the job. Neither of us wants to back away from Geekstuff.com. I can't wait to work there, and same with you."

He looks up at me then, and I can't look away. "I want to add one additional requirement onto this."

"Anything. Please, just don't back out." I scan deeper into his green-gold gaze, wishing I could read his mind.

"If you're going to hang out with me and my friends, you have to be nice."

"Nice?" I swallow.

"Nice. Like you're being now. Like you were yesterday—to everyone at the interview. To me."

I pull a face and prepare to blast him for calling me nice, but he holds up a finger to stop me from speaking as he continues, "If you aren't, no one will believe a second of this. And there's my grandmother to consider. As much as I've heard you say I've got a reputation as a player, *you* are rumored to be a huge 'capital-B'. I'd prefer that word not be part of how I bring you up to Gran—"

"God. Stop yourself." I swallow. I don't want to admit how much his words hurt. "I'll be *nice*, but you have to be nice back. And—I—I—won't let you blab about this contract—"

"Honestly. Stop *yourself* this time." He holds up his hand. "I'm *famous* for not talking about stuff. You've got no worries there. I'm not telling any of my friends about this—about you—about our contract." He seems to assess me. "If it leaks because of *me*, you can keep the money. How's that?"

"Do you think I'm going to be the one that blows our cover?"

He shrugs. "Trust me, and I'll trust you. It's as easy as that."

I have to work to get some steady sounding words to come out. Instead of layering on a snide comment, I hit him with the absolute truth: "I'll trust you. But know that I despise, down to my core, that I have to do that. I hate trusting anyone but myself. No offense."

I can feel him staring.

"*Jess.*" His voice is whisper low and sends goosebumps up the back of my neck. "You have my word. I won't let anyone—anything hurt you. This will work out. It will."

I risk a glance at him, feeling almost consumed by the concern I'd heard in his voice. For once, I'm sure I've read him right.

He cares. I don't know why, but he cares. Maybe it's the money, maybe he's just nice. But he seems to mean all that he's just said. I can only pray he's going to follow through.

I nod and rub the creases in my jeans flat over my knees. My throat is dry, and my eyes are heavy with exhaustion and unshed tears. I'm suddenly hot, then too cold.

I glance up again to find him still staring. "What are you waiting for? Write that all down so we can sign it," I manage, blinking.

He scrawls his name across the bottom of the paper and hands it over with a half-smile. "Your turn."

I sign my name next to his and hand it back. It's all I can do not to scream: *AWKWARD.* If only I could—but my voice seems to no longer exist.

Gray heads out from behind the curtain, and I stay put so I can get myself together. When I follow him out, he's turning on Mr. Williams' old-school printer/copier machine.

"I'm sure good ol' Coach won't mind lending us his personal paper stash. Not for this," he mutters. After a couple of false starts and stops, he figures out how to make it work, and hands me a copy.

"Well. That's it, *girlfriend.*" He grins, folding his copy of the contract and stuffing it into his back pocket.

"Mmmh." I nod. I'm still completely unable to form a sentence. I turn to grab my messenger bag and carefully place my contract inside. I don't want to wrinkle it in case I decide to frame it and hang it next to my future college diploma.

When I turn back, Gray's got his phone out. It's lit up like he's checking texts. His eyes are gleaming. "Let's exchange numbers. I'll text you at 7PM sharp." He tosses me another one of those perfect, heart-stopping winks and raises his eyebrows up high. "I'd hate for your parents to miss my charming message."

My face is so stiff from holding the same expression in place that my cheeks actually hurt. I wonder if I've cracked a molar.

God. Seriously? Gray Porter, my hired boyfriend wants my phone number so he can text me tonight. HA...

I shrug like this is no big thing and pull out my iPhone. "You first, *boyfriend*." I shoot him a wink of my own, doubled with a huge glare.

I'll call this new look the 'winking-scorn-glare.'

The result: Gray laughs like I'm hilarious.

Obviously, I need to practice this look in the mirror.

Or fire him immediately.

10

jess

It's now exactly *7:01PM*.

So far no text. None.

I'm hoping Gray's chickened out.

My eyes have bored holes into everything in this kitchen besides the location of my iPhone. I've plugged it into the charger next to the table. The whole family has iPhones, and we are all pretty territorial over our charging areas. The antique cherry sideboard station is where my dad, a university geology professor at the Colorado School of Mines, usually plugs in when he gets home from work.

Tonight, I'd distracted him from his usual pattern: walk in, drop laptop bag in front hall, wander into kitchen to deposit mail, plug in phone, and look for Mom (or tortilla chips). I was lurking at the sideboard. Took the mail out of his hands, and attacked him with a few cheerful and earnest *sedimentary rock* questions.

BINGO.

He'd been unable to resist. Within seconds I had him in his office and at his computer, looking up websites to show me what he said were, "some great photos". I thought the photos were just okay, but my dad is so cute when he's excited about geology, I'd never tell him.

Over dinner, thanks to all of our research, we shared our findings. We had a very nice, extended review of the area's 'Fountain Formation'. It's these cool, red, sandstone rocks that are the remainder of an ancient river that was once the size of the Nile. This formation covers huge parts of Colorado with diagonally angled rocks. It even makes up Red Rocks Amphitheater. Dad never tires of this topic. Rocks are his life. The Fountain Formation is like his personal church. And Red Rocks is the coolest place in the world to see a concert.

I lingered over Mom's dinner, one she'd made to celebrate my new job. Now both parents and my sister are sitting around, waiting patiently for me to finish cutting two pints of strawberries for shortcake. I'd used the words 'please' and 'family-time' in the same sentence to stick them to their seats and wait for me while I make dessert.

While I wait for Gray to text me in front of them all.

7:03

Dad's glasses slide down his long, straight nose. His head is propped on a hand that's buried in his wavy, gray hair. Because of geology-bonding session, the poor guy hasn't even changed yet. I can tell he's getting antsy. He looks overheated in his usual rumpled, tweedy-wool professor blazer. Mom hates Dad's blazers because he wears them every season. They're supposed to only be for winter.

Mom's a freelance nutritionist for large hospitals—a class act, and very into fashion. Because she travels a lot she's taken to only wearing black, white and gray. She looks like she's always stepping off some plane from Paris. Always. Her dark-brown hair is never messy. She wears it shoulder length, but it is endlessly pulled back into a fancy clip. Her other trademark accessories: round gold earrings, one matching gold choker, and one wide gold bangle. Her only color splash includes some type of seasonal scarf in an appropriate fabric to set it all off.

7:04

Now Dad's checking his email. A sure signal he's ready to head to his den, or worse, set his phone on the charger.

Mom's begun tapping her foot. I can tell she's working really hard to sit still. Most probably she's working even harder to not snap at me to *hurry.*

Kika's oblivious. Smiling, her spacey smile and watching the strawberries hit the bowl. Thinking about whipped cream, I'm sure.

"Hang in there, guys. I'm almost done." When I'm sure no one's looking at me, I glance at the clock again.

Still 7:04! Really?!

Longest minute of my life.

"No hurry. This is fun, isn't it, *honey?*" Mom asks my dad— her voice is tense.

I catch her gaze, and she shoots me another stiff smile.

Dad, no dummy when Mom's voice has that ring in it, has put down his phone and is sending my mom a pained look of his own.

"I'm not leaving until you deliver the gooey goods," Kika says, not once wavering her gaze from the bowl. "Don't forget, double whipped cream on my plate." Kika's long, blonde hair is coming out of her twin pony-tails. She wears them the same way every day. Pulled toward the front to hang over her shoulders. Like a frame for the picture on her most favorite wardrobe item: the graphic T. Today, it's baby pink with a picture of an owl on the front.

At *7:05* I breathe a sigh of relief and stop slicing the strawberries.

Gray must have gone back to work. I can't help but feel a little disappointed.

"Jess, you need some help? I can't sit here all night. I've got some papers to look at," Dad pleads.

I realize I've been standing frozen like a zombie. They must think I've lost it. I shoot him a grateful smile (one that's real). "Yeah. Sure. I think the day has finally sunk in for me. I'm tired. Thanks."

"I bet you are, champ. Finals are tough. Have a seat." He's smiling at me now with the same extra proud look he and Mom suffocated me with ever since I told them I got the internship. Now that I've got my contract with Gray in place, I feel like such a *good girl* to make them all so pleased with me. Heck, I'm pleased with myself.

I slide into my chair, grateful to be sitting.

Bzz. Bzz. Boing-donka-donk.

The entire family jumps at the same time. If I hadn't been vomiting in my own mouth, I might have laughed. My dad drops the knife and is eyeing the kitchen fire alarm with a bewildered expression.

Less than one second later, it happens again.

Bzz. Bzz. Boing-donka-donk.

"What *is* that?" Mom's jetted out of her chair and is looking around the room like a hawk, trying to gauge the source of the annoying sound.

"Sorry. It's my cell," I croak.

"Well, I've never heard that noisy sound come out of your phone before," Mom accuses. "What's wrong with it?"

I'm about to make a major dive for the phone but Kika beats me to it. I try to cover the fact that I just bolted out of my chair by bolting back into it.

Kika's staring at my iPhone screen as she walks it to the table. I'm hoping whatever's visible on the phone's monitor is not going to blow my cover.

The sound comes through again.

Bzz. Bzz. Boing-donka-donk.

My mom winces. "Can you change it? *Now?*"

"Yeah. Sure. I don't know where that came from," I lie, knowing full well I chose that tone for its incredible sound and combined buzzing effect.

Dad's head disappears behind the kitchen island and he's groaning, "Oh, the old gray knees are not made for this." He pops back into view, holding the lost knife. "Shortcake in two."

Bzz. Bzz. Boing-donka-donk.

"Whoever's texting you, sure has a lot to say." Kika smiles.

I want to crawl across the table to get the phone out of her hands, but I wait patiently for her to bring it over. When she does, Kika and I stare at the screen together: *Yo QT. r u there?*

I dart Kika a glance. "What does that mean? He called me a Q-tip?"

Kika laughs and sits next to me. "Read it out loud. It will make more sense."

"Yo-Q-T ru there. Q…T…?"

"Q T means *cutie.* CU-TIE. Jess, you're so out of touch." Kika's smile turns beaming. "This has to be a *guy!* A guy that thinks you're cute! OMG Who is he? Talk. Now. Talk!"

I want to kiss my sister for ramping in on my behalf. And for making me blush.

"You've never had text messages before," Mom says, her voice guarded, but her eyes betray her. They're already sparkling as the information gets her *Mom-Wheels* turning.

"I text Jess all the time," Kika protests.

"I mean—texts from a guy," Mom says. "Is it? A guy?" she probes.

"Am I paying extra for text messaging on all of our cell phones? Am I?" Dad pipes in, not at all getting it that *this* text message signifies a major turning point in my life. "Text messaging is just another excuse for teenage boys to score without actually having to ever speak to a girl."

"Dad! You're so old. What does 'score' even mean?" Kika rolls her eyes.

"It's true. No one says that anymore." Mom's smiling at me now.

We all laugh. Mom turns to Dad. "Text messaging is normal teen activity. We have unlimited text. If we didn't, we'd be broke just from Kika's texting habit alone. Jess sweetie, you don't need to limit yourself. Text all you want."

I choke back another laugh and hide it in a, "Cool. Thanks. Good to know." I'm so happy right now I'm grinning ear to ear.

With a few letters of simple text chatter, Gray Porter just launched me into the realm of what my mom calls *normal teen activity*! And I haven't paid him one cent—yet! Oh, but I will. This pretend boyfriend thing is going to be more awesome than I'd thought!

Mom leans in so she can see the message. I hold still so she can soak in the letters Q and T.

"So, who is this boy?" she asks with eyebrows still raised.

"It's the guy who got the *paid* internship," I remind them. "We exchanged numbers after the interview. No biggie." I bite my lip, and avoid their gazes for a second so they can't miss that this IS, indeed, A BIGGIE.

"He's calling you a *cutie* and you only just met?"

"Am I not cute, Dad?" I divert.

Dad's frowning as he scoops the strawberries he's just sugared onto the pre-formed shortcake pies. "You know what I mean. Do you have anything to tell us? Does Q plus T mean it's serious?"

"Please!" I feign my best gasp. "I don't even know him. He's sort of…nice. We had some conversations between interviews. I suppose he could be considered almost a…yeah…a friend." At least I don't have to keep trying to bring up a blush to scorching cheeks.

"A friend!" Kika's bubbling up into one of her middle-school giggle fits. "Who thinks she's cute!"

Mom's gaze has turned speculative. This is just the expression I've been expecting. "What's his name?"

"Mom. You don't need to know everyone's name," I stall. My stomach clenches as I try to remember the order of what I'm supposed to say next.

Bzz. Bzz. Boing-donka-donk.

Thank you, fake boyfriend. It's time to stop now.

I pull the phone away from everyone's view. "Sorry. I'll fix that ringtone." I tap into my settings. "Maybe I shouldn't have given him my number," I mutter, genuinely frustrated that Gray Porter rattles me even from a distance. I'm grateful for the excuse to concentrate on my phone and not meet anyone's eyes while I regroup.

As much as I've practiced all possible scenarios of this moment in my mirror—and as much as I'm elated my plan appears to be working—I'm suddenly scared to death.

I hate how far I'm about to go on lying to my parents. And what about Kika? She's on my team. She's the one person I've never lied to about anything. Ever.

My heart hurts just thinking about deceiving that kid.

"Text him back, Jess. Who cares about your ring tone? He's probably waiting for you to say something back!" Kika says.

I shoot her a glance. She's still beaming at me so brightly it strengthens my resolve.

For the first time in three years, Kika doesn't appear to be worried about me. She actually looks proud—admiring—excited. I like how beautiful, how normal, that looks on her face.

"What should I type?" I ask, working to smile back and keep my voice as breathless as hers. "I'm not good at texting."

"Lost cause." Kika giggles again. "Read what he said." Kika

pulls on my arm.

I've already established it's safe so I read it: "Why U so quiet? C U at school 2morrow. Got2 wrk. On a double. I'm as tired as U looked 2day. Go 2-zzzzzzzz, Jess Jordan."

"He goes to your school?" Dad asks.

Kika sighs and claps her hands. "*Ohmygod.* Text him back. Text him back." She's bouncing out of her seat.

"I will later. I can't do it with all of you staring."

"But texting is supposed to be immediately responded to," Kika protests. "I'll make you a list of easy text replies okay? You can study it."

"I like that he noticed you need to sleep." Mom smiles knowingly. "Maybe you *should* text him back something quick. You don't want him to think you don't like him, do you?"

I shudder. This *family bonding* thing has just gone way too far.

"I'm *so* not having this conversation with any of you. Mom, don't even try. I don't know if I like him. And—and—you guys are making me nervous. It's just a couple of texts, not a marriage proposal."

Dad's hovering over all of us, blinking at me with four strawberry shortcakes precariously balanced in his hands. "I don't know if I like this at all. Are you going to be constantly staring at your phone now like your sister does?" Dad asks.

Kika dives into her shortcake and chomps half of it in one bite. "I'm not staring at my phone now, am I? Gee, Dad." She's talking with her mouth full, but still manages to look cute.

I can't possibly eat, so I scroll up to view the first message that we all missed: *As promised. Hi GF. Sorry I'm late but ur boy is on duty. U There?*

I gasp and pull the phone into my chest. No need to read that out loud! My cheeks start burning a new round of fire.

"See? You're already hugging your phone and acting weird,"

Dad says, also speaking with his mouth full. Not at all his best look. He shakes his head, and gives me a sad look. "I'm going to miss you, honey."

Before looking up, I make certain the entire conversation is cleared. Deleted. Gone.

I think Mom's been watching me closely the whole time because she, like me, has not touched one bite of her dessert. "Come on, we're waiting for some details."

I wonder if this is what Gray sees in my expression when he calls me *relentless*. Who knew Mom and I had that in common?

Thankful I can still feel my cheeks flaming, I go for my *flustered and embarrassed* version of this scenario. It seems the easiest because I happen to be both right now.

I push at my plate and fold my arms over my chest, using what I call the 'therapy voice'. A voice I learned to use from my years with Dr. Brodie. "I need you *all* to do me a favor," I start and let out a long, patient—*time to communicate*—sigh.

Mom smiles. I know for a fact she loves conversations like this.

Kika and Dad *do not*.

They stop eating and regard me cautiously as though I might be about to have one of my flip-outs. I almost crack a smile because they are so darn funny. Both have forks in the air and whipped cream stuck on their lips.

"We're listening. Go on," Mom urges gently.

I turn all of my attention back to her. She's the one I need to convince the most. If I do it right, the others will take her lead. "I need you to *hear* me on this. Don't interrupt, okay?"

They all nod.

I flash the iPhone in my hand and begin the performance: "This is just a *guy*. A friend. Well, maybe a friend, like I said, I don't know. And, okay fine...I think I like him, as a *friend, of course.*" I hold up my hand in case anyone tries to burst in. "And, he thinks I'm…cool or a possible friend back. Or… something good enough to want to text me, anyhow. Okay?"

"Sure," Kika says.

"Okay," Dad says.

Kika and Dad resume eating their shortcake. I turn to Mom and blink, waiting for her response because I know she's going to pry. She just can't stop herself.

"Oh, honey, we think that's just great. Of course he's just a guy and it's no big deal. We only want to know—"

"Mom. Stop. Just stop." I've raised my voice, and now I hold out my hands like an orchestra conductor.

Kika and Dad pause again, this time with shortcake-filled forks halfway to their very open mouths.

This is going so on cue I could swear they'd studied their scripts beforehand.

I take in a long, tortured sounding breath and then head into my monologue: "Maybe I'm not being clear. I'm asking you guys to back off and let me enter into this friendship— whatever it is with this guy—*on my own.* And to also let me handle this new internship *on my own.* Meaning, all of you need to please stay off my back. Don't attack me with a ton of questions. I know you love me, but if the purpose of this summer is for me to *prove* that I'm going to be able to make it in college, you must let me give things a shot without analyzing my every move. Or text. I'm asking for some simple respect. Please, don't ask me any questions, spy on me or invade my privacy in any way."

"Well, you aren't going to have a teenage, summer rebellion spree, *young lady.*" Mom's turned all red. Getting fired up as usual—but I'm ready for this rebuttal.

Wait for it…wait for it.

Mom crosses her arms and goes into full-crackdown, argument-mode. "We're going to have to know some things about what you're doing! Asking for names is to be *expected*."

I flip the switch on her and gentle my voice into absolute agreement. "I know that, Mom. And you're right. I'm sorry if I'm being sensitive. I *will* tell you his name. But…let me *tell* you his name. Don't just force it out of me. I want this to be… natural. Okay? Give me some time. I'll tell you when it's right. You guys are so used to hovering over me. I feel suffocated, you know?"

My heart's racing and I think my dinner's about to come up, but I manage to keep a *pleading-sincere* look intact.

Mom crumples. "Sure, honey, of course. But we worry—"

I stop her again. This time I pick the practical-reasoning voice. "Mom. I'm going to go to work and come home. If all goes well, and with your permission, I might start hanging out with some new friends. But I haven't even made those friends yet. This isn't about me going to parties or anything like that. I swear. This is just about me being able to—"

"But—" Mom starts up again.

"Let her finish," Dad says gently. I can tell from the soft, sad look in his brown eyes he's totally on my side. Which makes me feel like the world's worst daughter. Because there are no sides to take. There's only me, lying to everyone I love.

Lying. Lying.

My eyes sting, but I have to finish my speech: "If this guy turns into something important, I'll tell you. Until then, I need to have something that is mine. All mine. And this summer, this internship, and even this guy's name seem so special right now."

I twirl my fork in my fingers. Unable to look at them anymore, I squash the whipped cream flat into the strawberries as I continue, "Maybe because I got the job and made this friend on my own—you know? Minus the weekly advice from Dr.

Brodie? It all feels…"

I pause for effect. Then, I paste on the *very-very-happy-smile* before I look up and say the last lines: "I don't know…it all feels so *normal.*"

Add in a small shrug, and finish with: "Am I making any sense?" Look up, tilt head to the side, wrinkle the forehead, play the music and roll the credits.

Oh. And remember to breathe.

"Honey, that's wonderful!" Mom is practically gushing. All feathers have been smoothed.

Kika smiles and wanders to the counter for seconds on whipped cream without a blink. I'm stunned she's not onto the fact that I'm acting really weird.

Dad's smile widens as he and Mom share a glance.

"Yes. Yes, it makes sense, Jess. We'll give you all the space you need. And we're really happy for you," Dad says.

I can't reply.

I've reached the point where if I get too much air on the back of my throat the crying thing is going to happen. I scoop up a pile of strawberries and whipped cream and stuff it into my mouth. It tastes like rocks and sawdust, but I chew with gusto.

Because it's pushing away the urge to cry.

And because they're all still staring at me. "Mffmf. Good. Thanks." I chew more.

"You let me know if you need me…or anything. We're here for you," Dad adds.

I nod, glancing between them.

Mom's expression is flooded with motherly delight, approval, and absolute hope for me. I can tell she thinks our family's balance is about to finally be restored. My heart clenches with remorse.

I toss a look to the ceiling, waiting for God, or lightning, or something huge to strike me down.

Unable to take more of this, it's all I can do not to leap out of my chair. Instead, I put my fork on the side of my plate and slowly stand. "Okay. Well...cool. And yeah. Last finals are tomorrow. I'm going to study, then I'm going to text my... *friend*...and go to sleep. I'm wiped."

"Well, you go on. We'll handle the clean up," Mom says, beaming as wide as Kika.

I have this sensation that if I asked them to give me a new car right now or twin pet monkeys—I think they'd do it. As I exit the kitchen, I search for some shred of comfort in the fact that two out of three of my last lines to my parents were true:

1. Finals *are* tomorrow. And after 24 hours of being awake, I'm so tired there's no way I'm going to be able to avoid sleep tonight, no matter how hard I fight it. Eventually, my body will betray me. So, —2. Yeah, unfortunately, I'm going to sleep. As for number 3? Texting Gray Porter my new friend, or employee, or whatever he might be to me?

That, of course, is not going to happen.

11

gray

Corey drops his backpack next to mine and slides into the desk on my right. "I hate the thought that this math final is going to kill our friendship."

"Huh?" I ask, only half-listening.

"I fail, and you go on to college leaving me behind. Will you still hang out with me when my career tops out as the assistant manager of Taco Delights?"

"Only if you give me free gelato-tacos. Besides, I think you could make manager." I don't look up. I'm texting Jess. I want this sent before Mr. Madsen, the math teacher, arrives and catches me with my phone out.

"The managers have to be able to count past ten fingers. Come on man, I need you front and center for my pity party. Don't you care that I'm about to go down in flames? You've been texting non-stop. What's up? *Who* is up?"

I toss him a look and realize the guy is a little pathetic today. His dishwater colored hair is rumpled like he just rolled out of bed. There's also more stress than spark to his usual, trouble-making expression. Poor dude. Math is his worst subject.

"Sorry. I've got a new crush, and I'm trying to work it. You'll rock the final, don't worry," I say as I send the text.

He nods toward my phone. "That text was long enough to be a novel. And again—who's the girl?"

Mr. Madsen's still nowhere in sight. The rumor flying around the room is that the main office copy machine broke. There's a chance our final might be rescheduled. During lunch. "What do you think about me having a *real girlfriend* for the summer? As in long term," I ask.

Corey laughs so loud tears come out of his eyes, and half the room turns to look. "Dude, you almost sounded serious," he adds when I hold silent.

"I am serious. What would you say if that text was to Jess Jordan?"

Corey laughs even louder. "No. Hell no. I'd freak. I'd check if you had a belly button just in case you'd been switched out by an alien race. I'd stage an intervention and get you the help you need. Tell me you're joking. Tell me you, acting like a complete weirdo yesterday and wearing her pink sweatshirt around after she lost it at lunch, was *not* about you wanting to hook up with that girl."

I shrug. "More than hook up. Date. I'm into her. Plus, she's hot as hell. You even said so."

"Yeah… meaning hot and *ice cold*. Or should I focus on the fact that you also said the word *hell* for the rest of this conversation? Dating *that* chick, even for a second, would be absolute hell. Do you have a death wish?"

"Hot and *sweet* actually. She's different. Not how everyone thinks at all. I like her. *Like, like her.* I swear."

"Dude. Show me your belly button right now."

Mr. Madsen saunters into the room holding a stack of stapled tests. "Sorry. Had to run these on the music department's machine. Pencils and erasers are the only things I want to see on your desks. Once you complete the first two pages, turn them in to me, and I'll hand you the last part of the test.

For that, you may use a calculator. Mr. Porter, when you've completed the entire final, report to Coach Williams. He has a bone to pick with you about something that might have been done to his personal copier. Know anything about that?" The teacher shoots me an accusing look.

My heart slams up and sticks behind my eye sockets. It's beating rapid fire. That means my eyes must be bugging out with a beat everyone can see. "Right. Sure," I choke out, already planning my escape out one of the side doors.

Mr. Madsen nods like he can read my mind. "He told me to tell you he'll be waiting, no matter how long it takes. If you don't show, he's going to call your grandmother."

⁘

"If I weren't a teacher who valued my career, I'd drop you with a punch so hard it would put you straight into the emergency room!" Coach Williams shouts when I enter his classroom.

"Bring it," I bluff, walking slowly toward him. "I'd love for a chance to help get you fired. Oh, and great to see you too."

"Explain this." Coach shakes the original copy of the contract I copied yesterday in my face.

I wince. I'd forgotten the original in the machine. *Shit.*

I'd have forgotten a screaming baby on that copier with that blue-eyed girl shooting me winks and calling me *boyfriend.*

Anyone would have.

"You know Jess Jordan is off limits. This is a contract that has you *dating*? *Dating!* Christ, Porter. What in the *hell* are you playing at?"

I eye the contract, wondering if I can just grab it and run, but I don't. I'm way beyond letting this guy intimidate me. I'm actually thankful it was Coach who found the contract and not anyone else. The guy knows as much as I do about Jess's situation. He was part of her situation, and mine. Part of not prosecuting the asshole senior that created her situation.

I level him with a stare. "I suppose I could ask you the same question, *Coach*. Why in the *hell* is Jess working every afternoon for your music program? You talk. I'll talk. I have a feeling her being in here every afternoon has nothing to do with college application credits."

"She's been working for me since freshman year—at the request of her *parents*. And she doesn't really work—mostly she—she—" He lets out a long breath and shakes his head. "We aren't discussing my arrangements—or hers. I want to know what you think you are up to even talking to that girl. You must have done at least that because you both signed this idiotic paper. What happened to your promise?"

"Jess does *what* in here? *What?*" I insist. "I'm not coming one-inch clean unless you go first. During the music program, Jess Jordan mostly *does what?*"

"She sleeps." Coach glowers and crosses his arms. "If she's having a good day, she helps out or does homework. If she's having a bad day, I give her free access to nap behind the stage curtain. Mostly, she has bad days. I watch over her until her parents are home from work. She does better if she's not alone."

"Holy shit. You aren't kidding." I let out a long breath and shake my head.

"Of course I'm not kidding. The girl has serious problems and you know that. You shouldn't be considering even one second of what's written on these pages. Your turn. Start talking."

He slaps the contract onto my chest, so hard I swear my heart rhythm goes off beat. I grip the paper and crumple it until it's smashed into a tight ball.

"This," I hold the destroyed contract in Coach Williams' face, "was her idea. It's a done deal. We mean to go through with it. I'm going to be her pretend boyfriend for the whole summer, and we're both looking forward to it."

Coach Williams lets out a long, low whistle. "Holy shit," he mutters not once breaking my stare. "You aren't kidding, either. Are you?"

I shake my head.

He sighs. "Does she know everything? About me—and what happened? And she remembers you and—*shit*. Is that why she's absent today?"

He suddenly looks way older. He's also shorter than I remember. That, or I'm just taller. It's been a long time since I've been anywhere near this guy.

"I don't know. I don't know what she knows or remembers," I say. "I'm 99% percent sure she doesn't remember *me* or anything that happened. She texted me earlier. She's sick. That's all. I can vouch for how terrible she looked yesterday. Said she had a headache and a bad lunch. Maybe she got worse?"

"Jess is not the type to ditch finals for no reason, so you must be right. But, if you messed with one hair on her head, I'll personally destroy your entire life."

"Whatever. That's already been done—thanks to your lameness. Which reminds me, isn't this about the time you suck up and offer me a spot to play on the hockey team next year? Let's just get *that* conversation over now, so you don't have waste my time and hunt me down before the last day of school."

My comment seems to take the fight out of Coach. He uncrosses his arms and runs a hand through the sparse pile of white hairs on his bald head. "The offer still stands. There's a spot for you on my team, anytime."

I'm the first to break our stare-down. I guess I'm surprised he still sounds sincere with that offer. The same offer he's made to me since I quit the team. Even after I just egged him on like that.

Nobody digs into Coach Williams like I just did and survives.

I look back into his serious, ice-grey eyes and answer, "I won't have a coward for a coach, and I'm pretty sure you're still the same guy as before. Right?"

Coach Williams turns away from me then. I count it as a win because I think I caught a grimace crossing his face. At least the guy still has some guilt—and he should.

"I'd thought after all these years you'd be able to understand my position," he says after a short pause. "I stand by my decisions and the decisions of Jess's parents. Nothing good would have come us exposing everything. Any further involvement would have hurt Jess, and destroyed the future of a young man who made some really bad choices on one night while he was drunk at a party—"

"Don't you dare defend that asshole to me!" I shout. "He's long gone. Probably graduating from college right now and living life just fine. From what I suspect, Jess is still falling apart on a daily basis because of *him*, because of *you*, and, because of her parents' chicken-shit attitudes." I pace across the room and lower my voice. "At least offering to blow the whistle and stand witness back then allows me some sense of self-respect. How any of you losers manage to sleep at night is beyond me."

"You still think your plan would have brought a better ending to any of it?" Coach Williams levels me with his steady 'game-time' stare. But his quavering voice doesn't match.

"Yes!" I shout and look down at the contract balled in my hands. My heart aches from too much pounding. I can hardly focus because I'm replaying how it all came down the last time I spoke to this man.

The room feels like it's sucking away under my feet.

When I speak again, I'm so drained I can only hold my tone just above a whisper. "Honestly, I don't know if things would have changed for the better. But none of you gave my offer a chance, so I guess we'll never know."

I push his chair out of my way as I pace the room again.

"Sometimes different is not better," he says, when I stop in front of him again.

"Does that apply to Jess? She's not looking or acting any better than she did when she first came back to school three years ago. Admit *that*, at least."

"You're right. Jess appears to be the same. I can tell you the kid who did it—he is a better person now. He's sorry. Very sorry. I've kept in contact with his parents."

"Why would I care? That fact makes it worse." I sit on the corner of Coach Williams' desk. "You and Jess's parents sacrificed the two innocent people in all of this so that a jerk could grow up to become a *better person*. Did he ever look Jess in the eye and apologize? Can you not see how twisted that is? He should have done some time for what he did."

"It was your word against his. He wouldn't have gone to jail because nothing happened. Nothing they could test for—beyond underage drinking. Drinking in which *you*, my whole hockey team, and Jess Jordan were also participants. I wasn't willing to drag twenty kids' futures, their college plans, and my career through the mud for something that couldn't be proved."

"Bullshit. You sacrificed honor and honesty to protect the hockey season and win state. The giant gold trophy down in the front hall is still front and center. Did you get a nice raise that year?"

"No, and I didn't get fired, either." Coach Williams shakes his head and paces the length of the stage before returning to face me. "You sacrificed yourself, son. No one asked you to quit the team. Next year is the last chance for you to undo the personal damage you created because of your stubborn impulsiveness. I know you still practice. A lot."

I cringe a little at that. His words—the truth—make me angry again; but we both know he's still talking crap. There's no way to undo any of the damage.

When I don't answer, Coach goes on, "You're good enough to gain a solid scholarship. I've heard you're holding up great on ice. And your inline wins are always top reporting these days. You're a high profile player and with that, you'd get noticed by top coaches—"

"Whatever, that's none of your business. I won't be bought out."

Coach Williams shrugs. "Your choice. In the meantime, I have to ask you not to participate in that ridiculous contract between you and Jess."

"This contract is going to help me pay for my first semester at college, minus your 'strings attached' offers. I'm convinced it's going to help Jess big-time as well. If I handle it right, I think I can get her to come out of her shell, make some friends."

"It's pure insanity."

I shrug. "I don't think you're right. I think it will make Jess happy. It already has. And money aside, I would never do anything to hurt her. I've only ever wanted to help. You must know my intentions are still the same where she's concerned."

Coach nods, his gaze is wary, but he seems to be hearing me. "Are Jess's parents aware of this?"

"Hell no, they aren't. They won't even know my name. Didn't you read the whole thing?"

He nods, and I laugh, because I'm sure Coach Williams read it more than once. He's probably got this thing tattooed to his ass, in blood.

"Why does she want this?"

"Jess believes that without some semblance of a 'normal summer' under her belt, her parents won't let her move out and go to college."

"That sounds like her parents talking, not her."

"Nope. It's all her. She wants out. Jess should get to move on with her life and *become a better person*, also. Don't you agree?" I throw his words back into his face. "If I can give her that, I will. Don't ruin it. You owe her something too."

"But what about you? It's not like you to participate in anything so underhanded."

"It's not underhanded if she doesn't remember. If I'm helping her. If *she* asked *me*. Besides, I stopped being a 'better person' when I messed up everything that night. You think I'm doing this just for her? I want to make up for some of that. I'm tired of feeling guilty. Aren't you?"

"Son. Gray. None of what happened was your fault, or mine. None of it. What if she remembers? You're putting me in a terrible position. I have to tell her parents."

"It's summer. You're off duty as of Friday. This has nothing to do with you. Me, dating Jess, will not occur on school property. You can check in with her any time while you run your practices at the complex. She'll be hanging around the rink and the snack bar. Safe. With me. If she remembers, then I promise to tell her the truth. It's simple. Give me a chance to step in and try to help. Please. If she hasn't remembered anything in three years, or in the last week of hanging with me, then she's not going to remember at all."

Coach Williams lets out a long, tired sounding breath of air. "Okay. I'll be watching. But you need to promise me one thing."

"Shoot."

"Make sure you help her get some sleep during the day."

"Why?" My mind is overtaken with the image of Jess snuggled up in her car at Geekstuff.com—of the image of her ashen face during the interview and yesterday after school.

"You can find that out on your own. Mess anything up, hurt her once, and it's over. This stays strictly on the friend level. I mean that, Porter. Don't step over the line with her."

I hate his threatening tone, and I hate that he knows more about Jess than I do. "I'm already more than her friend. As of yesterday, I'm her *boyfriend*. I will cross any line I want. You can keep this copy for reference."

I throw the wadded up contract into his chest as hard as I can.

He catches it without a blink.

12

jess

...

You're a very lucky girl.
Nothing happened. Nothing happened.
I thought he was nice.
C'mon. Dude. Let's get out of here.
What've you done? You're an asshole!
Nothing. Nothing happened.
I didn't do anything. I swear she wanted this.
Wait. Please. Please. Don't leave me here.
I'm sorry. I'm so sorry...I can't untie the knot...
It's not her fault. Jess, none of this is your fault.
But it is. I believed him when he called me beautiful.
Nothing happened. Not really.
I'm so sorry.
You're a lucky, lucky girl.

...

I'm covered in a fine sheen of sweat, about to vomit, but grateful to be awake.

When I sleep through the nightmare—when I make it to the part where my parents are standing around me and I'm in a hospital bed—then everyone in the house hears me crying in my sleep.

Everyone except me, that is.

I'd almost been to that point. I strain to listen for any footsteps or sounds that might alert me to my parents lurking in the hallway. The towel is still in place where I'd stuffed it under the door to block out any sounds I might make, so that means no one peeked in here either. Thankfully all is silent save for my racing heart. I allow the fear and voices crawling through every inch of my soul to wash over me so the rest of it can play out as quickly as possible.

As the spinning stops, I stare at my jellyfish lamp and count. Tonight, the words from the nightmare are worse—louder than ever. Repeating. Rocketing through my head.

•••

Lucky. Lucky. Lucky girl.
Nothing happened.
Nothing happened.

•••

I haven't heard them this clearly in almost two years.

The words belong to the people who were present the night I was drunk and almost raped freshman year. The night I snuck out to a party, lied to my parents, got drunk and brought all of this on myself. The nightmares and the voices are my memories. Or what's left of them.

It's always me, floating in and out of varied versions of the same scene. I'm half-naked sometimes. Often, I'm all wrapped up in a white sheet. Usually there's two faceless guys talking. The policeman is always around too. Sometimes, a nurse, and if I don't wake up, my parents appear when it moves to a hospital room.

In the nightmare, I'm forced to be everyone. I'm observing each moment from very far away—like it's on a small TV monitor. But as it unfolds, it's my *own voice* that's been dubbed over the words everyone else spoke that night.

It's freaky, but whatever. It's a *nightmare*. They're supposed to be horrible, right?

I work to sit up, still counting, and rest my chin on my knees so I can watch my nightlight better. The three tiny jellyfish spin aimlessly up and down, up and down, in their water-filled tank. The tentacles are almost distinguishable.

Almost. Almost.

How I hate that word and the way it defines me.

Almost raped. Almost over it. Almost normal.

I can almost forget. Way worse, I can almost remember.

I don't want anyone to feel sorry for me. Even though everyone says it wasn't my fault, I feel responsible. How can this messed up life not be partly my deal? I did wrong. I broke all the rules that night. And I'm paying the consequences for my 'bad choices' in this endless time-out. Nightmare. Punishment. Endless time out.

My parents used to make us do time-outs on a little bench in the front hallway. Mom and Dad's price for misbehaving: sit on the bench one minute for every year 'old' we were.

Six years old, six minutes.

Ten years old, ten minutes.

This used to really make me mad. I'm four years older than Kika, and she always got *free* four minutes earlier for the same crime.

A few months ago, as one of my stay-awake-projects, I ran the numbers on my current time-out. There are 52,560 minutes in every non-leap year. Multiply that number times the three years I've been stuck in this stupid limbo. Officially—according to the rules in this house—I've been doing time for my bad behavior at that party for 1,576,800 minutes.

This means, I'm 1,576,800 years old.

Sometimes, when every inch of my body aches like it does now—when I can't see straight from wishing I could sleep at night—I think that number is dead on.

Mom was *way off* when she'd called me a skeleton impersonator the other night. *Ghost* would have been a way better word. That's what I'll become if I can't regain control over my sleep schedule, and make the nightmare go back to a reasonable level.

13

gray

"A different name for me? Hmm. That's going to be weird," I say, motioning to the door of the minuscule office Jess and I have been assigned to share. "Can you move into the hall? I need to put this desk against the wall you've been holding up with your back."

I'm joking, but I'm also serious. Worried as hell about her, actually. She looks really pale and fragile again—like how she looked the day we made the contract.

I step around a box overflowing with brand new office supplies and shove it to the side, clearing the way for her to exit more easily. She trades one leaning spot for another and props her weight against the door. I know I won't be able to concentrate unless she sits down. Rests. Sleeps? I grab one of the wheeled office chairs and traverse the mess with it to set it near her.

"This chair is also in my way," I add, pausing to scan her face up close. "Maybe you can drag this out into the hall and just hang while I finish?"

She makes no move to touch the chair. "I'm good."

I'm certain she's lying. Coach's words haunt me as I scan the etched circles under her eyes. They're so dark today they look like bruises. Does Jess need to sleep, even now? It's not like I can ask directly, or call her on her answer. It's going to take some time before I can just *know* if she's having a bad day or not.

I wish she'd talk about herself. Most girls usually have no problem doing that. I've already deciphered that Jess is not like other girls. Her eyes haven't left the chair.

"Might as well take a load off," I encourage again. "This is going to take me a bit, plus I could use the extra twenty inches of space."

"Yeah, but you're doing all the work. I can't just sit and do *nothing*."

"Only one of us can fit in here while the big stuff is moved around. I don't mind being the grunt. I'm the *paid* employee. Remember?"

"Oh, I remember." Her tone is dry and possibly sarcastic, but I see her flush. She turns away to, *thankfully*, pull the chair out into the hallway and sit. She lets out a sigh, and when she leans into the seat like she's comfortable, I'm unexplainably happy and relieved.

I pretend to ignore her and shove the long, rectangular workstation into the center of the windowless office we've been given. It's down in the basement near the shipping department. Takes five minutes just to find it. Mr. Foley told us not to worry about the tight space or the bad location.

The office is supposed to be more of a room to store our things and a place to learn the database. Apparently, once we get through that, we'll be assigned to special projects and work in one of the larger warehouses. According to the smug dude I'd met in the employee lounge this morning, the *summer slaves* (as he called us) were usually stuck working on the jobs no one else wanted. Whatever. Bring it on. I can't wait.

"Names," I call over my shoulder. "Let's get it over with.

What are you thinking I should be called? I'm terrified." I grimace and raise my brows up really high like I'm worried. "Name me Edward, or Peeta, or Prince Charming, and I swear—I'll quit."

She laughs and it takes all of my strength not to look toward that sparkling sound. "We need to pull a real guy's name from our class," she says. "Once my mom latches onto the idea of me being into a guy—she's going to head straight for my yearbook and look him up. Kika will be right behind her turning the pages. Plus, I'm going to have to add you to the contacts in my iPhone. Right now when you text me, I have you listed as *InternshipGuy*. Meaning you aren't really *anyone* to me, yet. That has to change soon because my mom and sister have started tracking that already." Jess holds up this year's yearbook. "Let's just choose someone, anyone, I guess."

I glance up and watch her half-heartedly flipping through pages. "What if I think who you choose is a downgrade? Pick someone cool, or at least good looking," I joke.

"Did you really say that? You're so smug about how you look. Must be nice to be so perfectly put together."

"Ooh. You did not just say that." I smile and pause to rest. Does she really think that? "Might I return the compliment, Miss Jordan? Love the pencils you stuck in your bun. I can honestly say I've never seen any girl look hot in what appears to be...a 1940's school teacher outfit?"

"Shut up. I was not complimenting you, and we both know this outfit was selected to deter all hotness." She fingers one of the long, stick things coming out of her bun. "These are not pencils. They're a Geekstuff.com product called *Sushi-hair*. These chopstick bun makers are top sellers. DUH. How did you make it to the second interview round again?"

"Must have been something about my looks." I wink.

"God." She's turned bright red. "FYI, I do not need your ridiculous player-charm to be turned on all the time." She slams the yearbook shut and places it in front of her like she means to use it as a shield against me.

I can't help but tease her a bit more. "Maybe it's you that has all the moves, not me. When you say '*FYI*' all snide like that, and then shoot me the *hateful-looks,* my heart kind of melts. FYI back. *You* don't have to work so hard to catch my attention, chopstick-bun cutie. We're already dating," I finish, loving the way her eyes snap at me.

"Seriously?" She's sputtering now. "I really want to hit you. You swore no more joking like that. You swore."

I take in the tense set of her face and realize she's truly upset, so I tone it down. "Right. Sorry…jokes getting out of hand again. If you really have the urge." I point to my left cheek. "Do your worst. No extra charge. I'm sure I deserve it." I tear my gaze away from her distracting chop-stick bun, pink face, cute freckles—adorable pursed lips.

Hell. I'm positive. I deserve to be punched.

I think I just stared at her lips so long I wonder if she noticed where my focus had been stuck? I turn away to pull the desk out another foot, but my imagination flashes to the line of her neck, then back to her lips. She has really cute lips.

The blood in my head and body is pounding in a way that is about to have me really embarrassed.

"Finished," I say, refusing to look up as I force my interest and thoughts away from the beautiful girl in the room and onto the office supplies in front of me.

Pencils, printer, pens, paper.
Staples. Staples. Staples.
It's working.

"We can now easily share this desk. Let's set up our supplies," I say as though I'm still on track, as though I've been able to erase the image of her lips from my mind.

Inside I'm screaming: *printer cartridge, paperclip holder and paperclips!*

"Do we have any other choice than this?" She swallows, looking supremely uncomfortable and if possible, she's paler than she was five minutes ago. She's surveying my desk set up.

"What's wrong?"

"We'll be, like…two feet apart, and *staring* at each other. Kind of too close, don't you think?"

Hell yes. Too damn close, I think, before saying, "We'll have the monitors back to back. You'll see. It will create a sense of privacy. Plus, it's not as if I don't shower every day." I've snuck in another joke, hoping to put a smile back on her very worried face.

"No…it's not that." She looks at me, through me, into me. I can't breathe.

"It's going to be *fine,* right?" she whispers.

Her gaze is so open I think I can see all the way to her broken heart.

Does she mean the desk or the whole summer?

Either way, I only want to erase this terrified look from her face.

"Fine? Fine?" I grin. "It's going to be perfect, Jess Jordan, girl-who-worries-way-too-much. The signs of greatness are all here. Look at these babies." I pat the brand new twenty-seven inch Macintosh computers Mr. Foley brought us. "These boxes alone should make both of us scream like it's Christmas morning! Snap out of it. Santa came! Now we get to play with all of our toys!"

She laughs and appears to relax. "They are over-the-top, aren't they? I hope I don't hurt your feelings when I get mad at you for your…jokes. I'm just getting used to all this banter. I don't talk this much, to anyone. And the flirting, even though I know it's not real—that you're just pretending—trying to do your boyfriend thing." She flushes. "It's, um, very weird for me. Besides, I'm sure it's inappropriate at work. Can we put a hold on that kind of stuff until we're used to each other?"

"Uh...yeah." I swallow. "I suppose that's what I've been doing...practicing...flirting with you. You sure you want me to stop? Practice makes perfect. Plus, it's pretty weird for me too," I quip, knowing I wasn't practicing. I'd simply *forgotten*.

Forgotten she wasn't just any girl that I had a crush on. I turn and crack open one of the Macintosh boxes, pull out her computer and set it on her side of the desk.

"Honestly, it seems like you don't need to practice at all. Like you're a natural. So...how about you only do that when it's *important*, okay? Like when people are looking. And only after we are 'official'?"

"Right. Makes sense." I nod, wondering if any of this will ever make sense.

"Thanks. And...just thanks for understanding."

"You draw the lines and call the shots. I might joke around, but I promise to be a gentleman, okay? I don't want you to feel weird...or like I'm going to take advantage of you. I won't. Swear. Remember? We promised to trust each other."

She nods, but won't meet my gaze as she plugs in and turns on her machine.

Sensing a change of subject is in order, I dig into my own computer box, unload the beautiful machine, plug it in and power up. "I'm thinking we use my best friend's name. Corey Nash."

"Why him?" She leans on her elbow to peer around the two monitors so she can see me. My heartbeat doubles because she's right.

We are nose to nose. Entirely too close.

Don't stare at her lips, I command my brain. I pull back a bit to fiddle with my computer cables. "Corey Nash is..." I look up again.

She's chewing her bottom lip—oh man. *Don't stare at her lips!*

"Corey is the perfect choice," I say quickly. "He'll be hanging around with me—with us—at the rink. As you get to know me, you can observe him. Then you'll have a real reference point when you talk about *him*. I mean talk about *me* to your family. That sounds so twisted," I add, chuckling.

"Because it is so twisted." Jess laughs too. "How will I keep it straight?" She turns her eyes to the ceiling and taps her chin with one finger. "Your best friend. Hmm. Makes sense. He can even come out with us all the time. We could set up group dates—confuse my parents with your mass of friends."

"About that. My mass of friends is not that big. It consists of Corey and Michelle. That's it. Sometimes there's a few stragglers who hang around the rink and the bowling alley, but not often."

Jess scowls. "What about all those other girls I saw at lunch?"

"Michelle's cheerleader friends, not mine."

"That's it?" She rolls her eyes. "There's no posse? No gang? Aren't you on some sort of sports team...and don't teams hang out together and bond in a huge group all the time?"

"Yeah. I'm on an inline team, but the guys are pretty split up. Some drive for hours to get to Golden for practices and games. Plus the season isn't back on until fall. Because of my work schedule and Gran...I'm maxed."

"Oh, I thought you were way more popular."

"I did warn you," I add gently, but I feel ridiculously upset that I've disappointed her. "If it helps, Michelle and Corey are both awesome. You'll see. We always hike when we can. I also get free use of bowling lanes, skating rinks—whatever I want from the sports complex. Finding places to do the dates should be easy. Do you skate? Ice, or roller?"

"No way. Never. Neither. And it's not happening." She hits me with the dangerous 'back off' glare I'm getting used to ignoring.

"Lose *that* idea. It would make no sense if I didn't take my *girlfriend* skating. If we don't use the rinks, Corey and Michelle will know something's up. I think ice is more fun than roller because it's so much colder, and I'm so very warm," I tease and toss her a wink.

"Eew. And eew." She shudders. "That's flirting *again*. I swear I'll dock your pay. Don't forget the part where you said I could hit you. I have an extreme right hook. I'll use it. Final warning."

"Right. Bad habit, and complete accident, again."

She frowns, but doesn't answer. I can tell she feels betrayed, and she should. I only want this girl to trust me but I keep messing up. "I'm sorry. Truly," I plead again.

Should I tell her I want to hit myself really hard right now? Why does it only take two minutes of this girl smiling into my eyes to make me forget none of this is real? Not to mention she's just asked me not to flirt with her. "But you will skate," I add, forcing myself right back on task. "We'll do roller. Okay?"

She shrugs. "It's your funeral. Whatever you think will seem realistic, but know this: innocent children will die, limbs will break, and walls will come crashing down."

"Impossible." I grin, pleased she's considering it. "I won't let you fall. Besides, if you get hurt you'll miss the annual ThunderLand fun. It's an all day trip we always make to Fort Collins every summer. It's a perfect opportunity for everyone to witness...to our *love*." I wink, and then flush when she glares bullets at me. "Right. Sorry. Sorry."

She shakes her head and smiles. "ThunderLand!" Her smile changes into a huge beam that hits her eyes. I realize this is the first time I've ever seen this expression on her face. She still looks tired, but I think she's *happy*. Really happy. It's like all her defenses are down. My heart catches when I think some of that happiness might be because of me. Our contract. Because we are beginning to know each other.

She continues, "I've never been there. But we've been to Disneyland a few times. I love the coasters—going fast, cotton candy, boardwalk games, listening to the rides roaring from every direction...and..."

"Don't stop. And what?" I lean on my own elbow, enchanted by the dreamy excitement crossing her face.

"I don't know...to get to go with..."

Her eyes return to my face. She freezes for a second like she's been doused with cold water, and I wonder if she too, is forgetting off and on that this is a paid arrangement and we really aren't close friends. Real friends.

Yet. I think. Yet.

"To go...just to *go*...will be really cool," she finishes in a much more subdued voice. She reaches for her yearbook and finds our class section. "Does Corey have a girlfriend?"

I take note of her deliberate subject change and applaud her. She's as good at that as I am. "Corey's got a bad crush on Michelle, but she won't give him the time of day. I'm all for it if they go out. But...if they ever broke up and hated each other it would be the end of my world. I'm actually glad you and I are going to be a *couple* for the summer. It will be nice to have an excuse not to feel like such a third wheel around the two of them while they figure out what's going on."

"What is going on?"

"Michelle destroyed Corey's heart with the *'I just want to be friends'* line a few months ago. Personally, I think she's in denial. Girls go through that denial stage, don't they?" I shoot her a grimace.

"No idea." Jess grimaces back.

"Either way, Corey's still hanging around and doing back flips, trying to change her mind. You'll see. It's weird. Entertaining, but weird."

"Has any girl ever said the *just friends* line to you?"

She's asked it so naturally I see no reason not to answer truthfully. "I'm the one that uses that first. Like I said, I don't have that kind of time."

"Wow. Right." She blinks. "Can I be the first to use it when I break up with you?"

"Only if you mean it. It would be cool if we could be friends after this."

She doesn't answer. She flips to Corey's photo in the year-book. "*Nash*. Here he is. Cute. Blond, blue eyes—a great smile, and a little dorky too. My mom will be thrilled when she sees this shot. He's also in the chess club and an *Eagle Scout*! Believable, and *so* me. Nice to meet you, Corey Nash." She holds out her hand, and we shake. "And he won't know? Swear?"

"Swear. He's been like my brother since we were seven. If I do have to tell him, you can trust in his silence."

"No way. It's bad enough I have to trust *you*," she says.

I feel slightly sick because every time trust comes up between the two of us, I'm well aware I'm a hypocritical, lying freak. Coach Williams was right. This situation is going to be harder than I'd thought. I break her gaze and mess with my keyboard.

"Let's just try to do this without any other people knowing the deal," she continues. "I've had to lie tons to Kika and it's already been brutal. You're going to have to do the same. What have you already told Corey about me? Anything?"

"Corey's witnessed most of the text messages I sent during finals. He and *everyone* also watched me approach you on locker clean-out day. I bring you up every chance I get, but Corey thinks I'm nuts to be into you."

"God…how embarrassing. I want to know why Corey thinks you shouldn't like me."

I feel the back of my neck grow hot. "Corey believes you'll draw and quarter me. Eat me alive. Roast me on a spit, or spit on me?"

She smiles. "I'm glad someone respects the reputation I've worked so hard to set up. You deny yours as a player, but I'm proud of mine. What else did you say about me?"

I smile and shake my head. "I said I wanted to date someone *different*. That I'm geared up for a long summer fling. I also told him you're sweet, and I've had a secret crush on you since freshman year. Blah, blah, etcetera." I swallow as my chest tightens. I'm hit with the realization that everything I've told Corey about Jess is the complete truth.

And then some.

Jess's laugh is almost bordering on a giggle. "Such whoppers! See? You're a natural. What else!"

"That I can't wait for them to meet you—which reminds me—" I struggle to straighten my thoughts—keep my expression void of too much excitement. "What time are you coming to the rink tonight? I'm on at five, but everyone usually shows up at six. That's when I start the snack bar shift. It's dead during dinner, so I can hang out pretty easily until the late crowd shows. Do you know how to get there?"

Jess's eyes are now unreadable. I can't miss how she's tightened her shoulders. "Tonight? So soon? Is that normal…like if this were *real*, would that seem like a *normal* thing for me to do?"

"Of course." I nod and hold back an urge to laugh, because she's so darn serious. And because more than anything, I want to hang out with her, show her my rink and the other parts of my life. Tonight. Tomorrow. All summer.

"You sure?" She raises one eyebrow.

I sigh as though I don't care either way and turn it into a challenge. "Your summer is ticking away and I'm on the pay clock. Are you afraid you can't handle being nice in public?"

She crosses her arms, her eyes snapping as she rises to my bait. "Please. How dare you insult my talents? I'm the master at layering on any *state of being* to hide my whacked out self."

"I don't want you to show up faking it." I shake my head, feeling bad for calling her on this. But if anything, by the end of the summer, I want Jess to understand I'm not buying her act. "You don't have to layer on anything…just be yourself. I'm afraid you're going to show up and act like a too friendly Hello Kitty…or something creepy. Just be how you are. If today has been you, being crazy, I've liked it. And you. As is. Crazy or not, if that's the real you, I'm in. And guess what? You come across as nice by default. My friends will feel the same."

She laughs. "Well then, even you've bought into my talents. I'm never the real me—not today, not ever. That girl scares the hell out of everyone."

"You are so flipping cr—" I stop myself before I say the word she wants me to believe about her. I was about to fling it out there carelessly, and hurt her. And she knew it.

I call Corey and Michelle crazy twice a day or more, but around Jess I'm going to have to watch myself.

I shake my head at her glaring face. "Nothing. Whatever."

"Whatever back," she mutters, and glances at the table. "Will you be able to handle a girl visiting you at work that doesn't end up making out with you in the parking lot after?" She raises her brows up high in challenge, to prove she doesn't care.

But she does. And I do. And I think it's freaking us both out.

"I think I can manage." I shoot her a smiling glance. "Especially if you're wearing that bullet proof skirt. Don't get me wrong, it's attractive on you—but wrong for the rink," I say, hoping I can tease her from shutting me out completely.

"Maybe I will. Maybe I'll dress even more like a nerd. Get some glasses and my mom's eighties clogs on my feet! And was that flirting again?" She's got her hand balled into a fist.

I lean out of her reach. "Easy, there. I'm innocent." I have to work to keep my expression serious but it's difficult because she's hilarious-cute when she's pissed off. I continue, "Mentioning that something is attractive on a person is a *compliment*. Flirting, for example, would be *me*, mentioning that I believe *you* would be way sexy in all clogs. Even little painted, wooden Dutch girl ones."

"I get it, dork. But you're smart to stay out of my reach." She laughs and throws a pencil at me.

I laugh back. "No. Seriously, what you wear is up to you." I shrug, but in case she decides to call her own bluff and show up in a whacked outfit just to put me in my place, I press the point. "I thought the key to your success this summer is making yourself believably *normal?* If you step out of your house in front of your parents in that outfit plus ugly shoes, and tell them you're heading to meet *friends* at the sports complex, they're never going to buy it."

"Okay. Okay! This whole situation is demoralizing enough without me taking advice from you on wardrobe." She all but bursts out of her chair and paces the three steps it takes to cross to the door of the office and turns to face me. "I'll be there around six. And I'll be...*believable*." She gives me little disgusted snort and glances into the hallway as though she's about to bolt.

"You want to make any suggestions about what I should wear? It's only fair," I add.

"God. No. You're pretty much perfect—as is." She turns

bright red as she continues, "You…you…just do your job and prep your peeps for the oncoming summer of lies. I…I'm going to get a Red Bull out of my car," she says in an odd, strangled sort of voice. She's dashed out so fast I don't even have time to blink because all I can think about is how she'd just said I'm *perfect.*

The girl's delusional. If she only knew.

14

jess

As I inch my Jeep through the maze of parking lots that make up the Town of Golden Sports Complex, known to everyone as *The TOG*, I have the sensation that I'm an intruder on an alien planet. I've never been anywhere near a sports complex, and the only professional sporting event I've attended was a Bronco's game back when I was ten. And from that, I only remember the cherry snow cone my dad bought me, not the game.

To prepare myself for my trip to The TOG, I've researched the place. Go Wikipedia!

The five-acre complex is a mass of interconnected metal buildings, parking lots, and windowless field houses. It boasts two indoor soccer and inline arenas, two competitive ice rinks, and one giant recreational roller skating rink (here since 1956). Back then, ice skating used to be on the pond which now holds the gas-powered bumper boats. There's also an ancient bowling alley (here since 1962 and recently updated), one large set-up of outdoor batting cages, three areas for mini-golf and a two story driving range.

To add insult to this nightmare, a bounce house, laser tag, and birthday party annex was added last year. From the impression I got by looking through The TOG website, I mean to avoid *that* sector of my first visit to *planet hell* at all costs.

How can Gray stand coming to this place every day?

Up close and in live action, I think The TOG is just how I've imagined a prisoner-of-war camp might look: low barrack-like structures growing out of blacktop, dingy colors, and zero landscaping. Not even weeds.

Instead of prisoners, the place houses swarms of kids in lumpy hockey gear flanked by their personal parent-jailers. Each grouping of decked out, mini-athletes hauls some sort of strange, canvas, wheeled duffle that looks suspiciously like a body bag.

Intimidating hockey sticks take the place of machine guns.

I concentrate on avoiding the kids darting between the cars and scan for any signs of the indoor rinks. They are supposedly connected to the bowling alley and the parking lots by some long 'intake tunnels.' Gray had said to find the largest build-ing, but I can't tell which one looks largest. Instead, I focus on the warped, plywood bowling-pin creatively—if not danger-ously—attached to the metal rooftop and drive toward it.

Apparently, this crumbling bowling pin was not part of the recent renovation budget.

It's just past 6:20.

I'm a little late, but proud for having the courage to come at all. I turn off the engine and I can now hear, in addition to *feel*, my heart's incessant, painful pounding. It's been doing that since I backed out of our driveway. I'm starting to sweat underneath the cotton, v-neck t-shirt Kika made me borrow. It's too tight. The lace on the matching white cami she insisted I wear underneath everything also itches like mad.

Thankfully, my *getting ready show* went as planned. Heck, *better* than planned!

Kika had been *delighted* to share her fashion knowledge

and her closet full of clothes with me. Mom's antics had been comical during Kika's *wardrobe consult.* The woman pretended to stay out of our way and 'not be involved or listening at all' while she refolded the entire linen closet located in the hall outside Kika's room.

It's been a decade since anyone has cleaned out the linen closet.

I used the opportunity of Mom eavesdropping in the hall to plant the name, *Corey Nash* along with glowing descriptions of his blond hair and blue eyes. The family radar is fully activated. I imagine Kika and Mom are gushing over Corey's photo in the yearbook right now. To make the whole thing perfect, a text message titled 'CNash' came in on my newly adjusted iPhone while Kika and I were talking about *him.*

One that said: *YOU Coming soon? Can't wait to c u, QT.*

Always the *QT.* I'm not going to lie, I really like when he adds that.

I blush now, thinking about how badly I'd blushed in front of Kika when the text came in. So much so, that she went wild with giggles on me. Giggles and squeals I'm sure Mom heard.

Ah, *progress* again!

I avoid looking in the mirror because I don't want to be reminded of the eyeliner, mascara, blush—not to mention the squirt of some new glittery lotion my sister attacked me with. As much as I want to sweep my hair into a ponytail or up into my bun, I leave it alone. It took Kika a long time to brush it out. She curled each and every strand of my hair into (what I have to admit) are some cool looking loose curls. I must have been nuts to let a puny, giggling, twerp be in charge of my outfit. But it had made Kika so happy…

I take a few calming breaths and focus on the fact that I have no other choice but to go inside. I've been dressed to assimilate. And assimilate I will.

After all the work and lies—and lotion—it took to get me into this parking lot, I'm not going home without more success to add to my list. Even if Gray and everyone I'm about to meet think I've gone overboard.

I step out of the car and feel the curls bouncing around my shoulders. I swallow the ball of dread at the back of my throat because I know it's going to take a lot more than a new hairstyle and a clone outfit to keep the natives of this planet from tagging me a 'fake'.

I can do this. I can do this.

As I approach the door a flood of mini-hockey players and their parents rush past me, heading for the parking lots. I'm hit with a puff of cold, stale air as I work to get through the crush. For every step I take forward, the throng pushes me back. Just when I'm about to give up and retreat, a little kid dressed in hockey pads way too big for his small body saves me.

He stops, blinking up into my face, and holds the door. I peek around him, wondering if I'm close, but I can only make out the green plastic-turf flooring and the bobbing heads of yet another stream of sweaty hockey kids and parents heading toward me.

"You going in?" the kid asks, probably because I'm blinking back at him like he's some sort of scientific specimen. Because…he is. Is this how Gray started out? Buried in padding, all freckles, red cheeks and missing front teeth?

I smile at the kid. "Uh yeah. Thanks for holding the door."

"You're pretty," the kid says, lisping. Still blinking.

"Josh!" A man, apparently the kid's dad, catches up. "Sorry. He's a lady-killer. Knows what he likes. Son, you can't blurt out things like that to women."

"It's okay. He's pretty adorable himself," I say.

"What did I do? She's pretty. But I'm *not* adorable, lady. Sheesh." The kid's cheeks turn pink.

"Right. I'm not all the way a lady yet, either. So we're even. How about you call me a girl and I call you handsome. Deal?"

"Maybe." He glowers.

The kid's dad smiles at me and shakes his head. "Take the compliment, Josh. This *girl's* way out of your league." He pulls him off the door. "Let's go."

Relaxing a bit after my first encounter with this alien race, I head farther into the tunnel just as the second swarm of kids and parents envelop every inch of space around me. I hold my ground until they pass. Then, without looking back, I march through this second hallway as though heading for battle.

If this place is an alien planet, then I'm entering the mother ship. Gathering my courage, I stop a guy who looks like he's my age. "Excuse me…" I say, watching his gaze skirt over me and then land on the floor. "You know where the snack bar is?"

"Up there, smack in the middle." He flushes bright pink and rushes away.

15

gray

It's impossible for me not to spot Jess. She's emerged through the rink's EXIT doors and seems unaware she's entered in the wrong direction.

"Would you look at her hair?" I pull in a quiet whistle. I've never seen it down. The shine—the *length*—almost hits her waist.

The rink's horrible, seventies fluorescent lighting never flatters anyone, but Jess seems to be glowing under them. She looks around, and I can tell by the set of her shoulders that she's tense. Her hands are also gripped into tight fists. When she glances toward the open snack bar area where the tables are, I detect a hint of disappointment in her expression. She walks around each table as though searching for something and I realize that something is not me...she's too focused on the tables. What is she doing?

I guess I'm glad she hasn't noticed me. I'm holding two giant-sized cans of 'Pico Nacho Cheese Sauce' like a dork. I also can't seem to shut my gaping mouth, which only opens wider now that I've caught sight of her profile as she draws closer, making a slow lap around yet another table.

I ditch the cans onto a table and step toward her.

"Holy crap and double *wow*," I say under my breath. I can't move. My chest tightens and I experience a brief moment of panic. She's put on some sort of makeup. Her already remarkable eyes seem lighter and twice as large even at this distance.

And her lips! "Damn."

I can hardly breathe as I hide myself behind one of the support pillars. Her lips have been transformed by some sort of intriguing lip-gloss or lipstick or whatever it is girls use in their attempts to freak out guys.

Yesterday, I thought I hated that junk…but now…I'm not so sure.

No. Lip-gloss is still the worst thing ever invented. I still hate it. I do. I do.

"You're losing it, dude. Calm down. You knew what she looked like well before tonight." I decide on a new plan. I'll pretend I haven't seen her yet.

I quickly recover the cheese cans and head toward the half-door entrance into the snack bar. The snack bar counter will allow me three good feet of space between me and her. Then, I'll call her over. Call my girlfriend over. Yeah. My girlfriend.

My *pretend*, unbelievably beautiful, pretend girlfriend.

Pretend. Pretend. Pretend.

I close my mouth just in time and paste on my game face as she spots me and heads me off. She's trapped me on the front side of the counter.

Way. Too. Close. To. Her. LIP-GLOSS.

"Hey," she says.

"There you are." I cover my choking voice with a small cough.

Uncertain of where to look and where not to look, I concentrate on her eyes. On what she's feeling. Not on how she looks—not on how she's made my heart feel like it's in a horse race.

Her expression is wary. Somewhat hunted and very nervous.

As much as I want to play this cool and tell her this night is going to go perfectly, I can't reassure her because I've never felt this freaked out in my entire life. I have no idea how to talk to this amazingly beautiful yet vulnerable looking version of Jess Jordan. She's right. I have no idea who she is at all.

"Was the place hard to find?" I ask, hoping she doesn't notice the cowardly squeak in my voice. I skirt past her and dump the giant cans of cheese onto the counter and duck behind it. My senses are instantly overwhelmed by how she smells. Something is different. Not cinnamon anymore, but…

"Easy. I had a map." She follows me to the counter and leans on it. She's pretending to study the cans of cheese.

I do the same. It's like the drawing of the smiling cartoon green-chili-guy on the logo is the most curious and interesting thing we've ever encountered. When she leans forward, her hair curls against the counter top and I realize the new smell is coming off her hair. Some sort of amazing shampoo. I move my hands away from the glowing curls. Too tempting. They look really soft—and cool.

"Why were you looking over the tables so closely? Is something wrong with them?" I ask, breaking the awkward silence.

"I was hoping for a table where I could sit with my back to the wall." She looks up with her mask in place. Her little sassy challenge smile is also on high. "Since my back to the wall is not possible, tell me…where do you want me?"

Where do I want her? Where do I want her!

My head pounds. If any other girl came to meet me looking like *this*, asking me where I wanted her—I would've let loose on the flirting. But I can't even go there. I'm trying to honor her request. Plus I don't want her to feel more uncomfortable than she already seems.

My gaze drops to her lips. AGAIN. I take a quick breath and

look away, hoping she hasn't noticed. I have to cross my arms to resist the temptation I have to touch her hair again, or her cheek, or her small, nail bitten hands.

Instead, I bite my bottom lip to keep myself from saying the cheesy lines flooding my brain.

"Hmm, where *do* I want you?" I manage. And just barely.

"What? You're acting really weird," she snaps. "Is this the wrong look, or outfit, or what? If so, I can make it out of here before the others show."

"It's peaches," I say, realizing too late I should not have said that out loud.

"What?" She raises an eyebrow.

"Do you smell faintly...like peaches?"

Or should I say you smell like peach-cinnamon-heaven?

"God. Yes, I—I think I do. I'm sorry." She winces. A cute tinge of pink floods her cheeks. "Kika lent me some make-up stuff and slathered me with one of her odd fruit lotions. It's bad, huh? My sister is all about fruit-scented products."

"PIE," I say, and pull in a huge breath. "It's peach pie, isn't it? Like peaches with vanilla?"

"Uh...yeah. Guilty. But...is it really that bad?" She motions to her hair, then her face. "I can wash some of this junk off. Kika's in eighth grade and...well, she said all this stuff—this outfit—would be good for hanging out." Her mask is wiped away and now I feel terrible, because her expression looks panicked.

I pull myself together and try to say something sane to erase the crinkle of doubt and worry creasing her forehead.

"No. No! I love it. I mean—it's great. You—how beautiful you look. It threw me off. And, you have no idea how much I love peach pie, a-la-mode. Sorry...sue me, dock my pay, but damn, girl. You've turned me into a stuttering fool." I smile but cringe inwardly, knowing I've crossed over the edge of flirting with her again.

She glowers. "Swear you aren't lying? I knew I'd mess this up by trying too hard. I'm paying you, yes. But don't blow smoke up my ass if this is all wrong. I don't want to be humiliated here."

"No! Honest. I simply had no idea it was possible for you to look more beautiful than you look…normally. So…I sort of lost it there. And it's not often a girl shows up smelling like my favorite food."

She shoots me a sideways glare but appears to relax a little. "Did you get those lines from *slimy-ways-to-get-to-second-base-dot-com?* Please."

I laugh. "How bout *dorks-trying-to-talk-to-beautiful-pretend-girlfriends-dot-com?*"

She laughs back. "Odd apology accepted. Weird, horrible, ridiculous compliments are not. And…could you not call me beautiful?"

I shake my head and smile. "The beautiful adjective is an informational fact. I'll say it if I mean it. And I'm sorry about the flirting. I'm nervous just like you are, so I'm bound to lapse. Forgive me?"

"I won't forgive you. Try harder. And I never said I was nervous."

"Right…well…I am nervous," I repeat, unashamed of the truth. "Plus, I have to get into flirt-mode because I'm about to have to turn on all the charm in public. A little practice is a good thing."

"Do you think this won't work? Tell me. Honestly." The tremor in her voice makes my heart twist.

I don't answer because right now I'm not sure.

And—because Corey Nash and Michelle Hopkins are bee-lining it past the bowling alley lanes, and heading toward the snack bar, toward us.

I take in a deep breath. "My small posse is heading this way. We'll just have to run the dress rehearsal with a real audience. Ready?"

She shakes her head, darting a glance over her shoulder and then back at me. "I can tell by your eyes that you think this won't work. I should just go."

I duck out of the snack bar and block her path to the door.

"Play along and trust me. Let's see what happens. At least give it a chance." She pales two shades whiter. I lean forward and look into her eyes. "If you'll let me, I'm going to put my arm around you and sweep you toward them. I think that's the easiest."

"Like a broom?" She sounds alarmed.

I have to stop myself from laughing. "Yes. Permission to touch. Is it granted?"

She nods, stepping closer.

"Let's not mess this up, huh?" I whisper, wondering if those last words are for her benefit or mine. I gingerly place my arm around her shoulders and I get the sensation Jess is suddenly made out of glass. Worse, it's up to me whether she shatters or not.

Because it is. Crap. What are we trying to do?

She trembles a little, and I pull her close, noting that she fits perfectly under my arm.

She stiffens for a second, but doesn't resist further. My heart clenches when she glances up and her eyes meet mine. I can hear her heart.

"Courage," I whisper. "If it's too much, I'll back any excuse to get you out of here. With me?"

"Do I have any other choice?" She swallows.

Michelle rushes in first, talking to me, but her eyes rivet on Jess. "OMG. Gray Porter and Jess Jordan. It's true, then! You two *are* a couple. Corey told me everything."

"Oh, *did* he?" I stall.

Jess is taking long, slow breaths. I give her shoulder a gentle squeeze and glance at Corey. My best friend is in classic form, smirking already. It's also pretty apparent Corey is taking one, way too long and *very* appreciative look at Jess. His eyes are like a broken elevator. Up, down. Up, down. And up again.

I'm starting to get a little pissed off about it. I shoot him the 'back off' glare, and he grins back, totally uncaring that I'm pissed.

"How goes it, guys," I say, trying to sound natural.

"Not as good as it goes for you, dude," Corey says, ignoring my glare and heading in for another: Down. Up. Down. Up, and a quick bootie check.

Bastard. I will retaliate.

I smile even wider as I feel Jess's hand move tentatively around my back. Her neck rests against my upper arm. It's not lost on me, or anyone that she's blushing like mad. Her hand touches my waist for a second, and then moves off quickly.

I feel her entire body stiffen like she's really freaking out.

I hold my breath and don't move until she settles for gripping the bottom of my t-shirt.

"When did all this start? You've been holding out on me." Michelle tosses me one of her wounded looks. I know I'm going to hear about how upset she is that I didn't tell her *first*. Michelle turns to Jess. "I'm Michelle Hopkins," she says with her trademark, friendly smile.

"I'm Jess. Jess Jordan. I know you from pep rallies. You're next year's head cheerleader, right?" Jess asks softly.

I smile to myself. She actually sounded *nice*, as promised.

"Yeah. About the head cheerleading thing." Michelle makes a face. "My promotion was more of a pity move. There are only two seniors on the squad next year. The actual talent graduated. The other girl and I flipped a coin. Don't expect to see me in the front line. I suck."

Corey pipes in, "Michelle wouldn't want to hurt anyone with her loose-cannon kicks. She looks like the perfect, athletic cheerleader, but she's dangerous. Mostly to herself!" He laughs. "She kicked so high she fell backwards and hit her head last homecoming game."

"You did?" Jess tosses Michelle another smile, laughing. I feel her shoulders relax.

"Hard to forget that when it's on Corey's YouTube page. I'm up to 43,000 hits. You should check it out," Michelle says, laughing also. "Don't believe anything you've heard about me—especially if it comes from this one." She rolls her eyes toward Corey.

Jess shrugs. "I haven't heard anything, except that you're a great cheerleader. But, I recommend you believe *everything* you've heard about me. Right, *Gray*? I'm as mean, stuck-up and as horrible as they come." Her self-mocking tone tells me that she's ramping into her usual bravado.

Michelle tosses me a surprised glance, but recovers quickly. "Well...I've only heard about Gray's crush on you. And that your placement in the senior class next year has you at third. I'm sure that makes a lot of people jealous. How'd you pull that off, anyhow?" Michelle asks, blatantly ignoring Jess's reference to her brutal, super-bitch reputation.

Jess bites her bottom lip. "It happens by default when you read all the time and never go out. I'm actually going to be first in the class when the year starts. But only because the Alder twins moved. They held the top two spots."

I'm proud of Jess. Her nice meter is soaring.

"You think you can help me work on some Pre-Calc this summer? If you're hanging around, I mean. With us. You will be, won't you?" Michelle probes, meeting my gaze. I want to hug Michelle. She can always be counted on to make people feel comfortable and get conversations smoothed over.

I glance at Corey. He's staring at Jess's butt again. Drooling, actually.

"If I'm around, I'd be happy to help. If I can," Jess says, sounding pleased.

I shoot Michelle a grateful smile. "I'm glad you two came out tonight."

"You made such a big deal about us being here—how could we miss it?" Corey nods to Jess. "I'm Corey Nash, and *you*, Jess Jordan, have turned my best friend into one love-sick puppy. Now I see why." He scrunches up his face. "Were you this hot last week?"

I'm resisting the growing urge to kill Corey, but Jess's happy laughter saves the kid's life.

"Easy dude," I say. "She's off limits from your shady, creeper moves. If you want to live, go ogle some other girl."

"Ooh. Gray's staked a claim," Michelle says, as she punches Corey playfully in the arm. "This is why I will never go out with you, Corey Nash. Why *no girl* will ever go out with you. You have no finesse. What is wrong with you?" Michelle holds up a five-dollar bill. "Come on, Jess. Let's get *your boyfriend* to make us nachos, so we have something to eat while he and Corey duel over you."

Jess takes in a breath and her body has turned back to ramrod stiff. "I'm not—he's not my *boyfriend*. He's just. We're just…"

"Just what? Don't stop," I interrupt and beam a huge, fake smile at my friends. "Did you hear that? She said, 'we're'. As in: 'we are'. I have witnesses. I think Jess Jordan's admitted we— *she and I*—might be *something* after all!"

I give Jess's shoulder another gentle squeeze, hoping she can regroup and realize she's jeopardizing the progress we've just made.

"Dude. Why are you talking like a robot?" Corey grins.

My heart sinks as Jess pulls away from me. Has she changed her mind?

I try to meet her gaze. But her eyes are darting around the room, taking in everyone and everything but me. I stop her from bolting by holding on to one of her hands. When her gaze meets mine, I'm certain she's about to panic. Panic, and possibly cry.

I make sure her face is not in view of Corey and Michelle and take up her other hand. I run my fingers over the backs of her knuckles and wait for her to find her control—or game face. Whatever it is she does to mask her feelings. I don't know when or how I get lost in her pale blue eyes. I stare deeper, tracking the glistening tears and glimmers of fear on the fringes of the many expressions crossing her face.

I long to see that fear erased. "Please. Trust me. We can do this," I whisper. But I said it so quietly, I'm not sure she's heard until she flushes beet red and gives me an almost imperceptible nod. I smile and draw her hands closer to my heart, never once breaking her gaze, which causes her to blush even more.

"Aww. So sweet." Michelle's voice hits me from thousands of miles away.

"Dude. This is like a bad TV movie." Corey pretends to gag-vomit. "Make out already or cut us loose. If you drop down on your knees right now and whip out some jewelry—we are *so* done hanging out. Seriously…yuck."

Corey's sarcasm cuts through some of the fog between me and Jess and the rest of the world, but not much. I can't gather my swirling thoughts to play it off. Nor can I joke back at Corey's comments. This has all become extremely important to me.

"Shh. Both of you," I say over my shoulder, not once taking my gaze off Jess's. I put slight pressure on her hands and my heart flips, hell—it actually *stops*—when she allows me to intertwine my fingers with hers.

Jess smiles then, finally. And I know she's going to be okay because she says, "*God.* Corey's right. You're embarrassing all of us. Did you guys know Gray's such a romantic weirdo? He loves Jane Austen too."

"He is? He does? I never knew," gushes Michelle.

"And again: YUCK," groans Corey.

I let go of Jess's hands and turn so Corey and Michelle have a better view of her face while I try to shoot for my goal. "In case you two hadn't noticed, I'm still trying to get this amazing girl to take me seriously. Will you, Jess? Be my girlfriend this summer?" Jess swallows. I know her shuttered, closed off expression is her way of giving me one last chance to back out. Without a blink, I continue, "Please. Say *yes.* That we're going out. That you're my girlfriend. Officially, and right now. If you agree, I promise to tone it down."

"Man. Jess, agree or end my boy's pain before we all puke," Corey adds.

I'm the only one who catches her obvious slip.

The girl has been shaking her head with a definitive 'no' this whole time. Luckily, she answers, "Yes. Okay fine. Yes. Now, please. Make us some nachos."

16

jess

Tap. Tap. Tap.

I try to ignore the sound and pull my car-blanket over my head so I can go back to sleep, only I can't. It's not one of the usual sounds: not wind, not the soft patter of rain, nor the loud smacks that come with hail. It's...

Tap. Tap. Tap.

It's definitely not the scratchy sound branches make, either. Could it be a bird?

Tap. Tap. Tap. Tap. TAP.

The sound moves to the glass nearest my head. No bird could be responsible for that unless a spastic hummingbird is trying to make its way in to attack. I pull off the blanket.

Gray. Of course.

He looks all goofy. Smiling that heart-wrenching half-smile I can't get used to. A smile that has actually served me well the past few nights. When I'm about to drift off to sleep, just thinking about that smile attached to *him* gives me a huge adrenaline rush and saves me from falling all the way asleep.

Unfortunately, in daylight, and in person—the effect is double. Now, all thoughts of napping are erased by the usual butterfly monsoon that takes over my body when he's near.

And he seems so happy to see me, I can't be mad that he's stolen precious minutes of morning sleep from me. Why does he have to be so…perfectly made? It's annoying.

Acting as though I'd known he was there the whole time, I open my side door to force him to step back as I launch one of my bored sighs. "There's no need for you to stalk me. I said I'd be your girlfriend days ago. You're here early, what gives?"

He leans on the edge of my open door and smiles down right into my eyes.

Into my heart. Where I don't want him to be.

"FYI, spacey. We're actually a bit late. Besides, it's typical boyfriend activity for me to track my GF's car."

"It is?"

"Yep, got to be aware if you're playing me. If I didn't know you better, I'd assume you partied a lot and hid your hangover moments from your parents in your vehicle. Do you always nap before work?"

"I was meditating."

"Lie. No one drools like that when they meditate."

I turn back to get my bag along with two double-caffeinated Red Bulls and hop out. We fall into step, heading toward the employee entrance of Geekstuff.com.

"I hope that's not your breakfast." He points to my drinks.

"It's a snack. I ate cereal at 4 AM. Thanks for—um—stopping to walk in with me." I wipe the corners of my mouth. "Was I really drooling?"

"You're avoiding my first question. The one about you sleeping in your car before work—why? And why were you eating cereal at 4 AM?"

I contemplate lying, and then see no point. He'd already caught me snoozing like a dork twice. Could make things easier if he knew some of the truth. "I…I nap during the day. Dawn till dusk. Whenever I can."

"Why? Are you some sort of all night bounty hunting vampire/zombie slayer? If so…I'm still in, because that's sexy." He grins.

I stop one step above him and turn to halt his progress while I delete all the things I don't want him to know about me from my answer. "I don't sleep very well when it's dark because I sometimes have—like—night terrors. If I'm lucky, I manage to not sleep at all. So, I'm tired a lot. I use my car to catch up during the day. Any other questions, nosy?" I end it with a flippant smile.

"Wow. That sucks." He's frowning.

"It is what it is. Just part of being me." I tap my temple. "I handle it just fine." I look away from his too intense gaze and take in how cute his curls are when they're damp. I'm pretty certain the lime and freshness smell comes from his shampoo. One day, I'm going to be brave enough to ask him about it. Maybe.

"You'll let me know if you—you know—need help or whatever?" he says softly.

"Help *sleeping?* What gives you the idea I would need help with anything?" I snap, annoyed that this guy has the power to turn me into an idiot girl that contemplates boy shampoo.

"Nothing. But for the duration…if you need to talk…or…"

"Please. I've been napping in my car years before you came along. It is not a freaking 'cry for help' so back off, Sir Lancelot. Park your white horse at some other girl's life. I only told you so you'd stop bugging me to go hiking with you at lunch. I need that hour to sleep."

"Oh. Right." He looks away, and I feel kind of bad because I think I've hurt his feelings.

"Look, I do appreciate that you care." I soften my tone. "I'm very used to this situation. I'm fine. Great actually. This job, hanging at the rink…things couldn't be better. My first round of college applications is almost filled out. And, because your—I mean—*Corey Nash's* daily text messages bring a constant bloom to my cheeks, my parents are thrilled. Just keep doing what you're doing. It's enough. No need to volunteer where you aren't needed, that's all."

He shrugs but I can't translate the look on his face to save my life. I'm suddenly worried he's going to ask a ton more questions.

Instead he says, "You don't drool. I was teasing." He shoots me his sideways smile and the dimple flashes.

"Insufferable," I answer back, relieved he's dropped it.

"Stubborn." He grins.

We walk through the doors together and he adds, "But the way your mouth drops open when you sleep leaves room for possible future drooling. Thought you should know."

"Oh yeah?" I have to laugh because he's wiggling his ink-black eyebrows at me. "Well, the way your—"

"You two are ten minutes late." Mr. Foley catches us in the hallway that leads to our miniscule office. We both sober instantly.

I flush when I meet Mr. Foley's silver bullet gaze. "I'm sorry, sir. I take full responsibility. Gray was on time. He'd stopped to…help me with a problem in my Jeep." *As in, me. The problem in my Jeep.*

Mr. Foley adjusts his glasses, squinting as though he can hardly see us through the double-wide lenses. "Just don't make this a habit. You get one chance before pissing me off. Consider this moment the end of your one chance. Simply because it's called an *internship* doesn't mean it isn't a real job. You were the one who agreed to do this without pay, Miss Jordan. I will not feel sorry for you about the deal you made, nor will I expect less of your work."

"No, sir. It won't happen again," I say, vowing to set my

iPhone alarm onto a louder ring as soon as I hit the ladies room.

"I won't be late again, either," Gray adds.

"Good." Mr. Foley nods as though satisfied. "I'm putting you both on the DIGI-TOYTECH Tradeshow team, starting today. The last thing I need to worry about is one of you pulling a *no-show*."

"DIGI-what?" Gray asks.

"DTT for short," Mr. Foley says. "It's the tradeshow where we launch our new product acquisitions, and hopefully, attract some international vendors in addition to new customers. This year the tradeshow's on our home turf. Denver, July 14th. It draws over 100,000 people during one long weekend. You two will be unpacking and repacking a ton of boxes. You'll also be assembling our booth freebies. Those are the ultra quality Geekstuff.com mini-toys we hand out each year. We're going big because we won't have any shipping costs. If you work hard, I'll let you both work the booth during the tradeshow. It's a giant ocean of thankless labor with double-the-fun at the end. Any problems with the assignment?"

"Heck no," Gray says. "Beats being stuffed—I mean—beats sitting in that small office all day."

"How and where do we start?" I say, holding myself back from jumping up and down with excitement. "I've been to DTT once as a ticket holder. It's the coolest. Working that tradeshow in an actual company booth—in *your* company booth—is going to be unbelievable!"

Mr. Foley smiles. "Head down to the receiving bays," he says. "There are fifty-two boxes of frog-shaped USB drives that just arrived from our Chinese manufacturer. Each one needs to be unboxed, unwrapped, logged into the system, loaded with our newest marketing brochure, hooked onto a lanyard and lily-pad, and then repackaged to look like this." He tosses an object toward me. I flinch and miss the catch. A green blob hits the floor and skitters to a stop.

"Sorry, Jessica. I almost took your eye out!" Mr. Foley seems to be biting back a laugh.

I vow revenge when I hear Gray chuckling as I recover the bright green lily pad with the words "Geekstuff.com" printed on the outer edge. There's a brighter, neon-green tree frog nestled into a cool plastic white lily that's connected to it. A lanyard with black text imprinted with 'Geekstuff.com' as well, has been creatively attached to a small fly on the frog's slightly protruding tongue.

"Cool. But, what is this thing?" I ask.

"Pull on the tongue," Mr. Foley says.

I do. When it pops off, I see that it's a USB drive. "So cute," I say.

"Let's hope you think so after you've put together five thousand of them. Should take you two a couple of days just to open and sort the boxes. We've slated a whole week for assembly. It's the most complicated take-away we've ever handed out. The project after that will seem simple. You'll be attaching mini-camera ladybugs onto a sunflower. Not as complex but you'll be making twice as many."

"Five thousand frogs and ten thousand ladybugs?" Gray asks.

"Yup!" Mr. Foley takes back the lily-pad sample and holds it up proudly. "This little frog holds 64 gigs of data. The ladybug is even cooler. It's a camera as well as a USB storage device. It holds 128MB and it actually shoots two minutes of quality video with sound! The underbelly hides a stamp-sized color monitor. Wait till you see it. They were donated to us by Fitzu, our Japanese sponsor. Heard of them?"

"I have. Digital cameras, TV's and electronics," I say, intrigued. I can't wait to see the ladybug.

Mr. Foley nods. "Our booth is famous for having the coolest items. The ladybugs and the frogs are only half of what we'll pass out."

"What will be the other half?" Gray asks, but I think I don't want to hear the answer.

Mr. Foley's eyes are gleaming with excitement now. "We're going to put together mini-LightSticks. Only these are replicas that allow you to text message someone else with the same LightStick. Networks permitting, of course. The message is sent and received in the hilt with the sword portion lighting up every time. Very cool. There will be twenty thousand of those, total. We're hoping to give one to each family group who comes by the booth, and then sell *extras* to friends and family who want one back at home. We reached record sales on them last year."

"Did you say twenty thousand, sir?" I ask, trying not to grimace.

Mr. Foley nods. "Not a lot of work assembling those. You'll only have to attach the different colored beam covers over the light source. I'm planning on having you assemble extras to keep in shipping for any early orders we are sure to get the week during the tradeshow."

"Oh. Cool. Looking forward to it," I lie, feeling suddenly overwhelmed. How in the world will I be able to stay awake all day and build little plastic toys, head to the rink to 'date my boyfriend', and still manage to keep my eyes open, PLUS keep my mind off sleeping all night long?

Gray's smile holds power over me—but not that much power.

I'm going to crumble. Die. My eyes might pop out. My brain will melt.

"Yes, it's a lot," Mr. Foley's saying. "Every year the intern has managed to pull this project off solo, though we've never gone this crazy before. Should be easy for the two of you to accomplish together."

"You said this job would involve grunt-labor, sir. Happy, are we to be chosen," Gray says, using the funny Yoda voice.

I want to roll my eyes. He's so great at brown nosing at just the right times. "Yeah, this is going to be cool," I add, forcing my tone to sound as excited as Gray's. "If we get behind, could I possibly take a bunch home—to work on there?" I ask, thinking I could make up any slack on my part in the middle of the night.

"No way. The tradeshow toys are top secret. I don't want them off property until the big weekend. Just keep me in the loop on your progress. If you get behind, I'll pull one or two guys off shipping," Mr. Foley says. "Besides, I want you two to have some *fun* this summer. Work hard, but don't kill yourselves. Interns should not be taking work home."

I feel as though I've suddenly been sucked into a fog as Mr. Foley tosses the frog and lily pad combo to Gray. He catches it without a problem. Of course he does.

I sigh and shoot an envious glare at him.

Not because he's coordinated and has such good social skills—because he looks so wide awake.

17

gray

I eye the mountains of frogs on lily pads I'd carefully set up on the long metal tables in the Geekstuff warehouse. Considering Jess and I had been working on this project all week, and we haven't even begun to unwrap the lanyards yet, this frog task now seems beyond impossible to complete in the next two days.

I never want to see a frog dead or alive, and especially one made of *plastic,* ever again. As far as I'm concerned, the DTT Tradeshow project sucks ass.

Jess's initial enthusiasm has also dimmed. We've split the task to be more efficient. She opens the packages while I assemble. After that, we'll attach the lanyards and load on the data file together. A few more hours of frog piling, and we'd be able to switch from this monotonous task to the next one.

Jess has been distant all morning. Short answers and long sighs are all I've had from her since she disappeared behind the growing pile of packing materials on the other side of my workspace. Each stupid frog was shipped from China. They're wrapped and taped in enough cardboard and bubble wrap that you'd think they were made of glass.

I'm sure the things are worth less than their packaging, but at this point I don't want to know. I'm bored, hot, cranky as hell, and hungry for some serious man-lunch.

Burritos. Foot-long meat-stacked subs.

The largest icy Coke I can buy.

One whole large pizza and a side of wings.

A burger, dripping mayo and bacon, and an extra large icy Coke. Anything. Everything.

I throw a lily pad like a Frisbee over a stack of boxes and smile when Jess gasps.

"Two points if that made contact!" I yell, trying to get a rise out of her.

"You wish!"

I hear a small laugh as she whips the thing back over the boxes. It takes out one of my carefully stacked piles of frogs. "Easy there. It's called aim," I tease again. "Are you starving like I'm starving?" I ask, wishing she could come to lunch with me.

I don't bring it up because I know she won't. Can't.

"Eat this, why don't you?" Before I can defend myself, Jess whacks me straight in the forehead with a tape-wrapped ball of bubble wrap.

Damn, but the girl has a good arm.

"Missed completely," I say but know I've been busted when I see a flash of her blonde hair ducking around the far side of some yet to be addressed boxes.

The ladybugs. Our future hell project.

"Whatever you need to say in order to save your pride." She's doing that irrepressible giggle that makes me unable not to smile.

"Do you want me to hit you with another? Or are you done at one, you wimp," she challenges again.

I can hear her scrunching papers and stretching tape around another ball bomb. I imagine she's about to whack me with half a box.

"This one might hurt," she adds, confirming my suspicions.

She's full-on laughing now.

"Stop. Truce. If you knock over these piles this project will take longer. I'm sorry I started it, but I'm antsy. You've been quiet too long. Let's talk about where I'm going to take you for our first weekend date. It's in two days. Preferences?"

"I'd rather throw things at you." And she does. Pelts me with the giant wad of tape and paper. I catch it, but she doesn't emerge. I can hear her pouring plastic frogs into the wire baskets she's been using. "I have no idea. You pick," she says finally. All laughter has been erased from her voice. This makes me feel bad, sad…annoyed.

"Come on," I plead. "I'm not that terrible. You've spent every night at the rink with me for almost a whole week. I think it's been fun for you." I hook four more frogs onto their lily pads. I'm getting faster at this. "Hasn't it…been fun?"

"Fishing for compliments, as usual. You are the neediest guy I've ever paid to date me," she says.

"Funny. You're the most evasive girl I've ever known. Come on, answer," I insist.

"Yes. It's been fun. I already told you that."

"Good."

We work in silence for a long moment. "Did you decide?" she calls out. Her tone seems hopeful, but I detected a little anxiousness also.

"Hiking. A short trail. What works best for you? Saturday or Sunday?"

"Saturday please. Sunday is what my parents call 'family day'. But mostly we do yard work, clean house or do laundry. Sometimes church. Sometimes movies. Does that work with your rink schedule?"

"I'm on at five. We'll make a day of it. The picnic lunch is on me. Your job is to locate some hiking gear. Bring a water bottle, sunscreen, all that. The trail is a bit rough but the view is worth it. What's your favorite food?" I ask and my stomach grumbles again at that thought.

"I like everything," she says, but she sounds doubtful. "Don't forget," she adds, "for official dates, you have to pick me up at my house and bring Michelle and Corey. But on pain of death, stay in the car. My parents are getting viciously curious about you, *Corey.*"

I hate that she now sounds resigned, as though we just discussed some mandatory chore like toilet cleaning.

"Fine," I grumble, feeling slighted. "I'll have the car full of other people and distractions." I'm getting sick of Corey and Michelle being part of our equation. Our contract. Our new friendship.

My crush.

Hell. I just need to admit it. I've got it so bad for this girl that I'm jealous of any conversation, smile or time that Jess gives to my best friends. It's something that's making me feel crazy and it's gone way out of control. It's a crush I need to kill. But how?

Jess has turned out to be great on every level. Smart, perceptive, hard working and kind. And let's not leave out her soft skin, the hair she hides in those buns. The cinnamon-sunshine pie thing, and the way she lets me put my arms around her when Corey and Michelle are looking.

The girl has cast some sort of spell on me. One I've been vowing daily, *hourly*, to ignore. So far I'm having no success with that.

Worse, the boring toy building makes it easy to daydream… about her!

Just now I'd been thinking about the way she fits so perfectly under my chin and next to my heart when I pull her into a hug. The way she eats my nachos at the rink every night so carefully, but still manages to wind up with cheese on the corners of her mouth and all over her chin. *Damn*...that alone is beyond hot.

How am I supposed to just shut that cuteness down?

I figure my stupid imagination has allowed this crush to go way out of bounds. I know she's completely off limits. All I can do to keep under control is to remind myself of the night she was almost raped. Remember my part in it—what a chicken-shit loser I'd been that night.

I'd only wanted to be her hero; instead I'd been—crap! I'd been a complete failure. If I continue to entertain thoughts of *me*, being with Jess—as in—*for real*—then I'm a complete ass on every level. Worse, I will have failed her all over again. And I refuse to do that.

Wanting more from Jess is pure selfishness. This has to be about her. I need to be satisfied with just being what she wants—what she needs—what she's asked me to be. I'm going to figure out a way to stop my reckless imagination from coming up with impossible scenarios where Jess and I become a real couple.

Impossible.

Anything else would hurt her—would cause her to remember. She doesn't deserve that kind of pain no matter what. And not from me. I pull another pile of frogs over and snap them together, reminding myself of things that seems to be working for both of us.

As in, *I'm* working for her. We have a contract that makes us both happy. I'm getting paid a mega-load of money, and we're both going to college on our own terms.

I toss down the latest frog-lily-pad-combo and pull out my wallet to look at the $448.00 Geekstuff.com two-week pay-check simmering in there. I haven't put it in savings yet, but I will.

And then I'll ramp up being the best damn pretend-boyfriend in the world. Whatever she wants. Jess deserves to get the guy she's hired on task and in focus. The girl had no paycheck handed to her today. And for the past two weeks she's worked as hard as me. Maybe harder. While all I've done is daydream about her and wish things were different. They aren't. So I'm going to deal with that and go with what's real. Period.

Done with crush. And moving on.

"Hey, slacker. It's awfully quiet on frog island." Another volleyball-sized cluster of paper and tape lands with a tape-sticking thwack near my feet, pushing me out of my twisted thoughts.

"Head back to trash planet. I need a basket trade out," she commands.

"Coming boss-lady," I say and empty the few frogs remaining in the large wire basket onto my worktable. I head around the wall of boxes that house Jess's unwrapping empire. For the tenth time that morning, I stop, frozen, and stare.

All of my latest vows, promises and new resolves melt away. She's too cute. And I'm only human.

Humans get crushes. It's how we're programmed.

Today, she's twisted the length of her hair into the most epic bun of all. This one's tennis ball sized and making her little curly wisps of hair twist out in every possible direction. The whole effect of the odd hairstyle, not to mention the smooth skin along the long line of her exposed neck all but does me in.

I love that she has zero vanity checks like other girls do. She never looks at her reflection in mirrors or windows. Nor does she flip her hair around, blink her eyes all weird, and never blabs on and on about her clothes or shoes. Somehow, her careless attention seems to accent just how pretty and cool she is.

"What? You on a sugar low? Me too." She stops to shoot me

a grin while she twists one of the rubber bands tighter into that mad, sexy bun.

"Something like that," I mutter, stifling a groan as I will my body to move toward her when in fact, *I know* I should be running the hell away from her open smile.

Those lips. Damn! Someone shoot me. Please.

"You do look somewhat off." She shoots me a worried glance. "I've got an extra Red Bull in my car…though I'm not sure if your caffeine-free stomach will be able to hang with the big dogs." She grins up at me wider.

I'm gone. Lost. Done for. Crush is back on. Times two to the tenth power. Hell, yes the girl has cast a spell on me!

All I want to do right now is fall on my knees, tell her the truth, tell her who I am, what I did and apologize for all of it—just to see if she'll forgive me. Find out if we can start this all over. Then…touch her face, ask her questions like: Does she like me at all? Will she take out that bun so I can see how long her hair really is again? And do we, as a real couple, even stand a chance?

I shiver. There's no way.

We'd have to unwind time. Start over three years ago. It's way too late for that.

"Well? Do you want the Red Bull or not?" She arches one graceful brow, waiting. *Crap.* I've been standing here blinking down at her like a total, zombied freak.

"No thanks. I can wait until lunch," is all I can manage. I start forward and set down the empty basket at the edge of her crisscrossed knees. Christ, even her work-grubby knees are sexy as hell!

Help me, someone!

Unable to speak or meet her gaze after what I've just been thinking, I take up the full basket she loaded and turn to leave.

"How's it look out there?" she asks, not at all noticing my

absolute shut-down. She leans back into one of the mini mountains of paper, boxes, bubble wrap, and cardboard she's created behind her. The move catches my eye and I can't help but stare all over again.

Hell. I'm caught in a living hell.

She's blinking up at me and I realize I'm supposed to answer.

"We're...starting to show real progress," I choke out, working to ignore the surge of blood that's rushed into my head. It also surges into other places down lower. Places I do not want *her* to notice! It's like I'm back in seventh grade and not able to control *anything.*

"This is not half bad as far as comfort goes." She leans back farther with a yawn and stretches her arms over her head. I can't squelch the image of me pushing her back into that pile of packing material and making out with her. For a long, long time.

I'm a sick, sick, stalking bastard with a crush on a girl I can never have, and there's nothing I can do about it.

"You should take a little break," she says.

"Mmmhm." My throat has gone completely dry. I can't even swallow.

"I'm taking a little break right here," she adds, closing her eyes. This brings my attention back to her lips, and then of course, to the rest of her. "Mmm," she sighs again.

Everything in my body surges to max capacity and I don't even care.

Does the girl have no mercy?

Isn't some sort of devil in a black suit supposed to show up right here and suck me underground? Make me sign away my soul? Or did that already happen when I put my name on her insane boyfriend contract? That can't be right. When you sign away your soul you're supposed to get what you want for a little while. And I'm not even close.

I shove the basket of plastic frogs in front of my pants and all but run around the boxes to the safety of my waiting stack of lily pads.

Nothing like four thousand, hellish plastic frogs to calm a guy down.

Frog to lily pad.

Frog to lily pad.

Frog to horrible, boring, stupid, freaking Geekstuff.com plastic, lame-ass, lily pad!

Frog to lily pad.

Frog. Lily pad.

I shove one of the piles to the side and attack the next.

Now I'm the one dreading our date.

Jess was right. It *is* going to be a chore. If Jess is making me this insane while lounging around in recyclables, I can only imagine how amazing the girl will look in dusty hiking gear! Unless she decides to wear a frog t-shirt and a lily pad hat for the rest of the summer, I'm doomed.

I attach three more frogs to three more lily pads, but the pounding in my head and other areas will not relent. I brace my hands flat against the stainless steel worktable and sigh.

"I'm going to lunch. Are you good with me checking out for awhile?" I call over the boxes. "I'm seriously…dying." I grimace almost laughing at myself. "Jess, you planning to eat something today? I can bring you a sandwich for later if you're going to nap in your car."

She doesn't answer.

"Jess. Earth to Jess Jordan."

Crap. Crap. And crap!

My stomach growls then twists. There's no need to walk around the stack of boxes to confirm what I suspect.

She's asleep.

Which means many painful things.

1. I'm going to stay here to watch over her.

2. I'm going to resist the temptation to head back around those boxes so I can stare at her beautiful face and feel sorry for myself while she sleeps.

3. I'm going to ignore my stomach and build enough stupid frog-lily-pads to cover for both of us until she wakes up. No matter how long it takes.

4. When she does wake up, I'm going to play it off and get us both a snack from the machines in the employee break room so we can start on the lanyards together.

Because I have a paycheck and she doesn't.

Because we have a contract. And because she needs me to honor that contract.

Not for any other reasons.

No other reasons.

18

jess

The jellyfish tentacles in the lamp are in focus now, but something's still not right.

I unclamp my arms from around my knees and stand, wincing as the blood rushes back into my legs with thousands of pin-pricks. My comforter falls to the floor. I pad across the room, pausing at my desk to scratch the number 617 below the recent 456, and last week's winning number of 507.

All numbers I've logged since the internship started.

617. Record high. I'm on a bad up-trend.

To try and regain my breathing—my bearings—anything, I let my gaze travel through, into and out of each of my favorite movie posters.

Pride and Prejudice always comes first: Mr. Darcy, staring at the Keira Knightley version of Elizabeth while the sun beams over their shoulders. The last scene. Where they vow to never part from that day forward. I love the way he's got his forehead next to hers. In that whole, perfect movie…they only kiss once…

Next: Jack and Rose from *Titanic*. They face the ocean on the ship's bow. Soaring together, facing the world.

The most captivating poster of all is from *Romeo and Juliet*:

It's from the 90's movie that starred Leonardo DiCaprio and Claire Danes before they got all old. The whole play is filmed, word for word, in a modern, gang/mobster setting. My poster is of Romeo and Juliet staring at each other through an aquarium.

I've stared at this poster and watched the movie, not to mention the YouTube clips of this one single moment—the moment where they first meet—countless times.

Romeo sees Juliet first. His expression is so sure. He *knows* that he will never be the same because of this one moment. He's lost and in love with Juliet forever. With zero words exchanged, his course is set.

Juliet's expression is equally startled when she sees Romeo. She seems amazed—but cautious. Like she's smarter—at first. But if you watch the YouTube clips closely enough, I swear you can see in Juliet's eyes that she *knows* she's going to die because of how she feels for this guy.

I think this scene is where the true tragedy of the whole story lives. It's not because they both die in the end. The tragedy is all right there…in the very beginning when he smiles at her. When she instantly forgets. Forgets how dangerous he is.

You can't blame her for how it plays out. Romeo's so amazing in this movie—what he says to her—how he looks at her. She's obviously drowning in butterflies.

I know for a fact now, butterflies like that can be horrible, beautiful things. I tear my gaze away from the posters and head for the door. Leaning my head against it, I breathe in as deeply as I can, willing the voices to stop. It's not working—nothing is working tonight. The flashes and voices won't quit.

I even think I heard Gray's voice in my nightmare! He's become so tangled into my messed up life, it makes sense that he'd wind up inside my head. Trapped in my nightmares—my dreams and the in-between parts of my mind where I hide secret, unspeakable wishes. I suppose he's mixed in there forever now, with all the rest.

The most amazing, best thing, floating through everything that's the worst.

That thought gives me this incredible surge that I hate Gray. Hate him a lot.

Then I wonder if I've started to go crazy. This time—crazy for real.

That has to be what's happening to me. Why I can't get control. This is all too much. How long can one person live on a few hours of stolen sleep each day before going bonkers? Hopefully a few more weeks. That's all I need, and then this madness can be over.

I shudder because I'm afraid. Afraid like I haven't been in a long time. What if I can't make it? What if I'm stuck in this bedroom for the rest of my life?

I fling open my door and head out on shaking legs to my sister's room. I need help. Some sort of solace. Kika's the only beacon of light I trust. I know she'll at least distract me from the tornado of confusion that's attacking me.

Her room's lit up green from the fish nightlight she's had since she was six. Even though it's summer, she's afraid of insects and keeps her windows closed tightly. It's a phobia that makes her room endlessly suffocating. That's just what I need. To be suffocated so my thoughts don't have any more room to breathe is just perfect.

"Kika? Can I snuggle in? Just for a bit?" I whisper.

"Mmph." Kika scoots to one side as she holds up the covers. "Time is it?"

"You don't want to know." I snuggle in back-to-back, not caring that she'll feel my shakes. I resist the urge to cling to her and cry like a baby. "What's that smell?" I ask instead.

"My lotion. BathLand discontinued it," she mutters as she

yawns, waking up. "I bought all they had."

I smile a little. "Is that the lotion you hit me with before I went to the rink the other night?"

Kika taps her nightlight one notch brighter and turns to look at me. "Peach Cobbler."

Her light blue eyes, so much like mine, sparkle even in the dim light. Her feather-wisp brows are drawn together and she's frowning. Watching my face.

Kika always tracks me with the same worried expressions Mom uses. Their voices are also exactly the same. On the phone, no one can tell them apart. But unlike Mom, Kika seems to know exactly what I need after my nightmares. She's quietly watching and waiting for me to get myself together—minus any sort of question and answer torture session.

No judgment, no speculation on 'what it all means'. I love her for that. For everything.

"So…you liked the lotion?" she asks finally. She must have discerned that I'm not going to bawl all over her or flip into a deeper level of shaking like I've done in the past. She snuggles back into her pillow. "I'll lend you more if you want—for any other *special occasions* you might have coming up," she hints, but her voice is too low. Heavy. She's worried about me.

I try to joke, "I appreciate the offer, but I think that lotion should only be worn on a consistent basis if you're thirteen, trying to repel insects, horrify guys and attract bears all at the same time."

"Hey now…"

"Not that I'm saying I won't need to do all of that…some day. I'll let you know."

"Should I mention there is only one *gallon* left in the whole world? And it's going fast," Kika huffs, insulted. "I'm sure it doesn't repel guys. Though you might be right about the bears."

"Just in case, you might apply that stuff with a lighter touch. Although…" I take in another breath, feeling steadily better. "Corey—he—knew right away your lotion was peach—he guessed pie, not cobbler, though. Said he loved it. So you could be on to something," I add, shaking my head, remembering.

"It worked and you *mocked* it? How dare you make me doubt. You should bow to me, right now."

"Tomorrow. I promise. I'll be your slave."

She giggles and my heart swells with warmth. The nightmare can't compete with my sister. She's always had some special brand of magic. Asleep or awake, any space she occupies somehow instantly becomes the sweetest place on earth. Right now, that place has morphed into this messy, peach-infused, darkened room.

Kika moves her shoulder closer to mine before speaking again. "I heard you cry out. You practically shook the walls," she whispers.

"Ugh. That loud?" I sigh. "If Mom heard, she's probably emailing Dr. Brodie right now, trying to get me an appointment."

"I was going to come in, but you quieted right away. I figured you'd gone back to sleep. Was it bad?"

"The usual," I lie. But now that I've had time to process it, I think the nightmare has changed more than I'd thought. The images had come at me faster. Clearer. The police officer had been wearing a gun in a black holster, and he'd had a walkie-talkie thing too. I've never remembered looking at those so clearly before.

Dr. Brodie told me the dream, after all this time, could easily be a mixture of current memories and past ones. He told me I shouldn't trust them as any sort of definite truth or memory. He also told me that despite how drunk I'd been, if I truly ever *did* remember, that it would all feel *different*. I'd simply know what was real and what wasn't real.

Remembering is remembering. Not a foggy, messed-up dream.

Only I don't want to remember anymore. I haven't wanted that for a long time.

At first, I'd spent every waking moment trying to decipher my nightmares. Wishing I could remember. But last year I'd decided to ignore the whole thing. That's when things started to get better. I don't obsess over the past any more. I just want to move on.

Kika asks, "Is it getting to be like before? You sounded like you did when—"

"No! Not even close." I refuse to let her finish. I don't want to talk about how it was when I'd lost it. Screaming and crying night after night, month after month. That was when everyone in our house had circles under their eyes—not just me. When they all thought I'd be crazy—forever.

"It's just a bad night, fine—a bad week. But that's bound to happen sometimes, right?"

"If you weren't shaking so badly right now, I'd believe you."

If I weren't shaking so badly, I'd believe myself, I think.

"Don't tell Mom and Dad. They'll just act all weird. I'm off my usual schedule because of the internship. Things will settle. Honest. I'm fine." I turn to stare up at the ceiling fan and Kika finds my hand. She holds on to it extra tight until the last of the shudders have left my spine.

"Wish one of my checklists could fix you," she says in a voice as deflated as I feel.

I force my tone to sound cheery. "You have fixed me. Because of your last list, I'm well on the pathway to normal on all fronts. I've got places to go, people to see and a cute boy's texting me every day." I ramp up my subject change. "Which reminds me, I need the list you promised me about the text messaging. What does g-t-g mean?"

"Duh. 'Got to go?' You're hopeless. I'll get it to you first thing."

"Thanks."

Kika sighs. "I know you want privacy and all that, but will you at least admit you *like* this Corey Nash? At least tell me *something* about him? You owe me for the lotion that trapped his heart, after all. I want details."

"Okay." I smile and turn to lean on my elbow so I can peer down at her. I'm stalling. Searching for something true to tell her after two weeks of evasiveness and full-on lying. "He's tall. Lanky, but solid and strong looking. And he says I make him laugh. That part is annoying really, because you know that I pride myself in being NOT funny." Kika giggles as I continue, "He also mumbles to himself. Like all the time. It's cute. And his voice. OMG. You should hear it. It's all low rock star... and...shiver-worthy. And his eyes. I can't even explain them. They're magic. Dark forest—sparkling green."

"What?"

"I mean *blue-green*...really deep blue with teensy blue-ish flecks mostly. They change all the time. And he's growing out his hair to look surfer shaggy," I add quickly, trying to recover from my slip. I've said all along Corey's got *blue* eyes. Because Corey Nash does have blue eyes. My bad.

I conjure Corey's face and hold onto it, pushing away all thoughts of Gray. "His personality makes him very impish. And he's—how can I explain him—he teases everyone. He's sweet, and he kind of flirts all the time. But not in a creepy way. He's charming," I add.

"Nice," Kika says, still half lost in her giggles.

"Yeah...well." I meet her gaze. I'm grinning back, but I can't hold on to Corey's image.

As I continue, Gray's face hovers in my mind all over again.

"The way he *looks* at me—sets off major heartbeats. If you must know, standing still, this guy fills my brain with taffy, makes me act like a fool, and stops my heart with butterflies at least twice a day. I have them just mentioning the guy, if you must know."

And I do. So annoying.

Kika grins. "Wow. Really? Butterflies mean you have a serious crush. I know that much!"

I swallow, denying it to my sister and to myself. "I'm not going to make a big deal about a few tummy flutters because… dead people, old people, even furniture would get butterflies if they met this guy. You should see him in person. The yearbook does not do him any justice. I wonder if he's my type or if I simply enjoy looking at him?"

"It sounds like he's your type. And I like the yearbook photo. I can see what you're talking about."

"He—um—asked me on a date. I think I'll go."

Kika, chomping on the bait, smiles and claps her hands. "OMG! OMG! What will you wear? OMG! A date? Do guys actually say: 'Do you want to go on a *date* with me'? It sounds so awkward."

I turn over and tuck the blanket tightly over both of us. "He asked me to go hiking. I think he used the words *group date*, so it probably means nothing. He did say he'd pack my lunch. That's something sort of sweet, isn't it?"

Kika sighs and flips over so we're both staring at the slowly turning ceiling fan. "What if your first kiss with him is on a mountainside with the sun shining, and there's green grass and little wildflowers all around, and birds are chirping and—"

"—and we live in Colorado at the end of June? So you can add in a bunch of dust, delete the green part, turn the flowers to dandelions and brown grass, and kill the chirping unless you mean squawking Magpies. Add in the rest of our friends staring at us. And don't forget to throw in a torrential afternoon lightning storm followed with quarter sized hail?"

She laughs. "Oh yeah. Kissing in the rain! Awesome romance!"

I laugh too. "I'm not kissing any guy on a 'group date' after I've been sweating like a trucker from hiking. What if—he's had garlic in his lunch?" I'm blushing bright red right now and thankful for the dark room.

It's too weird imagining a first kiss with Gray…or is it?

The guy is my boyfriend, after all.

My chest squeezes…how I wish I had the nerve to make him kiss me as part of the contract. But I was the one that made up the zero benefits rule. Although, I did reserve the right for changes.

No. No.

Kika saves me from my insane thoughts. "As long as you've had garlic, the kiss could still be a go. There's a chance you'll be saturated in the same ingredients 'cuz he's making your lunch." Kika giggles.

"Holy…that's true." I meet her gaze and we both bust out laughing.

19

gray

Hey, GF. I'm 2 blks away. Warning: Flying solo. Sidekicks ditched us.

I've pulled over onto a side street in Jess's neighborhood and send my text message *as promised* just before the scheduled 9AM pick-up. I'm a bit worried she's going to flip when she sees I'm alone in the car.

I breathe a small sigh of relief when she answers right away: *K. Red D. Warning!! MOS DOS!!*

I have no idea what *MOS DOS* means. Maybe it's Spanish?

Jess's texting skills have become a point of argument between us. Her little sister gave her a whacked list of texting acronyms. She brought it to work on Friday, but I'd refused to 'study it'. It was the first 'no' I'd given her about anything. Man had she been ticked off. Yesterday, when I'd asked for a translation of one of her cryptic messages she'd responded with all caps: *AWGTHTGTTA?!!!*

Apparently that meant in full shout: *Are we going to have to go through this again?!!!*

At least she's consistently hilarious.

I pull up in front of her house. Before I have a chance to put it in park or honk, the girl is slamming into the passenger seat.

"Let's go." She's out of breath.

I'm so disoriented by her short, dark brown hiking shorts that my foot slides off the clutch and I stall the car.

Legs. Smooth, tanned, long, beautiful legs.

"What are you doing?" she asks. Her eyes dart away as she gestures wildly toward her house.

Cinnamon-sunshine, legs, and...car died.

My mind clears a little. I follow her pointing finger in time to spot two people who'd trailed behind Jess and were now heading straight for us.

Parents. Parents!

She starts waving and smiling, but is talking to me through her smile. "Drive away. As in NOW, or you'd better be ready to pretend your name is Corey Nash and explain why you don't have blond hair and blue eyes."

My heart has never pounded so fast.

Jess's mom calls out, "Honey, wait! We'd love to meet your *friend.*"

I remember this woman's voice from years ago and panic. Explaining my looks are the least of my worries where these people are concerned. If they recognize me, I'll be shot on sight.

I slam my foot into the clutch, throw the car into neutral and turn the key, revving Bessie, my 84 Honda Accord, back to life in a way I know might make her stall again.

The car complains and shoots out her triple backfire, but she stays alive. The exploding noise seems to startle Jess's parents, and they freeze momentarily on the walkway.

"Honey! Young man? Yoo-hoo. Corey? Just one minute please." Jess's mom jerks forward like she's been released from an invisible catapult. Her father is frowning and shooting me and my car a heated glare that rivals one of Jess's.

I pull my ball cap down and hunch my shoulders, pretending not to hear. In two seconds I back out of the driveway, pulling away from the curb with a lurch.

Jess leans out her car window and calls out, "Bye! We're late. Got to pick up the gang. See you this afternoon!" She waves wildly, smile on double-high now.

I can't breathe at all.

We don't speak for three whole blocks.

On my part, the silence is for two reasons: 1. I think I've swallowed my tongue, and 2. Jess has stretched and crossed her ankles, which makes me notice her legs again. I make the mistake of glancing over at her just then.

Crap!

Three reasons now: 3. Her cute, prairie-girl braids are over-the-top adorable and are playing a part in another one of my complete mental shut downs!

This girl is perfect…my crush will be forever.

"Holy crap!" It feels good to curse out loud. "And crap!"

"I tried to warn you. I texted *MOS DOS*," Jess says, wrongly assuming I'm talking about what just happened. "That should have tipped you off."

"MOS DOS means *parents*?! Girl, are you deliberately trying to kill me or simply get me killed? If you'd typed MOM and DAD you'd have used the same number of letters, and that would have actually made sense!"

"I didn't think of that." She looks so surprised and then chagrined, I feel bad for yelling. "But…everyone in the texting world knows that MOS means *Mom Over Shoulder*. And DOS means—"

"I get it. I officially flunk you on texting. Delete all memorized text message abbreviations from your mind. And accept no more texting advice from your eighth grade sister. She's a menace and you know it." I shoot her a grin and finally, have to laugh. "I almost had a heart attack back there. MOS DOS?

Really?"

"Oh my God." Jess laughs along with me. "I *am* sorry." She bursts into a long fit of giggles. The happy, bright sound brings the air back into my lungs. "You should have seen your face," she adds.

"You should have seen yours. I can't believe you told them we were going to get the *gang*. This is not 1955. And, *gosh golly*, I don't want to bum you out but, today, there is no *gang*." I shoot her a glance. "Just me. Michelle bailed for a shopping trip with her mom, and Corey's grounded for back-talking about chores. You okay with that?"

"Oh. Yeah, I'm good." She shrugs as though she doesn't care, but I've spent enough time with her now that I can tell otherwise. She's nervous. I take note of the dark circles under her eyes. She also looks really tired.

"How was your night?"

"Good. Actually."

She's nodding—too much. I'm sure it's a lie.

"I want to know what a *good night* means to you." I dart a glance directly into her eyes, wondering if she'll open up. Her expression has turned wary so I keep my attention on the road. "Did you sleep?" I add.

"Not much, and that's why it was a good night." She stares out her window.

Shit. Her answer is worse than any lie. I sigh, finding myself at a loss for words.

"What did you bring for lunch? Can we eat first? If I don't eat real food with these babies, my tummy hurts." She flashes two Red Bull's nestled inside her pack, obviously taunting me away from feeling sorry for her.

"I hate that you always drink that stuff," I say, letting her win on the subject change. Today is my attempt at 'turning it all off and getting back to business'. I can do this. Despite her damn legs, I can do this.

"Red Bull's tasty," she adds. "You should try some. Maybe it will get rid of that glazed look you've had since Thursday. If you ask me, I'd say you're the one not sleeping," she teases.

I shrug, wishing I could tell her that 'glazed look' is *me*, trying to fuzz-out my gaze so I can't see her cute face so clearly. "Tasty or not, that stuff isn't exactly a recommended pre-hike drink. Will you be able to hike after not sleeping all night?"

"Honestly? I have no idea. But I can't attempt it without my daily dose of caffeine *assistance*, so back off my staple food. I need it, and I love it." She closes her bag.

"Deal. Will you tell me more about the nightmares? Why you have them?" I ask gently, risking a glance at her now closed off and defensive expression.

"Pfft. Tell me why you don't like Coach Williams? Or, how come you don't play ice hockey for our school anymore? Corey and Michelle told me you're really good. As in, you're free-ride-scholarship good. I saw Coach Williams at the rink the other night and asked him about you. He said he's holding a spot for you on his team. Anytime."

"Did he, now?" I cover, not surprised that Coach made good on his threat to check up on Jess. This is my chance to shut up and leave it all alone—but instead I decide to tell her some of it. If I open up to her, maybe she'll open up to me. "Coach Williams and I had a fight. It's stupid, simple, and private. But it was big enough to put me off ice forever, okay?"

"Whoa. A fight? About what?"

"Nope. Your turn."

"I don't like talking about my nightmares. They're stupid, complicated and private. Just like yours. You wouldn't understand. Let's just say those buggers put me off sleeping for life," she quips, tossing my words back at me.

I cringe as I catch the truth and meaning behind what she

said. "Tell me a little? Are you some sort of insomniac?" I try again.

She crosses her arms. "No. Well…yes. But not a willing one. I crave my bed like some people crave chocolate, but if I fall asleep when it's dark outside the nightmares are worse—dreadful, endless. So I try not to encourage them."

She looks at me through her lashes—like she doesn't want me to notice she's watching my reactions to what she's saying.

"Go on. Please. Explain a little more."

"After three years of therapy and never being able to understand them, staying awake all night is way easier than chancing my random nightmares. And it works. I don't get them if I nap during the day. That's it. Nothing deeper." She lets out a long breath. "You'll think I'm crazy now. People who are sane don't do therapy year after year. Oh—and newsflash—the therapy never worked on me."

I feel slightly sick. Helpless. "I'm sorry. Really sorry."

She shrugs and stares out her window. "Don't be. I don't want pity. I don't deserve it. The nightmares—they're partly my fault because I can't get over them. Not directly, of course, but after my parents spent thousands of dollars, after I've tried every pill available, we've all found out I'm simply not curable. In the big scope of things—it's not so important."

"What?" I almost shout, angry that she seems to totally believe that. "*You,* not being able to sleep is major important. Jesus, Jess."

She shrugs. "Other people have way worse things to deal with than nightmares and not sleeping. Like poverty, cancer, war. There's people who live with no legs, or a family member dying. My random sleep schedule is small in comparison. Besides, I'm used it. I'm like an ER doctor. Always on the night shift. No big deal. Honest." She pulls her arms tighter over her chest.

"Yeah, but you're on the day shift with me," I say softly.

"Yep." She laughs a wry little laugh.

"So…you're exhausted, all the time?"

"Like a model's always starving," she jokes, but I'm not laughing. "I try to hide the *not sleeping* from my parents. During school I can pull it off, but this summer…it's been more difficult. With the internship plus my clingy new boyfriend I can't catch up. I've been forced to sleep at night…only that's not going so well."

"Because of the nightmares. You've been having a lot of them?"

"What is this—my tribunal?" She rolls her eyes at me and her expression is so comical, that I almost laugh.

Almost, because I know she's doing that to play off the seriousness of what she's told me.

The girl is falling apart and it's my fault.

My heart twists as she finishes, "I have to work out the kinks. I won't slack off again, I swear. Sleeping while you work for both of us was a one time thing, if that's what you're worried about."

"Hell! Is that what you think?" I grip the steering wheel and turn onto a two-lane road marked with a sign that reads: *Red Rocks Hiking Area, 4 Miles Ahead.* "Will you tell me what the dreams are about?" I venture again.

If she says *yes*, then I'll park this car and tell her the truth. Here and now.

"Never."

"Never?" I draw in a half-breath and hold it. I wish she hadn't just slammed the door so hard on me. I'm not surprised. The girl is so strong, so stubborn…so alone.

"It's nothing personal." She meets my gaze. "I've learned the hard way that 'sharing' any specifics stops my *progress*." She taps her head with an index finger. "After years of messing with this baby, I keep the lid on Pandora's Box locked tight. Don't even attempt to crack me. Stronger people have already tried and failed. Plus, I'll hate you if you try." The look she gives me is wide-open and deadly. "I'm serious—I've told you enough, okay?"

"Sure. Of course, but that means I can't tell you my secrets," I try to tempt her.

"I don't want to know yours. Mine are hard enough to deal with." She smiles but it doesn't reach her eyes.

I nod, keeping my own fake smile in place. "Topic closed. I wouldn't want you hating me. I mean that. And—well—" I forge ahead...just in case. "If you ever want to talk about it, about anything, please don't hold back. I'll listen. I will."

"Thanks." Her expression is weighted. She's beyond sad. She's tormented. But I swear she's stronger than anyone I've ever known.

Does she remember? Does she remember me at all?

I drive on, reaching the end of the paved road. My mind clouds like the dust picked up by my tires. I'm again, remembering that night—her—how she looked, how she'd cried. What I could have done better. Cold sweat, sadness and my guilt should push me through the floor of this car and swallow me into the road.

I'm such an asshole. A coward. I should tell her. I should... but I can't risk causing her any more pain.

"Can I say one more thing, though?" she asks after the quiet and the dust threaten to choke us both.

"Anything."

She takes her small pack onto her lap and fiddles with the straps. "I like that you know. About me—like we're friends. We are, right?"

"Hell yes, we're friends. Money aside, Jess...*yes*. You don't go to Geekstuff.com plastic-boot-camp together and not end up friends." I pull into the parking area and kill the engine, then turn to face her. "Just ask me if you need to sleep. I'll help you find a way. I mean it. I'll cover for you. I hate to think you're tired all the time. It's going to kill me if you don't let me help."

She flushes. Her ice-blue eyes hold me fast. "I don't know why, but with you, things always seem so easy. The past two weeks, our contract and even this day." She points to the hiking trail. "I can't remember the last time I went hiking. If it gets bad, I'll tell you, but don't get all parental and worried. That would kill me. You have no idea how much fun I've had this summer already."

"You have?"

She sighs and puts her hand to her forehead. Her cheeks go one shade pinker as she continues, "Yes. I'm being a dork. Just...thanks for everything. You didn't have to participate but you did. I might be tired all of the time, and I *know* that kind of freaks you out—but, I'm great. Happy. It's thanks to you, okay? I...really trust you now, and...thanks for letting me have this summer."

"I...wow...uh." My mind's reeling. What can I say?

Not the truth. That's decided.

"Jess..." I start again, searching for the right words but I can't think thanks to the brutal ache in my heart.

I'm stuck in the middle of everything. She'll never give me a chance to be with her if she knows what I know, what I've done. And if she ever figures that out, it will become apparent that I don't deserve a chance to even be in the same room with her.

So...what am I? What does this make me—today? I wonder. Am I her friend? Or am I the worst person in the world, past and present. For not coming clean on the truth.

I should. I will. I can do this.

But what truth should I go with first? That I'm biting my

tongue bloody so I don't tell her how much I love how she smells? How about telling her I've got my hands glued on this steering wheel so I don't lean in and take her face in my hands, allowing my fingers full access to the wispy curls that I've been dying to touch since day one!

Yeah. That ought to be a great starting point.

Or, should I mention I've spent eons of time wondering what it would be like to kiss the perfectly sexy bottom lip she's been chewing since I parked this car?

Oh, God. What is the right thing to do?

If telling her what I know is the *right thing*, hanging out with her so I can make her smile—being this girl's friend—has become my personal *everything*.

Which will help her more? Truth, and more pain—or hanging out and having a fun summer? Together. As friends. A summer she just told me was amazing. I admit, I'm also being selfish. Greedy. And weak. Fine. I can own that not telling her seems much easier—for both of us.

Besides, if I come clean, here and now, I won't get to do this hike with her. I'll never get to take her skating. It's doubtful she'll ever let me put my arm around her shoulders again, either. Having her next to my side, smiling up into my eyes or better, glowering at me will be over too.

"Jess…" I start up again and realize I've been staring at her lips this whole time. "I'm…I don't know. I'm just happy you consider me a friend, that's all."

It takes her a second to meet my gaze.

Hold up. I could swear she'd been staring right back at my lips!

Impossible.

"Okay…good." She flushes and tosses me my favorite 'back-off' glare. One I completely welcome.

The girl is so good—and so dead on.

If only she'd punch me in the eye right now, I'd feel a bit less like the devil.

Instead she says, "Let's just do this hike-date-thing before I start snoozing on you. Glad we had the talk but eesh…can you say *awkward moment?*"

"Yeah. And, awkward moment."

She rolls her eyes and we both laugh.

Without looking back, she dashes out of the car, heading for the large wooden trail map. She calls over her shoulder into the open window, "Which one of these hikes are we going to do?"

"You pick." I pretend to be busy turning the old fashioned crank on my window while I untangle my thoughts and deal with the fact that my legs have turned to Jell-O. It could be a side effect from my new level of pure self-loathing. But it's also a side effect of all of the blood rushing out of my head and into other embarrassing places.

My fault for staring at her lips.

Or is this one her fault for staring at mine?

"H-U-I-M-S," she shouts. "That means: *Hurry Up I'm Starving.* I just made that up! Good, huh? I wonder if I can get that approved on the national board of text messaging?"

"Don't quit your day job," I tease, glancing up as I reach across the passenger seat for the other window. She's tossing an empty Red Bull into a recycling bin as she cracks open a second. She beams me with an extra cute *I dare you to bust on me for drinking this* smile.

I grip the crank, almost snapping it off in a white-knuckled panic attack as she crosses in front of the car aiming for a covered picnic area.

Legs. Legs. Long, tanned, smooth legs.

"What are you doing? This baby needs more fuel." She points to her flat stomach and flips her long braids over her shoulders.

"I'll be right there." I hold up my cell phone. "Checking messages. I have to leave one for Gran so she doesn't worry," I lie, and close the second window faster, suddenly wishing it were some sort of force field. One that could protect her from my thoughts.

She shrugs and turns to mess with her pack.

I let my eyes travel up and down the length of the super sexy girl waiting to go hiking with me. She's my *girlfriend* after all. Shouldn't I stare? Shouldn't I shower her with attention...compliments...whatever I want?

"Dude. After today, you're so far on the dark side you'll never get back," I mutter, openly admiring her delicate profile as a small bead of sweat rolls down my temple.

My head starts pounding.

With both windows closed and the sun heating my dashboard, the scent of cinnamon coming from her seat crashes all around me.

Legs. Unbelievable legs.

I lose control all over again and groan, resting my head on the steering wheel. I close my eyes so I can't see her anymore, but that makes it worse. Now all I can see are her lips in my mind.

"Crap!"

I might never be able to leave this car.

20

jess

You're a very lucky girl. Lucky. Lucky girl.
Let's go. Dude. Nothing happened. Let's go.
I'm sorry. I'm so sorry...Jess...Jess...

•••

"Jess! Jess. Wake up all the way. Jess! You were screaming."

I can't—I can't—I can't—breathe in. I can't breathe out.

My face feels like wet wood, my body is concrete, and my eyes won't focus. The images and voices are cutting into me from all directions. *...Seashells, glass, beige walls, and white. Too much white. And Kika's pulling on my shoulder.*

Tears. Sweat. Shuddering panic, and I still can't breathe.

"Oh my God. Jess! Please, say something or I am *so* telling Mom." Kika's voice shatters into my head, releasing me from the nightmare. Releasing my lungs.

"No! I'm okay," I gasp out, fighting to control myself. I know I need to act as though I'm okay, but I'm disoriented by the sunlight streaming across my face.

It's not dark. What's happening?

I find my clock. 4:35. My eyes burn as I search the room.

Where's my lamp?! I need the lamp.

The jellyfish lamp is turned off! It's too bright in my room.

I must have fallen asleep at my desk.

During the day. During the day. There should be no nightmare.

I gasp and gasp again, fighting tears and a new level of panic. I've never, *ever* had the nightmare during the day. The room shifts, darkens at the edges of my vision, and I catch myself from falling out of my chair by landing an iron grip on Kika's arm.

"Oh God…I'm getting Mom. You don't look good."

"Please. Wait with me, wait." I cling to her, hoping my grip will be enough to keep her here while I click on the lamp so I can decipher the level of aftershocks about to hit me. Thankfully, the three bobbing jellyfish are only half out of focus. I can see their tentacles pretty well. This realization calms me more than anything.

Silently, I start to count and let go of my sister so I can stand. My legs ache, already beginning to shake uncontrollably. I make it to my bed and clamber under the covers to hide the worst of shaking from Kika. I work to breathe and count silently as I force the voices and the images from the dream away. After a few moments I'm able to refocus and see that Kika hasn't moved. She's been standing there, crying—crying for me—and I hadn't even heard her.

"Don't *you* cry. That's what I do," I croak. Her expression makes my own tears launch. I don't have the energy to stop them.

"You. *Oh Jess*. You screamed so loud. You sounded so…*awful*." Kika gulps and moves to the foot of my bed.

"I'm okay. *I am*. Come here, Sis. I swear, it's over and I'm okay."

Kika uncrosses her arms to climb in the bed with me. She wraps her arms around my trembling shoulders, and I lay my head against her shoulder, breathing her warmth in. "Please let me say something to Mom and Dad. I heard you the other night…and you sounded the same. It's too much for you to handle alone."

"I'm not alone. You're here. I'm so glad you woke me up." I hug her tighter.

"You've never screamed like that—not before."

"I don't know. Maybe because the dream seems to be changing. Everything is different. New. For the first time, I think I saw faces. And I heard the voices. Voices that weren't my own." I shudder. "Maybe I'm finally remembering. The voices were as clear as day. Dad kept saying: *She's going to be fine, nothing happened. Nothing really happened. Right? She's going to be fine, right?* He was talking to Mom like a broken record while I was in that hospital bed."

"What else? I want to know." Kika pulls the covers higher.

"Mom. Crying. I heard that the other night for the first time. It was terrible. Mom sounded like a broken record: *Jess. Our Jess. She was almost raped. Almost raped. Almost raped.* And then more crying. I think Dad cried too."

"Dad? Holy." Kika's eyes fill with tears again and my heart clenches.

Our dad doesn't cry.

"The worst was everyone saying: *nothing happened, nothing really happened* combined with all the old stuff."

"The old stuff?"

"Yeah. Like how the police officer said I was *so lucky* and that I'd be *fine.* He's always there…saying that. The voices were all so real—like I could tell them apart. One in my ear kept repeating my name, and then he said: *I'm sorry. I'm so sorry.*

I finally met Kika's gaze.

My terror is reflected back in her eyes. I hate that look and I hate myself for not being able to erase it.

"*All* of that's new?" Kika asks.

"Except for the voice in my ear. That's always been there.

Even three years ago when you all thought I was permanently whacked. Right in my ear like that. Endlessly apologizing. Dr. Brodie suggested that maybe it's actually *me*. My *subconscious*. Like I'm talking to myself. Apologizing for my drinking and lying. All the stuff I still feel guilty about and for totally screwing everything up for our family. I think he's wrong. Even *that* voice had changed. It was someone else. Whispering. I don't know."

I moan and put my hands over my ears as tightly as possible, pulling my legs up until I'm curled into a ball.

How I wish I could just push it all out of my head and forget. "I have no idea what's real." I'm crying again. "I'm such a disaster of a sister. I'm sorry if I scared you."

"Jess. I'm the one who's sorry—sorry you go through that night after night."

I shoot her a grimace through my tears. "Maybe I screamed because I wanted them all to shut up. To stop saying I'll be *fine*. I won't ever be that, obviously. Sometimes, I think the whole thing would have been easier to deal with if I'd actually been raped. Instead of just *almost*. Then there'd be a concrete reason for why I'm this much of a failure at life. There are no 'almost raped' support groups or 'almost better' from 'almost being raped' websites. No blogs, Twitter feeds, and no 'almost-crazy-but-not-quite' Facebook support groups either. I feel like such a loser that I can't get over this."

"I could make you a Facebook page, if you want. Or Google the other stuff. Bet there's something. I'll compile a list."

I flip onto my back and use the blankets to dry my tears. "I love your lists. It sure can't hurt." We share a grim smile.

Kika takes my hand. "I'm glad it didn't happen. That you *weren't* raped. I can't imagine how I'd live knowing someone had hurt you so badly." Kika grimaces. "It's hard enough to know what you did go through."

"Yeah. You're right. I shouldn't have said that. I can't imagine how much heavier and broken my heart would feel if that had been the case." I stretch out and sit up a little, shooting Kika a grateful smile. "I'm fine…for now," I say. "Thanks for sticking around."

She throws her arms around me again. "You *will* be fine. You will. You are! You need more time. More help. Someone better than me to talk to," Kika hints.

I pull out of her hug. "There is no one better than you. Unless you want me to stop talking to you. I don't want you upset or afraid for me."

"No, I like that you talk to me. But I'm just a kid—not a doctor. I can only listen. I didn't even *get* what really happened to you until this year."

"You mean what really didn't happen to me," I try to joke.

"No. It happened. All the way or not, it happened and it was real and terrible."

"I wish I could take it all away. Have a *do-over*." I meet Kika's gaze. "I know it's wrong to heap all my garbage onto you; but I'm asking you not to tell. I want to figure this out on my own. Please. I'm begging you. If I can't solve this, then I'm sure Mom's going to catch on soon enough. I can hardly hide the fact that I'm screaming in my sleep for very long, right?"

"Keep screaming like *that,* and the neighbors will know," Kika agrees, but she doesn't seem convinced. Her stony, freaked expression tells me the kid is going to be blabbing to Mom before bedtime unless I can take her mind off what just went down.

"Look. Aside from the nightmares, everything's going perfectly for me." I point to a stack of papers on the corner of my desk. "My essays are done and ready to be typed. I'm working on getting my letters of recommendation lined up now. The internship is better than I could ever imagine. And," I let out a practiced, gushing sigh before continuing, "*Corey Nash*—he's amazing. I have a secret."

"What is it?" Kika arches her brows, interested but suspicious.

"I'm totally, completely, and absolutely falling for him."

"As if *that's* a secret. You text the guy every six minutes, and you blush like a little kid if we bring him up at all."

The shaking has almost stopped. I slap on an embarrassed smile. "Well, *he* texts me back every five minutes. I think he's falling for me too. He's asked me out again. Roller skating!"

"Really!" Kika grins. "Date number two can be an appropriate place for a first kiss, you know?" She grins wider.

"It's not a movie. I'm not going to kiss him on the second date. Your first kiss is when you find out he's not a creeper. That discovery should take a really, REALLY, really long time. We aren't even close to that. Yet."

"OMG. OMG. You said *YET*! Meaning...you *want* to kiss him?"

"I...sure. Yeah. I think I do." I crack a real smile and blush thinking about it. There's no need for me to say anything more. Kika gets me, so I don't have to fake this.

"OMG!" Kika squeaks and is sucked into one of those contagious middle school giggle-fits. I burst out laughing along with her.

"What's all this noise in here?" Dad pokes his head into the room. "Mom sent me up because she thought she heard you two screaming and fighting. But I see no evidence of sibling war."

"Jess is going on another *date*. Roller skating...with a guy. *The Corey guy.*" Kika chokes on another giggle.

"Hiking, now roller skating? I will say 'no' if the next one involves a zip line or rock climbing." He smiles. "That explains all the screaming, I suppose. Is this true, Jess?" He steps into the room.

"Dad!" I quickly pull the covers over our heads so Dad will think I'm embarrassed instead of hiding mine and Kika's blotchy, post-crying faces. "It's true. Okay?" I call through the comforter. "It's not that kind of date. We're friends, going skating *with* a bunch of other friends. That's all. Hear me? *Friends*. And I'm telling *Kika* all about it, not you, Dad…so carry on… report back to Mom, please."

Kika giggles in the dark next to me. "Yeah Dad, this is girl stuff," she adds.

"I assume we will get to meet this mystery guy," Dad says. From the sound of his voice he hasn't budged.

"Nope. You're never going to meet him!" I shout, and mean it. "He's just a *friend*. No reason for anyone to meet the parents. Yet," I add.

Right on cue, Kika giggles again. "Unless she *kisses* him, and he becomes her *boyfriend*. Then we get to meet him. You promised."

"Because that's not, at all, EVER, happening," I say. "If I do kiss this guy, I'll bring him by the house so Dad can kill him. How's that?"

"Sounds perfect." Dad laughs while Kika bursts into another fit of giggles. "And kill him I will," Dad adds, which makes Kika laugh louder.

I try to laugh too, but I'm about to suffocate. "Okay, Dad… I'm humiliated enough here, you can go anytime."

Thankfully, when I peek out of the blanket, Kika's still sighing and giggling. Her threat to tell our parents about my nightmare is forgotten, and Dad is long gone.

Divert successful.

21

jess

My first time roller skating has gone way beyond my low expectations. I've actually given it a rating of *perfect* despite the fact that the entire place is kind of whacked. Everything off the rink is covered with blue carpet and smells like old socks and stale sweat masked with Pine-Sol. It also blasts eighties pop non-stop, and has headache-worthy seventies disco lights.

But to me, it's become Cinderella's ballroom. I'm the girl crashing the party and dancing with the prince. This is total *progress*. Icing on the cake: Thanks to this date, I'd faced two other major *teen firsts* besides roller skating tonight: 1. An 11PM curfew and, 2. My new interrogator-style parents.

It's like the worried, *do-whatever-you-want-sweetie-pie* parents I used to have never existed. Tonight I'd been slapped with real live crankiness, a deadline and a long lecture about safety and *making good choices* before I'd left the house.

Double *progress*. This second date with Gray has earned me a first class ticket on the normal train! But it's also come with an unexpected price. Because my parents are worried I might have a boyfriend, my perfect 'give me privacy' set-up is now at an end.

I knew this would happen eventually, but the third week

into my contract with Gray seems way too soon for the prying to begin. I suppose it's my fault for being too good at all this lying.

In order for Mom and Dad to allow me to leave the house at all, I'd promised that I'd bring *Corey Nash* home for a barbecue next Sunday. Worse, *Corey's* supposed to pick me up and drive me the next time we go out. The speeding away from the driveway trick really pissed off Dad. They said if I was officially calling these outing *dates*—a word I'd used more than popcorn at the movies the past few days—then my *boyfriend* needed to man up. "Unless you're hiding something, *honey*," Mom had said, suspicion dripping off her.

I search for Gray, who'd offered to get us drinks but now seems to have disappeared. Gripping the half-wall that separates me from the zooming people skating on the rink, I half skate, half walk, toward a sitting area. I'm trying to imagine scenarios that might work to delay the barbecue.

Maybe Gray could convince Corey to be his 'stand in' for one night; but I shudder at that thought. It would mean involving Corey in our contract, and I'm starting to like that everyone believes we're a real couple. Plus, Corey would blab the truth to the whole planet. Maybe not right away, but somewhere he'd slip up. The guy is just that type. Plus, I'd already imagined going back to school with only Gray and I holding onto this secret summer.

That feels safe—livable. Corey Nash...in my front yard eating Dad's special chili slapped on a grilled burger while pretending to be my boyfriend? That feels like the worst idea in the world.

I've run out of rink wall so I gingerly hold my hands out wide for balance and *tap-clump* my wheeled feet toward the rest area. My head's spinning. Partly due to the music and lights, partly due to the barbecue dinner problem, but mostly, because as of tonight, I'm admitting that I have a major, huge, impossible crush on Gray Porter.

It's not Gray's fault. He's simply been himself. His *paid self*, that is, which is probably not even really how he truly acts at all. Either way, my pretend boyfriend has been someone so amazing tonight, that he's sent my heart into unrecoverable space.

I don't know if that's a good thing or a bad thing, nor do I care. Who can think straight when you're melting from happiness? Not me. I love how being near Gray paints me with goose bumps when he touches me—when he smiles into my eyes. He's done both, nonstop for the past hour. I feel my cheeks tingle and heat.

I've crossed so far over into my self-constructed land of madness and lies that I'm sitting here admitting that what I have is way more than a crush. Somewhere, between testing the ladybug cameras at work all day and holding his hand all night, I've fallen in love with Gray Porter. Or my fake life, or my fake boyfriend.

Whatever it is, whomever he is…what I'm experiencing is real, exciting, and the best feeling I've ever had in my whole life.

This has to be love.

I'm a casualty of my own war. Unexpected, that's for sure.

And now, in hindsight, I see it was probably unavoidable.

Today, when Gray had been handed his second paycheck, I'd been given a lame pity-smile from the HR lady who passed out the envelopes. But that woman had no idea what my pay-off is. I'm the richest girl in Golden, CO.

I'm out on a date with the most beautiful guy in our whole town, and he's treating me like I'm enchanting, priceless, beautiful and breakable! Gray has earned every penny of his money tonight. He's made sure not one of my knees, elbows or my butt has once hit the slippery smooth roller-skating rink. He's also laughed at every one of my jokes. He even laughs when I'm not joking—like he's truly happy to be hanging out with me.

Even real girlfriends don't get *that*. Do they?

Once I'd figured out how to skate a little, he'd spent the last hour patiently pulling me around the rink, making certain I was safe from colliding into the walls or the other skaters.

It might be a 'fake' situation and I might be a little crazy, but I'm still a real girl.

One with a beating heart who's not immune to sweet, green-eyed smiles and tons of attention from a gorgeous guy. I feel my cheeks heat to burning. I think of his hands…hands I've been holding for hours and blush even more. Suddenly the rink grows silent and all I can hear is my own voice swelling inside my head.

I'm in love. Love. Love.

I pause to cover my cheeks with my hands and work to breathe normally while I console myself with the thought that it's only a mirage. I'm living fiction. It's perfectly okay to be in love with any and all fictional boyfriends, even if they aren't yours.

Boys in books are NOT better than fake dating GRAY PORTER.

I know deep down, Gray and this *feeling* are not really mine to keep. My current happiness is stolen—bought. It's only a matter of time before the clock strikes twelve and all of my magical sparkle wears off. That's the part where everything turns back into mice, a pumpkin, and a ragged girl who had a really fun summer once.

I don't mean to leave a glass slipper behind either. My parents forcing me to bring *Corey Nash* to a barbecue is a bleak reminder of how soon I'll be out of this world and back to reality.

I've got eight days before the game is up. Unless I can come up with a way to buy myself more time, this princess is getting forced out of the ball early. Besides, my Prince Charming, nice as he might be, is in this for the money. Gray would be horrified if he knew where my thoughts, my heart, led me tonight.

Love.

Ha! He'd run so fast and so far away from me if he knew. What guy wouldn't? But he's not going to know. So there's no harm in me thinking what I want, or in gathering as many memories as I can for later reference. When we'd made this contract, Gray was the one that told me it's not a crime if we have *fun* together. So, as much as it's scary to feel this way, and even though I feel a bit guilty about it all, it is fun. Me, being in love with Gray Porter, is sort of my personal, private, secret fun binge! And I'm totally okay with it.

I make it to the round, carpeted bench without any embarrassing leg twisting incidents and I sit. A small, pent up laugh escapes because, *really,* this whole situation is sort of hilarious. I kick my skates against the carpeted floor as fast as I can. When the wheels are humming, I lift my feet high to watch them spin and I can't stop grinning.

I spot Michelle and Corey. They're still on the rink and lined up as finalists in the limbo contest. I toy with the idea of standing to watch, but I don't trust myself not to fall so I stay put, waiting for my *boyfriend.*

Because I love him.

That thought has me laughing out loud, grinning and spinning my skate wheels all over again.

He emerges through the crowd and skates toward me. He's so good at skating, the carpet doesn't even slow him down. His dark curls are wild, and his sun-bronzed cheeks are flushed. He's smiling at me again. He always does that.

My heart clenches as I smile back. To combat the rush of excitement surging through me, I roll my eyes at him as though I'm thoroughly bored waiting for him. Without even a slip, he executes a perfect, hockey-half turn and slides on to the bench next to me. "Sorry it took so long." He hands me a Coke.

I don't trust my voice so I sip the drink, wondering if he ever feels out of place—or like he's losing his mind. He always seems so comfortable in his own skin. Does he ever have to keep his face straight while he's screaming inside his head?

"Tired?" he asks.

I still can't answer.

"Jess, what's up?" He bends down.

He's used *that voice*. The one that is sort of private and says he's speaking only to me. The one that's probably the reason I'm so nuts over him because he's been using it all night.

He moves closer, those amazing eyes scan my face.

"Okay. I'm a little tired," I say and meet his gaze with my most serene expression.

And I'm so in love with you my heart hurts.

"I knew it." He's watching my face like I'm some sort of lab rat.

I look up at him, shocked. *Did I say the love bit out loud?*

"And my ankles ache," I blurt out and hold up my feet to distract him, just in case.

He eyes my feet. I can tell from the look in his gold-green eyes he's worried. "The ankle thing is normal, but you'll tell me if the tired part becomes unlivable. We don't have to stay here. We worked a long day and—"

"No…I'm good," I insist. "Look, Michelle's bombed out of the contest." I'm happy that he cares. That he knows me. But no way do I want this date to end—no matter how tired. I smile and try to joke, "Are all of our dates going to be this sporty? My dad wants to know."

"Yes. Unless it's too much for you?"

"What are you planning next?"

"ThunderLand. Saturday. We're all going. You with me. Michelle with Corey. A few other couples might meet up with us there. It's tradition. I know we have this contract between us, but I really want you to come—with me—as my date. Will you?"

He sounds so earnest…like he's worried I'm going to turn him down. "We already talked about this outing as part of our contract, so of course I'll come." I say, "But if I can't make it, I'll let you delete one weekend from the list. Deal?"

"Why wouldn't you be able to come?" His face falls like I've said the wrong thing, and I suddenly can't read his expression anymore.

"The contract is in crisis. The parents said they have to meet you, or should I say they want to meet one *Corey Nash* face-to-face before we have any other dates. Someone's supposed to make good and shake my dad's hand. That someone needs to look exactly like Corey Nash from the yearbook."

Gray pales. "Oh no…"

"Oh yes. Epic, family barbecue. Next Sunday. My dad's already planned the menu. That's the day *after* ThunderLand. I'd rather skip that date weekend. Avoid the barbecue completely, make you fake sick or something and try to prolong our contract for another two weeks or so."

"Crap. If you don't come, I might as well not go. And that would be completely sad." He scrunches his face into a pout.

"It sounds like a long day for me, anyhow. The hiking thing almost did me in. I'd probably ruin your fun unless there's a special *napping* area in the amusement park?"

"I'll let Corey or Michelle drive. You can sleep in the car both ways. If you're too tired we'll simply stop and hang out until the others are finished. As for your parents, tell them it's not a *date*. It's a bunch of people going to ThunderLand. Friends. General, *normal,* summer fun. Tell them you're going with the 'golly-gee-nice-gang' you've invented. Of course we'll pick you up with Corey in tow. As long as we're quick we should be able to manage an appropriate 'Corey sighting'. That should put them off, right?"

I smile and almost crack up, remembering the look on Gray's face when my parents almost attacked his car in the driveway. "Maybe…but whomever drives better not have a stick shift vehicle. Dork."

He laughs. "Whatever. It will be easy for me to fake some cotton candy overload and pull a tummy-ache-no-show the next day for the barbecue. Then we can have a fight or something and that way you'll still get a couple more weeks without me needing to show up at your house?"

"You make it sound so simple." I lean back and nod. This idea might just work. "If we're still alive after Mr. Foley and the LightStick project chews us up and spits us out next week, I'll do it!"

"Yes!" He beams. "Awesome."

Goosebumps tickle my spine when he smiles deep into my eyes. "Swear you'll fake sick, though. Make it believable? Maybe even talk to my mom on the phone to give your regrets the next day?"

"I could do that. No problem." His smile dims slightly.

I don't blame him. My mom is scary. I stretch my back. "Oww. Everything hurts."

"Where? Here, especially?" He reaches forward and squeezes the muscle just above my knee.

"Yes, there. Oww. Stop!"

"Or how about here?" He moves in on the other leg.

"Don't even!" I haul onto his forearm to stop a second squeeze just as Michelle skates in and plops down next to us.

"Aww. Aren't you two just the cute-cuddly-skater-daters? If you were about to kiss, save it. Your moment is ruined." She laughs and moves closer so she can see the rink through the thinning crowd. "Aren't you going to watch Corey take the limbo trophy?"

"He's won it three times. In case you didn't notice, I'm *really* comfortable here in my girlfriend's arms."

Gray has moved his hand casually onto my knee and I realize I'd been practically hugging him. It must look as though Gray and I are getting *very* close. My heart races. I let one hand drop to my lap, but then I force myself to remain still and leave my other hand on Gray's arm. I try to keep my expression calm and lean into him as though I'm completely used to hanging all over him.

He smells amazing…again. *Always. Ugh!*

Gray's fingers trail across my knee and I gasp, feeling almost burned where he's touching me. He tosses me a wink as he does it again. "Ahh, Jess Jordan's *ticklish*. Good to know," he whispers, and his breath is hot against my ear.

Goosebumps. Butterflies. Panic.

"Uh. Michelle, do you want the rest of my Coke?" I pull away from Gray and offer the giant cup to Michelle, knowing full well my entire face has just flamed cherry red.

"Thought you'd never ask!" Michelle takes it and flips the plastic top. "Limbo's a workout," she says between gulps.

I toss Gray a glare and he winks at me again, adding in one of his amused smiles like he knows he's rattled me.

Michelle continues, "Corey's only winning the trophies to impress me. He told me so." She looks up, pausing to chew on an ice cube. "It's kind of cute, really."

"Would you go out with him already? You're reaching cruelty status," Gray chides.

"A couple more limbo trophies and I just might give him a

chance," Michelle says.

Gray laughs and moves in close to me again. He takes one of the hands I've fisted tightly in my lap and opens my fingers until they rest flat against his. I figure he's trying to remind me to look relaxed in front of Michelle so I uncurl my other fist and remember to breathe. I feel like I've swallowed a helium balloon. There's a chance I might simply float up to the ceiling and not be able to stop myself. I manage another long, calm breath.

"I'm glad Jess didn't make me wait forever to date her," Gray says, tossing me a wink. I'm sure he's just working to fill the awkward silence I've created.

"Michelle, the summer's in full swing. Give Corey a break," I add. "The guy's bonkers for you."

"Maybe I'm really enjoying how hard he's working. If I give in, I'm worried he'll stop all the cute stuff he's been doing to get my attention. Do you know he sent me flowers?"

Gray frowns. "If you don't invite my man to the 'couples skate', you're going to break his heart. He told me you dogged him last week and skated with a random twelve-year old."

"Hey, that was a charity case. I couldn't say *no* to that dude. I explained that to Corey. The kid asked me first."

The crowd cheers and then breaks into applause. We hear Corey announced as winner over the loudspeaker.

In seconds, Corey skates up, dips onto one knee and offers a small plastic trophy to Michelle. "My lady. Your prize," he says, comically bowing his head as though she's the queen of England.

Michelle, biting back a smile, takes the trophy. "You rock, Nash."

"Thanks."

The room dims as the flashing colored lights are replaced with silver-white, spinning circles of light created by the rink's giant disco ball.

"That's so cool. It feels like the whole room is moving," I whisper. Gray squeezes my hand.

The DJ, housed in the farthest corner of the rink, announces: "Couples skate. Couples only on the floor, please. This session has been dedicated by Corey Nash, tonight's limbo winner, to the beeeeautiful, love of his life, *Michelle*. Because we all agree, Michelle Hopkins is so beautiful. This is your song."

The strains from Jo Cocker's *You are So Beautiful* fill the rink.

Michelle blushes, shooting Corey a pleased look. "Aww. Romantic." She punches Corey playfully in the arm and then holds out her hand. "Let's skate."

"Sweet. Does this mean we're going out?" Corey, beaming now, leaps up and takes Michelle's hand. They skate toward the entrance to the rink.

Now that we no longer have an audience, I figure Gray probably doesn't want me to maul him any more, so I work my captive hand out of his.

He frowns. "Was it? Romantic?" Gray sighs, looking at me with that hooded, unreadable gaze again and crosses his arms. "You're the expert. How'd that rate?"

"Completely dorky."

"Thought so."

"Wait! I'm not done. The trophy presentation—on his knees—plus getting the DJ to say all that stuff, combined with the song choice rates a total romance approved *ten*."

"No. Impossible. You said dorky. Completely dorky."

"Adorkable. It's in its own category."

"What?"

"Corey's so *out there*. So unashamed to tell everyone Michelle is the girl for him. It snowballs into perfect. Girls love that stuff."

"I'll never understand women." Gray slides his skates forward and does another cool skating move so he can stand up looking all smooth. "Since I didn't think of anything *adorkable,* I'm going to have to use the old-school tactics to impress you. Skate with me, girlfriend?" He shrugs.

"You don't have to think up special stuff. As long as I'm paying—I'm sort of a sure thing right?"

He shakes his head as though he's not happy with me bringing up the money. "After this song, there's going to be two more to complete the couples set. Will you? Skate them with me?"

He's holding out his hand and it feels rude not to take it, so I let him help me to my feet. "Two more songs?" I grimace, eyeing the rink. Couples are going around, hand in hand. Some are intertwined and facing the same direction, while the better skaters are actually dance-skating face to face as they complete the circle. "I might hurt you or someone else," I mutter, filled with doubt, but loving once again how I feel when he's holding my hand.

"Oh my God. Look at them." I laugh as I spot Corey and Michelle whizzing past full speed, laughing their heads off. They're holding hands like the other couples, but yanking their arms as hard as possible in an attempt to make the other person skate faster and fall.

"So much for their big romantic moment," Gray says. "So… will you? Skate. With me?" he asks again. It's almost a whisper.

When I meet his gaze I wonder if the longing I see in his eyes is coming from him or from my reflection? I nod and he propels me to the rink entrance.

As he steps down onto the rink he lets go of my hand. The loss of momentum causes me to flail. I careen toward him, almost falling off the step face first. Before I can recover or even gasp, he's picked me up entirely and is holding me tightly against his chest. He sets me down gently in front of him as though I weigh nothing.

As though it was perfectly natural for my entire body to slide down his entire body!

I can't breathe. I don't remember how.

"Sorry, I won't let you go again. Promise."

Without a pause, he skates behind me and before I can blink he wraps his arms around my middle. I think I might prefer falling. Extreme pain and a broken nose might be much easier to bear than the blood melting right out of my heart.

I'm flooded with too many feelings all at once. I wonder if I'm going to cry, or simply die from happiness, from fear, from embarrassment. From love.

He's talking softly behind me. Teaching me how to skate all over again. I've only heard half of what he's said. I try to focus on the rest and not at all on how warm he's made me feel.

"Just lean back. Use me for balance. Hold your legs steady and straight while I push you along until you get the feel for the music. Once you've got the beat, you can skate along with me. But only if you promise not to trip me up. Ready?"

I nod and lean back slightly, but as he starts off I feel like my backbone and limbs are made of wood. "How many girls have you skated with—like this?" I'm using my cynical, joking tone to see if I can trick him into answering. To see if I can get my heart to stop beating so fast.

"Do you really want to know the answer to that?"

"Billions…trillions?" I ask.

"Jess, I'm not, nor have I ever been the kind of player you make me out to be."

"Whatever," I say covering my aching curiosity with sarcasm. I want to look into his eyes and ask him if he's ever been in love with anyone before, but then, I suppose it doesn't really matter. Instead, I add, "You're so good at this. Like you've done this a lot. Tell me...how many."

"None." He wraps his arms tighter and draws me closer. I don't even care that he's probably lied to me. I force myself to relax against his faded, soft, navy t-shirt, and go with it. With him. What harm can come from me pretending this is all real for a few moments? I breathe in and try to memorize his scent.

Right now, thanks to our drink break, he's lime-cola awesome.

My heartbeat races as he picks up speed on the turn.

"There." His breath moves the hair beside my ear, causing the ever-erupting flurry of butterflies and goose bumps to rage through me. "You've got the hang of it. Want to try to move your legs along with mine?"

"No. I'm good...if that's okay?"

"It's great." He speeds up and holds me even tighter. The silver lights swirl around and over us. The music, some sort of European electronic techno with no lyrics, fills my head.

My limbs, my soul. I'm flying.

I stare at his arms wrapped so confidently around me and I gently move my hands until I've placed them over his. I lean farther into him, trusting that I won't fall. Trusting him.

"Doing all right?" he asks.

"Perfect." I close my eyes as he propels me around the next corner, content to let someone else be in control for once. I smile as cool air pushes against my face, rushing through my hair. I can feel Gray's heart beating near my temple.

"Jess Jordan...do you ever wish...wish that we...that you and I...whoa! Watch out!" He pulls me to the side and skids us both to a stop, lifting me slightly so his skates won't collide with mine.

I open my eyes and freak. The person we almost hit is my sister!

My stalking, smirking sister!

"You need to skate in the same direction as the other skaters, okay kid?" Gray says.

"What the hell?!! What are—" I'm already yelling over him, but change my mind because Gray's still holding me, or hugging me, or—I'm hugging him.

He has no idea who this is! I make my entire body go limp into a complete dead weight. It throws Gray off balance and he releases me. I hit the floor with a huge thump.

"Oww. Kika, what are *you* doing here? Besides trying to kill me?" I cover.

"Sorry. Sorry!" She's out of breath and scrambling to stay on balance. "I was trying to catch up! I've been looking for you, but was focused on couples with tall *blond* guys?" She darts a confused glance at Gray before rushing on. "I'm at Holly Basker's bowling party. Only the bowling alley didn't schedule it right. Instead of bowling we have to skate." Kika skates closer to Gray. "Are you Corey Nash?"

"*Grmry!*" I deliberately mumble his name. "Meet my sister, Kika."

"Nice to meet you but—*are you*—Corey Nash?"

I struggle to my feet. "Kika! God!"

"No. I'm not Corey, but he's here somewhere," Gray answers, looking around evasively.

"Yeah. He was just here," I add glancing around. "He's... hmmm..." I swallow and paste on a smile and point off into the dark distance. "Over there."

"If you aren't Corey, then how come you were all snuggled up close like that with my sister?" Kika's glowering at Gray now. "That's really going to make her *boyfriend* pissed off."

I gasp. "What are you saying? I got too confident and told Corey to do a lap without me. Only I can't really skate and I got stuck way out here. I'd just asked my *friend* to transport me safely to the exit. Which is what he was doing. And it's where we're still going, because I'm sick of humiliating myself on this rink. Can we please move along?" I grip Gray's arm on one side and Kika takes my other hand. We skate toward the rink exit. I struggle to paste on my best poker face. How am I going to talk my way through this one? I start in with some defensive tactics. "All right, little sister, confess. How much did Mom and Dad pay you to come here and spy on me?"

"They didn't pay me a thing." She smiles but looks slightly guilty.

"Spill it. They totally told you to check up on me, didn't they?"

"They said, if I *saw* you, that I should say 'hi'. That's all! And *boy* did I see you. But it really is Holly's birthday. See? There she is. *Holly!*" Kika yells and waves. Holly Basker has been Kika's best friend since fifth grade. She doesn't see or hear Kika over the music as she whizzes past. "And there's Kimmie, Keva, Maddie, Masha, Kenzy and Saoirse and—"

"We get it," I say. "Shouldn't you be with all of them—as in, *now*?" We make it to the exit and I breathe a sigh of relief, feeling safer on the carpeted area.

"I'm not leaving until I meet your boyfriend. Don't you want me to?" Kika's bottom lip has set into a stubborn line. I can tell I've hurt her feelings. "Where is Corey Nash?"

"Did someone say my name? Corey Nash, at your service." Corey and Michelle have exited the rink right behind us. The two are grinning like fools in love, and even worse, holding hands. Kika hasn't missed that.

"Corey!" I fling myself at Michelle and Corey, purposefully disconnecting their hands with a body slam, knowing my voice sounds way too over-bright. "Did ya miss me?"

Kika's face scrunches and twists. I can all but hear the motors turning in her head. I want to scream but instead I ramp up into the widest fake smile I've ever created.

"Sorry—hold me up, *Corey,* would you, cutie?" I grab onto him like a psycho. I don't even have to pretend to lose my balance because my heart is racing so fast I'm about to have to sit on the ground. "Oh, and meet my little sister!" I squeak out. Thankfully Corey's put his hand around my waist to steady me.

Kika smiles at Corey. "Jess has told me *a lot* about you."

I keep my grin stapled on and ratchet one of my hands onto Corey's shoulder as I turn back around, bumping Michelle toward Gray.

"Well hello, little sister," Corey says, shooting me a startled glance. "Nice to meet you. Kika? Did I say your name right? Jess has mentioned you also. You're going to make quite a hit next year as a freshman if you're planning on showing up sporting those pretty, big, blue eyes."

"Corey!" Michelle glares.

Kika laughs and blushes. "Thanks."

I want to hit Corey and kiss him because he's diverted Kika from all coherent thinking with that statement. "Don't you dare flirt with my sister." I have to say it before Michelle starts waving the *my-man-is-taken* flag. "If you or any of your jock-cronies even think about coming near her—or any of her *little* friends, I'll simply kill each and every one of you," I say. Deep down I mean it. His comment to Kika has given me a mini-anxiety attack.

"Jess!" Kika blushes even harder, embarrassed and obviously annoyed with me. "He's just being nice. Gee. Don't call me *little.*"

"Yeah, Jess. I'm just *saying.* Besides, I'm drunk on love and heading into a long term relationship." He shoots Gray a smirk. "The two most dangerous guys at school are off the market, so the freshman girls are safe. Don't worry, Kika, think of us as your future guard dogs. Any dudes that want to meet you have to pass through our gauntlet first. Deal?" He winks.

"Awesome. Thanks." Kika's all but gushing at Corey, clearly charmed to her toes. "Jess told me you were really nice and cute and so sweet," she adds.

"She did?!" Corey blinks at me. I find myself grinning and nodding at him like a bobble head doll.

"Of course I did," I say, wondering what Michelle's thinking right now.

Kika goes on, "Yeah, and she told me that you—"

"Easy. Corey knows he's adorable. Let's not make his ego get out of control," I half-shout.

Gray steps to the side and puts his arm around Michelle's shoulders in the classic 'buddy hug'. "Have you met Michelle?" Gray pipes in. I know he's trying to change the subject, but his move brings all of the attention back on him. How gorgeous, and completely uncomfortable he's acting. Does the guy have to choose this moment to turn bright red? I glance wildly between them all.

Gray looks stiff, almost frightened with his arm around Michelle. I'm assuming he's afraid of her. Of me. Of my little sister. Heck, I'm scared to death right now.

Michelle's back is ram-rod straight and her expression is blinking from confused to royally pissed off. Corey looks as though he can't decide whether he's my new best friend, if I might have a stalker type crush on him, or if he should punch Gray for touching his woman.

Kika's frowning and has met my gaze. She's about to ask another question.

I can't handle one more question so I start blabbing, "Um. So, yeah…anyhow…um. Yeah."

"Will all skaters in Holly Basker's birthday party report to Birthday Room number 26 located in the bowling alley complex. *Happy Birthday Hoooooo-lleey Basker!*"

Saved.

"Oh. That's me," Kika says, looking around.

"Get off me, Porter! Your arm's heavier than a dead ox. What's wrong with you?" Michelle wiggles out of Gray's grip.

Kika's eyebrows shoot up. Thankfully, at that same moment, we're surrounded by the swarm of Kika's giggling, eighth-grade friends as they exit the rink.

"*Kiiiika.* There you are! OMG. Did you see me fall flat on my face?" A girl with long, dark braids laughs.

"OMG. Did you see *me* fall flat on that *old* guy? I felt so bad about it," says another as they all crowd around.

The girls erupt into a fit of giggles. "I saw you both," gasps Holly, the birthday girl. "Hi, Jess."

"Happy birthday, Holly," I answer with a small, stiff smile, wondering if I'm going to faint.

"Wow," Holly whispers to Kika too loudly, as though she wants to be heard. "That guy's hot! Introduce us."

I know she's talking about Gray.

"Guys, this is my sister's boyfriend and her other...friends." Kika points somewhere between Gray and Corey.

Was that a note of sarcasm in her voice?

"They're both simply...wow." Holly giggles, eyeing Gray as though he's in an aquarium or something. "Are they—aren't you all going to be *seniors*?" Her voice is filled with awe.

"You know it," says Corey, puffing out his chest.

"God! Corey, you're such a Neanderthal." Michelle punches his arm.

"Hey. It's not my fault I'm so endlessly admired by future freshmen." Corey winks at the girls and they all giggle again.

I feel my stomach tighten with more misplaced anxiety.

Three years ago I'd acted exactly like these girls. I had been fascinated with seniors. I thought the boys my own age were just skinny dorks. So much so, that I'd lied to my parents, snuck out to go to a *senior party,* and drank the drinks the *seniors* were drinking. I'd even followed a *real live senior* to an empty upstairs room, and got to lose my mind and my memory ever since.

Of course, *nothing* happened. Let the record show. I shudder as bile moves into my throat. I can't believe my little sister and her friends are really old enough to be high school freshmen in a couple of months. I shoot Kika a look. Did I look as young as she does now? Did I act as old and wise as Holly Basker seems to think she is?

I work to keep my expression in check as I try to curb the larger panic attack hanging over me. The memories wash in.

I concentrate on breathing slowly.

Kika is not me and she won't get herself into any bad situations. I'll protect her.

She's going to be fine. Fine. Fine. Fine.

I shudder again and dart a glance at Gray through my lashes. I read concern in his eyes. He can tell something's not right.

I toss him an annoyed glare—which makes him smile a strange, sad little smile.

"You better go, guys. Party room twenty-six," I say, reminding them.

The girl with the braids looks back as they move past us. "If that's what the boys look like in high school, then I can't wait for the summer to end. *Seniors,* huh? *So cool.*"

Holly Basker giggles and looks back too. "Which one's your sister's *boyfriend*? The blond or the dark-haired one?"

Kika turns and meets my gaze. "Does it really matter when they're both so amazingly hot?" Kika answers. She brushes past, shaking her head.

I hold my ground next to Corey, feeling suddenly like I'm the younger sister and Kika's some sort of grown-up, successful attorney. Judge. Executioner.

I wish for the floor to open wide and swallow me whole.

If I can't come up with a plausible explanation for why I was cuddled up on the couples skate with Gray, Kika's going to take everything I've built and destroy it with five simple words:

Mom, guess what I saw?

22

gray

"I'm dead. *We* are so dead. I can't believe I let my guard down like that."

Jess is groaning like she's in pain and rubbing her eyes while I back Bessie out of the rink's employee parking lot.

"I don't think it was as bad as you're making it. Your sister couldn't possibly have figured anything out. I think it went rather well if you don't dwell on the part where Michelle almost blew the whole thing by decking me." He laughs.

"This is *so* not funny. What about the part where *my not-boyfriend, Corey* was holding hands with your *not-girlfriend, Michelle?* That was hard to miss. Worse, I wonder how long Kika was watching me skate like that—all wrapped up snuggled and happy in your arms."

"Were you? Happy?" My throat tightens as I regret asking that. I try to meet her gaze, but can only catch her darkened reflection in the ink-black passenger window. It's not light enough to read what she's thinking.

"Why?" she asks. Her tone has taken on a skeptical drawl. "I'll pay you even if I'm not happy, you know. My happiness was never put into the contract, okay? Where are you taking me? We still have two hours before my curfew's up. It's bad form to be home before my little sister."

"I need Band-Aids." I hold up my fingers.

She gasps. "Do you have blisters like that on both hands?"

"Yep. Those lanyard hooks from the last batch of ladybugs wouldn't hook on without a bit of brute force mixed with skin."

"Why didn't you tell me? I just thought you had really rough man-hands. It was so dark in the rink I never thought—I've been holding your hands all night. I probably made them worse."

"I do have rough, manly, and mannish, man hands. So glad you noticed," I try to joke, but my voice sounds forced.

She laughs, apparently not noticing that I'm acting like a freak.

"I'm taking you home." I wiggle my fingers. "Gran will still be awake. I'd love for you to meet her."

"No. Not your house! No way!" She grips the sides of her seat.

"Why?"

"I don't think I have it in me to…you know…*pretend* for another second. It takes a lot of energy for me to fake it. Seeing Kika at the rink took it all out of me. I can't possibly betray a sweet, old lady after that."

"We're already here. Don't worry. You won't have to pretend anything around Gran."

"Does she know? Did you tell her about the contract? About me?"

"I've told her I've got a crush on a girl who's playing hard to get. That's all. I'll show you my house, fix up my fingers, and then it will be time to drive you home. No biggie."

I pull Bessie into our long driveway and park in front of the detached one-car garage. My house can't compete with hers, but I know that Jess doesn't register any sort of materialistic stuff as important. Another reason I like her too much.

"I don't want to go in," she whispers and meets my gaze. The front light is streaming into the cab of my car. I recognize Jess's expression. She had the same tense, yet vulnerable look on her face the first time she'd come to meet me at the sports complex.

Beautiful. Terrified. And exhausted.

If only I could erase the last two things. I seek solace in the fact that she's letting me see what she used to work very hard to hide.

"We'll keep this low key. Gran's great. You'll love her."

"And if she doesn't like me?"

"Impossible." I wink, trying to get a smile, but instead she leans her head against the seat and closes her eyes as though she wants to block me out. It's too tempting not to stare when I'm this close. And when she's not looking. "You're the kind of girl she's always hoping I'll bring home," I add. My heart catches when she smiles, eyes still closed.

"I bet you've used that line on every single girl you've had sitting in this very spot." She opens her eyes and meets my gaze. The warm evening breeze blowing in through the windows gently ruffles the curls that frame her face.

Crap, do I love those wispy curls...those blue eyes.

Her.

I wish I could say it. Instead, I smile back.

My gaze wanders along the curve of her cheek and I follow it down to her neck. If only I had the right to kiss her.

Or at least, the courage.

Maybe I do.

I lean slightly forward. Her eyes are heavy, staring at my lips. She moves an inch closer to me and I hold my breath. That's when I spot the flash behind her shoulder.

"Crap!" I sit back, completely freaked out. "And *crap!*"

"What?" She's looking around. Her cheeks have flooded into

glowing fire. Mine are in a similar state, I'm sure.

Right now, every inch of my entire body burns with longing.

She's facing forward in her seat with her back pressed straight against it, and she won't look at me.

Did I almost kiss Jess Jordan?

Did she almost let me?!

"And *crap*," I mutter again. I talk as quickly as I can, pretending the moment never happened. "Gran has been staring at us from the window this whole time. Sit tight." I open my door and leap out. "She'll never forgive me if I don't do this right."

If I weren't so stressed, I'd laugh at the irony of that statement. I've never been able to do one thing right where Jess Jordan is concerned. My botched attempt at kissing her is a perfect example.

"Do what?" Jess asks. "What?"

I talk to her through her open window because she's still so gripped, I'm afraid she's going to deck me or scream. I wouldn't blame her for either.

I go for the Mr. Darcy accent I know Jess loves: "I must, in the presence of a lady, act like a gentleman if my grandmother is watching."

I'm afraid to look into Jess's eyes just yet so I swing her door open with a flourish, holding out my hand for her to take. "Humor me, and try to look pleased. If I mess up, Gran will grill me for weeks. But don't get used to this," I add, dropping the accent.

She takes my hand and shoots me the back-off glare. "If you try this again, *ever* in front of anyone under the age of 70, you'll need to get used to *me*, hurting *you*. This is completely embarrassing, you know?"

"And super awkward. You forgot that." I grin, relaxing

slightly when she laughs. I close the door behind her.

"What about the part where I don't want to go inside?"

"Too late for that. Hurry. Gran's a stickler for propriety. Any seconds that tick past the 9PM mark will be held against me."

Gran is opening the door and speaking through the screen as we make it up the front steps. "Young man, you'd better have an excuse for showing up here at this hour and with a guest. You should have called me on that cell phone of yours."

"Sorry, Gran. It was an emergency. Plus you tell me not to call while I'm driving. I needed some first aid," I say, holding up my fingers so Gran can see the blisters.

"Oh my. Well. Come on then you two. I've got a pot a tea already brewing." She drags Jess into the kitchen and I follow.

"I've waited a long time for Gray to bring home a girl. You're the first," she says as she bustles around, pouring about twenty miniature cookies onto a plate and hovers the plate in front of Jess's face. "Please, have one and take a seat." She points to one of the chairs.

Jess flushes, takes one of the cookies and sits, looking around the room with wide eyes.

She's still sporting some very red cheeks. It's not lost on me that she's very cute with powdered sugar coating her fingers. She's also sitting in *my spot* at our antique, slightly battered kitchen table.

I love her in my spot.

"My, but you're a beautiful young lady." Gran smiles.

"Thanks," Jess says and eats the cookie.

"Now, where does your family live? Near here?" Gran starts in, picking up her own cookie and moving a chair closer to Jess. My stomach clenches. Why in the hell have I brought Jess here? Gran is going to connect the dots and flip out!

Worse, she's going to blow my cover.

I cough and clear my throat. "Uh…Gran, I hate to ask for

help and sound like a wimp in front of my girl, but do you think you could give me a little assistance?"

Under the kitchen light, my two blisters look puny. It's pretty obvious I could handle them alone, but they're the only distraction I've got to get Gran out of gossip-granny-mode.

I blink helplessly and try my puppy-dog eyes. Gran loves it when I *need* her. "I can't open the cabinets and dig around very well—please?"

"Oh, my poor boy." Gran's bought it like a humming bird aiming for red. "Jess, you watch the teapot and pour when ready. We'll be right back."

23

jess

I wait a good five minutes, pour the tea, drink the tea, and demolish a surprising amount of the crumbly cookies. Sitting here with warm tea swirling in my stomach has pushed me past the point of exhaustion and into a dangerous zone of near oblivion. I've almost fallen asleep twice already. I'm not going to let them return to find me head down and zonked at the table.

This means I'm going to have to move.

The clock on the microwave reads 9:30. I rearrange the remaining cookies to fill the gaping hole on the plate and head out of the kitchen.

Only another hour-and-a-half until my curfew's up.

I can make it. I can make it.

I head into the hallway and pause, taking in the wall photos. It's like a shrine—to Gray. I stop and stare at each and every one. There's years of cute little toddler Grays all dressed up in brand new outfits. Then kid-sized Grays holding various lunch boxes as he's heading off to his first days of school.

So cute.

Farther down the hallway toward the staircase, I come to the ice hockey photos, arranged by age, little to big. He must have started playing ice hockey around age five or six. The most recent are of Gray, as assistant coach for the junior level hockey teams at the Complex.

The last photo holds me rooted to the spot.

It's Gray, probably a freshman and as a team member of our high school's ice hockey team. Not a formal shot, but rather the *fool-around-and-make-faces* photo snapped by a parent. Gray's standing to the far left. He's much younger than the other players, but he has a varsity jersey. I figure he must have been good to have made varsity; but it's obvious he's the odd man…or should I say, odd *boy* out. The guy was beyond puny before his growth spurt.

Stranger yet, his arm's around Coach William's shoulders and they're laughing like they're best friends. Weird.

There are no ice hockey photos after that. Only shots of Gray playing inline hockey at the sports complex, and a really sweet one of Corey, and Michelle with Gray, standing in front of this house.

As I turn away, black spots rush across my vision and the room tilts. I hold onto the wall for support. I feel like I'm about to black out. This happens often when I become this over-tired. My body morphs into a two-billion pound slug and I start to collapse from the inside out. If I can't catch a nap soon, I could lose all control. I don't want to do that in front of Gray. Anyone. Hearing voices at the top of the stairs, I grip the wooden banister and start up. I'm moving slowly in case the urge to faint returns, plus, I'm not a fan of falling down stairs.

Gran's voice reaches me before I hit the landing.

"Gray Porter, you've lost your mind!"

"Okay. Maybe I have. I know I shouldn't be taking her money, that's for sure. But it's not an easy thing to bring up, and I mean to. I will."

My throat tightens when I realize this conversation is about me.

He drops his voice to a whisper, "We're starting to be real friends and I care about her. I'll figure out a way—soon."

"Oh, the poor girl. What have you gotten yourself into with all of this? Oh, the poor, poor girl. She seems so sweet. Poor little love."

My chest crushes inward like I've been hit with a bag of sand. Pity sand.

My eyes burn with unshed tears. Embarrassment fills my lungs to the bursting point. Pushing back my exhaustion, I clear my throat and force my tone into one of teasing sarcasm. "You two done with the amputations?"

I'm well used to conversations dying like this in front of me. *Because* of me.

Gray's grandmother opens the bathroom door wide. Her soft, rounded cheeks are flushed. Gray looks completely ill. I shoot them both a straight-faced look, daring them to discuss the contract and my fake relationship with Gray to my face.

After people have been told I'm 'different', they never act the same around me. And I'm sure a girl who has to hire a boy-friend for the summer must come across as 'different' to Gran. I shouldn't care...but I do.

"I...uh...finished my tea. Hope you don't mind I came looking for you," I say, surprised at how steady and bright my voice sounds. I must be on autopilot.

Gran comes out of the bathroom with Gray in tow. "No. No. I'm sorry. We got to talking and we just abandoned you, didn't we?" The woman's face is shifting to brighter red and I can read that she's wondering if I've overheard them.

I meet Gray's shuttered gold-green gaze. He moves to my side and takes up my hand as though he means to apologize. If I weren't feeling so light-headed I would have shaken it off, because on principle—if his grandmother knows about the contract—there's no need to pretend he's my boyfriend any-more.

But I'm sinking, and the feel of his palm against mine is the only thing keeping me afloat. Desperate, I squeeze his hand hard. I hope he understands I'm at the edge of an abyss. "Gray, can I have a tour of your room?" My voice quavers. I point to the closed door at the end of the hallway—the one with the giant hockey stick attached to it. "I want to see your trophies and all that," I manage, hoping they won't bring it up again.

"Sure. Gran? Is it okay?"

I think Gran looks almost relieved that the *crazy girl* isn't going back down to the kitchen with her. "Door open. And no funny business," she says with a smile that doesn't reach her eyes. She's staring at my hand in Gray's. I can sense she's wor-ried. Maybe about Gray, or our contract. Maybe she's wonder-ing just what, *exactly*, I paid for. As if.

"Gran!" Gray sighs. "Jess has an eleven o'clock curfew. We'll listen to music and talk for an hour. Promise. Door open is no problem. I'm a gentleman."

We head into his room and I catch sight of a wall of medals and trophies out of the corner of my eye, but my real attention is riveted on the bed. His comfortable looking, neatly made bed. "Your room is so clean," I mumble.

"Easy to keep it up when I'm never in it."

"Mine's the opposite. I refuse to leave it unless forced. It's always a mess."

Gray frowns. I regret that slip of information. I release his hand and flop onto his mattress. "Do you mind?" I ask. "You said if I ever needed to nap I should tell you…and I need a nap. Now."

My eyes are already closed. I won't be able to move if he does mind. I've already kicked off my shoes. "I don't feel quite right, sorry."

"Did you hear what we said?" he asks. I hear him walking around the room, moving things. His pillow smells great—like him.

"I don't mind that you told her about the contract."

"Is that what you think I told her?"

"It's pretty obvious you told her the truth. What else would make her so angry and freaked? I bet she's not happy that you're a *paid companion* for the summer, huh?"

"I'm not going to lie. She's not exactly thrilled you and I are hanging out. But for other reasons." His voice moves closer. "A blanket," he says and I'm draped in soft, blue fleece. I feel safe. Like I'm wrapped on all sides in a secret version of Gray Porter's lime scented heaven.

"Truth is easier. But it's also a bummer...don't you think?" I ask.

"What do you mean?" His voice sounds tight, like an over-stretched rubber band.

I open my eyes.

The room and he are slightly out of focus. I know I shouldn't answer him without planning what I should say, but right now I'm too tired to mask anything. "Look. Until just a few minutes ago, I got to be the *first-girl Gray Porter ever brought home'*. It was awesome to get to be that girl in someone's eyes, even for a moment. I didn't like to disappoint your grandmother, that's all. So...if I'm feeling bad that she knows the truth, you probably also feel like crap right now. Am I right?"

When I catch his expression he looks stunned, like I've dead-on read his mind. And that he might be worried that I'm feeling like crap.

Quickly, I try to recant the implication that this has hurt me in any way. "Don't worry about it. I'm good. Now I can imagine how it will be when one day you really do bring a *first-girl* home. It's sweet, actually. Gran will get over this. We all will,

I suppose. It's such a strange situation. It was bound to get to this level of extreme-awkwardness eventually, huh?" I add in a small, careless sounding laugh, only I suddenly want to cry so much my throat burns.

That also happens when I'm over-tired.

"Jess...no. You've misunderstood completely." He drops to his knees beside the bed. "Don't say that. I have so much I want to tell you. You are—I mean...I want you to know—I told Gran that you're—" He looks away and runs both hands through his hair. "How can I say this? I don't know where to start."

I close my eyes against him. His face—the adorable chin divot—the intensity of his eyes are altogether, too overwhelming from this viewpoint. "Please, stop. I'm too tired to listen. I'm good. I shouldn't have made you feel bad about things. It's all right. Whatever you told Gran about me being messed up couldn't even scratch the surface of what's real about me. Not much gets to me. Crazies have really thick skin."

"I hate that you think that about yourself."

"I hate that you never believe me." I curl onto my side and face him. "But...don't feel sorry for me. Not like the others do. Like my parents, like your gran just did. I couldn't stand it if you suddenly treated me like that."

"Why?"

"Because you've always treated me differently. Better. Like I'm just fine. Fine the way I am."

"You are! Better than fine. And just the way you are. Jess, you're awesome. There's a lot you don't know. I need to tell you so much."

"No. I just want sleep. If I didn't feel so positively like dying right now, I'd suspect you might be crazy like me. My head kills so badly. I think it's your fault. I *know* it's your fault. All that spinning me around the rink, feeding me only Coke and cookies? It did me in. Stop trying to make me think, and let me sleep. Just a bit."

He lets out a long, heavy sounding sigh. "Sleep. It will give me a chance to figure out a way to say things better."

He shifts forward onto his knees and moves my hair back from my brow and temples, letting his fingers trail into my hair, over and over. I open my eyes again at that, but I don't say anything because I'm afraid he might stop. It feels so nice.

He says, "But when you wake up you have to let me talk. About the truth."

I shake my head 'no' and reach up and grip his forearm, feeling suddenly desperate.

"Gray," I start. I'm afraid to ask him this question, but I have no other choice. My level of exhaustion is terrifying me. I meet his gaze, hoping, wishing, praying he can read my mind. My fear.

"What is it?" he frowns, concerned.

"You have to wake me up if you think I'm having a dream. *Any* dream at all. It's dark outside and I...*you know*. Please. It's important. Don't leave me here alone."

He nods and his face goes pale. "Of course. Don't worry."

"Promise?"

He takes in a deep breath and gently takes my hand, giving it a squeeze. "I'm not going anywhere. Because when you wake up, we *are* going to talk."

His voice already sounds too far away.

My eyelids feel as though someone or something is turning a crank to force them shut.

"Don't leave me here. Please. I don't want to be here..."

...

Wait. Don't leave me. Please don't leave me here.

A white sheet floats suspended over me like a cloud...like a snowstorm, a shroud.

It descends over my body and I'm cold. Afraid. Alone.

Wait. Don't leave me. Please don't leave me here alone!

I fight and claw against the white but I can't move my arms or my legs. Terror sets in.

I do not want this. I do not want to be here. I shouldn't fall asleep. I think Gray's hand is still holding mine …but the white has already taken over and I'm crying, but I mustn't…I shouldn't cry…I need to stay in control.

Don't leave me. Please!

You're a very lucky girl. Lucky. Lucky girl.

Let's go. Dude. Nothing happened. Let's go.

I'm sorry. I'm so sorry. I can't untie the knot.

I'm sorry. Jess. I'm so sorry… Jess…

...

"Jess. I'm so sorry. Are you okay?"

Someone's screaming and crying.

Is that *me*? Is that ME?

I open my eyes.

Gray is holding my hand and his eyes…his face…his voice, all of the voices from the dream are inside me and outside of me at the same time.

Oh God. Gray's voice. His face. Why is he here with me? Now?

He looks as frightened as I feel. I don't understand anything beyond the images pulsing through me: *A silver belt buckle. Seashells in a crystal bowl. The bright line of red seeping down my arm.*

I can't figure out what's real. I let my gaze travel past Gray's face to the room. I'm searching for my clock, my jellyfish lamp. My posters. The shaking sets in like I've been hit with a train.

Suddenly the sounds in the room are all too loud as I realize what's happening.

I'm crying uncontrollably. Awake in Gray Porter's room. He's holding my hand, and I've had a terrible nightmare.

I'm not okay.

I try to gain control of my body but it's too late. I'm crying so hard I can hardly begin the counting...*one... two... three...*

Everything goes black as the nausea sets in and my stomach rolls. I bite the insides of my cheeks as hard as possible.

Four. Five. Six. Seven. Eight.

Breathe. Breathe. Breathe.

I haven't vomited after this stupid nightmare for almost two years. No way am I going to do it in Gray Porter's bed!

Nine. Breathe.

Ten. Breathe.

Eleven. Breathe. Twelve...

My focus clears a little when I reach 100. For the first time, I notice Gray's grandmother is standing in the doorway. Her face is distorted with anguish, fear and possibly repulsion.

All for me.

Gray hasn't left my side. As if he could have with the iron death grip I've had on his hand. His mouth has been moving constantly.

I strive to make sense of his words.

"You were sleeping so deeply—and then—*shit*. Jess. Talk to me. I'm *so* sorry," he says, like this is somehow his fault.

Make him stop saying that!

I want to scream as the images return: *The police officer's gun snapped to his side, a blue tie on my wrist, and white. Too much white.*

I purse my lips and work to swallow the lump of bile.

I'm so sorry. I'm so sorry.

You're a very lucky girl.

I'm going crazy. Someone help me stop my thoughts. The images. Stop everything.

I place my hands over my ears and press as tightly as I can

until my ears throb. I count and count until the only sound I hear is a rushing river of buzzing. Until floating numbers are the only images flashing through my head.

I take stock of what I *can* feel which is mostly a terrible ache in my bones from trying to suppress all my shaking. My heart hurts as well. There is also Gray's other hand gently smoothing-smoothing-smoothing the hair against my temple.

Knowing Gray has already seen the worst, I meet his gaze and let the tears fall unchecked.

"Shh. Shh. You're okay. Jess. You're okay. It's over."

I cry until the pillow under my head is soaked—until I reach number 789. But still the terror won't fade away. I wonder if there's a possibility I'm on the brink of remembering, or if this is simply *me*, running through the last shreds of my sanity.

If I've transposed Gray all the way into the end of my nightmare then I've gone over the edge. I'll never be better.

I'm *worse*. Way worse.

789 is beyond any number I've ever recorded. Maybe I'd gone too far, not sleeping and imagining things I shouldn't. Like, me being with Gray. And now, whether I'm asleep or awake, I can't sort out what is real and what is not.

I cry louder. Harder. This is totally my fault.

"Honey. Are you going to be okay?" Gray's grandmother moves closer to the bed.

No. No. I'm never going to be okay. Never!

I continue to sob and count. I'm at 862, with no end in sight. God, how I want my jellyfish lamp right now.

"Jess. I'm right here. Look at me. You're not alone. I'm here."

His hand in mine is the only thing that feels right in this whole mess. I work to focus on the little specks in his irises. I tell myself to wait until I see the gold appear, and then I'll be able to talk.

"Jess. Can you hear me?" I grip his hand tighter, and hope he understands that I do.

He's using the back of his other hand to gently wipe away some tears. "Don't cry anymore. It's breaking my heart. Should I call your parents? Nod if you need them here."

I shake my head and stare only at his eyes. They're helping.

"I'm going to call an ambulance and her parents. I think she's having some sort of breakdown. Gray, this could be dangerous." Gran walks nearer and bends toward my face. "Honey. Can you *hear* me? Give us some sign that you can hear us. Please."

I gasp, trying hard. "Almost over. Wait. D—don't call anyone." I finally find the strength to pull in a full breath. The images fade slightly and the shaking begins to subside. "I'm okay," I manage to lie.

I stopped at 932. There's nothing okay about 932.

"I'm sorry. I think I screamed." My throat feels like shredded sandpaper. "That was me, right?"

"Yes. But mostly you cried. I couldn't wake you." Gray's voice is shaking too. He looks so distraught, I feel sorry for him.

Though I'm not near ready, I sit up, hoping to assure him and Gran that I'm okay.

It's a mistake. The room and the bed spin in opposite directions. The black spots return with a vengeance. I can't balance at all. Gray moves to sit beside me, places his arm around my shoulders and draws me into him. "Jesus. Hang on." He says, voice lower than low and he tightens his grip.

"Don't worry, I know how to do this," I lie again, leaning all of my weight on him, beyond grateful that he's there.

Gray grabs the blanket, covers me back into the soft blue warmth and rests his chin on my head.

"I've got you."

Gran appears, offering me a damp washcloth. I take it and wipe my face. "Thanks."

"This happens often?" Gran asks.

"Gran! She doesn't have to talk about it. You don't have to talk about it if you don't want to, Jess." Gray takes the washcloth out of my motionless hand and wipes away the latest flood of silent tears.

I meet Gran's gaze. "The screaming started this summer, but the nightmare is not. Unfortunately, the crying part is a constant, lucky side effect. Sorry you had to witness it." I pull in a ragged breath. "I've gone through endless variations. When I wake up, it's always like this. Shaking, sketchy balance, inability to walk or speak. But not for long. You'll see. It's almost over."

I eek out a small smile and try to make light of it, but my voice is not quite ready to rally into quip mode. I sound like a rusted gate, as I continue, "I'm like a CD that plays only one song. One with a skip in it. It's not so bad. Really. Lots of people have recurring nightmares. I'm just one of millions, I suppose. Hope I didn't scare you too much."

Gray's breath moves the hair on top of my head. I wonder what he and his grandmother really think now that they've seen me like this.

"I'm... um... do you have anything I could drink?" I ask, when neither seems able to respond.

"Oh. You poor, poor dear. I'll go re-warm that pot of tea. Gray, will you be okay with her alone?" Her voice says she thinks there's still a chance I'm going to float up to the ceiling, let my head spin around, and spit knives at him or something. I feel him nod. When Gran leaves the room, I lay my head on Gray's warm shoulder and close my eyes.

He holds me like this until the shaking stops.

He holds me until I can't imagine facing another nightmare

without him holding me—just like this.

I shudder at that thought.

It's a bad thing for me to stay in his arms, feeling this safe and good. I need to stop leaning on Gray. When did I start relying on him so much? He's made me so weak. I can't find the girl I used to be before I hired him. The one who'd been able to haul loads of personal crap around all alone and still maintain a 4.0 GPA.

The girl who is *not* and never *was* in love with Gray Porter.

This guy being my boyfriend is fiction, so my love must be fictional too. Right? I have to close the book and find myself again or I'll be lost forever.

I pull away from him. With the terror gone, all that's left is my shame. I think I slobbered gallons of tears onto his pillow and shirt. I'm also embarrassed because of how I still feel about a boyfriend that isn't even real. I suppose that might never go away. I mean, I still love Mr. Darcy, and it's been a long time since I read that book or saw that movie.

I stand, but stumble a bit.

"Whoa. Are you steady enough?" His voice sounds different—stiff. Awkward. He's probably embarrassed too.

This time, he doesn't move to catch me.

"Fine. I'm fine." Cold slams into my back. Gray and I both stare at the goose bumps on my arms—like we can't look anywhere else. It's making the humiliation of what Gray just witnessed—how I'd behaved—even harder to bear.

I step away from the bed and try to read his expression through my lashes, but his eyes are unreadable as usual. Had he seemed almost relieved when I'd moved away? I'll make it easy for him—for both of us. I cross my arms over my stomach and choose my coldest tone. "If you don't mind. I'd like to go home. I can still make curfew." I pretend to study the clock.

"Jess. You promised we could talk. Gran's getting tea."

"You're delusional if you think we're going to have some chatty tea party right now." I suppress a shiver and met his gaze. "I'm tired and I absolutely don't want to talk. Not about this, or us, or anything."

"Well, what if I do?" He's hurt. I can tell.

"I'm the one in charge of *this*." I fling my arms wide. "Of how *us*, progresses. It's in the contract, remember?"

"I know you've just been through hell, but that gives you no excuse to suddenly act like some sort of evil dictator." Gray stands as well, and his eyes are snapping. His voice has lost its carefulness. Good. This will be easier on both of us if he's pissed off.

"The correct term for me is: *boss*," I reply. My own anger is building and giving me strength. Gray doesn't need to know that I'm mad at myself, not at him. Any anger will work. "Our *friendship*, or whatever it is between us, is over. I can't do it. Not after tonight. I'm sure you'll agree one of us doesn't have enough marbles to balance the load. Friends should be give and take. I only have enough to take."

"You're just upset. Of course we're still friends. You'll calm down and we'll talk. If not today, tomorrow."

"No. I've talked my ass off in therapy for three years. It never helped. Why in the world do you think *me*, talking to *you*, is going to make me or what happened in this room any different, or better?"

"I'm not trying to make it better, I'm—"

I don't let him finish. "Newsflash. I pull this same freak show once or twice a week. Sometimes more. I'm sorry if it surprised you, and I'm sorry if I'm hurting your feelings, but I can't, *won't* be your friend anymore. Not like I think you want."

"But—"

"No, *buts*. We only have to survive three more weeks plus

working the DigiToyTech conference. Then I'll break up with you in front of everyone, *as written*. I'm cutting out all other extra hanging out, including my time at the complex. You should be happy to have some of your life back."

"What will I tell Michelle and Corey? What will you tell your parents?"

"How about we both just tell them the truth. I'm sick. Sick and tired. Really tired. It's the truth, let's try to use it to our advantage. My parents will believe me as long as you keep texting me to string them along. I'll send myself some flowers once… or maybe twice. And then, I'll see you on the weekends. That leaves only two 'dates' until the tradeshow. In the meantime, I need space."

"Space?" Gray crosses his arms and yells, "What about the internship and all of the work days ahead? Are we not supposed to *talk* during that? What about the fact that we're building the ten-zillion LightSticks together in the same room next week? We're a team. We're supposed to man the tradeshow booth *together*. We have fun *together*. We *are* friends, no matter what just happened, no matter what you say! You can't just turn me off like you've flipped a switch. This is just a front. I won't let you get away with it. It's not fair."

I don't yell back. There's no point. "You don't have a choice. It takes two people to be friends. It was a mistake for me to mislead you. I just thought…." I sigh and look away. "I forgot that there are some things I can't handle. Friends are exhausting. I'm sorry. I take the blame for hurting you. Shouldn't have tried."

"Don't say that. You don't owe me any apology. Ever." His voice has also lost its fight.

Gray walks to the window and stares out. When he speaks again he's so quiet I'm not sure if he's talking to me or to himself. "I'm not a puppet, you know. I don't know if I can do what you want anymore. Maybe we should end our contract right now."

"Please." I walk over and look into his eyes. "Don't blow it all now because I'm finally being honest—because you finally believe me about the crazy stuff. I'll figure out a way to make it so it's not awkward at work. If I can't, then I'll quit the internship—if that makes this easier on you."

"What?! Easier on *me*?!" He turns red. I can read that he's truly upset but I don't know why. I'm offering back flips and a red carpet exit. What does he want from me?

"Don't quit. Don't do this…Jess." He's lowered his voice into *that voice*, and he moves toward me.

Butterflies whisper down my spine and flood my heart.

I'm ready. Every step he takes, I make sure to back away one.

He stops when he realizes what I'm doing.

My next step will have me exiting his room. I murder the butterflies, and take on his green-gold gaze as though I'm suddenly at war with him. Because I am. I layer on my coldest glare. "Back the hell off. I'm serious."

"You won't mean any of this tomorrow. You're still wrapped up in your nightmare. You could try. *We*…could try? C'mon. So what? So you had a bad dream in front of me. Jess, we are friends…"

I shrug, but his earnest expression almost crumbles me.

I allow my gaze to travel over him, memorizing each line of his face. I'm thankful he can't see inside my mind right now. The terrible images of him inside my nightmare still float there, threatening to resurface. That alone is strengthening my resolve. If he shows up in my nightmares again, it will completely destroy me. I need to make him understand this is life or death.

If only Gray Porter had never wandered into my dreams.

Including the good, waking ones.

I want to let him hold me again—to fling myself at his chest and cry in his arms. Try to explain. But I know none of that was real. And he knows it too. My heart wrenches as a new round of shivers return. The goose bumps increase and I wonder if I'll ever be warm again.

"I will not change my mind," I say, finally swallowing the huge lump in the back of my throat. "Can't you see…I did try, and…" I bore my gaze into his and tell him the truth. "It's hurting me. Inside and out…please. You don't understand how much."

He sighs heavily, and he looks at me like what I've been saying has finally sunk in. "I—yeah. Okay. Okay. Hurting you in any way—it's unthinkable." He runs a hand through his hair and meets my gaze dead on. "Tell me exactly what you expect, and I'll deliver. What do you want? Need. Just say it."

I want you. I want it all to be real. I want to be someone else.

Somehow, I answer in a steady voice. "I want to complete the contract. I know you're honorable enough not to blow that off as long as the paychecks keep coming. I want us—*I want you*—to stay away from me unless we're out in public."

"You're seriously not going to ever let me talk to you about this—about what happened here tonight?"

I shake my head. His eyes grow dark and he looks away. I continue to press it home. "This is not about you. It's for my personal survival. Despite what you witnessed, I still think I deserve the chance to follow my dreams for college, and so do you. The contract will get us both what we want. Let's just stay focused on that. Everything else muddies our goals. You have to admit that's true."

"Okay. I'll do anything." He looks lost. Deflated. Resigned. But it seems he's not angry at me anymore. That's something, at least.

I answer sincerely, "If you mean that, *truly*, then take me home so I don't get in trouble with my parents for being late. If I'm grounded from *my boyfriend*, I'll miss more *normal teen activity*. Being grounded will delay my progress. Okay?"

"Fine," he says.

"Fine."

24

gray

I throw LightStick number five thousand and *save-me-from-this-plastic-crap* into the box with complete disgust, drawing a look from *Percy-from-Shipping*.

Percy-from-Shipping is my newly assigned work partner. He's twenty-two and a high school drop out. He's been filling in for Jess since Monday. Monday. The day Jess officially ditched me.

Monday was a bad day.

It's been three days since I've seen Jess. Of course the girl hasn't returned even one of my texts or phone calls. Not one. Because Jess is *sick and tired*.

Sick and tired.

That's what I'd told Michelle and Corey to explain her absence at the rink. That's what I told my grandmother when she caught me moping around.

I, of course, left off the part where she's sick and tired of me.

"Eff-ing three days with eff-ing *Percy-from-Shipping*," I mutter as I assemble the next LightStick, remembering just how easily Jess had shut me down and pushed me away on all levels.

She'd also fully abandoned me here in Geekstuff.com's plastic sweatshop. Alone.

Percy starts whistling, "This old man...he played one...he

played knick-knack on my thumb..."

Worse than alone.

Apparently, Jess had begged Mr. Foley to have a week on the *back end of things*.

He told me the whole story. Said he just couldn't deny such a *motivated and heart-felt request*. He'd sent her straight to study the order fulfillment and call center processes without question. He did ask me if I minded first. I told Mr. Foley what he wanted to hear.

That *I didn't mind at all.*

I about cracked a molar faking that answer and keeping my face straight. I have no idea how Jess has any teeth left in her mouth after the manipulation and lying acts she puts on every day. The girl didn't lie about one fact, though.

Faking that you're happy and everything is 'super-awesome' takes way too much energy. I've never felt more exhausted in my whole life.

I glare at Percy's back. We're each assembling our own tables of LightStick parts. "At least *you* don't have to stop for *narcoleptic naps*," I say.

"What? Narcoleptic? What's that?" Percy looks up.

"Nothing. I was saying that we will probably be done with these by Friday. Don't you think?"

"If we're being optimistic. It's a possibility." Percy eyes the piles of yet to be assembled toy parts and shakes his head. "I'm sort of regretting my trade out. I never thought I'd admit to missing my cardboard boxes and computer after only three days away from shipping."

"Three days! Eff-ing three days! GOD!" I throw another LightStick, green this time, into the box. "At least you didn't have to do the ladybugs and frogs."

I jam the next topper, blue this time, on so hard it almost cracks. To test it, I push the *on* button once, and pause a moment to study the completed product. When lit, the blue version has the exact same hue of Jess's eyes. "The stupid blue ones piss me off."

I toss it away from me into the box near *Percy-from-Shipping*.

"I refuse to do any more of that color. Are you okay with that, dude?" I shout. "I'm off the blues."

Percy shoots me an alarmed look. "No problem. I suppose I hate the red ones. You do the reds, I'll do the blues?" His voice sounds cautious, like he's humoring me.

"Deal," I say, trying to calm down. Percy isn't such a bad guy.

Tuesday, he'd actually been kind of fun.

Tuesday had been the day I'd convinced myself to stop being pissed off and agree that Jess's plan to totally ignore me was the only plan that made sense. I'd actually made myself believe that too. It is *her contract*. They're *her nightmares*. Tuesday I told myself I should simply be grateful and walk away. I know for a fact, that after the interviews had taken place, this would have been *her internship*, not mine. Tuesday, I'd told myself I was lucky to still be getting paid.

"Stupid Tuesday," I mutter, throwing another LightStick. "But today is suck-ass Wednesday, isn't it? *Percy-from-Shipping*. It's Wednesday today, isn't it?" I'm shouting louder now.

Percy darts me another look. "Dude. Maybe you should take a break."

"I'm just fed up. Fed up! What about what *I* want?" I yell again, hardly registering what Percy just said. I fling another completed LightStick into the box like it's a missile, wishing it would explode.

"Porter. You're freaking me out. Are you some sort of mental case?" Percy backs away from the workspace.

"Sorry." I shake my head as I pick up another LightStick.

I decide to just tell him my deal. Percy-from-Shipping *likes* it when I want to *talk*. "I know I'm acting crazy but I'm in love with this girl. Major love. And I have no idea what to do about it, so it's messing with my sanity."

Percy lets out a long breath as he walks back to his table. "Ah. That explains it. You've been sketching me out all morning. Love, huh? Poor bastard. Have you told her?"

"No. I'm planning to, though. That's why I'm all agitated. I have no idea how to do it."

"Just man up. We all have to put our hearts in the fire to get the ladies. No danger—no dates."

"We're already dating. Sort of dating. Only, I think she broke up with me last week."

"Ah. Was it the *let's-be-friends* scenario? Brutal. Like anyone wants a friend over a girlfriend. Girls suck with that line."

"I don't even rate the *friend* option. She's just done with me. Won't even try."

"Sorry, kid. But on the flip side, if she's on that trip, then there's nothing left for you to lose. Play the wild card and make a fool out of yourself. See what happens. It's not like she can double-un-friend-you."

"It's not that simple. I've got so much shit I need to come clean about. Once she knows my deal, there's the chance she might never talk to me again."

"Holy shit. Did you sleep with her best friend or cousin or something?"

"Hell no! Nothing like that." I laugh.

He shrugs. "Then you're good." Percy tosses his next LightStick into the box extra hard along with me. "Women. They mess us all up."

I spin one of the LightSticks in the air. "The girl is going to cost me a ton of money too."

"Money? Don't they all cost money?"

"I'm going to lose out on four thousand dollars. I'll possibly have to delay my college start date to make things right too."

Percy lets out a long, low whistle. "And if she still rejects you? Is she worth risking that much?"

"More. So much more."

"Dude, you're pathetic. And you're toast. You know that, right?"

"Yeah. I know."

25

jess

I snap open my eyes when the tapping starts on my side window. I haven't been able to sleep anyhow. That's mostly because when I pulled in, Gray had been parked nearby, reading in his car. Pretending to read, that is.

All this time, I've been pretending to sleep, so there! I can't believe he waited this long.

I grab my bag and open the door, trying to ignore him. But ignoring Gray Porter is like ignoring an elephant in a tutu. A really hot elephant—in a very manly tutu.

Of course I have to look. Especially when I've denied myself the sight of him for days. He's perfect in his brown cargo shorts, sporting the black Star Wars tee Mr. Foley gave us last week as a bonus. I pull my cardigan tightly closed over my middle. No need for him to notice that we're wearing matching shirts.

The sexy smell of limes is coming off his damp hair in waves right now. I never noticed limes before Gray Porter. And now, when we're in the supermarket I sniff them like a psycho and then put them back. It's a shock how often limes are on TV too. They're everywhere. My favorite burrito shop even uses fresh lime juice to make the salt stick to their hand-fried tortilla chips. UGH. I used to be able to resist eating more than a few, but lately, I've become a lime-chip-aholic.

"Did you get enough sleep?" he asks.

"Because it's easy to nap when I'm being stared at?" I snap. "Why are you here?"

"Jess..."

I meet his hurt, way too intense gaze. I'm unable to hold it for long. It's been only seconds and he's already got my defenses malfunctioning on every level.

I solidify my expression to flat. Bored. Dead.

He sighs. "I wouldn't have to hunt you down if you'd text me back. I've called every night at seven. And left messages, every other hour. Why won't you talk to me?"

"The contract states you must text and call *me*. There's nothing in there about reciprocating."

"That's *why*?"

I stare at him unblinking.

"God. You're serious." He crosses his arms and glares. He's standing so close I feel heat radiating off him. Heat I've craved like an addict after being wrapped in his arms the other night. I pull a Red Bull out of my bag and pop the top right under his nose. Thankfully, he takes the hint and steps back.

"I can't believe you're sulking around the parking lot like this," I cover. My heart rushes into my throat because I've made the mistake of looking into his eyes. I chase it away by gulping down the remainder of the Red Bull. No matter how fast he makes my heart race, I'm not going to fall for his magic this time. "I—you—said we're late. I need to get inside."

"I do too. But—I miss you. Can we please have lunch today? Get Mr. Foley to transfer you back to LightSticks and the DigiToyTech stuff. I know we can work this out." He gently grabs my arm and turns me to face him.

"No," I say, pulling away from his grip to start walking

again. He follows. "Gray, no hard feelings about me skating on the tradeshow project. I want to be in Shipping. I'm here to *learn*. As for lunch, I can't. Thursday is the department's monthly meeting. All staff members are required to attend. They give us free food."

"Whatever. You're probably making that up."

"Not. They're going to preview a new box-taping machine. The thing is awesome. Tapes over 400 multi-sized boxes per hour. Mr. Foley's asked me to run the training slide show. I've been memorizing the bullet points."

"Tomorrow, then. Noon. I know Foley gave you the afternoon off. Meet me in our office, if you can remember where that is. Back hall, first closet on the right. Your desk is the one squished up next to mine. Face to face." His voice sounds half angry, half accusing. "We'll talk. I'll bring sandwiches. Say *yes*."

"I said, no! Why can't you get the message through your head? I can't be around you."

"Why? Why are you treating me like this?! God, do you piss me off!" he shouts.

I turn my expression to stone but it's almost impossible to hold. My brain is firing off different versions of what I'll say next to make him permanently understand me; but he jogs in front of me forcing me to stop again.

He grabs onto my hands.

I glance at his sneakers—not his face. Too dangerous. I'm panicking because my mind has been wiped clean by the simple feel of his palms against mine. I love that feeling.

"You're being unfair. You owe me at least the respect to hear what I have to say," he says.

His voice is gentle…and low and rumbling. Zero anger.

Damn him and that voice and his hands.

I want to scream, "foul" or "off sides, or any sports call that could make him stop weaving his way so easily into my soul. I try to regroup, but…his hands are so gentle on mine. I move my gaze to his fingers, and let my mask drop away.

"You're blisters are almost healed."

"Yeah." His thumbs traverse the back of my palms. I should let go, but I simply don't want to. I glance at his face. Any remaining defenses I'd stockpiled against him fold under the absolute anguish and confusion I see in his eyes. I've caused this. I've hurt him, and he's right. I do owe him at least some sort of explanation for why I pushed him so far over a cliff. I shiver. Could I simply tell him the truth about myself? If he knows all, he'll understand my permanent limitations.

"Tomorrow." I nod. "Twelve noon. I'll really listen. But you have to *promise* to listen to me right back. Even if you don't like what you hear, you need to hear me back. Deal?"

"Okay. I will. I will." He smiles and the dimple flashes. The relief in his voice makes his eyes seem over-bright as though he's feverish, or holding back tears.

But that's impossible because I'm the one doing that.

I feel like a floating puff of mist. One so fragile and light, that if this boy blinks, I could easily disappear—be lost forever. But I know it's too late. I've been lost since the day he smashed his backpack into my car.

Stupid love. Stupid color green.

Why does Gray have the power to make me feel like this when I'm intelligent enough to *know* it's all a mirage? I wonder if this feeling will crush me when the summer's over. When I'm not allowed to hold his hands anymore. When he walks past me in the hallways at school with his *real* girlfriend. Will we smile and laugh about our shared secrets? Or will I die because I have to breathe his same air?

I work my hands out of his, and together we walk inside. It's impossible to recover my *back off* mask, so I don't even try. "Um. Thanks. For…you know…finding me. I'm glad I'll get the chance to explain better. What happened at your house—all I said that night. I'm sure I wasn't making any sense."

Gray lets me pass in front of him through the lobby. "Jess, I'm the one who needs to explain. Everything. Why I've been acting like a complete weirdo around you. I tried to give you space. Do what you wanted, but I can't. I know we can be friends. And— well, I think, I hope, you might want that—"

I bump him shoulder to shoulder to shut him up.

His whispered words have wreaked havoc along the back of my neck. I'm covered in goose-bumps. Worse, blushing like mad.

The GeekStuff.com receptionist has overheard Gray's indecipherable cluster of words. She's giving us this knowing smirk. Can't blame her, as we'd been holding hands for a really long time out there. I flush even more. "I uh…gotta go."

Gray, looking more flustered and awkward than I've ever seen him, shakes his head. "Right. I'm an idiot. Tomorrow."

His voice follows me down the hallway. "When I text you tonight—will you answer? Please?"

"No." I don't look back. If I see his face I'll change my mind. I have to be strong. He'll understand where I'm coming from, eventually. Maybe we can be friends after this is all over like he says.

But not until he knows the truth about me.

26

jess

"Jess!" Dad's voice trails up the stairs. "I need some kitchen help."

I head out of my room and meet Kika in the hallway. She's hauling a full laundry basket to her room. "Any idea why Dad sounds so extra industrious? What did you see down there? Is it bad?" I ask.

"He's making that marinade sauce for the meat from scratch this time. The chili meat. For the burgers on Sunday?" Kika arches her brow and turns the laundry basket to the side so I can't move.

I pretend to ignore her attempt to block me and try to squeeze past, keeping my voice light. "Oh. I should have known! He wants me to chop the onions." I force a smile but my heart has turned to weighted stones.

Dad always makes his special super tenderized meat before a big BBQ. He makes it when he wants to impress someone. That someone is supposed to be my boyfriend, *one Corey Nash*. To be delivered in person in three days time. Just because things have been off between me and Gray, doesn't mean I was stupid enough to cancel the barbecue plan. Yet.

"Jess. I'm waiting," Dad calls up again.

"Be there in a minute," I match the sing-song voice Dad's used and meet the challenge in my sister's eyes. "What's up?"

Kika won't budge out of my way. "What's up with *you*?" Her tone is sarcastic and angry.

"Nothing." I push the basket forcefully out of my way and head for the stairs.

"Oh no you don't." Kika drops the basket with a thump. She catches me on the upper landing. "He's coming, right? To the barbecue?"

"Corey? Of course he is." I blink slowly and shoot her my best 'what's-wrong-with-you' glare and head down the stairs. She follows. "No. Not *him*. I'm talking about your *boyfriend*. Is *he* coming? And don't try to pretend. Anyone could see that guy, *Corey Nash*, was into that other girl and not into you."

We stop in the front entrance. "I have no idea what you mean."

"I mean *the other guy*. The black haired, model-looking dude? Did you not see him, because I sure did. He's tall. Got green eyes, and he's major hot and very in to YOU. The one you were skating with, and you *know* it!" she shouts.

I check the hallways for signs of our parents. "Who do you think you are, butting into my life? You don't know anything," I whisper.

She doesn't whisper back. "I'm your sister. And I know a whole lot. Seriously, I'm about to blow up. Start talking."

"Tell me what you *think* you know."

"And give you the chance to twist your story again?" Kika crosses her arms and shoots me her little death glare—the one that wouldn't even wilt a daisy. "You tell me the *truth* first, starting with his real name, and then I *might* tell you what I mean to share with Mom and Dad."

I admire her answer. The girl's quick, and she's also scaring the hell out of me. I motion Kika to follow me into the deep, bench-lined alcove that makes up the area inside our front door. "This is really none of your business. What have you already told them?"

"Nothing. But if the right guy doesn't show on Sunday afternoon, then you're going down. I'm done covering for you, especially when you haven't even told me one single thing."

"You're seriously threatening me?"

"Yes. I'm completely freaked. You don't even know how horrible it sounds when you scream in the middle of the night, because you're asleep. But I've been listening to you lose it all week. You're so lucky Dad's deaf and Mom was at a conference. Or they'd already be involved. I should have told Mom the second she hit the driveway. But I didn't. Because I thought you'd talk to me—about stuff—about what's going on. Jess. WHAT'S GOING ON?"

"Come on. It's not as extreme as you're making it out to be. That other guy—you don't understand. It's not what it seems...or...it's just confusing, that's all. As for the long nights. I'm sorry if you couldn't sleep. You know I can't control that."

Kika's face crumbles into complete worry and anguish and she starts to cry. "I don't care about sleep. Do you know I've been trying to stay awake in case you need me? But you don't. You never ask for help. You never come to my room anymore." She gulps. "You haven't talked to me—you haven't even *looked* at me—since I saw you at the sports complex. I miss you. I'm scared for you."

My heart sinks. We hardly ever fight. And, she's right. I've never shut her out of my life before. "I know—" I start, but she won't let me finish.

"What I don't get is why you've played this really weird *boyfriend* prank on our whole family. I can only think you're, like—doing *drugs*. Or you're in some sort of trouble. Are you pregnant?"

I gasp. "This is not a prank. And this is definitely not *me* on drugs. I can't believe you'd think I was pregnant! Not even close. My entire life is at stake right now. It all rests on how things go for me this summer. Sue me if I've been a bit distant, but I've been busy working on my future. And it's not going very well. That's all. It's not personal, or against you, or Mom or Dad. Nothing like that."

She shakes her head and her eyes are icy cold. "Give me one reason not to tell on you right now. Say something *real*. Honest. If you even know how what that means anymore."

How could I let things get this out of control? I hate myself right now. Mostly for breaking my sister's heart like this.

I can't lie to her anymore. "You want real? Fine." I sigh. "Let's start with the fact that I'm in love. Head over heels in hopeless, horrible *love*. And with the absolute—most gorgeous guy I've ever known. He's perfect actually. You saw him at the rink."

"I knew it. I knew I was right about him and you."

"But you aren't right. Truth is, I'm paying that guy to be my pretend boyfriend for the whole summer. And he's done an amazing job making everyone believe he and I are the real deal. He's so good at his job, that I've fallen for him, the mirage of him being my boyfriend, all of it. Like everyone else. Like an idiot."

Kika's chin drops. "No way. What's his name?"

"Gray Porter. His best friend is Corey Nash, the other guy you met that night. We just traded their names to keep you and Mom confused. Corey and Michelle—they don't even know what we've done. No one does. Except you. I can't let Mom and Dad find out none of this is real."

"What about the internship? Please tell me you've been driving to a real job every day."

I grimace. "The internship's legit. That's why I'm so tired. Why the nightmares are so strong. No time for car naps. I was thinking about quitting early. I just want to finish out this week. Make it to Sunday. But if you tell on me today, you'll ruin everything I've worked so hard to set up."

She throws her arms wide. "How can I ruin everything, if your nightmares are back and your boyfriend isn't even real. Sounds like you're pretty much a total disaster, right here and right now without my help."

I sit on one of the benches and let out another long sigh. "Yeah. I know." I lean back and meet her gaze. She sits on the bench across from me as I continue, "If Mom and Dad find out what I've done—if this information leaks at school—I'll die from the humiliation. I've pulled back from everyone because I'm trying to salvage some of the situation. My self respect, and my plans for college at the very least. But now, I don't even know if I have what it takes to make it to college. Maybe Mom's right. Maybe I'll never be able to move out of this house."

"Oh. My. God. This is so messed up." Kika pulls in a ragged breath.

"I stayed away from you because I didn't want to admit that you were right about the dreams getting worse. I knew you'd worry too much. You always do. I'm going to ask for help. Soon. I'm asking you to wait three more days. You have to believe me, by Sunday's barbecue the entire thing with Corey Nash and Gray Porter will be solved. Over."

"How?" She arches one brow.

"I'm planning on breaking up with my *boyfriend* before the barbecue starts."

"But which one will you break up with? Corey? Or Gray?"

I feel my cheeks grow hot. "Both. Gray, I guess, and Michelle too. You'll never see any of them again so it doesn't matter. And I'll be back to—normal. Back to *my kind of normal*, anyhow. I'm begging you. Give me the next few days. Real or not, this time is all I'm ever going to have with this guy. Heck, with any guy, and I know it's selfish of me, but I really want those days to happen."

Kika sputters, "So—no one—*no one at all* is coming to this barbecue except for our family?"

I nod, working to swallow the lump in my throat. "Just us."

"What in the heck do you plan to say to Mom and Dad on Sunday?" Kika jerks her head toward the kitchen. "Mom's been cleaning the house and acting like a crazy homemaking freak. She's making me plant more flowers with her out front! What are you going to say to make any of this okay?"

"Easy." I shrug. "I'm going to tell everyone the truth. Then, I'm going to shell out the answer I always use: *I'm sorry*. Because, Kika. *Ugh*. I *am* sorry. You know I am. Then, our family can have a nice *talk* about all the shenanigans I've pulled. How I've actually made no *progress* at all. And what a sad, messed up, mental-case I'll always be."

I look away from her astonished gaze as I go on, "Dad will retreat into his office, Mom will cry, and you'll try to make everyone happy by being the nice, perfect one—as always. My college will be on hold, of course. I'm sure Dr. Brodie will have me back on his couch by Monday afternoon."

I stand, keeping my face a mask of serenity. But inside, I've become so heavy I'm amazed the weight of my permanently messed-up life doesn't simply push me through the wood floor. I wish it would. Being sucked into the molten-core-center of the earth has to feel better than this.

Kika crosses her arms. All of her angst fades away as the realization of what I've said sinks in. "OMG. That completely sucks. I think *you* completely suck."

"Yep. You're always the last to believe the truth about me.

I'm glad you've finally ramped in. Newsflash: I've sucked for three years. I'm sorry I lied to you, though. I won't do it again. Of course—I won't expect you to believe in me again for a long time. If ever. It's only fair."

I head out of the alcove, but Kika grabs my shoulder. Her face has mottled to patchwork pink and white. A signal that she's about to have a major cry session. No more words are going to come out of her mouth.

My heart breaks to look at her. I soften my tone and beg again for her silence. "Don't tell on me. It's only three more days. I want a chance to say goodbye…to Gray…to the job. To the best summer I've ever had. Gray and I have plans to hang out all afternoon tomorrow. And then, Saturday we have a date to ThunderLand. I've never been there. Even though it's totally fake, every second with that black haired, green-eyed boy is better than anything I've ever known. You must understand a little why I don't want to let it go. For me, this is all I'll ever get to have."

She's shaking her head back and forth as though she wants me to deny all that I've said. As if she wants to say more. But she knows what I've said is true.

I whisper, "Just go upstairs and put away the laundry. Plant the darn flowers Mom wants you to plant. Play along, Kika, please. Let me have just a couple more days of being in love before I have to go back to square one. Please."

Without a word, she shoots me a tear-filled glare and runs upstairs.

27

gray

Jess. IK ur reading these. Txt me bk. Txt me bk. Plz.

I click send, and then cut and paste the same message into my phone and send it again. And again. No response.

"Damn her," I mutter.

"She's still sick? What does she have? Chicken pox? The plague?" Michelle leans on the rink's snack counter. Her smile tells me she knows there's something bigger connected to Jess's absence.

"Yeah. She's got it bad." I pretend to check my email, unable to meet her eyes.

"Dude, you're major whipped. I think you've checked that phone a total of sixty times in the past two hours." Corey shoves a dripping nacho into his mouth. "Send her some flowers, make up already. I miss the girl bossing me around."

Michelle punches Corey's shoulder lightly. "Shut up, would you? They're fine. You guys are not breaking up, are you?"

I open a can of cheese sauce to refill the pump, thankful the complex isn't busy tonight. "It's—not what you think. We're not fighting. She's been really run-down. The girl's not used to so much activity. We've had some long days on the tradeshow project, and she's been moved into the shipping department until the tradeshow next Monday. All the new info has over-whelmed her. I'm going to see her tomorrow. We've both been given a half day off for good behavior. We just need to hang out. Reconnect. You know how it is."

"I've never seen you actually moping after a girl," Michelle says. "It's so cute."

"Jess won't text you back. She won't pick up your calls, and you are saying things like you *need to reconnect*?" Corey sticks his finger down his throat and fake-gags. "Smells like trouble in paradise to me. You kiss her, yet?"

I shake my head and open the next can of cheese sauce.

"Porter, you've held back all summer long on that move. Go for it, show her some skills. That should cure her from what-ever she's got. You should just mmm....and mmm, and then—ooh, yeah."

I don't have to look behind me to know that Corey's making faces and being a complete ass, because Michelle's giggling like he's the funniest thing ever.

He goes on, "Plant a big one—right smack on her lips and then—"

"Dude. Shut up. I told you—she's *sick*."

Michelle coughs. And then coughs again. I realize she sounds really odd. Corey suddenly coughs too.

Something's up. I turn, surprised to find Coach Williams standing at the counter next to my friends.

"Hullo, Coach," Corey stutters, fidgeting with the napkin holder.

I meet Coach Williams' steely, accusing gaze with a small nod. "Can I make you something, Coach?" I ask, pasting on a tight smile, wishing I could punch Corey.

"Nash. Miss Hopkins. Good to see you both." Coach Williams nods. "Mind if I have a word with Porter, *alone*?"

"Sure, Coach." Corey shoots me a look as he grabs his nachos. He's all but running to a table with Michelle. Traitors.

"Is she really sick, or is it true you're having some sort of fight?"

"It's true that I've never tried to kiss her yet," I offer.

"That's something."

"I had an interesting phone call from Jess's father this week. After what Corey just said, I'm not sure what's going on. I thought maybe you could enlighten me before that man ambushes me again?"

My heart feels like it just got tossed in a blender. "No. What did he say? Did you out me? Did Jess tell him about our contract?" I ask, wondering if this is one of the reasons Jess won't text me back. "Would have been nice if you'd warned me."

"The guy called me, and he has no idea about the contract. In fact, the guy sounds happier and more hopeful than I've heard him since...since...you know." He looks away.

"Still afraid? I'll say it for you. *Almost raped.* Since his daughter was *almost raped* by your star player."

Coach clears his throat and leans over the counter so only I can see his face. "Jess's dad told me you were going to their house for a barbecue day after tomorrow. Only there seems to be a bit of confusion on the invite. He told me Jess is bringing a kid named Corey Nash to the party. He asked me what I thought about *him*." Coach flips a glance at Corey and Michelle who are currently holding hands and pretending, very badly, *not* to watch us.

"*Crap.* I'd forgotten about that barbecue. What did you say to that?" I hold my breath and try not to blink.

"I told him Corey is a great kid. A bit goofy, but nice enough. Thankfully, that's all the man asked. Had his questions gone any deeper, I don't know if I could've lied to him. You attending a BBQ at the Jordan house this Sunday, or is that dumb-ass standing in for you?" He shoots Corey a doubtful glance.

"Jess and I already have a plan in place. No one is going... thanks to some future food poisoning. At least, I think that's the plan."

"Hell, Porter. Maybe I'll call her dad back and tell him what I know."

"Don't. Please." I run a hand through my hair. "I need to handle this carefully. I've fallen for her. Seriously."

"Why are you telling *me* this? It only makes me want to kick your ass from here to Kansas."

"I don't know. I guess I'm asking for your blessing, or help. I want to tell her the truth. About me, about that night. And I'm scared to death I'm going to mess it all up. Mess her all up. You know?"

"Are you out of your mind!" Coach Williams roars, causing everyone in the room to stare. He lowers his voice and leans in. His fists clench on the snack counter and his eyes are spitting fire. "Hell yes, you could mess her up! You could put the girl over the edge. You have no idea what you're doing. She's going to need a therapist standing by, or something more serious than some *misguided,* love-sick Boy Scout opening a can of worms all over her head."

I don't even flinch. "I've already witnessed her flipping out after a nightmare. It can't be worse than what I saw her go through the other night. I've never known anyone as strong or as brave as Jess. Don't you think she should know the truth?"

"Yes. If she wants to know it. But Gray, why do you think you have the right to be the one that tells her?"

"Because I want to protect her. Plus I have everything to lose if it goes badly! I'm the one who's in love with her. Because I was in love with her freshman year when it all went down. If the truth about *me* trickles down into her head from the mouths of her over-protective parents, or even from *you,*

I'm sure it will be twisted forever. You'll ruin all the good stuff between us. And believe me, it's there. It's fragile as hell, but it's completely real. She hasn't said anything, but I think she feels the same way abut me."

"I don't know, son..."

"Please. Either way, when she finds out she's going to flip out some, right?"

"Probably." He swallows.

"Wouldn't you want her to flip in my arms where I can catch her? If she has to go through finding out what happened that night alone, it will hurt her even more. I'll do everything in my power to not let her fall. If she does, then I'm going with her. All the way."

Coach sighs. "When are you planning to tell her? And where?"

"Tomorrow. We have a lunch date."

He grabs a pen and scrawls two phone numbers onto a napkin and shoves it at me. "You call me and her dad if anything goes wrong. And, would you please call me when everything goes right so I don't have to worry? I'll be pulling for you...and I'll add in a prayer or two. Or three. Deal?" Coach Williams starts away.

"Coach?" He turns back. His brow has furrowed, giving his face the look of a crumpled piece of sandpaper. He nods once for me to continue, as though he can't talk. As though the guy is choked up and about to cry!

"Thanks," I say. My heart is slamming into my chest with relief and with something that feels like respect. "Just, thanks."

28

jess

I can hardly wait to have lunch with Gray this afternoon. I'm starving…but more for him than for the sandwiches he's promised. I hadn't seen his car in the parking lot when I'd pulled up this morning. I figure that's because he's trying to give me the space I'd requested.

I feel half excited and half scared that we're going to have this talk. I'm even hopeful that he might be right. That we can be *friends* after this is all over. Despite my secret crush on him, of course. But he doesn't need to know about that. Even when—*if*—we do become real friends.

I've dashed to the bathroom after my shift to apply some make-up so I won't look pasty when he shows up. Now, like a vain weirdo I can't stop myself from trying to decide if I should wear my hair up, or down, or back for the rest of the day.

For him.

My heart flutters because I've imagined his face. I watch in the mirror as red heats my cheeks. He'd been so happy that I'd agreed to talk to him. I frown at my reflection and undo the tenth ponytail. I shake it all out and settle on wearing my hair down with a small clip holding back the front layers. In case I'm tempted to primp even more, I run out, making it into our tiny office at exactly 12:00PM.

Then like a dork, I sit there, staring at the back of Gray's computer monitor, and drawing in a little breath of excitement each time I hear a footstep in the hallway.

After an entire half hour has passed and still no sign of Gray, I break my own rules and text him: *YGTS—OW?* I wait sixty seconds and try again: *That means: You Going To Show — Or What? Where RU?*

My tummy's rumbling. Sitting in this office chair is getting dangerous. To stay awake, I head on to Google and randomly type: *Where in the HELL is Gray Porter?*

I slam the return key, enjoying the satisfying 'click' the keyboard makes. While the results load, I grab my iPhone and check the battery. It's green. Gray simply isn't responding. I figure he's giving me a dose of my own medicine for ignoring his texts all week.

I know I deserve it. But heck, the land of 'No Text Back' is truly a cruel and lonely place. Turning back to my monitor, I'm surprised by the search results.

There are tons of pages featuring Gray Porters!

One appears to be a back issue of our high school's news journal. It's actually got the title: *Where is Gray Porter?* Weird. And WTF!

I click the link and stare at the photo in the article. The kid in the shot is so scrawny and hidden in gear that it could have been anyone. But, because of the pictures I'd seen at Gran's house, I know it has to be Gray. The puny, freshman him, anyhow. The text under the photo reads: *Star red line winger, Gray Porter, chooses club inline over varsity ice hockey and leaves our team in the lurch.*

Before I can delve into the article, someone enters the room.

"Finally," I say, popping my head out from behind the monitor. It's not him. It's Michelle? "What are you doing here?"

"This place is a maze. Took me eons to find you." She pauses with a smile and looks around our tiny office. "So, this is where the magic went down?" Michelle plops into Gray's chair and gives it a half spin. "Nice, and cozy. No wonder you two got *so close, so quickly.*"

"Not even. We've been down in the loading warehouses. That's where they keep us caged most of the time. What are you doing here?"

"Gray sent me. The guy was a tragic bundle of nerves. He was literally freaking out and then freaking out again."

"And that means, what? Where is he? What happened?"

"Gran had some sort of episode this morning. Severe muscle cramps and tremors. Enough to make them both think she was dying—having a stroke, heart attack or something worse. Gray rushed her into the hospital. He's been there ever since."

I leap out of my seat, eyes already searching for my bag. "What hospital? Is she okay? Poor Gray, he must be out of his mind. I should go help."

"Hold the fire, woman. That's why I'm here. She's good. He's good. After a slew of tests, they realized it was simply a strange vitamin problem. She'll be released tonight after she gets some sort of drip put into her. Potassium, I think Gray said. She'll be right as rain by tomorrow, but you know how hospitals are. It's going to take forever."

"Why didn't he call me himself?" I wonder if he'd changed his mind and sent Michelle here as a smokescreen. But Gray wouldn't lie about Gran—about anything. Not his style.

"The hospital is a black hole. Zero service. The nurses took pity on him and let him have one phone call, prison style."

"So he chose to call you over me?" I look away.

Michelle laughs. "Hiss hiss, *jealous.* It was well thought out. He called *me* because I'm an unemployed, late sleeper. A sure thing. You're much more difficult to track down. He begged, seriously, *begged* me to meet him at the hospital to pick something up for you. I've been ordered to hand deliver *this*."

She waves a large white envelope as she roll-scoots Gray's desk chair around to my side. "This must be seriously mushy stuff. He ordered me not to open it so many times my fingers ache to break my word. Another five minutes in my purse and I wouldn't have been able to resist."

I smile and take the envelope, trying to play it cool like I don't care what's inside. My name is written across the front in Gray's scrawling print.

"Thanks. I missed you last week," I cover, trying to steer her focus away from the envelope.

"Back-atch-ya." Michelle smiles and points to the envelope. "Gray said you two had a date. He didn't want you to think you'd been stood up. He said if you thought that, then you'd never speak to him again. I suspected you two were in some sort of tiff, but four days of not talking sounds like break up to me. Did you? Are you? What's going on? Open the envelope."

I flip the envelope over and suck in a breath. The back had been sealed with some strange, medical tape. It says: "Whatever you do, don't open this in front of Michelle."

I look at her and Michelle quirks a brow, holding back a laugh. "*I know, right*?! I think he wrote that to torture and tempt me. I should get a freaking medal for not breaking into it! Seriously Gray sucks! Who does that to the most curious person on earth? He's such an ass." She laughs. "It's probably some disgusting love poem. Gray knows if I see any romantic drivel I'll ridicule him for life. And I will. It's my sworn duty to mock him. It has been since we were five. But okay. Fine. If you want to open it, right now in front of me, I'll try not to vomit." Her eyes are glittering with mirth and curiosity.

I grin but shake my head. "I'll wait…if you don't mind." I trail my fingers over where he's written my name.

Michelle leans in and stares at my computer. "What are you looking at? Holy, no way! That's from freshman year." She laughs. "Look at the guy. I'd forgotten what a little peep he was. That helmet honestly looks like it swallowed his whole head."

"Yeah. And the scarecrow body—wow." We both laugh.

"But he was good. Really fast," Michelle says. "He was supposed to be varsity's ticket to state. They called him *Bullet*. He was so speedy that no one could touch him. His shots always scored. Still do. He's still amazing at ice. But he only skates alone at the complex, or to teach the little guys." She pauses and scans the article. "This is about when he quit the team. The entire senior class had a death warrant on him. The principal caught some senior players beating the stuffing out of him just before he quit. Shoved him into lockers, pulverized his face just before Halloween. Do you remember all that? People talked about it for weeks."

"I came in after Christmas that year so I would have missed that." I swallow and flip the subject back to Gray. "Do you know why he quit?"

"He never talked to me about it. Far as I know, he's never talked to *anyone*. Even Corey. He was one angry, messed up little dude in those days. Corey and I almost dumped him. It was like hanging out with the Grim Reaper. I asked him about what happened often enough. But after awhile, his double black eyes disappeared. We gave up trying to get the story out of him. He chilled out by sophomore year."

She leans back in her chair and smiles. "Our hockey team managed to keep the state title without him. That's what probably saved his life. After the season ended, everyone forgot about it. Except for Coach Williams and Gray, of course."

"Wow. He told me he and Coach had a fight, but I didn't know about the other stuff."

"Gray's never been very good at sharing his feelings. He also hates gossip. He's such a *guy* about keeping silent. He and Coach Williams were really close before that year. Kind of a bummer. Coach was sort of a father figure to Gray, and then— they became enemies." She shrugs. "They were going at it all over again last night at the rink. You should have seen them. Just like old times. Shouting, flexing biceps. Staring each other down."

"Really?" I shake my head.

"So, let's talk about you." Michelle brings her knees up and spins her chair. "What takes a freshman a whole semester to get back to school? Were you sick? Are you still sick? Is that why you're always so tired? Why Gray treats you like you're made of glass? Did you go through chemotherapy or have bad kidneys or an organ transplant or something extreme like that?" She blinks, waiting.

My stomach clenches. I break out into a cold sweat. No one's ever asked me this. No one's ever seemed to care. "I... uh...um...well..." I fiddle with the computer mouse.

"Sorry. I'm always putting my foot in it. You don't have to tell me. I'm so nosy. Sorry." She flushes.

"No. It's okay. It's sort of gruesome. But if you want to hear it, I kind of want to tell you." I take a deep breath and meet Michelle's gaze.

She nods, her eyes turning grave.

"I was almost raped." I swallow. "At a party. Almost. Nothing happened. *They*—I mean the cops—found me. No clothes, half passed out, even tied to a bed. Supposedly, it was quite a scene. But nothing major happened—to me, that is."

"Oh my God. What do you mean *nothing major happened?!* Wow...Jess. I'm so sorry." Michelle has tears in her eyes.

"I don't remember much. Don't even remember who did it. How I got in the room, on the bed, none of that. My parents think I was drugged, but we never tested because I had definitely admitted to drinking so...yeah." I shrug. "I suppose not remembering is a good thing. I'm always tired because I have nightmares about that night. I try to only sleep during the day. Lots of cat naps. The nightmares are the worst. And they scare me. A lot. The clinical term is Rape Related PTSD. My term: suck-ass isolated, napping, loser-lifestyle."

"And the guy responsible for it all? Is he in jail?"

I shrug. "I don't know who he is. I couldn't remember his name or his face. I didn't...I don't want to remember him. Any of it. I used to want that, but now, I wish that night would just disappear out of my head. We—my parents—didn't press any charges, or whatever. An 'almost rape' is nearly impossible to prosecute. I was so out of it, I guess I was partly responsible. Made bad choices and all that stuff they say not to do. Well, I did them all that night."

"Duh. No! *AND NO.* You were not responsible." I'm surprised Michelle's wiping away tears now. "Freshman year. We were so dumb, that's true. But come on. Any kind of rape is never the victim's fault. You were young—probably punier than old Porter in that newspaper article. How old were we freshman year? We were like sitting ducks back then."

"Fourteen. And cluelessly trying to be so cool. Trying to get noticed by boys." I remember the pink Converse I'd made my mom buy me for the first day of school. I'd worn them to that party, thinking they were so awesome.

Michelle nods. "Fourteen was baby-land. I was so scared freshman year...even to go to lunch. I can't imagine how you must have felt at that party. What you went through." Michelle pushes her chair back and comes to hug me. I let her. It feels nice.

"Want to know the sad part?" I ask, when she sits back in her chair.

"What you've told me isn't the *sad part*?" Michelle's face is so anguished and freaked that I have to smile.

"I've still never been kissed. It's the only thing I'm sure about from that night. The guy—he—never actually kissed me. The rest, it's all a blur. Voices. Images. Stupid stuff. Like, I have an odd seashell phobia now. I hate them. And I have no idea why."

"That's so messed up. But if you ask me, the *no-kissing* is the good part, not the bad part. As if you'd want that creeper to be on your *first kiss memory bank*. First kisses should be special. Perfect."

"Yeah. You're right." I feel suddenly light-headed, but not in a bad way! Like I'm happy. Saying everything out loud made my problems seem…smaller. That, or I feel bigger. Stronger.

Holy. I blink at Michelle.

Is this what real, live *progress* feels like? Too bad it's too late to make any sort of dent in the disaster I've made of my life.

"Jess. I can't believe—we all assumed you were some sort of stuck up, straight A—you know—a total—"

"Bitch? Yeah, I *know*. I wanted people to think that. It was easier than having to explain myself. Easier than having to make conversation. It's hard to chat when all I ever want to do is sleep. I like my reputation. It keeps me alive."

"Wow. Does Gray know all this?"

"No. Well—he knows I don't sleep at night. Not why. It's one thing to tell another girl. But Gray…" I swallow and meet her gaze. After all this honesty, I don't want to start up the lies again, but I have no choice. I can't bring up the fact that I have a signed *boyfriend contract* with her oldest friend. Even cool, like Michelle is, she would eventually tell someone. I mean to survive senior year without people finding out I paid a guy to date me.

I try to skirt around the lies with half-truths. "Our relationship is complicated. I told him I didn't want anything physical. He's respected that so far, which is really sweet. But now, I think things are changing between us."

"Aww. You really like him, don't you?"

I nod. "I'd have to tell him what happened to me. And I don't want to. I think I should break up with him before he gets too serious. Before both of our hearts get broken."

"After how he acted today, I promise, Gray's beyond serious about you. He won't care what happened. I think he's fallen for you big-time. He's never been this bonkers over any girl. Ever."

My chest constricts. "It doesn't matter. I don't think I can... you know... *kiss* and do all that other stuff that's required for the next level. It won't work. I'm like... broken now."

"Why?"

"I'm worried I'll have some sort of relapse or act crazy if he touches me when I'm nervous. And to hit the next level, I know I would be really nervous because he would be touching my lips with his, right? Hello. It makes me nervous to just say it out loud."

"Oh. My. God! Yeah." She laughs.

I blush but continue, "My therapist said with stress and PTSD, anything could happen to me. I would just die if I freaked out in public. Or, if Gray... if he ever looked at me like I were truly crazy—it would break me. I can take being called a bitch by anyone; but I can't look in Gray's eyes if he believes I'm whacked. I think I'd rather cut and run before the inevitable goes down."

"But, Jess, he wouldn't! You wouldn't react to him like that! I've seen you wrapped in his arms countless times, and you've looked completely happy about it. I'd never suspect you had any issues. I think you should go for it. Tell him. Or if that's too extreme, take a chance and kiss him once. To find out. Before you decide to walk away, you have to give it a chance. And then—even if you did go nuts—you'd have your first kiss with a boy you really like. So…it's worth it either way, right?"

My heart races at the thought of me just planting one on Gray. "No. I've already sort of flipped out on him once on accident. The look on his face afterwards almost killed me. It's why I backed off. I prefer preventative medicine to public open heart surgery. No way am I going to try and kiss that guy!"

Michelle shakes her head. "You're in love. *Open heart surgery* is how it feels for everyone. And if you're in the stage where you're both still unsure and not committed, it is scary. It also hurts like hell whether you're sane or not."

"Then, I don't think I can handle love. It feels just awful."

She laughs. "From the look on Gray's face an hour ago, he wasn't doing so well himself. He and you have matching dark circles under your eyes. You two have it so bad, it's hilarious." She laughs again.

"Thanks. You suck. But it's not going any further than this. Not for me. He wants us to be long term friends, and I guess I can consider trying that. But I have to make him understand that friends, *JUST friends,* has to be my max exposure to him. To any guy."

Michelle grins and leans back, spinning her chair again while staring at the ceiling. "My mom says everyone has se-crets—like personal demons—they have to battle. You'll just have to overcome them. I know you can. If you *try.* But it's your choice whether you chose to go to war or not."

"Pffft. Whatever. What if I'm my own personal demon? How do I battle myself? It's impossible."

"I'll ask my mom and let you know. Which reminds me, I'm supposed to pick her up. She lent me her car." Michelle stands to leave. "You're still on for ThunderLand tomorrow, right? I'm driving us. Total score. It's a minivan. Plenty of room for catch-ing up on sleep!"

I smile. Content that she knows I'll probably have to take her up on that offer. "I'm in—if Gray still wants me to go. If Gran's okay, all that. It will be a perfect time for me to talk to Gray."

She shakes her head. "Don't break my boy's heart. We can't be friends if you do that."

"I won't. I'm going to let him down easy. I just need him to shut up and listen to me."

Michelle rolls her eyes. "Blah, blah, blah. You are so far gone over him, you're never coming back down to earth. I'm hoping whatever drivel he put in that envelope will fix things, so you two can patch it up and start making out already." She winks and pulls a face. "I'm late. If I don't go now, Corey will have to drive us to ThunderLand because my mom will revoke my car privileges. And none of us want to be in that situation." She bends and looks into my eyes. "You going to be okay? You could come with me…?"

I smile. "No. I'm fine. I think I'll go home and nap so I can be fresh for tomorrow. Thanks for listening."

Michelle nods. "One day, I'll spill my own tragic, *parents-got-divorced* story on your head. Though next to yours, my story isn't even sad. It was cool of you to confide. Your *secret-demon-monkey-war* is safe with me. I'll never tell. Pick you up at eight?"

I let out a long breath, relieved that I didn't even have to ask her not to tell. "I'll be ready."

Michelle pauses at the door looking lost. "Point me out of this hole."

I laugh and point to the right. "At the end of the hall take two lefts. Follow the exit signs to the top of the stairs."

29

jess

When I'm home, twenty minutes later—and safe in my room, I pull out the white envelope and tear into it.

Jess, if you're reading this then Michelle came through.

Sorry about today—and the old-school delivery, but it's all I can do. Gran's good. Don't worry like I know you will.

Maybe it's for the best we can't talk face to face. In a letter, I can say what I need to say without your beautiful eyes distracting me from my point. Like they always do.

And my point is this: It's OVER. I mean the contract, not us.

I never should have signed it in the first place.

I can do college a million ways. I don't want the money this contract brings me anymore. My goals have changed. And not one of my goals will work without you in my life.

You. You + Me.

I'm asking you out. For real. Say yes. Take a chance, even though you'll find out quickly that I don't deserve that chance, or even deserve to be in the same room with you. But I still want that chance…want to be with you. I know you thought I wanted us to be friends. But I don't.

I want more.

Tomorrow. ThunderLand. I'm hoping it will count as our first real date.

I have much more to say, so much to tell you. But I need to be holding your hands, and looking into those distracting blue eyes to say the rest. And yes, as promised, I'm ready to listen to you. But whatever happens, hear me first and...don't hate me after.

Please. Never hate me.

It's wrong of me to ask that favor in this note, because you don't even know what I mean yet. Or why. But...this is GAME ON for me, Jess. And this letter is my first major play to keep your heart forever...so please, remember: Do. Not. Hate. Me.

Play number two is also in this envelope.

Tonight—when you're trying not to sleep—though I wish you would—I'm asking you to think about us. US. Us being together, how good we are as a team. How much fun we have as FRIENDS, because despite your stubbornness—we both know we're already that.

God, I wish I could see your face when I ask you this question. Here goes: Is there a chance you could love me? Even a little?

Because I do—love you. And I think you know that already too.

Either way, no matter what happens tomorrow—I'm not taking any of what is in this envelope back.

Love. Seriously. Love you. With all my heart.

See you tomorrow.

Gray

⋅⋅⋅

My heart's pounding. My eyes burn with tears, frustration, anger, and of course, absolute longing. How could I not be dying with *that* after reading what he'd written.

His words change everything.

Unfortunately, they also change nothing.

As much as I wish I could accept his words and his love— neither can change me into someone else. Someone different. He has no idea whom he's asking to date. If he did know the real me, he wouldn't have asked in the first place.

A boyfriend, love, and any sort of normal relationship is not for me. I'm not allowed to have that. If I were, I'd have cured myself long ago.

A second, rectangular shaped, light-blue paper is still stuck inside the envelope. I pull out the paper and open it. It's a personal check.

From Gray Porter, make payable to: Jess Jordan, the sum of $4,000.00

On the bottom left hand corner, he'd scrawled *internship payback*.

I grab my phone and text him, hoping that when he gets out of the hospital where the network can find him, he'd read it immediately.

WTF. No need to stay up all night wondering. My answer holds.

No. No. No. NO. I'm not keeping this money. Thx, but no. To all of it, no. I don't love you. You don't love me. You don't even know me. And you promised you wouldn't back out on the contract.

I'll return the check tomorrow.

⋅•⋅

It's not until much later that night while I'm staring endlessly at the ceiling fan going around and around in my room, that I finally receive Gray's reply: *Home with Gran. All is well. Not taking 'no' as an answer from you until we talk. I do know you. And I do love you. You'll see this is right. Be there at 8AM, GF.*

Before he can text me again, or worse, call me, I power down the phone without replying.

For the first time all summer, I'm easily able to stay awake all night long.

Because who could sleep when you have a letter like mine to read, again and again?

30

jess

"And who's driving, *exactly?*"

My mom's on a roll. She'd been plucking dead leaves off the houseplants and making up random conversations so she can haunt the front entryway while I wait for *the gang* to pick me up.

"Michelle. Michelle Hopkins. She's a good friend. She's driving her mom's new Honda minivan. It has air bags all over it. We'll be perfectly safe."

"And what time do you plan to be home?"

"The place closes at eight, it's about a two hour drive. I won't be past my curfew. I promise. Plus I need to wake up early to help Dad cook, right?" I add that in to keep her focused on the idea that she's going to get what she wants—*tomorrow.*

"Yes. Oh, I can't wait to meet your boyfriend. I just can't. I wish you'd invite him in this morning."

"*That* would spoil the surprise," I quip.

Kika wanders through on her way to the kitchen. She's heard my last line to Mom. She snorts once, very loudly, and keeps walking as she tosses me her most scathing glare.

Mom shakes her head and whispers, "I think your sister's a bit jealous. She's been acting very much like a sullen teenager for two days."

"I heard that!" Kika yells. "YOU BOTH SUCK! If you want to say something about *me*, then say it to my *face*." Kika slams one of the cupboards.

Mom shoots me a knowing glance. "See?"

I grimace and break Mom's gaze. Thankfully, a very shiny black minivan pulls into the driveway. I bolt for the door. "This is me...oh great," I mutter. Michelle has pulled all the way down the driveway to our porch. I'd texted her *specifically* to park out on the street. Teenagers—it's true—we never listen. Not even to each other.

"What's wrong?" Mom's followed me out the door.

Of course.

"I...nothing. I hope Michelle knows how to back up without hitting your flowers. That's all," I cover.

Corey Nash is sitting up front waving at me like an overly excited seven year old. "Let's go, Jordan! ThunderLand opens in exactly fifty-eight minutes. We ride the Super Splash first." I smile and wave back like I'm just dying in love.

"Is that *him*?" Mom whispers, smiling at Corey. "He seems *very* cute."

I answer only half of her question. "Corey's cuter than cute. It's his specialty. Bye, Mom!" I dash down the steps, knowing Mom would try to follow. I leap through the van side door and into one of the bucket seats, but the door keeps doing some electronic self-opening thing when I yank on it to close. *WTF!?*

"Drive already! Before my mom blocks the driveway," I hiss, not caring that the dumb door is still open.

"I told her not to pull in," Gray says, sounding as stressed as I feel. I shoot him look. He's lounged in the third, bench-like back seat. I'm careful not to let my gaze linger on his intense gaze. Michelle pushes a button up front and the door finally slides closed.

"See you tomorrow, *Corey*!" My mom is waving at the front of the van like a dork.

Corey, thankfully, just keeps waving back. "What did she mean about seeing me tomorrow?"

"Heck if I know. She's constantly confused these days," I divert.

Michelle carefully backs the minivan into the street.

"Jess, don't buckle up there. Sit back here with me," Gray calls out.

"God. *So* whipped. Move back there—cuddle buns. I like to make my seat go flat so I don't have to watch Michelle's lack of driving skills on the freeway." Corey reclines his chair, almost crushing me. When I don't budge, he glances back with a questioning look.

Unable to come up with a reason not to move, I weave back to the far bench and scoot next to Gray.

Corey pulls out his iPod and plugs it into the jack that connects it to the stereo. "Any requests back there?"

I try to buckle, but Gray is leaning in, apparently to scan my face. "Play something quiet. Soothing. If Jess is tired, she's going to need to nap." He picks up my hand and clicks my buckle in place for me.

"I'm *not* tired." I pull my hand away to adjust my strap.

"I can tell from your face that you didn't sleep last night. Don't deny it."

"I've got *you* to thank for that."

"Ha! It must have been that loooooove letter," Michelle pipes from the driver's seat. "And what about *your* face, Gray Porter. I can tell you didn't sleep much, either!"

I give Gray an assessing glower. He does look tired. "Hard to sleep when your girlfriend won't text you back," he says quietly.

I whisper, "I'm not going to be your—"

"Shhh. Don't start."

My hand moves to my pocket. "Wait! Michelle, can you go back? I forgot my phone." Panicking a little, I picture where I'd left the phone. I'd been meaning to plug it into the kitchen charger during breakfast, but then I forgot. Hopefully it's camouflaged within the clutter and magazines on the mail table and no one will spot it. If they do, Mom and Kika won't be able to resist messing with it.

"Heck no! We will not turn back. You can use one of ours if you need to," Michelle insists.

"Dude. It's probably for the best. Last year I dropped my phone into the Lazy River. It freaking sucked," says Corey.

"Dude. She's not a dude," Gray grumbles.

"Whoa. Someone's cranky back there." Michelle makes a face at Gray in the rearview mirror. Michelle continues, "Here's how this is going to go. Anyone who's tired had better catch up. I won't have people pooping out on me after lunch. We only get ThunderLand once a summer. So both of you whiners, snuggle up and nap it out. You know you want to."

The strains of Pink Floyd's *Dark Side of the Moon* fills the van.

"How's this for mellow?" Corey calls out.

"I love this," Michelle's voice has faded, far to the front. "Turn it up, would-ya?"

"I bet you don't love this album as much as I love Y. O. U." Corey turns the volume knob until I can't hear their conversation.

Gray quirks a brow. "I could use a little shut eye, but if you want me to stay awake, and watch over you..."

"God. Don't you dare use that voice on me. It's not fair."

"What?"

"You know how you sound when you talk all quiet like that! All low, sexy and rock star, brainwashing perfect. You do it on purpose to mess with my head."

He laughs. "You have to know you're the only one who

has ever spouted such ridiculousness. But I'm glad you like my voice." He puts his arm around me. My back is ram-rod straight. I don't know if I can take him touching me like it's normal. But I also don't know if I can take it if he doesn't. "You read *none* of my text messages last night? None?" he asks, looking deeply into my eyes.

"Honest. I turned off my phone. Then the charge died because, yes, I slept some and forgot to deal with it. So I plugged it in the kitchen during breakfast."

"And?" He raises a brow.

"And because I didn't want to talk to you—or read any more of your writing. That letter was difficult enough for me to handle."

"You aren't making this very easy on me. Do you want to read what I said on my phone? Now?" he offers, holding up his cell. "Or are you going to make me repeat everything?"

"No matter what you texted me, I won't budge. We're at an impasse. I also brought back your check," I say. But my resolve is weakening and I am unable to resist settling back against his too comfortable arm.

He sighs, looking frustrated. "Keep the check. For today. Let's just try to hang out minus the money hanging between us. It will be just us. Two people, on a date, at an amusement park. One step at a time. You read the whole letter though. Every word of it?"

"Yes. Every misguided word." I wonder if he can tell by looking at my face that I read it three thousand, nine hundred, and ninety times.

"And you do, don't you? Love me just a little? Because I'll say it again. Right now, to your face. I straight up *love* you, Jess Jordan. I'll shout it if it will help plead my case. But I have to at least get that point across before one more minute passes."

My face grows hot as he continues, "Answer. Please. It's important. Everything aside. What's in your heart—how do you feel about me?"

I meet his gaze. "I've had a crush on you from the time you told me about your Star Wars bedroom. And now I love you so much it scares me. Okay?"

"Yes! I'm so happy right now—"

"No. Don't be. It makes me feel terrible, and it doesn't change anything. I won't go out with you. I can't. I can't, and I won't."

"But you will go out with me today?"

"Yes. But today is in the contract. It's just part of the deal."

"It's good enough for me."

"I'm serious. When today's over...*we* are over. It has to be that way." I look away from the hurt simmering in his eyes, but I soften my tone. "It's too much for me. No matter how much you want it, and even if there are real feelings between us, I can't want this. Yes, I've fallen for you this summer, but I need to un-fall. So do you."

"Why?"

"We've fallen for something that doesn't exist."

"Jess...is that what you really believe?"

The sound of his ragged breathing crumbles the rest of my resolve. "No. I don't know what I mean. Let's just get through today, and we'll see," I say.

He tightens his grip on my shoulders and I cling to him, soaking up his warmth.

"Thank you," he says, and again his voice sends shivers down my spine.

31

gray

As Jess sleeps I spend my time going through the various ideas on how I should come clean. My fingers have trailed through her long, blonde hair and down the pale warmth of her cheeks until my imagination has gone mad with the smooth feel of her skin. I can't take my eyes off the little twist at the edges of her lips that make her look like she's smiling even when she's asleep.

I long to kiss this girl. I'm drunk on cinnamon and sunshine. On her...on the possibilities of us truly working something out. I've also decided to take my own advice. I will not bring up anything serious until the end of the day.

Us, being together or not, is going on hold for a few hours. When she pulls away and shuts down, it scares the crap out of me. I have this day to make her see, no *feel*, that we're right together. That breaking apart is the last option.

We pull into the parking lot of ThunderLand and Corey launches his battle cry of summer: "Honey....I'm home!"

Michelle laughs and I roll my eyes. Jess wakes up in my arms and smiles so sweetly, I think I might die. First, from wanting to kiss her even more, and second, from knowing there's a terrible possibility looming over me that I might never have the chance.

I push that second thought aside and stare at her mouth, vowing to kiss this girl at least once today no matter what happens.

"That was fast." Her sleepy, soft eyes alight with excitement when her gaze takes in the coasters.

"You okay?" I ask, remembering the last time she woke up in front of me.

She grimaces. "Stop fretting over me like an old lady. I don't have bad dreams all the time. I feel great, actually. Let's go!"

We pour out of the van. "My girlfriend rocks for getting us tickets," Corey shouts, as we head for the gate.

"I can't believe Jess has never been here," Michelle says as we pick our way through the cars in the giant parking lot. "You're going to love this place. The Funhouse is awesome. And when we're sick of rides we can do the boardwalk games. Corey! I won't rest until these girls are the proud owners of some cheap, large, horribly ugly, random stuffed animal. Last year they had giant dragons. Remember?"

"Two giant softies for the ladies. I will not fail them." Corey grins.

"I'll be winning *my girl* her own hideous animal," I add.

Michelle hands the tickets to the gate guy. She and Corey are already holding hands, so I take Jess's hand too. I hold it firm in case she tries to pull away. Encouraged when she doesn't, I stop just inside the gate.

"Guys, do you two mind if we split up until lunch? We can meet in the Blue Atrium at noon. You know, the one by the bigger Ferris wheel?" I shoot Jess a wink. "I'm going to trick Jess into going on the *couple rides*. Alone."

Corey sneaks me a knowing wink and says, "Heck yes, because I have my own plans. Remember the kiddy *Dinosaur Planet Train*? Sooner than later, huh Michelle?" He wiggles his eyebrows.

Michelle laughs. "If you don't eat three pounds of Fire Hot Wings first, like you always do, I'm in."

"You know you love me spicy," he jokes. "Jess, watch out for *Porter*. The Fairy Garden is where he leads the ladies into trouble."

"Nash. No need to give her the game beta. What's wrong with you?"

Jess shoots me a funny look. "Where's that ride?"

"It's not a ride at all. It's a contrived nature trail with all kinds of hidden make-out benches," Michelle says and jumps on Corey's back. "Now come on, we're wasting ride time."

Corey grabs onto her legs, keeping her there piggyback. "My woman much cute. Light as feather. Hot like volcano." He spins her a few times until she cracks up.

"Oh, sexy caveman…do you know where I can find the nearest dinosaur viewing area?"

"Ugga. Buga. Score! No need to ask me twice. See you two at lunch!" He lopes off, Michelle in tow.

Their sudden exit has somehow paralyzed us both.

We watch people enter the turnstiles and walk past us. It seems we can't look at each other, but at least she hasn't dropped my hand yet.

"Well—wow. This is beyond awkward, huh?" Jess says, finally.

I swallow. "I didn't mean it about getting you on those couple rides. I was just trying to get rid of them."

"Oh, I know that. I know. Yeah."

"Unless you want to?" I offer with a small, teasing smile. Only I'm not teasing.

That did it. She dropped my hand. I'm an idiot. I wonder if she'll finally punch me like I deserve.

Instead, she looks me straight in the eyes without a blink and says, "Let's start with some bigger rides first?

32

jess

The coaster roars past our place in line and we watch the people scream as they're dropped down a small set of hills and dips.

"Girl, do you ever make up for lost time. After that last ride, I'm not at all psyched to get on this again."

I laugh at Gray's pained expression. "Last time. Swear. Then I'll do the Pirate Boat, even though it's just a big, fancy, baby swing. Deal?"

"Done. But stop making fun of my favorite ride." He steps closer from behind and grabs me around the waist gently.

I smile and lean back against him, loving the way he feels so strong and solid.

We've ridden all the bigger rides in the park and every coaster at least twice. ThunderRoad, the one we're lined up for now, is best because of the creaking sound the wood structure makes as the cars fly down the tracks.

My least favorite ride so far is the Chicken Drop. A three story, rectangular metal *coop* that draws about twenty-five riders up and up in a metal cage.

Up means, two hundred feet WAY up. All while chickens cluck in the speakers by your ears every second.

At the top, a whiny farmer voice screeches, "Everyone knows chickens can't fly! Good luck *cluckers!*" The entire coop is then released into a free fall device that catches all the screaming, half dead, heart attacked *chickens* back down at the bottom. But not until it's flipped you upside down and dropped hay on your head.

Gray, who'd known full well how terrible that ride was, had laughed at my pasty faced, unable-to-walk reaction afterwards. But he'd also taken me to a bench and held me, wrapped in his arms until I stopped threatening to murder him.

The ride had sucked, but the time on that bench had quite possibly been the best twenty minutes of my life. Until the next best twenty minutes happened, that is.

And the twenty after that.

And this moment right now.

Because he's just pulled me closer and whispered, "Jess…do you know how amazing you smell?" using *that* voice.

He'd also spent over forty dollars determinedly throwing softballs at metal milk containers until he'd won me a giant, bright blue orangutan! We'd met up with Michelle and Co-rey at the Burrito Barn for lunch. Michelle had been happily toting the green version of my same orangutan. Her smile had been as wide as mine. Gotta love the boardwalk games. So fun.

After we ate, Gray had transported the stuffed animals to the minivan so we didn't have to lug them around. And, after a few rides with Corey and Michelle, we'd split up again, promising to meet at the gate at eight to head home.

Gray's only humoring me on this coaster because I told him I want to try the front seats and he agreed I should have that chance. I've never felt so spoiled and happy.

I vote this date is better than hiking, or the roller skating date. Mostly because, all day long, I've let myself buy into the idea that Gray and I could really be in love.

The fact that we've both said it has made this day simply perfect. For today. *Only* for today. I'd said that too.

I hope he listened.

To remind myself that this is all just temporary—an event with a time stamp and a price—I'd kept Gray's four-thousand dollar check in the little green bag I'm wearing. I try to look at the check after each ride. To keep things in perspective.

The guy is getting paid. I'm paying the guy. That's what's happening here today. And that's all.

It's our turn. After a few cycles, we're allowed into the first row seats. Gray draws down the safety bar over our knees. He takes my hand and squeezes it next to his chest, acting like he's holding onto it for dear life. "Why do you have to adore the most terrifying ride in this park?"

I laugh, enjoying the fact that his face is slowly turning pale and we haven't started moving. "It's not half as scary as the upside down coaster," I say.

What I'm really thinking, though, is that this ride is not half as scary as staring into his eyes right how. Because, by the look on his face, when this day is over, I'm probably going to hurt him. A lot. I'd never meant to get close enough to this guy to do that.

"This coaster is waaaaay worse," he argues, unaware of my turmoil. "The upside down one is made out of pure, strong and silent metal. ThunderRoad terrifies me, because it reminds me every second that it was made in 1936 out of soft, break-able, burnable, *bug-eatable*, rickety WOOD. You know, at any second, part of it might shatter? That would send us tumbling to our deaths. Not to mention, it was built before there were any sort of proper safety codes."

"I'm sure they have those codes in place now," I say, frowning a little.

We stare at the empty stretch of track ahead of us. Ancient, rusted track, that is.

"Oh God. I *hate* the front row. You are so going to owe me." He swallows as the 'stay in your seats at all times' announcement plays on the loudspeaker.

A long bell sounds, followed by an odd, 1936-sounding clunk!

The coaster cars release and they click-clack slowly around the first corner. The front connects to an odd pulley mechanism that hauls the weight of the coaster up the first and largest hill. That's when I, the fearless coaster crusader, start to lose my nerve.

"This pulley contraption seems to have been made hundreds of years ago, not just in 1936," I say. "What do you think?"

I can tell by Gray's face he thinks I'm teasing him. "Crap! Did you have to say that now? Relentless, cruel girlfriend!"

We both reach for each other's hands as though this were our last moment on earth.

The old chain has yank-click-yanked us all the way to the top of the first, huge drop. Gray puts his head on my shoulder and closes his eyes and says, "I want you to know if we die right now, I won't be able to distinguish if I've made it to heaven or not, because I'm already sitting here with you. Like this."

Before I can accuse him of finding that line on the Internet, we whoosh down the huge hill. Everyone's screaming, including me. We fly into the next set of hills and turns.

Gray points to the huge looking moon rising over the sea of suburban houses in the distance. Too soon, the ride shoots us into the long mine shaft tunnel that marks the end.

Gray finally relaxes the death grip he's had on my hand. I love how he doesn't let go completely as we get off the ride. When we step out of the exit, the amusement park sparkles in the twilight. And still, he's holding my hand.

Every tree, bush and ride structure has been strung with a zillion small lights. I feel strange. I'm happy, inside and out. It's a feeling I haven't had in a very long time. And it's real—every bit of it. If only I could have it for keeps.

I look at Gray through my lashes as we walk along the lit pathways.

How does he make everything seem so easy. So possible?

I waver on my break-up plan, wondering, imagining that I could truly be with this guy. As his girlfriend. Would he truly be okay with my random panic-attacks? Would he be patient and wait for me when I sleep in my car during and after school? Would he get bored, or annoyed if I could never change that? Aren't couples supposed to eat lunch together and hang out, and both be awake? Would his friends notice or catch on—make fun of me? Would I care about any of it if Gray was by my side? Defending me? Loving me? What if I'm wrong? Am I giving up too soon—failing both of us—without even trying, like Michelle said?

"Do you want to rest?" he asks. "I know you're running out of steam. Maybe we should call Michelle and Corey and meet up a bit early? We've done everything there is to do."

"Not everything," I say, pulling him along, scanning the signs that mark the way around the park. "I still haven't seen the Fairy Gardens."

He skids his feet and pulls me to a stop. His expression is tense and he can't hold my gaze. "Jess. I—we need to talk."

"We will. But first, I think… I want to, um, yeah." I bite my lower lip and nod my head. "I definitely *need* to kiss you. Soon. In the Fairy Gardens." Determined not to give him room to back out of this, I drag him through the tree-lined entrance before finding the courage to ask:

"Do you want to? You know? Kiss me?"

33

gray

"I want to kiss you more than anything."

My heart is beating in time to the leaves fluttering in the bushes along the garden's entry path.

Did the girl really just say she needs to kiss me? Soon? Now?!

"Holy wow. Beautiful!" Jess gasps. We enter the main part of the Fairy Garden where the pathway opens wider. It leads us to a giant fountain trickling through a back-lit pond that's filled with hand blown glass flowers in various colors, shapes and textures. A three foot bronze statue of a fairy with paper-thin glass wings holds court on a small island.

"This is amazing." Jess's eyes are shining bright. "Look at the ground! Her wings—everything sparkles. How did they do this?" She releases my hand and dances across the paving stones, turning in every direction with her arms outstretched. She looks every inch like she belongs in this garden with all the other magical creatures.

"It's been embedded with mica and fool's gold. I asked last year."

She frowns and regards me solemnly. "How many girls have you brought here for the sole purpose of making out?"

"I haven't come here with *you* for the sole purpose of making out," I evade, wondering if she can hear my heart.

She scrunches her nose, arches a brow, and meets my gaze dead on with her cutest challenge glare. "Well that's why I've brought you here."

I laugh. "Pinch me if this is a dream—only not just yet. If there's going to be kissing, I want to wake up after it's over."

Her cheeks turn pink as she paces around to the other side of the fountain and back. "Where do we—where do you— normally do this? Is there a *best* spot for kissing in this place? This is my first time, so I really want it to be perfect."

My heart speeds even faster. "Honest. You've never?"

"Is that a problem?" She looks away as though I've embarrassed her.

"No. But this is added pressure on me." I shake my head and lower my voice. "What if I mess it up? This is giving me a huge anxiety attack."

"*I'm* the dork who's seventeen with zero kisses. *I'm* the one who's wondering if *I'll* be able to handle this—or—or—even measure up to all of the zillions of other girls you've probably kissed in this same spot. You're not allowed to have an anxiety attack. You're the best kisser in our whole school! Everyone knows that."

"What?" I'm completely thrown off guard. "Where in the world did you get that twisted information?" I laugh.

She shrugs. "Gossip on your exploits, not to mention your kissing skills are a constant topic in the hallways. And in the locker room! Now buck up and sweep me off my feet before I bolt. No joke. I have a huge urge to run away right now."

To distract myself from how large and luminous her eyes seem right now, I take her hand and pull her along to the far side of the garden. "Weeping Willow, or stream side?"

"I love weeping willows." Her voice is almost a squeak as we duck under the long branches. I can feel her hand trembling in mine.

Thankfully, the other couple who'd been occupying the weeping willow alcove leave when we approach. I lead her to a carved wooden bench made up of intertwining leaves and branches.

"Um. So. This is a really pretty bench. Yeah. Very cool. Hand made, I bet." Her eyes flit in every direction that doesn't include me. She pulls her hand away from mine and crosses her arms over her chest. Then she uncrosses them. Then crosses them again.

I try not to notice—or laugh.

Her next words come out in a whispered rush. "I think I should tell you there's a huge possibility I might act all weird or freak out. It could happen after we kiss or even during. Okay? So, I just want you to know that. About me. Okay?"

"I know," I say, breathing a sigh of relief that I'd finally said those words to her. It feels so good that I say them again. "Jess. *I know.*"

"You know? What do you know? Am I acting too nervous? How embarrassing. Why are you never nervous?"

I reach forward and grab both of her hands. Her gaze is fixed on my lips. Her light blue eyes are shimmery as though she's holding back tears and reflecting the tiny lights from overhead. I lower my voice, fearful that she's going to run on me. "I know everything. Let's just talk. I'm nervous too. Very."

"I don't want to talk. Just, kiss me. Kiss me, right now. Then we can talk. Please. I can't concentrate. My stomach's doing these horrible twisty-flips and…your eyes are so green I can't focus…"

Before I can move an inch, Jess moves in and places her lips against mine.

I register softness, heat and the sounds of our heartbeats intertwining. Gently, I kiss her back.

I let go of her hands so I can pull her closer. Her arms go around my neck and she's coiled her fingers into the back of my hair. The soft trembling feel of her lips sends lightning down my spine. And I soar, fly, and die of happiness all in the same second.

I pull back and look down at her sleepy, half-closed eyes. "How was that?" My voice has come out hoarse.

"Wow," she whispers. "Can we try it one more time?"

Lost in the trust I see in her expression, I bring my hands to her cheeks and draw her in again. She presses her lips deeper, and I risk darting my tongue over her lips and into her mouth.

She gasps at the contact, and I take the opportunity to deepen the kiss and move my own fingers into her blonde curls.

She melts into me, unresisting, trusting. She kisses me back like she knows exactly what to do.

The back of my mind registers my favorite scent: sunshine plus cinnamon, and the idea that she tastes as good as she smells. A half second later she timidly runs her tongue along my bottom lip. This move shakes me and I disappear into sensation.

Time stands still, and we kiss, and kiss, and kiss, until I feel tears on her cheeks.

She's crying! *Crap.*

Startled, I pull away. I try to make out her expression as I work to recover one shred of my senses, not to mention some semblance of control over my body.

"I'm sorry," I whisper, horrified that I might have hurt her or scared her somehow. I try to back away even more, but Jess's arms are clamped around me like a vice. Her tear-stained face is breaking my heart. "Are you okay? Jesus, I'm such an ass. I'm so sorry. I couldn't stop myself. Please stop crying."

Her breathing is as ragged as mine. "No. I'm happy. I know

now that—I do love you—I do! You've made me feel like I'm not afraid of anything anymore. Not anything!" She smiles up at me. "It's all because of you—and that kiss. OMG. Kissing. Kissing *you*...is awesome."

She lets out a long breath of air.

I fight back the sensation that I'm tearing up too. Did she really say that she loves me? Have I finally cracked through her mask for good? I pull her legs up and over mine so we're closer and I wipe away some of her tears.

"You're wrong to credit anything to me. You're the most fearless person I've ever known. There's nothing to be afraid of anymore. Not between us. Let me tell you what I've wanted to say for the past few days. This is not going to be easy to say, but you have to know some things about me. About us."

"Okay—but first, kiss me, again," she commands. Her eyes are full of her impish teasing.

"No. You'll have to wait. Jess, I'm trying to be serious."

"No. You'll have to wait," she pleads, tightening her arms around my neck and scooting closer. "Come on, just one more?" She closes her eyes and actually puckers up old-movie-style.

I groan. "You're killing me. Stop distracting me and listen. You promised me this."

"Fine." She blinks up at my face, frowning.

I disengage my arms from around her waist and lean back as far away from those lips as I can. Which is difficult because she doesn't seem to want to let go of me. I take in a long breath, searching for courage. "How do I start? I have a lot to say."

"You're so cute when you're nervous. I love when you let me read your expressions." She peers into my face. "What? *Holy*. You really are freaking out right now. How bad could it be?"

"That's for you to decide. I guess I need to begin with when I first met you. Do you remember meeting me, freshman year?"

She shakes her head. "I think I would remember meeting you—meeting those eyes anyhow. Or your voice. At the very least, that."

"We did meet. I actually formally introduced myself to you once. Like a complete dork. It went something like, *Uh...hello...you're...uh...uh....Jess Jordan, right? Duh...duh...I'm the biggest loser in the world?* Something like that anyhow." I smile. "My voice wasn't quite changed yet. I'm afraid I still sounded like a choir soprano that year."

My chest thumps with fear, watching her face for any sign of recognition.

She furrows her brow. "There's no way. That never happened."

"Oh it happened. You destroyed me. Walked away with a, *Yeah, nice to meet you*, and you never looked back. I had such a painful crush on you back then. One I've never truly gotten over. Obviously."

Jess tilts her head, her face still shrouded in disbelief. "If that's true, then why have I never seen you at school? You don't seem the type to give up after just one brush off? Or was I that mean? Why didn't you try again? I never even see you in the hallways. Did we have a class together?"

"No. No classes. I wanted to try to approach you again, but...I...I...*Crap*! This is so difficult."

"What?! What is it?"

I put my arms back around her waist. My heart is racing so badly I can hardly speak, but I know that I can't chicken out. "Let me start over. Forget about when we met. Let me start with now—with this summer. The internship. The boyfriend contract and why I agreed to do it." I brush the hair out of her eyes.

"Okay?" She shoots me a look that tells me she thinks I'm

nuts, which is fine because I actually feel crazy right now. Crazy in love and crazy scared to lose this girl.

I start up again, hoping she can feel I'm giving her my heart and every inch of my honesty. "I never thought I'd get to have this moment with you. Let alone having just kissed you. Finally. Do you even know how many times I've wanted to kiss you, all summer long?"

"Well, that goes for two of us, then."

She flushes and looks away as I continue, "So you can see where this is overwhelming me. Tonight, with you admitting that you love me, I'm about to die of happiness. I don't want to chance losing you. I still don't. I love you so much. And I'm scared. If I tell you this the wrong way then there's a chance that you'll never even—"

A loud cough and then Corey Nash's fake, overloud, "EHEM" explodes like a bomb on the other side of the willow tree branches.

"Porter. I have to stop you there. I can't have Michelle hearing all this romantic *talking about your feelings* crap. You're seriously turning into a freak. So, yeah. FYI. We're standing right here and I bet you DON'T want us to hear this anyhow. So…this is your official, shut-the-hell-up, we've ruined your moment intervention."

Corey comes through into the alcove with a giggling Michelle in tow.

"Aww, look at you," Michelle says, smiling at me. "Sorry for interrupting."

"Your timing sucks," I say, hating them both at that moment.

"We've been looking everywhere for you two." Michelle is beaming from ear to ear and silently sending some sort of super-secret girl code to Jess. Jess unwinds her arms from my neck and pulls her legs off me. She's smiling and nodding, voicing some secret language back to Michelle. If I weren't all tangled up inside my head and about to flip out right now, I'd swear Jess had actually given Michelle the thumbs up!

"Guys. I just need a few more minutes to talk to Jess. Can we just meet you in the car? Please," I say, shooting my own super secret-silent-language to Michelle. I mouth: *Get lost*.

Michelle shrugs, her expression apologetic. "No can do. There's a possible Gran emergency. I'm sorry. It's serious."

"Gran? What's wrong?" I leap to my feet.

"She called through to Corey's phone. She just kept saying for me to find you and that you needed to come home right away. If she hadn't sounded so freaked I'd let you two have more time in the old love garden. But Gray, you'd have killed me if I hadn't found you."

"Yeah. You're right." Michelle knows me so well. "Thanks," I tell her as I pull out my phone. The monitor's gone black. "Stupid battery. What if she's had a relapse? I should have stayed home with her."

"Gray, the doctor said she'd be fine. And Gran sounded okay. Just sort of panicked," Michelle adds.

"I hope so." I turn to Jess. "We can try to talk in the car, but what I have to say should not be said in front of these two. It's private. Can you wait?"

Jess relaxes against my shoulder. "I can wait for the talk-ing part, but could we try that kissing thing again one more time before we go?" She grins. "You guys promise not to look, right?"

"Oh. No. You. Did. Not. Just. Say. That," Corey groans. "I refuse to witness your sappy, creepy conversations and public making out with my best friend." He smirks, before going on. "But if Jess wants to kiss Michelle in front of me...now *that's different*."

Michelle socks him in the arm. "You freak. I don't kiss girls, ever. Our life is NOT like what you see on TV. Get OVER that stupid show you saw, or move to New York City and see if you can find girls to kiss in front of you. And good luck with that. Do something, Gray. He's so out of line."

I stand and punch Corey's other arm as hard as I can.

Corey winces. "Bullies. Destroyers of dreams."

I ignore his glare and put my arm around Jess's shoulders when she stands and shoots me a smile. Her cheeks are bright pink and her eyes tell me she's remembering our kiss. I pull her closer.

"Have I mentioned to you two how much in love I am with this girl?" I say.

"We know, dork." Michelle laughs. "Now let's go."

"What have you done to my best friend, Jess Jordan? And when can I have him back?" Corey rolls his eyes.

"Never," Jess says. "He's mine, now."

I love the sound of that. But without finishing our conversation, I can only hope she means it.

34

jess

I have no idea how I make it to Michelle's minivan for the ride home. I can only float across the parking lot like I'm a helium balloon tethered gently to Gray's hand. My lips and cheeks burn as my mind replays and replays *me* kissing Gray! Gray kissing *me*!

Every inch of my skin is on fire. I swear I still feel his hands brushing against my cheeks, his fingers lingering on the back of my neck and running through my hair.

Kissing is amazing…weird…beautiful! Everything I didn't expect, but all that I'd dreamed about. My cheeks burn all over again. I know I've been in a constant state of 'blush' since Corey and Michelle interrupted us, but I can't seem to stop.

I don't want to stop.

"Tired?" Gray asks as we wait for Michelle to find her keys and unlock the van.

For the first time ever, I feel no need to lie. "Yes. Very."

He smiles, but his eyes are dark, troubled. I can almost see the tension radiating from his expression.

"Don't worry. I'm sure Gran's just fine," I say, hoping to calm him. We open the van door. I call out to Michelle who's on the other side of the car, "Michelle, let Gray borrow your phone to call home. He's beyond stressed."

"Yeah…hang on," Michelle says.

"It's not that," Gray says, lowering his voice. His eyes flash and cloud more. "I'm—I need to finish our talk. Really. I have to know we're on the same page here."

I brush a bold, quick kiss on his lips before stepping up into the van. "We are. I'm in. You win. I'll give it a chance. I'll trust you," I say over my shoulder. "Just call Gran first so you can talk to me without that weird, completely upset expression on your face."

I work my way past the bucket seats to the bench, grabbing the giant blue orangutan Gray had put in the car earlier. I shove the monstrous thing into some semblance of a ball while Gray makes it into the van and takes the seat beside me. "I love my new pillow. Thanks again for winning him."

Without a word he squishes the awkward stuffed animal half onto his lap. "This time, you buckle into the middle. I'm your pillow too. If you can't accept that, the monkey dies a terrible death."

Pleased, I rest my head on the monkey and lean my weight on Gray. I've never been so aware of how long his legs are. He smells like limes and warmth as usual. But this time he's got a cotton candy tinge coming off his shirt. I sigh, feeling completely safe and unbelievably comfortable. Happy, all over—again. I kind of want to scream. My heart is whirling like a pinwheel.

OMG. I kissed Gray Porter and it was AWESOME. And he's my boyfriend!

Michelle starts the car and turns to toss her phone to Gray. "We probably won't have signal until we get closer to Denver," she says.

He catches it with one hand, leaving the other entwined in my hair. "I thought you said Gran called Corey's phone. If there's no signal—how did the call come through?" Gray asks.

Corey pipes up, "We were making out in the SkyChair—it's the only place that gets signal. We were at the turn-around point. Gran ruined my 'hand-up-the-shirt-move'."

"Corey! Can't you just tell them we were enjoying the view?" Michelle says. "As for your *move*, I sure didn't notice it."

"Oh, it was in full play. I was about to let my fingers enjoy the view of the lace on your shoulder strap and *then*, I was going to check out that little spot on the side of your neck that my lips like so much. And *then* I was going to look for more lace and try a little—"

"Shut it! Or you're about to enjoy this ride home from the bumper."

Corey laughs, totally unashamed. "What? A guy can dream."

"As long as you keep them to yourself. Otherwise, my dad will be happy to help you adjust the dreams you have regarding me and the lace on my underwear any time."

One of them turns up the music, drowning out the rest of their flirt-argument.

I sigh again. Enjoying the moment, the warmth of Gray's body so close to mine, and the goose bumps travelling up and down my arms. Gray's hand—the one that had been playing with the ends of my hair—has wandered to my cheekbone. It lingers there a moment and traverses the length of my shoulders so he can gently rub my neck.

I completely relax. It feels so wonderful...

...

Nothing happened.
Let's get out of here.
You're a very lucky girl...lucky, lucky girl.
"There's someone in here."
The man's voice is far away.
Suffocating white is the only thing I see.

My stomach flips and rolls with nausea. I need to find some air that's not overheated. Everything begins to spin. I try to roll over, because I think I might vomit, but I can't seem to move very far. Confused, I stare up at my arm. It's caught—*tied*— above my head. On the other side of the white thing that's suffocating me.

My hand kills, and I can't move.

I pull down on my arm hard as I can.

And I remember. I remember. Pulling doesn't work.

I'd already tried to pull my arm free hundreds of times. My latest attempt has finally cut into my wrist. Now blood is staining the sheet above me. My blood. On the sheet.

That's what the white is…a sheet. A sheet…

I stare at the long trickle of red that has soaked through. It's dripping a slow a line down my arm. I hear the voice again: "Appears passed out. Wonder what the hell happened in here…"

"Help," I croak. The back of my throat feels shredded—like it's been hit with a blowtorch. "Can you please get me out. Untie me. Please. I want out."

I look down at myself and realize I'm only wearing panties. No bra. My cheeks are wet like I've been crying for a long time.

Shame, panic, and absolute dread solidify the lump in my throat until I'm choking.

The fear has me frantically pulling at my arm again. I don't care that it hurts. "I'm over here. Is anyone there?" I call out again. Why won't my legs move? "Please…"

I hear keys, the clash of metal, and a strange, noisy static sound growing louder. Light hits my face like a punch, and I cringe against it as the sheet is pulled off me.

"What the—!" The policeman's voice is so loud it cuts through the air like pointed knives.

Cold slams into me and I close my eyes. I'm only able to turn slightly away from the police officer.

"You're safe now," he says. I feel the sheet come quickly back up to cover my nakedness, but he keeps my face clear of the fabric.

Only I wish he wouldn't.

I wish he'd hide my face. Make it so I can't breathe again, because now, I think I want to die. I don't want to talk to him.

I don't want to be here. I don't want to be here!

"Young lady, can you tell me what happened? How old are you? Do you know your name?" The voice is kind, but the reflective flashes of light glinting off his badge, his handcuffs, his belt buckle, and even from the small snap that hold his gun in place make it hard for me to find his face when I open my eyes again.

The static buzzing increases and blips. I realize it's the officer's walkie-talkie, which is right next to my ear. He kneels next to me, and shines the light right in to my pupils, then on to my tied wrists.

"This is O'Connor. I'm requesting female officer backup ASAP. Upstairs—master bedroom. I have what appears to be a 261 or 261A."

More loud buzzing, and then, a metallic reply: "Pulling up outside." It's a woman's voice. "Can you hold for two? Over."

"Will hold. Request ambulance to scene. Code 50. Basic transport. Victim is conscious and breathing. Wait for possible injury update."

"Ambulance dispatched," a third voice runs through his radio.

The officer leans closer. I can finally register his face. He looks worried. He's older than my dad. His eyes are kind. Safe.

I'm safe. Safe. He said I was safe.

All that I've been holding back—the pain and my fear—

washes over me and I start to cry again. "My arm," I moan. "I—I'm going to be sick. My arm and my hand—it hurts so much. Please help me get my arm down."

"Stay calm. Do you know where you are? Can you tell me your name?" His hands move to the knot tying my hand to the bed.

"Jess. I'm Jess Jordan. I'm at the Peterson's house. At a party."

"It's a flipping necktie," he mutters, letting go of my wrist. "I'm going to have to cut the knot off with my knife. Are you okay with that? Can you hold completely still?"

I nod. He pulls out a large, black pocket knife and slices through the knots. My arm flops next to me like it's not part of me anymore. It takes all of my concentration to pull it under the sheet. It's so numb I can only register the weight of it pressing onto my bare chest.

"That looked pretty bad." He holds my gaze. His eyes are scanning my face. I look away and see my clothes heaped in a clump near his feet and my head starts to spin all over again. "Are you hurt anywhere else? Have you been raped?"

"Almost, I think. Almost," I whisper.

"You sure?" His voice lowers. "I'm assuming you weren't tied like that of your own free will?"

"No." I cry harder. My arm is slowly waking up…it's pins, needles and knives. Thousands of them, all at the same time. I groan as the room spins above me.

He sniffs at the half-empty glass beside the bed. "This is pure vodka. How much have you had to drink tonight? Do you remember if you took any pills? Smoked anything?"

"No. No. I drank those lemonade things downstairs. And I didn't feel good. He—a guy—told me if I came up here where it was quiet I'd feel better. He told me that was water. He *made* me drink it. And then I couldn't move at all." I'm gasping for breath between sobbing. "He made me drink so much of that,"

I gasp. "He...*said I was...*"

He said I was beautiful.

"Who was it? I need a name. Who brought you up here?"

"I don't know. I thought he was nice."

I lean over and vomit on the carpet. On the officer's shoes.

On my tangled, inside-out, brand new, blue shirt that's crumpled in a heap next to the bed.

"Shit!" The officer moves back. "Okay. Okay. Breathe slowly. You're okay. I'm thinking you're a very lucky girl. You're going to be fine. Nothing happened. You're going to be just fine."

He walks into the bathroom and returns with a small, silver wastebasket lined with a pink, powder scented plastic bag and places it under me.

I vomit again—this time all over the wads of tissue at the bottom of the basket until there's nothing left. "I need to go home...but I can't move my legs."

"Okay...hold tight. We're going to get you out of here by ambulance. There's a possibility you've been drugged."

I stare, and stare, and stare at the seashells next to the bed in a crystal bowl.

I make myself believe that if I stare long enough, I might wake up a second time at the beach and none of this night will have been real. This is all just a dream. The room spins all over again.

A dream. A dream. This is all just a dream.

I tell myself this over and over until my voice chanting these words is the only thing I hear, and the seashells are the only thing left in the room.

A second officer, a woman, enters the room.

She bends next to me, blocking my view of the seashells in the bowl. More questions.

I try my best to answer: "Jess Jordan. Fourteen. No. Didn't smoke. No needles. No pills. I live on Ridge Road. Number 55. I don't know. He made me drink something. He had brown hair, black eyes…and he was tall. Really tall, and so strong. Too strong. He made me…*he said I was…*My mom's cell? 443-8763."

The first officer comes close again, his face still apologetic. Sad. His voice has turned gentle, but he says it again: "She's a very lucky girl. You *are* a very, very lucky girl."

"You are honey," the woman officer agrees.

I close my eyes.

Am I? A very lucky girl?

I'm done talking to them.

…

Lucky. Lucky. Lucky.

Lucky girl.

The memories wash over me.

My hoodie being unzipped and pulled off.

"It's pretty hot up here to be wearing that," he says, laughing after I'd choked back half of the acid tasting drink he's forced down my throat.

He smiles as though he hadn't just been very mean. As though we're friends. My upper arms ache where he's still gripping me. "There you go. Have just a little more."

He pours it down my throat again. I try to not swallow. My t-shirt front is drenched. I cough, and some goes down my throat. I push at him and try to stand—to run—to hit him, but instead, I fall onto the carpet with a thump.

That makes him laugh. "Whoa there. That's right. Give it a minute to settle in."

He reaches toward me and pulls the hair band out of my pony-tail while I'm there—lying on the Peterson's beige carpet.

"Nice," he says, running his hand through my hair and pulling it out around my face.

I try to stop him but my hand is now made of wood. It only moves a few inches and then stops at my hip.

"You're almost there. I'll get you some water," he says.

He smiles and pulls me up, depositing me onto the bed easily as though I'm a rag doll. He's whistling as he walks into the bathroom—like everything's normal.

I manage to drag myself up and hold onto the bed frame. My eyes are on the door, but I can't move toward it. He returns, but not with what he'd promised. He looks into my eyes as though he's looking for something; but I can no longer register his face, or what he looks like. Where I am…and possibly…even who I am fades away into the buzzing that's filling my head.

All I can see is a swirl of black eyes and a strange, knowing smile that I don't like at all.

He pulls my blue shirt up over my head, then, my cami. My bra comes next.

"No." My voice is only a whisper. My limbs won't move.

He touches me…and I am not able to stop him…and I can no longer see his face…

"I'm going to make you feel really good. And you're going to make me feel really good. It's going to be fun."

"No. No. I don't want this. Please," I moan, managing to push his hands off my body and I sit up, but he easily pushes me back down.

"Shh…shhh." That's all he says while he ties my arms to the bed.

The only apology he makes to me is that he's sorry he'd taken too long trying to decide which of Mr. Peterson's neckties he should choose.

Blue. They're blue ties. Both of them.

He peels off my jeans.

God, how I want to scream because his hands are rough, scraping against my bare skin. I turn my face away from him. My parents and the Petersons are friends. This is their bed. This is their son's party. I'm supposed to be at a sleep over down the street. Not here! Everything is in its place, but I'm not supposed to be here. We snuck out...I'm not supposed to be here. And I want to go home.

Dark wood, dark fireplace, dark furniture, dark eyes on the guy who won't stop touching me.

There's a painting of windswept dunes hung on the far wall.

And beside the bed, Mr. and Mrs. Peterson's bed, are polished, purple-tipped seashells glowing, translucent and fragile in a crystal bowl. Beside the bed. Beside the bed where I'm being touched and I can't move.

Seashells...

His hands work to tug down my underwear. He steps away from me for a second and I think maybe he's going to stop. But the light glints off of his silver belt buckle, and I know enough to understand what's next.

I try to scream again. Move. Nothing works.

A crash and a door slamming into a wall has us both looking to the sound.

Someone is in the room. "You need to stop, right now!"

"What the hell? Dude. Get out!"

"The police are heading in. Someone tripped the alarm or something. There's three squad cars outside."

"Seriously? Damn. Back out of here. I've got time."

"No. No." My voice makes it to the surface, released from the dry leaves that were holding it hostage. "Please, no," I whisper, as my gaze searches for the person connected to the shadow by the door.

His voice cracks when he says, "Stop. Dude. Stop. This is going to blast you off the team in every way. I thought you had a scout coming next week. Just walk away."

"Look at her. She might be worth it. I'm about to explode. She's not even fighting me. She's so messed up."

"That is the doorbell."

"F—ingGodDamn!" He walks to the window and I can finally breathe in because he's away from me.

I feel some motion returning to my limbs. I want to get my arms free. To run. I pull against the ties, but the exertion exhausts me. The other guy walks nearer.

Mortified, because I'm naked, I close my eyes.

"Dude. She's cut on this arm. What do you mean she isn't fighting you?"

"Well—she wasn't complaining. Maybe I'll ask her to prom. Have a do-over. You know her?"

"Yes—I do. And I recommend you stay the hell away from the girl you just tried to rape! You asshole."

A loud crack rings out as a sheet unfolds and floats above me. It hangs suspended in the air for what feels like forever, finally draping over my nakedness.

"You're a brave one, for a ninety-pound newbie. Come on, calm down. Nothing happened."

"Piss off, you bastard." The new guy paces around the bed.

"Nothing happened…plus she won't remember. A guy I know gave me some stuff for her to drink. She won't even be able to place my face or yours. Shame to waste it all for nothing, though."

"Crap! What have you done?"

Hands. Different hands. Shaking. Shaking exactly like mine are shaking. They pull on the tie holding the arm that hurts the most, but when it won't budge, he moves around the bed to pull at the other.

"Crap! These things are not budging."

"We don't have time. Let's just get out of here."

"Hang on. You're going to be okay," he whispers to me. One knot comes free and my hand drops onto the bed.

I can't do anything but cry as he tugs on my other arm. I am not okay. Not. Okay. The new guy is getting upset. Shouting now. Not at me. Maybe for me. I don't know.

"She's practically comatose—we can't just leave her here—not like this. You can bet your ass if she doesn't remember, I'm going to fill in the holes. You are going down! If you think I'm not going to tell, you're delusional."

"Whatever. It will be your word against mine. I didn't do anything. Maybe I can say you did all of this to her. Try to tell on me, and I'll crush your dumb, loser, freshman ass in every way."

"Do your worst, and I'll do mine. You drugged a girl and tried to rape her. Has that registered yet? Or have you done this before you fucking-felon-freak! I'm going to make sure you rot for this."

"Does Coach Williams know you're this much of a squealing baby? Let's go. C'mon. Leave her already. I'm not getting caught in this room. She'll be fine. I lost my head. And maybe this was a bad idea. Either way, nothing happened, right? I don't know what I was thinking and I didn't go through with it. Just—come on. Nothing happened."

"Help me untie her other arm first."

"If you don't leave with me now, the whole team will have to sit out the next three games. And state. Isn't that why you came in here—to warn me? One for the team?"

"I'm not here for you." He speaks to me then, his voice is low… scared…angry. "You're going to be okay. You're okay. Jess, I'm so sorry. I can't get his knot out. I don't know what to do."

I stare at his anguished, golden green eyes. "I didn't. He made me—"

"Jess…I know. I know. I'm sorry. I'm so sorry."

"Porter. If you don't walk out of here with me, then I'm going to pin this whole scene on you."

"Don't leave me here. Please. Don't leave me here alone," I whisper.

He lets go of my arm and steps back. "I'm sorry, but I—I— you're going to be fine. The police are outside. I'm so sorry…"

Their footsteps fade. The door closes. And I'm alone.

I command my free hand to move. After a very long time passes, I manage to pull my underwear back up. Then, I yank at the arm that's still tied to the bed.

When it won't budge, I stare and stare at the seashells.

I tell myself, over, and over, and over again that this is all a bad dream.

A dream. A very bad dream.

...

I wake up gasping for air inside the van. Silent screams fill my head.

It's all I can do to keep them inside.

For now. Hold on. Hold on.

Nausea floods my body; but I keep very still, striving to get my bearings. The van is silent and my skin is covered in a light layer of ice cold sweat. Gray and Corey must be asleep. Streetlights flash through the window. The stop-start-stop motion of the van tells me we're off the highway.

I remember. I remember.

I realize we're in my neighborhood.

Almost home.

Almost raped.

Almost. Almost.

I unbuckle and scoot into one of the bucket seats. I need to be as far away from Gray Porter as I can possibly get. My head spins double-time. I grab the door handle and pull hard, but the safety locks hold it closed. "Michelle. Stop the van. I need to get out."

I hear Gray wake and shift in the seat behind me. "What's up, beautiful?"

That stupid word triggers the panic. It hits me like a bomb.

"Don't call me that. *Never* call me that," I yell. "I said stop the car. I need to get out."

Michelle glances at me through the rear view mirror. "But,

we're almost to your house—just hang on—"

"STOP THE VAN. NOW. I NEED TO GET OUT. NOW! NOW!"

Gray sits forward. "Jess. What's wrong? Jess!" He places his hand on my back just as Michelle swerves to park.

I hit the button that opens the door. "DON'T TOUCH ME. DON'T TOUCH ME. EVER. EVER. Oh my God. OH MY GOD."

I fling myself out of the van. He's following me. I run a few feet down the sidewalk before the nausea wins out. I double over and vomit into the street.

Gray, Michelle and Corey catch up. Gray's already squatted down next to me and is trying to pull me into his arms as another round of nausea takes over. I scream and kick and punch him away.

"No. No. Don't touch me! Don't let him touch me. Michelle, please. Don't let him touch me. Please. Don't ever touch me again! I remember. I remember YOU!"

Gray pulls his hands away.

I vomit again. I can hear Corey's voice somewhere near. "What do you think's wrong with her? Too much candy?"

"Tell them. Tell them," I choke out.

When Gray doesn't answer, Corey whispers, "Dude. Gray. What's going on? What is she talking about?"

Michelle sits next to me on the curb and puts her arm gently around me. I put my hands over my eyes, trying to stop the crying and gather some strength from Michelle. She helps me to my feet. "Was it one of those dreams you say you have?"

"Not a dream. A memory. I remembered."

I notch my chin up as high as I can and I make myself look at Gray.

I want to watch his expressions while I say this. "Freshman year, I was at a party and a senior—*a senior hockey player* almost raped me. He took me upstairs after calling me beautiful. He forced a bunch of laced vodka down my throat. Then he tried to rape me. And Gray was there."

Gray takes a step back.

"And you saw. And you *knew*," I sob, crumbling again. "Why. Why didn't you tell me? Why have you known every single second of the worst night of my life, and I'm only finding out tonight. WHY? God. You knew for *years*."

I look wildly at Corey and Michelle. "Did you know too? Michelle, when I told you about it the other day, did you already *know*?"

"No. I didn't. I swear," Michelle says, darting Gray a questioning glance and I sense with some relief that Michelle isn't lying.

Corey's looking at me as though I'm two steps from a straight jacket. It's pretty obvious this is the first time he's heard of it as well.

"Jess…" Gray's voice is shaking. "I promised your parents I wouldn't tell. And then, I was afraid that I was going to lose you. Please, let me explain. I did try."

The world under my feet falls away as his words register. "*My parents*? My parents knew about this—YOU? MY PARENTS KNOW YOU?!!"

"Coach Williams knows also," Gray answers.

"No way," Corey mutters.

"Do all of you also know the name of the kid who did this?" Gray nods.

"No wonder you didn't want to meet my parents. Were you *trying* to make me crazy? Was all of this some kind of sick joke?"

"No. God no! Jess, don't think that. You said you were going to hire another guy to be your boyfriend if I turned you down. I couldn't let you do that. If you'd gone public with that ridiculous checklist—I thought, because I knew about you that I could keep you safe from more gossip. And I wanted to make up for what happened to you."

"You wanted to make up for what happened? You jerk! You can never make that up."

Corey barks out a laugh and crosses his arms. "I knew something was up. You're not even her real boyfriend? She hired you? Man...this is freaking *epic*."

"Shut the hell up, Corey!" Gray shouts, walking nearer to me. "Jess, I thought I could help you. And, at first I wanted the job and the money. But then, you turned out to be so awesome. It was fun...and...I never knew we'd fall in love. But I did want very much to be your friend. I still do."

I wish I had some sort of immunity pill I could take against his cajoling, now evil sounding voice and perfect face.

Damn his green eyes.

Tremors from the dream begin to take over. I pull out the envelope that holds his check and throw it at his feet.

"You thought you could *help* me?" I ask, slowly, not at all trying to hide the desperate tremors and tears in my voice. Let them all hear it. It's not like I can fall any lower than what they've already seen. "Oh, you helped me all right. I've been hearing your voice inside my nightmares all summer long. And screaming in my bed at night because of it! Don't you get it? I thought I was going crazy. Really crazy."

"I didn't know. Why didn't you tell me? Say something?"

"Because it's none of your damn business! Or at least I thought it wasn't. But maybe it IS. You suck! And I don't love you. I take it all back. I don't even know you!"

"Jess...if I'd known—"

"What? You would have made up better lies?" I look up at the darkened tree branches overhead and bite back a scream of anguish. I gather my thoughts and quaking body and draw strength from my absolute fury. "How could you have written that beautiful letter?" Tears are falling unchecked down my cheeks. "How could you have kissed me like that? When all the time you knew." My voice cracks. "You knew that we could never be. All along, you've been lying?"

"I've never lied. I just couldn't figure out how to tell you the whole truth without losing you. Without hurting you. I could not bear either option."

"You had no right to do what you did. You had no right!" I scream, hardly recognizing my voice. A porch light near where we'd parked flips on. My heart crumples to the size of a marble. "God. You just lost me. And you hurt me. Beyond belief."

"I...." He lets out a long breath.

"Let me help you get back to the van. We'll all go to your house and talk this out," Michelle offers.

"Jess, please, Michelle's right," Corey starts in. "We—you guys can work through this."

"No. No. This is *so* over. This whole summer. The internship, all of it, OVER. Send my regrets to Mr. Foley. I won't be coming back to work. I won't need his letters of recommendation, either. Imagine what the dorm monitor would think of me? Screaming in the hallways every night is not a good plan for academic success."

I manage to laugh a little then—not wanting them to see any more of my complete devastation. I ratchet on what I hope looks like an uncaring sneer. "Michelle, Corey, you two should be equally pissed off at Gray, and at me. We've been playing you all summer, more than you know."

"What?" Corey frowns.

"In case Gray decides to withhold information from *you* like he did from me, I think you should know that we added you two into our contract. You were an added value-pack. Like a *friend-bundle*. He probably owes you some money for your time. Make him pay you. You both did an awesome job."

I smile at all of them, and force my tone to scathing. "Oh, and before you write me off as a complete lunatic and buy into Gray Porter's *broken heart* act, you should know one more thing about your best friend."

I walk right up to Gray. This time my gaze into his eyes is unwavering. "Tell them. Tell them what you did at that party."

"Please. Don't do this. Not after what we said to each other tonight. Come on, Jess. You don't know the whole story."

"Oh, I think I do. And, if we're sticking to the truth, then you can correct me if I'm wrong." I blink and step even closer so I can see his face under the street light before I continue, "Tell me it wasn't you in the nightmare I just had. Say that you weren't there," I whisper, letting my gaze memorize every line of Gray's face. The dark curls on his forehead, his wide shoulders, the chin divot—and those terrible, lying lips.

I press on, "Tell me that I didn't beg you to stay with me in that room. That you didn't cover me with a white sheet like I was some sort of corpse. I was alone, afraid, naked, and tied to a bed! And you left me there after I begged you to stay. If you can say that person wasn't YOU—*then*—we can continue this conversation," I gasp out, working to control my breathing and the next wave of tears welling up inside my whole body.

The whole time, I make sure to never waver from Gray's green-gold gaze, wishing with all my heart he will deny what I've accused. But I know the truth. I know these eyes and every stupid gold fleck inside each one. I've seen them in my nightmares for so long.

Dr. Brodie said I'd know when my memories were real. *And I know.* I choke back a sob. *Oh God. I know.*

A tornado of emotion crosses his face. "It's what happened. That was me. I'm sorry."

Michelle gasps.

Gray seems to be shaking as hard as I am. He holds his hands out like he wants me to take them. "Jess...please. We've got so much—"

I put my hands over my ears. "Stop. Just stop! Don't you see? I've hated you for three years! Every single time I've had that nightmare, you've been in there. In my head! I've hated you all along. Hated you for years. And now, after this summer I—I—"

My legs almost buckle as the enormity of my whole summer with him becomes clear.

"Oh my God. That letter. You totally *knew* I'd hate you. How could you possibly think I wouldn't?"

"I had hope." He drops his hands and looks away.

I turn my back on all of them so they won't see how badly I'm crying now.

And I run.

35

gray

Nobody moves until she's disappeared.

"*Shit*. Porter. What the hell? Should we follow her?" Corey asks.

I'm just able to get control of my breathing. I don't want to bawl like a baby in front of them. "No."

"Is all of that true?" Michelle whispers.

"And then some. She has every right to hate me forever. I totally suck. I was a selfish bastard." I shrug, crossing my arms, trying to absorb some of the pain thudding through my whole body.

"You never told us *anything*," Michelle says, sounding half pissed, half overwhelmed.

"Like I said, I'd made a promise not to talk about it. I keep promises. The entire thing was so messed up."

"Obviously," says Corey.

I shoot him a glare. "And if you ever tell anyone what you know about Jess's past, or the contract. Or any of this entire summer, I'll personally shred every ounce of your stinking ass—"

"I won't. Jesus. I won't, you freak. Chill." Corey balls his hands into fists. "I should be royally pissed that my own *best friend* had me so out of the loop. I feel like I'm looking at a stranger right now. You took her money even though…wait a minute! Gray…holy shit." Corey lowers his voice to continue, "*Jess Jordan* is why you quit the hockey team? Why you got your ass kicked freshman year?"

I look away. "It wasn't directly her fault. But yes."

Corey goes on, "You're the best ice hockey player in the state, you have no team and no scholarship money. And it's all because of that whacked-out girl?!! And you *still* set up a deal where she'd be your *girlfriend* for the whole summer?" Corey whistles. "Like I said, I think I have no idea who you are. Dude, you're insane."

"Corey. He's not. He's in love. Didn't you hear him?" Michelle puts her arm around me. "I'm so sorry. I can't believe Jess would strike a deal like that in the first place."

"She was desperate." I push her arm away. Annoyed they both seem to want to blame Jess for a situation that is my fault.

I have to make them understand. "Her parents weren't going to let her go to college unless she could prove that she'd finally become 'better' or 'normal' or whatever lame prerequisite they came up with for her. I found out about her plan and signed on. How could I not? Knowing what I knew, I felt obligated to try to help her. She didn't remember me. I thought it would be okay…until I wanted more. This is my fault for wanting what I shouldn't have wanted."

"She wanted it too, Gray. She told me so." Michelle says.

"Whatever. It's pretty clear she's not even close to normal," Corey says, looking as shook up as I feel.

"Don't ever say that about her. She's perfect. You got to know her pretty well. Aside from her being tired all the time, she's the most amazing person I've ever met. And you guys liked her too. So what if she has bad dreams? Everyone has something. Doesn't mean they can't still be awesome."

I feel completely empty and worry Jess must feel the same. Worse. I put my hands on my face, and groan.

"Crap! Crap. And Crap! I let her down in so many ways at that party. And tonight I just let her down again. *Crap.* Do you think there's any chance of me ever getting her back?"

"Maybe you can catch up to her in some hospital mental ward, because that's where you're heading dude, if you try to follow up on this one."

Michelle steps between Corey's face and my fist just in time.

"Guys. Do not have this fight. Let's go home before we all do something we will regret."

"You mean something *else*," I say.

36

jess

I stop running when I reach my front steps. I sit, taking in a deep, very quiet, breath. Rather than fight against the dream— the memories—I do something I've never done before.

I welcome the voices, the images, the sounds, and the smells from the nightmare. From the worst night of my life.

I play it over. Sifting and sorting it into consecutive order until the entire memory solidifies and makes sense. Start to finish.

I even piece together what my parents said at the hospital that night. Every word uttered when they thought I'd been asleep is now burned into my brain.

...

Mom. Crying: "The doctor told me nothing happened. She doesn't remember how she got upstairs in that house. They think she might have been drugged. But we'd need to test for that."

Dad, next. Shouting. Accusing: "No. No tests! What's the point? They pumped so much alcohol out of her system she could have died. She can't even remember who's to blame for this. She lied to us. Jess is lucky as hell. Lucky as hell! I hope she learned a lesson."

"She was almost raped! What lesson is there in that?" Mom, sniffling again. More tears.

Dad. Angry. "We've told her how to behave! We've told her not to drink, and that parties are not allowed. The first chance she gets to walk out of our house as a high-school freshman and she pulls this stunt? She put herself in the wrong place at the wrong time and this is what happened."

More sobs. Mom falls apart. "I can't believe she was almost raped."

"Almost. Thank God. Almost. Nothing happened, right? Honey…you know I don't blame Jess. I just want to kill someone. Our poor girl—"

And then, a sound more terrible than any of the others: My father, crying.

"Poor Jess. Poor Jess. What she must have been through. I hope she doesn't remember. They said she might not. I hope that's true. I never want her to remember. I just want her to be fine."

...

I wipe away my last few tears and pull in a long breath, wondering how long I'd been sitting out here. Wondering if I'd missed my curfew yet.

As if that matters anymore. I hope my parents ground me forever. The safety of my bedroom is all I want right now. I swear I'll never leave this house again.

My entire body feels hollow.

I can't feel my heart. I can hardly feel myself.

I slowly open the front door and walk into the entryway. Mom peeks out from the kitchen, as though she'd been sitting in there waiting.

"Jess. That you? I didn't hear a car pull up," she says, walking closer. "How was it?"

I don't try to hide my tear stained face. At least I don't have to pretend I'm upset. I need this to go quickly, so I pull in a long shaking breath and say, "Oh, Mom."

The tears start falling all over again.

Mom ramps right in. "Honey! What's wrong?"

"I walked from the corner. We—it's over. We broke up."

"Why? I thought things were going so well?"

"It's me. I couldn't deal with it. It was all just moving too quickly. He and I are too different."

I can tell by Mom's expression that she's completely on board. She hugs me. I have to admit her arms feel wonderful. I cling to her, wrapping my arms tight around her and hold on for way too long. And then, I remember what I need to do.

"Mom." I pause and sniffle again, pulling away. "Will you tell Dad? The barbecue is going to have one less guest. And I'm sorry. I just want to go to bed."

"Oh, honey, of course. I'm so sorry too."

I cringe at those words, and head up the stairs. More tears rain down. I make no attempt to wipe them away. The lingering smell of lavender and the warm feeling from Mom's hug has me stopping and calling out to her just before the landing.

"Mom?" I turn back; she hasn't moved. "Tomorrow, if you have time, I really want to talk to you and Dad. I need to tell you some things. Some major things. Some are not so good."

Mom's face brightens. The expectation in her eyes almost blinds me. "Yes. Of course! Dad and I had wanted to talk to you tonight, about your boyfriend too. But now, it's late and Dad's sound asleep on the couch anyhow. Maybe morning is best. We'd be happy to hear anything you want to tell us."

"Good," I answer, feeling slightly lighter that at least I hadn't lied on that last one.

I stop in the hall bathroom to wash away the sticky, drying tears with cold water before I brush my teeth. When I reach my room, I quickly put on the softest pajamas I own, throw my hair into a bun, and head for my desk.

Without even pausing, I take my final college application essays and throw them in the small trash can under the desk.

Maybe I can apply to some online school…

No matter how I try not to think of Gray, I can't purge all of the terrible things I'd said. How he must hate me now. I'd sworn to hate him. But I don't. No matter how hard I try, I can't.

I also can't blame him for leaving me alone that night.

He'd just met me, after all. Or…I think he'd just met me. Sadly, I still can't remember meeting him. I wonder if that moment will be erased forever. Gray had tried to tell me about it. Now, I'll never be able to know the rest of that story. I picture Gray as a freshman, all scrawny and puny. I *must* have blown him off like he'd said.

I pull out my yearbook from that year and flip to my photo. I'm amazed at how young I'd been. I looked a lot like Kika does now. I'd been sporting a major set of braces too. Plus I had some big attitude that I was a complete *woman* who could handle anything. Even sneaking out to parties—drinking and talking to *upperclassmen*.

My thoughts tumble, and my head begins to hum and spin as my endless tiredness sets in.

All I want to do is close my eyes and fade into blackness.

I stand and pace the room, fighting the sleep monster. The monkey on my back. I'm so tired of having this war with myself.

My gaze scans all of the things that usually make me feel better after I've had the nightmare. First, I watch the plastic jellyfish bobbing aimlessly up and down inside my lamp. They swim and twirl in the changing colored light, but they bring me no comfort because I've realized—even my pets are fake!

I sigh and move to study the movie posters: Mr. Darcy with his hand on Elizabeth's cheek does nothing for me but make me want to spit. He might love her, but for his whole life, Mr. Darcy means to be who he is—just an endlessly cranky dude.

Edward Cullen, with his arms protectively around Bella while Jacob glares at them, makes me want to puke. And they named their baby *Renesme?*

PLEASE. Worst. Name. Ever.

Jack and Rose from Titanic have me clenching my fists.

Rose should have ditched him day one. If she had, she would've been fine never knowing Jack and all his electric passion for life, all his love for her.

Romeo and Juliet seem like idiots to me now. They knew it wouldn't work out. Romeo should never have gone back to her balcony. It was his stupid fault. He KNEW. If he had simply not tried, they both would have lived. And who drinks stupid poison to solve problems? Lame. Pathetic. All of them.

The faces in the posters seem to be mocking me back.

I should not have tried, either.

Who hires a stupid, fake boyfriend to solve problems? Huh? Huh? Oh, I know. A lame, pathetic person like me, that's who.

I've been an actor just like them, all summer long.

Stupid stories. Stupid summer. Fiction. All of it. Not one shred of it real.

I peel the BBB, *Boys in Books are Better* bumper sticker off my wall and scrunch it into a ball. I've learned one thing from all this though: Boys in books are not better.

Not better than Gray Porter holding my hand.

Before I can register what I'm doing, I've reached up and pulled out the tacks on the Pride and Prejudice poster. I watch it slide down the wall and curl onto the carpet. I pull down the next, and the next, until all are down and rolled up in the closet. I do my calendar photos next. Then all of the torn out magazine pages of characters from films who have stolen my heart. Everything—until my walls are completely bare.

As I admire my work, I'm feeling better, like I can breathe. I'm well past the point where I should be counting. For the first time ever, I don't bother. That's when I realize I'm actually not *afraid* anymore.

I'm just pissed. Also, I'm annoyed and tired. Minus my usual shake-and-quake crying party!

Finished with the walls, I head for the jellyfish lamp and unplug it. The LED back-light fades out and the silicone jellyfish stop swimming blindly in circles. In seconds, they float to the top with their tentacles spread wide like they're dead. Even turned off, they're too freakishly realistic. It's not right.

I grimace, wondering why—or how—I ever liked this stupid plastic lamp at all.

I walk the thing to my trash can and pull my college essays back out. Gingerly, I place the lamp at the bottom of the basket so none of the water leaks out. But I don't put the essays back in. I close my laptop and push it to the side of the desk. It almost covers the long, scratched-in column of 'nightmare numbers'.

Tomorrow, I'm going to sand them away. I can paint the top of my desk over, and rearrange this entire room. I'm done counting. So done falling for fictional guys. At least the ones *I've* made up, anyhow. I'm also done with nightlights too. And I'm officially done being afraid I might have a bad dream!

Bring it on.

Hugging the college essays now, I walk over and stare at my bed. My heart pounds with a small anxiety surge as my bravado fades away.

Am I really not afraid anymore?

I admire my beautiful, sage green comforter…the soft down pillows.

The clock reads 11:37 PM.

Can I do this? Can I just crawl in?

I already had the nightmare while I was in the van. I've never had it twice in the same night. Besides, it's not like I will ever go through an episode bigger than the ordeal I survived after the van ride.

Vomiting aside, I think I handled it well. *Or not.*

I shake my head. *Whatever.*

I set my essays on the bedside table, and bravely clamber into the bed, pulling the covers up to my chin. The warmth and softness of the blankets envelope me.

I feel strong. Again, I acknowledge I'm not one bit afraid!

Not of myself and not one bit afraid of falling asleep! Nor am I afraid of what might happen if I do.

I pull in a deep breath.

The nightmare holds no power over me anymore. Now that I remember, I feel like I'll be able to handle it when, or if, the nightmare ever comes back.

I flip off my light and stare at the empty walls, imagining how I'm going to place the furniture tomorrow. I'll ask Kika to help me with the bed, and ask Mom to help me patch the little holes my tacks left in the walls. Maybe Dad will help me with the sander. *After* I apologize to them one hundred more times, of course. And, when really Kika's speaking to me again, I'll tell her every second of my summer. ThunderLand. The contract. How I got my first and last kiss, and how bad it feels to have my heart broken.

I sigh and turn on my side, already planning to re-hang my Pride and Prejudice poster, because...well...I might have gone a little overboard. Poor Mr. Darcy...

And maybe, if I'm ever done being grounded, Mom will let me get a little goldfish or a couple of those tiny swimming frogs. They're cute...and real and alive...novel idea, that. Pets being alive...

❖

I wake to the sound of Dad calling up the stairs, "Jess. Wake up. We need you down here."

It takes me a second to recognize whose room this is—that I'm in my bed, under the covers with my head on the pillow. I've slept the whole night. And I feel pretty good, except the part where my heart hurts really bad.

My stomach rumbles as the smell of Dad's hot maple syrup hits me at about the same time the memories of last night sink in.

Here we go again, back to square one.

Same old, same old.

As I swing my legs out of bed, my gaze lands on my college essays packet and my heart speeds up. I realize suddenly that I feel pretty good.

And that nothing feels the same. Nothing at all!

Yes, I can feel the weight of my broken heart; yes, I'm about to get permanently exiled when I tell my parents what I've done. But the sun is shining across the bare walls of my room. I slept in my bed all night long, and I've trashed my jellyfish nightlight!

More importantly, I don't feel one bit tired, not one bit afraid of what I have to do today.

All this, and I've remembered. Everything.

I grin, and walk out of my room.

37

jess

As I hit the bottom step, I hear a low rumble of voices along with my mom's higher pitched whisper. All coming from the formal dining room that adjoins our large front hall. I roll my eyes, figuring my parents must have invited people over for Sunday brunch. They always do that.

Figures. I've got tons to say and now I'll have to wait.

Worse, could they not have warned me? I'm still wearing jammies. How embarrassing. Turning quickly, I move to escape back up the stairs to change, but my mom sees me first.

"Jess. Good." Mom's face looks pinched. She also does not have the supportive, sympathy-filled look I'm expecting after our shared *moment* last night.

It only takes a few seconds to decipher the reason behind the attitude change: Mom's holding my iPhone. From the look of the currently lit monitor, it's now completely charged. And I can tell from here she's in my text messages.

So much for the fleeting minutes when I thought I wasn't afraid of anything anymore!

My mind reels with the possibilities of what she's read. I have no idea what's on there.

If Mom has read any of the conversations between me and

Gray, then she's probably seen awkward *love* messages he'd sent after the hospital. Messages that I haven't even seen yet!

Those aren't a big deal because they'll seem legit. They'll back up my too-fast-too-soon break up story. *But Holy.* Who knows what madness that guy might have tried to text me last night? I'm sure he couldn't resist sending something.

Which means…if they saw those messages, then I've been scooped.

I *need* to read what's on that phone to get my story sorted out.

I go for a *calm* expression combined with a steady voice. "Oh, you found my phone. Great. Can I have it?"

"Not so fast. Your sister plugged this in for you this morning. It went so crazy with incoming messages, your dad and I thought it had been taken over by one of those virus-things."

Kika is coming down the stairs behind me, but stops on the third step from the bottom as though she's too afraid to approach. I dart her a glance. Has she told? If she has, then that changes my story even more! But if she hasn't…if she's just standing there to listen to me confess like I promised then…

My eyes are drawn to a movement by the dining room door. *Holy. What THE F-oh-no. No. No. No.*

A stressed-looking Coach Williams steps out of the dining room trailed by my father.

"This is just perfect," I say. "Perfect."

I push past my mom and turn to face them all in the front hallway. "Couldn't you guys at least have talked about *me* in front of my own face?"

Coach Williams clears his throat. "We'd only just begun. That's why we called you down."

"Does this mean we aren't having pancakes?" I ask, shaking my head at Coach Williams and working to cover the extreme anger that's threatening to blow to the surface.

Not counting Kika, these *people*—people I trusted—have been lying to me for years.

I speak to Kika first, deciding to play this straight. "What have you told them? What do they know?"

"I didn't tell them anything. It was your phone that started it all." Kika shrugs, her face a mask of tiredness and stress.

"Your sister refused to say anything until we woke you up," Mom says. "Coach Williams just got here. We called him because he is very well acquainted with Corey Nash." She holds up my phone. "This morning—because you were so upset last night, I read your text messages. All of them. I'm concerned, honey. From what I read, things were getting too serious. Is that why you ended things with Corey last night? Did he pressure you to do something you didn't want to do?"

"You broke up?" Kika asks, her tone hopeful.

I almost laugh. My parents still don't even *know!*

I risk a glance at Coach Williams. I can tell from his darting eyes, and his uncomfortable throat clearing that the guy could easily be prepared to spill it.

I'm going to need to divert him and talk first. I decide to use the typical teen tantrum to buy myself time: "My messages are private. *Private!* How could you have read my texts?"

Mom responds right on cue. "We've always told you girls that we'd check your texts and emails if we felt as though you'd been lying to us. And Jess, we think you're doing just that. The way Kika's been protecting you makes me sure of it."

I flick my eyes to Coach Williams. "And what about *my favorite teacher?*" I know he's heard the sneer in my tone. "Does *he* think I'm lying? What has *he* told you, exactly?"

"Nothing. Yet," Coach answers, confirming what I'd thought.

My dad is next. "Honey, this kid seems to be pressuring you." I roll my eyes because Dad's using the 'good guy' voice.

"It's obvious that this Corey's fallen for you. Which is not a bad thing. But from what your mom and I can tell, you seem to also have feelings for him. We don't think it's a good idea. For someone like you—with the past you've lived through—you're—"

"Don't say it, Dad. I know I'm a lost cause and I can't have a boyfriend but I don't need to hear it from you!"

Dad shakes his head. "No. That's not what I mean. Let me finish."

I meet his gaze and shrug.

Dad continues, "For someone who's been through what you've been through, you've got to really be careful and honest with your boyfriend *as you go along*. Maybe you haven't actually lied to us, but you've kept some information from us. And Mom and I hope you haven't done the same with your boyfriend. I called Coach last week and asked him a few questions about this Corey Nash and he told me Corey was a nice kid, so that's good."

"You did what!? You were trying to get the scoop without just asking me? *Dad!*"

Dad shrugs. "You've been pretty evasive. I only called Coach to ask his opinion on the guy. I was curious."

"About *Corey Nash*?" I say, almost laughing. I risk some guarded eye contact with Coach Williams. "They called you, about *Corey*? And you knew what you knew—but you didn't tell the whole story? Why not?"

Coach speaks to me as though the others aren't in the room. "He wanted the chance to tell you first. Told me he loves you. Said he wanted to tell you so he'd be there to catch you if you freaked out and fell off the deep end. He didn't want you to find out alone or from anyone else. And most importantly, without him there to help you."

"Oh I freaked out. And then I fell, Coach. Major. And nobody caught me or helped me. Not my boyfriend, and not my parents—that's for sure."

I dart an accusing look at Dad. "I fell hard. Crashed and burned, if you want the report straight from the lips of your *crazy* daughter."

I feel tears welling into my eyes as I remember Gray's hands dropping to his sides as I screamed for him not to touch me. Is that what he'd been doing? Trying to *catch* me? I push all thoughts of him being anything but my enemy away. I can't think of him. Not now.

Dad's turning all purple and he's shouting at the top of his lungs. "What does that mean? Coach, what is there to tell? Someone say something that makes sense. What in the hell is going on here? Jess, start talking—your mother and I have already assumed the worst."

I pace into the front door alcove and look out at our lawn.

"Fine. I've been lying to you all summer," I say.

"I knew it," says Mom.

I turn. They're all waiting, arms crossed like a jury that's already found me guilty. Well—I'm about to flip it. This is my trial against them, not the opposite like they think.

A whisper is all I can muster for my first accusation, "You've been lying to me too."

Coach Williams shifts his feet. My dad looks away. Mom's blinking really fast.

I move closer and muster more courage, more decibels for my voice. "Dad…what have you assumed would be the *worst*? Between me an my boyfriend—what's your definition of the absolute *worst*? I'm curious."

I can tell Dad's pissed but trying to keep it together. He humors me with an answer. "My worst, Jess, would be that your Corey is some sort of player who's taken advantage of you. I read the guy's over-the-top declarations of *texted-love*. And, frankly, I'm suspicious as hell. You say you've broken up with him; but his last two messages were sent less than an hour ago. And he's been apologizing for how much he hurt you since last night? Did that kid hurt you?"

My heart twists. And I can't speak. Think. Breathe.

Did Gray hurt me? Did he ever really hurt me? Never.

Not once. I think it's been the opposite.

I imagine Gray's gentle smile. The endless concern for me in his eyes. Even before I'd proposed the stupid contract. How he'd thought he was waking me up so I wouldn't miss the interview—even though he knew exactly who I was. Yesterday, his hands were so gentle. And his lips. Soft and urgent, but so careful against mine in the Fairy Grotto. Then the pain in his eyes as I screamed in his face. Told him I hated him.

I hurt him. Not the other way around.

It's all I can do not to cry.

I solidify my expression into my default *bored* look and concentrate on breathing.

Dad shakes his head at me. He's annoyed because he thinks I'm not responding to him on purpose. As usual, I want to tell him it's not that, I simply can't open my mouth right now or air will hit the back of my throat…and then we'll never get to finish this conversation.

Dad tosses a glance at Coach Williams. "Coach will confer that high school guys are schemers. You know what I mean. My worst, *Jess*, is that you've fallen for this silver-tongued devil. And you don't want us to know how far things have gone. If he hurt you then I'll—"

"Stop. *Dad.* I'm a senior. Not a middle-school kid." I've got control of my tears now, and I realize I'm blushing. "This type of *parent-speech* is way too late for," I pause to nail Dad with my best glare, "—*someone totally messed up like me.*"

"Jess, don't you speak to your father like that. Answer our

questions," Mom yells.

I shake my head. "What's the question? Holy! Are you and Dad actually asking me if I've *slept* with this guy? We're going to talk about how many bases I've been to, in front of Kika and Coach Williams?" I bark out a laugh. "I suppose it's fitting that Coach knows the details of my summer make-out session. Because he knows all my other exploits, don't you, Coach? Why not the new ones?"

"*Jessica*. You are out of line," Dad says.

"Am I?" I turn to Mom whose face has opened up in shock, like she's registering what I've just said. I press on, "Let's just get one thing straight before we continue. *My boyfriend*, treating me badly, or pressuring me, is the least of your worries."

I hold Coach's gaze next. "*My boyfriend* never even tried to kiss me until last night. And I had to make the first move to get him to do it. Which didn't go so very well because all he wanted to do was *talk! Talk, talk, talk*!" I fling my arms up in the air. "The *talking* part, not the *kissing* part, is why he's now my ex-boyfriend."

"What?" Dad's sputtering so badly now, I almost feel sorry for the guy.

I continue, "I fell asleep in the car on the way home; and I had my nightmare. But this time—it was not a foggy dream. It was minute by minute. I remember everything. Like it happened yesterday." I cross my arms and look around the room. "And I know that you lied to me. All of you!"

"Oh, Jess. We didn't lie!" Mom gasps.

I have to work to keep my face straight because I want to crumble. Have the world's biggest tantrum and hate them all. But I don't do any of that. I'm trying to fill up my emptiness with something—with someone—new.

I want to be the girl who's done hiding her feelings and lying and being lied to.

When I speak again, my voice is calm and resigned. "I'm kind of hungry, but before we eat, let's all just take a moment to fill each other in on the truth for once, shall we? Who wants to start? Mom? Dad?"

Neither parent seems to be able to meet my gaze.

"Coach? Kika? Or should I carry on?"

"I'll start." Kika sniffles. "Jess isn't dating Corey Nash. She's dating a black-haired, green-eyed, tall guy. A guy named Gray Porter. Corey Nash is Gray's best friend and he's dating a girl called Michelle," Kika chokes out.

Mom's put her hand on her heart and her eyes have gone wild with worry and disbelief. "Gray Porter? Gray Porter!! *That's* the guy on the text messages? Impossible. Tell me it's impossible."

She paces across the entryway toward me. I avoid her and her probing gaze by crossing to the opposite side.

"It's no wonder you've had such a huge relapse," Dad adds.

"You knew my nightmares had returned?" I ask, incredulous.

Dad nods. "You'd said you wanted us to back off. We were trying to respect your privacy. Waiting until you came to us. A mistake, obviously."

"You seemed so happy in all other aspects of the summer. We thought you were learning how to work through things on your own—" Mom starts.

Kika starts crying. "I thought I was the only one who knew. Why didn't you guys tell me you knew? I was so worried about Jess."

"You kissed *Gray Porter*, yesterday?" Dad's ramping up again, his arms are flinging around like he's some sort of octopus. "That little punk! Gray Porter? Holy shit." His eyes go wild and he looks at Coach. "I'll murder him."

"I won't let you," Coach shouts. "Gray had Jess's best interests at heart. And he does love her. I believe him."

"He's seventeen. What does that kid know about love? Jess is not allowed to be in love with that kid. And you—YOU KNEW!" Dad moves before anyone understands what he's doing.

He shoves Coach Williams by the neck until he's pressed up against the wall. One of our family photos tips to the side and then slides down with a crash. "You knew who Jess was dating when I called you the other day? I'll murder that kid, but first I'll kill you right here!"

Dad slams Coach into the wall again, and Coach Williams pushes back. Hard.

Dad goes flying clear across the entryway, but starts back toward Coach like he really does mean to kill him!

"Daddy!" Kika screams, hysterical now.

"Stop. Stop. Stop!" I shout. "You're all acting crazy."

Dad trips and falls with a thump at the foot of the staircase. He makes no move to get up, just shakes his head and stares at me. "What the hell? Jess—did you really date Gray Porter all summer?"

"Dad. It's not what you think. I *paid* him to date me. I didn't know who he was. Not at all. He never told me. I met him at the interview. It was me that offered to help him get the paid internship, but only if he agreed to be my summer boyfriend. You and Mom wanted me to prove I was 'better' only I wasn't better at all. Gray needed the money. He didn't hurt me. He didn't hurt me once."

My heart hurts as I walk to sit next to my dad. "He tried to be my friend. He even tried to give me back my money, long before he ever tried to kiss me. He's good. He's honorable. I'm the one who sucks. He tried to tell me everything. I wouldn't listen."

"That kid promised to never approach you or speak to you

again! What in the hell was he doing trying to tell you any-thing?" Dad's eyes are filling with tears. If he cries in front of me I'm going to lose it.

"Why would you make such an agreement with anyone?" Mom interjects, voice shaking.

I glance at her. "Why would you make Gray Porter promise not to speak to me? Why would you and Dad *hide* the details of what happened to me three years ago? You gave me no names. Why did you and Dad not let me be tested for drugs in my system? That guy put something in my drink and you knew it."

"Jess…it was a complicated decision. We had so many reasons not to pursue prosecution. We wanted to protect you," Mom says.

"Well I had reasons for what I did too. I want to go college. I thought if I could pull off what appeared to be a 'normal summer' including a boyfriend, then you guys would back off, stop the helicopter parenting, and let me go. I want some sort of life, messed up or not, I want to move *on*."

Mom takes the now sobbing Kika into her arms on the staircase, while Dad struggles to his feet and helps me up. He shoots a pointed glare at Coach Williams.

Coach Williams glares back.

"It's my fault. This was all my idea," Kika pipes in. "I made Jess a 'How to Be Normal' checklist before the interview. It was a joke. One of my suggestions was that she land a boyfriend. I never knew she'd use it. This is my fault. Don't you see?"

My heart clenches. "This is nobody's fault," I say. "Isn't that what you all have been hammering into me for three years? This is nobody's fault. It's pretty clear we all did some stupid stuff, and we all lied. Or didn't tell—or whatever. But it's all about what happened three years ago. I finally believe this is nobody's fault. Not even mine. I could blame you, Mom and Dad, and you too, Coach, for the whole summer. Three years ago, you should have told me everything. If you had, I'm certain I would never have asked Gray Porter to sign onto my scheme during that interview, that's for damn sure."

Mom starts sobbing harder than Kika.

"We couldn't tell you. It was too terrible. And since you didn't remember anyway, we thought we were helping," Dad says.

"I know, Dad. But if any of you are holding back other secrets about Gray, or that night, then I want to know. I deserve to know," I insist. "It's important. Please."

"Gray Porter offered himself as a witness to your attempted rape. He even confirmed you'd been drugged because the other kid told him. But your therapist and the police advised us not to prosecute," Mom says between breaths.

"Why?" My heart sinks and I'm flooded with a new wave of anger.

"Gray's offer made legal action possible, but you were so depressed. Our attorney said you wouldn't be a credible witness. You had no concrete memories of the event, and because you'd been drinking, we were told the other attorney would tear apart your reputation."

Mom chokes up so badly she can't say more.

Dad continues, "We didn't want to drag you through the courts—we didn't want you to have to face kids talking about it at school when you didn't remember the events yourself. We thought it best to leave it all alone. No one knew what you'd been through besides all of us, the bastard who started it all— and Gray. But he promised to keep your secret," Dad says.

"And the guy who did it? He—never even got in trouble? How did you shut him up?" I ask Dad.

"Our attorneys worked it out. If he'd ever approached or spoken to you we were on standby to prosecute. After the team won state and the kid signed to a university, they moved out of state. No way was anyone in that family going to talk. Not with the kid's college hockey on the line."

"I couldn't kick him off the team, but you can bet I tried," Coach adds. "Your family would've had to fill out a school district *incident report*. A report that would have exposed the details of that night; but again, even the report might not have held any weight. It all happened *off* school property, and you didn't remember." Coach sighs. "The kid denied everything, of course. His parents hired one of the best attorneys in Denver. The school superintendent told the principal that if I continued to make noise, I'd lose my job. I had my family to consider," Coach mutters. "And Gray, well he—he went through a lot after that. He hated me after the file was closed. Hated everyone. Hated hockey."

"Oh my God. Oh my God." I imagine the puny version of Gray Porter confronting my parents and Coach because of me and that night.

I meet my sister's gaze and whisper, "You were so right the other day, Kika. I suck. I completely suck," which only makes her start crying all over again.

"Gray—he got beat up—because of me?"

Coach nods.

I put my hand over my mouth to stop myself from crying as I remember the magazine article and what Michelle had told me about Gray quitting the team. The realization of what he gave up hits me. "He needed the money from the internship because he has no scholarship money. Because of me. Right?"

"I wouldn't go that far," Coach says. "Gray made his own choices. I've offered him a spot on the team every year. He just hates me too much to accept. He's got a great heart and he's a talented kid, but he's also stubborn as hell. I won't let you take the blame for his bad choices, Jess."

I let my own tears crash in. Gray has every right to hate me. Double hate me. Only he'd sworn all along that he loved me—that he'd been trying to protect me—that he simply wanted to be near me. To help.

"Oh, guys. I treated Gray so badly. I said so many terrible things. I told him—I told him that I'd hate him forever. But I don't. I don't hate anyone…I don't," I sob.

Dad takes me into his arms. "Honey," he croons, wrapping me up into a bear hug. I sniffle against his shirt, while I get control of my tears. "Jess, you were so young—you're still young to me and Mom. After—you were like a wounded bird. We only wanted you to forget. Hell, we all still wish for that."

"But none of us can forget, can we?" I ask, looking up into Dad's face. "It happened, and none of us are ever going to forget. It's made us all—even Gray—completely different people. I'm so tired of everyone blaming everyone. I want it to be over."

I pull away from my dad and sit heavily on the bottom step.

Dad follows suit. "I'll never be able to forgive the kid who did this to you. To all of us," he says. "I can't."

I meet his gaze. "I want you to try. Mostly, I need to forgive *myself* for lying to you guys when I snuck out. I need to forgive myself for getting drunk that night. I need to forgive myself for being stupid enough to believe that jerk when he called me beautiful. I need to forgive my body for not being able to move after he'd drugged me. I couldn't fight him, you know? I hate that the most. I was wide awake, and I couldn't move."

"Oh, Jess," whispers Mom.

"Mom, I've hated myself for that part of it for so long. I don't want to do that anymore." My voice cracks.

Tears course down Mom's face. "I'm sorry—for everything. If there's anything else you want to know, I'm here."

I meet her gaze and resist my ingrained habit of keeping her at a distance.

I don't paste on any practiced expressions. Though it feels strange and a little scary, I go with what's real and smile through the last of my tears. "No. I'm good. I'm really good. I think the only fact I don't know is the guy's name. And I don't want to know it. It doesn't matter, does it?"

"No," Dad says. "As long as you're fine with that, it doesn't matter. He's long gone."

"I promise never to lie again. If you guys can consider trusting me again—after you get over being mad about this summer?"

"We will consider it, Jess. Apology accepted," Mom says.

I smile again. "There is one *good thing* I have to mention about all of this. I finally believe what you've been saying all along. That I was lucky. Lucky I wasn't raped. Lucky that Gray stopped it."

"Jess, you don't have to talk about this," Dad says.

"No—let me finish—I need to be clear with you guys, but also with myself. I was almost raped, and you all lied to me. I got an internship, and a fake life, and I lied to you."

I stand and look at each of them and smile wider. "I'm actually happy right now. It sounds crazy, but I'm even happy Gray couldn't figure out a way to tell me the truth all summer long. I can hardly believe I've meant something to him from the start. You know? Any other way might not have worked. And he meant it—he means it. I hope he means it. Do you think he still does?"

Everyone's looking at me like I'm crazy—that's nothing different—but this time, I'm crazy in love—not just plain-crazy, and it's the best feeling I've ever had!

"Jess. What's your point?" Dad asks, his gaze moving rapidly between me and my mom. "I can never understand the girls when they get like this. What's my next move? Do I pulverize some poor boy named Corey Nash, or kill Gray Porter? Does she like him or hate him? What do you want us all to do?"

I walk over to Mom and hold out my hand. "Mom, I really need my phone—so I can read Gray's messages. I also could use some advice on how to approach a guy without offering him money to hang out with me. And Dad," I rush on, before Mom can answer. "Do you think—if I can get Gray to agree— do you think we could still have that barbecue this afternoon?"

"Whether he agrees or not, honey, the grill will be on at four."

"And you promise not to kill anyone?" I ask, raising my brows.

Dad shoots me a small smile and a nod. "Coach, you up for one of my chili burgers? I believe I owe you an apology and a beer or two...or three."

Coach lets out a long breath. "I'm in, but we're only good if you let me buy the beer."

My mom and I lock gazes. "The phone, Mom. Please."

She sighs and hands it to me. "You have one day of reprieve. But tomorrow, you'll turn this phone into me, and you will inform Gray Porter—friend or foe—boyfriend or not—that you are grounded. Deal?"

I throw my arms around her neck and hug her tight. "Deal. Thanks, Mom." I pull away and quirk a brow to my sis. "Kika, I'm going to need a checklist, an outfit, some make-up and a huge squirt of that peach lotion to get me through this. I can't do it without you. Please. I'm sorry I ruined the summer."

Kika still looks wounded but then catapults herself into me and we hug. "We still have a few weeks to turn it around. And now that you're grounded we can catch up on the lost time," she says. "Let's eat, and go Google 'how to fix your break-up'. I can't wait to meet your boyfriend," she adds. "No way any guy would turn down a second chance to date you."

"Please." I laugh. "I don't want to wish for too much after all I said to him yesterday. But at the very least, I hope he wants to still be my friend."

38

gray

We're all gathered in Gran's front sitting room watching the clock tick. We usually aren't allowed to sit in this room. I actually avoid it. But today, gathering among dangerous, spindly-legged furniture, breakable glass thingies, and the spotless white couch feels simple compared to what we're about to do.

I survey the arsenal of people I've assembled to crash Jess's barbecue.

My first weapons: Corey Nash, overdressed on purpose in his dad's blue blazer and a hilarious button-down shirt. Michelle Hopkins is equally decked out in a flowered dress, and low heels lent to her by Gran. The wicker purse is a bit much, but Michelle swears it will work as a decent whacking tool before I'm caught and murdered by Mr. Jordan.

I'm also dressed like a grandpa going to church on Easter. My button down shirt and blazer are in place, only I've chosen slippery polyester for mine. Hopefully, when Jess's dad gets his hands on me, I'll be able to squirm out of this lame outfit before he can drag me away completely. And I mean to be standing in front of Jess and talking fast when that happens.

Because that's the goal.

Corey and I have practiced the, *"Hello, sir. I'm Corey Nash,"* introduction with Michelle standing in for Mr. Jordan over twenty times.

As we go in, I'm going to huddle up hidden behind Corey and Michelle. When they're in full talk-mode, I'll slip around them and try to gain access into the house and search for Jess. If the "shake and howdy dash" doesn't work, I'll have another excellent weapon in place: one screaming little old lady with a fake cane and a flowered hat.

I just dare Mr. Jordan to match wits—or cane moves—with my grandmother.

Gran, now fully recovered from her hospital stay, has agreed to back me. Even if that means she has to fake a stroke on the Jordan's front porch in order to let me have my chance to talk to Jess. She's currently passing around a plate of her lemon cookies and fretting over exactly what she's going to do if Mr. Jordan actually does hit me.

"I'll smack him right back, Gray. No one hurts my baby boy," she says.

God, how I love Gran.

"It won't come to that. Don't worry." I toss Gran a confident, lying smile. What if this doesn't work? What if Jess refuses to see me?

My phone starts buzzing and lights up on the coffee table. "It's from Jess! I can't believe it. She's texting me back."

My heart twists when I read her message: *Do U h8 me 4 what I said last night?*

Michelle and Corey crowd around the phone.

Gran is only two seconds behind them. "Gray, what does that gibberish mean?" She's leaning on my shoulder to get a better view.

"She wants to know if he hates her," says Michelle.

"Poor little dear," says Gran.

I don't move the phone away while I respond: *Have I not*

made that clear. *I don't—won't—can't hate you. I love you. R U ready to talk?*

The phone dings back quickly: *No. No more talking.*

My temper flares as my heart rate increases from total frustration.

We will. I'm on my way. And we R going to talk—this time with MOS DOS.

NO!! NO!! NO MORE TALKING. IOTP. KO KO!

I share a glance with Michelle. "What in the hell does that mean?" she asks.

"No idea," Corey answers.

"It means she's relentlessly stubborn," I fume, shaking my head and pulling away. "I'm going over there. If this goes badly, I'll be back for you guys. I need to see her, *now*."

I search for my keys in the basket by the door with one hand while I awkwardly thumb-text: *Translate: IOTP and KO? Plze. I don't understand.*

"What about our plan?" Corey asks. "You need us."

"Like I said. I'll circle back and get you either way. Please hang tight just in case."

Not finding my keys in the basket, I head to the kitchen and scoop them off the counter. Racing through the living room, I toss a half smile at Gran and meet the gaze of a very worried looking Michelle. "Wish me luck?"

"Luck."

As I whip open the door, my phone buzzes and dings again.

I read her reply as I run out.

IOTP=I'm on the porch.

KO=Kissing only.

Then we can talk.

39

jess

The door opens and Gray careens into me with a loud, "Oooof!"

He's so huge, he' knocks me back. The door slams behind him so quickly it sounds like a gunshot.

His phone goes flying. "Crap!" he says. I catch a glimmer of his surprised green gaze flickers over me as my iPhone shoots out of my hand and lands somewhere behind me. I try to track it, but that move puts me even more off balance.

I'm about to fall off the porch steps. I fling my arms out, searching for the railing, but the back of my hand connects to Gray's chin with a crack instead.

He says something again that sounds like, "Ouwff*crap*oof."

I hold my breath, grasping for anything that might stop my fall. All I see is the concrete landing and wonder how it's going to feel when I hit.

Gray dives at me and crushes me against his chest, breathing fast. "I've got you. Oh my God. I've got you! What are you doing here?"

My nose is pressed flat into his shirt. My *Kika-arranged* hair has fallen in a mass cluster over my face. His arms suddenly tighten around me to the point I can hardly breathe. I cling to him harder than I should, but I can't help it.

Is the wild thumping I hear coming from my heart or his?

"Uh…" I say, finally, when after a long moment he still hasn't moved to let me go. "This is not at all how I'd imagined this conversation. And believe me, I'd actually planned for a few scenarios. Practiced them in front of a mirror too," I add, breathing in his warmth.

"Ditto. I also wrote a script."

"Please." I laugh and look up. He's smiling down at me through my tangled hair. "Gray. I'm sorry. Can you ever forgive me for what I said?"

He pulls me closer. "You've got it backwards. If only I could replay the whole thing. Please, accept *my* apology. Forever. I'll always be sorry."

"I do. I do. Okay? That's why I'm here. And I want to apologize right back for not understanding. For not listening."

"Well, you're going to listen now." He takes in a huge breath. "How is it you manage to always smell so good? Is that the peach pie stuff again?"

"To be exact, it's cobbler. And well…you smell like limes and…happiness to me." I feel suddenly shy and my voice wavers even more. "I came for one of those—those. Um. You know? Make up kisses? I heard that's what you do when you have a fight with your *boyfriend*. If, you are….actually…still my boyfriend?" I hold my breath.

He breathes into the top of my head. "Hell yes. Yes!"

"Hell yes you'll kiss me? Or hell yes you're my boyfriend?"

"Both. God…Jess…both." He hugs me tighter.

I try to pull free, wanting desperately to see his face, and I realize my hair has become so tangled into the buttons of his shirt that I can't move my head more than two inches away from his chest.

Of course I can't.

"I'm stuck…my hair is caught on your buttons," I say into his shirt. "Are you wearing a suit?"

He pulls back. "Wow. It is stuck. And—I'm wearing a blazer…yeah."

"Ouch. Easy…" I grumble as I feel hairs pulling out.

"It's bad. Hold still." I can hear the laughter in his voice. His fingers move into my hair. I'm actually glad he can't see my face because I'm still processing the fact that Gray Porter's said he's my boyfriend! Which means *I'm* Gray Porter's girlfriend!

His fingers move to the button near my nose. "I kind of like you stuck to me like this."

I quip back, "Good. Then get used to my moves. I have hundreds of ways to keep you tethered. I take the words 'old ball and chain' very seriously. From here on it gets ugly."

He breaks the last strands of my hair free and, for the first time, I'm able to look at his beautiful green eyes. He smiles down at me and caresses my face. "I was hoping you'd say that."

I reach up to loop my index finger gently through the curl on his forehead that's always out of place and move it up high with the others. I let my hand fall softly against his cheek, feeling the roughness of his morning beard against my palm, while my thumb explores the divot in his chin and my eyes travel to the strong curve of his lips. "I *need* you to kiss me. Right now. Please." I know I sound desperate, but I don't even care. All I want is some assurance that this moment—that *we*—are real.

My heart races when he leans in. Faster and faster. Our gazes tangle and I read his expression. It matches what I'm feeling: longing, mixed with happiness.

My heart soars and I lean toward him too.

"Not yet," he pleads with a long, shaky breath and places his hands on my shoulders. "You got to kiss first yesterday, and it caused pure chaos and confusion between us. I can't have you melting my mind with those lips, and then expect myself to have any sort of coherent conversation. And stop looking at me like that until I say what needs to be said."

"Are you serious? I'm not going to beg you twice..." I blush and look away.

Gray laughs. "Buck up. I'm still under contract and according to *that* document I'm not allowed to kiss you at all." He reaches into his pocket and pulls out an envelope flashing the contents to me. It's full of hundred dollar bills and a copy of our contract! "No more checks for you to destroy. Take this cash. It's yours, and then tear up the contract."

I make no move to touch the envelope. "I don't want that money. You—you need that for college. You are not changing any goals just because me."

"It's important. I want the contract ended. Taking your half of the money from the internship is the only way to make it fair in my mind."

"Yeah, but you earned it fairly. You don't even really know what this—what *we* are. And we sure don't know how things will work out. So...maybe I like the contract as is. We could re-write it? Add that we're dating on a trial basis, and then you could continue getting paid. Because we are both going to finish working the internship, right?"

He raises his brows. "I'm calling your bluffs from now on. We both know exactly what is between us, and how it will work out. We don't need a paper to bind us together. You *love* me, Jess Jordan, and I've been head over heels in love with you since freshman year. Let's at least come clean about that. Our contract is over, and you have to take back this money."

A lump has lodged into the back of my throat. My heart has swarmed with two billion butterflies. I pull out the contract and look at our names scrawled on the bottom of it.

"Waiting." He sounds annoyed.

"Okay. But this is really hard for me to say," I snap. "I'm afraid."

"Don't be. I want to hear that you agree." His eyes burn into mine.

"The contract is over," I say in a rush, feeling my face go hot all over again. "But...it seems sad to tear it up. I want to save this. It's so cute. Now...how about that kiss?"

He shakes his head and shoots me a warning glower. "Don't try to distract me. Finish saying what I need to hear."

I cross my arms over my chest. "I love you. Okay. I love you, and I get it. That you love me back. Happy?"

He grins so wide the sunlight seems to sparkle off every inch of him. "Almost. I can't move one more inch," he says, holding up the envelope. "Not off this porch, not on with my life, and I will not kiss you ever again if this money is between us. Take it back."

I manage an expression that matches the seriousness in his voice even though inside I'm having a *mini-scream-for-joy-party*. "I'll take the money if you agree to play on Coach's team and shoot for a hockey scholarship."

Gray's eyes flash first with what looks like surprise, then anger. Then it changes to what appears to be hope. He nods once. "It's a fair arrangement. Provided he'll have me back."

"He will. He told me so."

"But you dump me, then I'm quitting again."

I take the envelope full of cash and shove it into my pocket. "There. Deal complete. Pucker up, *boyfriend*."

He sighs, and looks deeper into my eyes and I can sense something's still wrong.

"What?"

"What I did, freshman year...it's haunted me. Now that you've remembered, can you honestly say that nothing's changed about your feelings toward me? What if you can never forget me—what I did—what I didn't do…"

"Stop. I don't ever want to forget you being there. Never. You were afraid, just like me. And I shouldn't be mad at you for that. You stepped up. You were my hero that night, and I see that now. You stopped him. Gray…you stopped him from hurting me when I couldn't." My voice breaks and my eyes well with tears. "I can't imagine who or what I'd be if you hadn't come in that room. You saved everything. And I was wrong to say I hated you for any part of that…."

He takes me into his arms. "Shh. Jess. *Crap!* I didn't mean to make you cry. I'm nobody's hero. I don't know how to forgive myself for leaving you like I did that night. For not killing that guy. Believe me, I tried. I started a fight that got me beaten to a pulp. I attacked him and his friends first. I was like a Yorkie going up against a gang of alligators."

Two tears escape down my cheeks.

"Jess—"

"No. I have to say this. We were just kids. Fourteen. I've seen the photos of you back then. You were smaller than my sister is now! *I* was smaller than my sister is now. I—just—*thank you*. Thank you so much. For fighting for me, for not telling anyone all those years. For taking a chance when I was such a jerk to you at the interview. You're the most honorable person I've ever known. To do something like that for a girl who wasn't even nice. And I wasn't at all nice that day."

"You've always been nice. I knew you were fronting. I'm not honorable. Not like you think." His eyes grow dark and I can see he's holding back his own tears. He shakes his head. "I didn't tell you the truth at the interview. And all summer long, I've been checking you out. I've had thousands of the most *dishonorable* thoughts about your legs, your eyes, your lips, that damn peach cobbler smell, the curls that gather around your temples and the back of your neck. God, the back of your damn neck drives me insane."

"Seriously? Like what else?"

"Like wishing I could kiss you, or run my hands along your skin. And I've had those feelings every five seconds we've been together. When the whole time you thought I was just 'doing my job'."

A shaky laugh escapes me. "We're even then. I've been staring at your lips, your gorgeous gold-green eyes and your amazing smile too. And I've been loving the way you smell and your low voice since the interview. So there. You can't change my mind. You also just saved me from falling off the porch. Honorable hero, through and through. End of conversation. My parents told me how you offered yourself as a witness—"

"Crap. I'd forgotten about them. What *about* your parents? Should I start digging my own grave?"

"No. They—they're good. I told them everything. My dad almost choked Coach Williams to death in our front hallway, though."

"No shit?" Gray pales. "*Coach* came to your house?"

"It's okay, they made up. I told them everything about the contract and about you—the *real you* including your name. They're also backing me on college. If I think I'm strong enough, then I get to make the call, not them. We understand each other so much better because of all this. Don't you see? I was lost, really lost. I couldn't get myself out of what I'd become until you signed my contract and stood by me."

"That was all you…finding your own way out. But we can argue about that later, after we make-up." He pulls me close again.

"Finally," I say, puckering up my lips like a fish.

He laughs, and places a warm hand on my cheek.

I put my arms around his neck. A trail of goose bumps forms where he runs a finger along the side of my neck. His expression becomes so intense, I feel as though I've melted into a rushing green river. He leans in and I close my eyes, afraid for a moment that I'll forget what to do.

"I love you, Jess. So much."

His lips brush against my cheek first. Surprising me, making me tremble in anticipation. The warmth of his lips travels across my forehead, my temples, my neck, until finally he finds my lips. I melt into him and wrap my arms tighter, kissing him back until the world spins under my feet.

He pulls me closer and his hands move down the sides of my waist.

My body is pressed against his. He's holding all of my weight and I kiss him again until I'm floating with thousands of butterflies, tasting bits of fire on my tongue and walking on stars.

I deepen the kiss, and let my fingers tangle into his curls.

Maybe because he's already been in my dreams for so long, it feels to me as though we've always been together.

In love. Love. Love. Love.

He pulls back and all I can manage is a dazed sigh. It takes me a long time to register the details of his face. "So…that's a make-up kiss. Let's have another fight soon."

"I'm the happiest person on earth right now," he says.

"No. That would be me. You have to kiss me again. It's so— it's so…*so*…wow. And I might be holding just the smallest of grudges that you'll need to wipe clean." I lean in.

He groans as though he's in pain and his cheeks have turned bright red. "I can't. We can't."

"Why?" I aim for his lips and he sidesteps me!

"We have an audience. If we don't stop, I'm going to royally embarrass myself in more ways than one. I have no control where you're concerned. Please. People are staring us down." He shoots a pained smile over my shoulder.

I turn to look. Corey, Michelle and Gran are standing at the window grinning like fools. Michelle's actually jumping up and down, doing one of her cheers while giving me the thumbs up. "Why are they all here? Why is Corey wearing a suit? And Michelle—what's up with that flower dress?"

"I told you. We had a script. Those are the costumes. You have no idea what we'd planned to win you back. That crew was about to crash your dad's barbecue."

"Even Gran?" I laugh and smile at Gran.

She waves back with a strange looking cane.

"Especially Gran. She'd vowed to go after your dad *if,* I mean, *when* he tried to kill me."

I giggle and open the front door. "As soon as we find our phones, dinner's on my parents. Who's coming to the barbecue to help me introduce my new/old boyfriend to the family?"

Corey walks out the door, snorting his obnoxious chuckle-snort. "I thought you two were going to make out for hours. Gran says she's gone for her purse, but I think she had to rinse the vomit out of her mouth. I know I did," he adds, shooting me a huge smile and a wink. "I'm sorry it didn't work out between us, Jess. But I didn't know we were going out until today. Hope you're not mad I cheated on you with Michelle this whole time."

"I'm already over you," I joke.

Michelle, following him out, bumps his shoulder. "Yeah, because I'd have killed both of you if you didn't break it off." She shoots me a look. "If you ever keep a secret this big from me again, we're no longer best friends."

I hug her tight, and I can see she's not mad at me. "I promise. I'm sorry. And thanks for understanding."

"Already history." Michelle hugs me back.

Corey grins at Michelle and puts his arm around her. "I'm *so* gone on this girl. Has anyone noticed that?"

Gran makes it to the porch and locks the door. She looks happy, but choked up like she is not ready to talk just yet.

"I'll never forget you, *Corey Nash*," I say to Gray. He laughs and hands me the iPhone he's recovered. Gray puts one arm around me and the other around Gran before placing a quick kiss on each of our cheeks.

"I'll make sure you forget every guy but me, *Jess Jordan*. And that's a promise I mean to keep."

Oh, that voice.

40

gray

"I didn't think it could be done, but you two pulled it off." Mr. Foley pauses to survey us unpacking the last boxes for the *DigiToyTech* tradeshow. The Geekstuff.com booth is almost complete. "If either one of you want a real job next summer, all you have to do is call. It's been one hell of a good thing having you two work for me this summer."

I set down the giant titanium basket overflowing with plastic frogs and ladybugs, and start dialing my phone.

"I'm leaving you a message right now, sir. I'd love a summer job. But hopefully, you'll let me work during the rest of the year too? Percy says you always have spots in shipping for people who need a flexible schedule."

I nod at *Percy-from-Shipping* who's arranging the LightSticks. The tradeshow doors haven't opened yet, but we'd all seen the huge line of people outside when we'd pulled into the Denver Convention Center's loading dock. It's now or never for me to seal next year's job. Mr. Foley's happy with my work and running on a pre-conference high. Hopefully he won't refuse me.

"I think we could work something out. Why do you need the flexible schedule?" Mr. Foley adds, tossing me a suspicious glance. The guy misses nothing.

"Varsity ice hockey. I need to be available for games, scout showcases, anything that will help me hook a scholarship. I'm hoping for DU."

Mr. Foley grins. "That's where I went to college, son. You pull off the grades to get in to that school *and* score a spot on the DU Hockey team, then my company will match whatever scholarships you bring in. We do it for all employees. And heck yes, I'll give you a flexible schedule—but you'll have to get me DU versus Colorado College game tickets. Remember, hockey's what got you the second interview, but those tickets in my hand could launch your career," he jokes.

"Oh, I remember." I smile, shooting Jess a wink and running to help her haul a second titanium ladybug and frog filled basket to the back side of the booth.

"And that reminds me," Mr. Foley continues, "Porter, those puck protectors and your other interview product suggestions are still something I would like to consider. Let's schedule some time to revisit those before the summer ends."

"Awesome." I nod. "I'd be honored to see some of my ideas turned into products."

"*That's* what you had in that backpack?"

Jess fires one of her darkest glowers. I grin wider as Mr. Foley moves to the far side of the booth. The girl is so cute when she's making that face.

"*That's* what you never showed me?" She's ranting on. "Mr. Foley *was* going to hire you over me, and you knew it."

"He was not. The bumper stickers were way better," I argue, leaning forward to breathe a small kiss into her ear. "The job was all yours and you knew it," I add. Though she's working hard to keep her face straight I can't miss the goose bumps I've caused on her arms and the sides of her neck.

She shivers and I could swear she's staring at my lips as some twisted version of revenge against me.

And it's working.

Undaunted, I shake my head and smile, whispering in her ear again, "If you keep staring at me like that, we're both going to get fired because I'm honestly about to plant one on you in front of the boss. Later, can we trade badges so I can sigh at your photo for the rest of the day?"

"Shut up." Her cheeks turn that adorable pink shade I love. She turns to pull her basket forward a few feet and tosses her hair to the side so it's out of the way. The ends of it brush against my arm and I'm hit with a whiff of lethal peach cinnamon heaven, and I have to concede.

She's won. Killed me, actually.

It's all I can do to keep my face calm while I fight against my own rush of goose bumps and rush of other things. I meet her too-knowing smirk and retreat a few steps. I vow not to stare at her lips or get near her again until I can thoroughly kiss every inch of that cute smile away for revenge.

"This is going to be one long tradeshow, isn't it," I mutter. Bitter and already breaking my vow as my gaze consumes the small upturned corners of her mouth. "*Damn.*"

She giggles. "I love when you talk to yourself. So cute."

"*You're* so cute."

Percy clears his throat and sighs behind us. "I'm glad you worked out your problems, but *man*, are you two disgustingly annoying."

Jess giggles again and I step away before she accidentally double-destroys me. I'm two seconds from needing ice thrown on my head—or down my pants.

Mr. Foley, who'd missed all of our blatant flirting, turns and calls over his shoulder, "Jessica, Gray's product ideas reminded me of yours. Once this tradeshow is finished, we'll try to bring some of those bumper stickers to market as well. *Those* we can have in the works and heading for the website before you finish the internship. How's that sound? You guys have really upped the scale for what we'll expect out of next year's interns."

Jess beams at Mr. Foley. "You mean it? That sounds awesome. Thanks!"

She shoots me an odd look, marching over to where Mr. Foley is setting up the Macintosh computers that are for the online order kiosks. "Mr. Foley, do you think you can tell me…which one of us you would have hired for the internship? You know? If you could have only chosen *one* of us? Would it have been me or Gray? Do you remember?"

"Relentless, stubborn one," I whisper.

Jess hears me and notches her chin one inch higher as she shoots me her best smirk.

Mr. Foley stops and taps his finger on the table in front of him. "Yes. I remember."

"And?" She blinks.

I hold my breath, wondering why this hurts a little…why she cares?

"Does it matter?" Mr. Foley's brow creases as though he doesn't want to say. "It all turned out so well."

Jess, like she'd been holding her breath too, takes in a deep breath, smiles a genuine smile at Mr. Foley, and gives her head a little shake. "No. No. You're right. I never want to know. It's been perfect. Every second. I don't know why I asked."

My heart starts beating again and I let out a long breath.

Jess hears me, and sends me a teasing smirk. Then, she clears her expression to one I know is really *her*. She looks at me— into me—and smiles all the way to my heart.

I'm happy too, because I know that some of the light-blue sparkle in her eyes is connected to her love for me. She told me so, last night, over and over again. Said she likes my dimple, my eyes, the shape of my chin and, well…me! I'm the luckiest guy in the world.

She won't stop staring, but I can't look away either.

Because I can't kiss that smile until we're off the clock, I return it and add in a slow wink that causes her cheeks to turn pink.

She also admitted that she loves my winks.

Well, I love making her blush.

the end

resources

1 out of every 6 American women has been the victim of an attempted or completed rape in her lifetime. 77% of all rapes are acquaintance rapes and only 2% of these rapes are ever reported. (14.8% completed rape; 2.8% attempted rape)*.

17.7 million American women have been victims of attempted or completed rape.*

(*From the National Institute of Justice & Centers for Disease Control & Prevention. Prevalence, Incidence and Consequences of Violence Against Women Survey. 1998.)

31% of victims develop some form of Rape-Related Post Traumatic Stress Disorder. (National Center for Victims of Crime & Crime Victims Research and Treatment Center, 1992).

The numbers here are based on USA 'reported' cases only.

The unreported, the unmentioned, & 'never told' numbers are devastatingly higher than what is listed here.

If you've experienced your own *ALMOST* or worse, you're not alone.
It was not your fault. Please report it. Talk about it if you can.
Tell a parent, a school counselor, or a trusted friend who will help you.
No matter what, please don't let what happened define who you are, take your future, or allow it to defeat your beautiful spirit.

for more information contact:

Rape, Abuse, and Incest National Network (RAINN)
National Sexual Assault Hot line
2000 L Street, NW, Suite 405
Washington, DC 20036
Phone: (202) 544-1034
Toll-free: (800) 656-HOPE (4613)
info@rainn.org
www.rainn.org

National Sexual Violence Resource Center
123 North Enola Drive
Enola, Pennsylvania 17025
Toll-free: (877) 739-3895
Phone: (717) 909-0710
Fax: (717) 909-0714
TTY: (717) 909-0715
www.nsvrc.org

National Center for Victims of Crime
2000 M Street NW, Suite 480
Washington, DC 20036
Phone: (202) 467-8700
Fax: (202) 467-8701
TTY/TDD: 1-800-211-799
www.ncvc.org

Men Can Stop Rape An awesome non-profit group I discovered after Almost launched. (One of their followers found me thanks to the character Gray Porter, stepping up.) Most men and boys would never harm a woman. This group and others like it work hard to educate men and boys, and moms, and sisters, and friends to set expectations, teach men and boys just how to take a stand, to be proud of their strength and natural protective abilities, and to be part of a partnership solution that ends violence in the world including bullying. They are especially devoted to ending violence against women. I don't work for them or anything, I just love their message. Have a conversation with a guy. Ask a guy you know *to take a stand.* Check out **www.mencanstoprape.org**
Tweet to follow: @mencansttoprape #I<3GoodGuys #loveOVERangerHEALS

These are just a few of the amazing support resources available. Sorry these resources are only US based. Wish I could list more. On most high school and college campuses there are rape crisis resources already formed. Ask, search on twitter, Facebook, or ask a friend where to look in your own country. If you feel like you need more check the Internet, Google your local rape crisis center or search the web or a local phone book in your city name and "rape crisis".

And again, ask or tell someone. It helps. It does.

acknowledgements

To my amazing family: **Tom, Kika** and **Wilson**: You suffered through many last minute trips to the burrito place because of me and this project. You held my hand every time I wavered, you edited pages (even Wilson), stared at cover art, convinced me not to quit with your notes, poems, quiet support, cute "keep-writing" crafts, and your never-ending belief in me. Seven years is a LOT of burritos, empty refrigerators, epic neglected laundry and mail piles, and even more love.

Thanks and Thanks. I love you guys so much.

To my parents, all four of you: **Louise & Louis Nelson, Chuck & Connie Powers**, my dear in-laws, **Bob & Jackie MacFarlane**, and the rest of my **awesome-huge-family** including those far away in **Canada, Italy** and **Spain**. Thanks for believing and sharing this ride with me for all these years. I love you all so much.

Please, everyone: Try to stop getting older. I do not like it.

To **Lana Williams & Michelle Major Duytschaever**: Dream sharers, writing warriors, master storytellers, story structure lovers, moms, and true friends. If we'd never met, or if one of us had quit (and I know we've all been on that fence) I would've never laughed so deeply, cried so hard or learned so much without you two in my life. I'm truly grateful for you two. Thanks for the tribunals, the 10PP, the vision boards, making me live The Secret, holding on to my heart so carefully, and reading and editing everything. Again. And again. And again. @ThrivingWriters, I love you.

To **Dawn Nash, Cathy Sheldon, Susan Clark, Erin Weller** and **Susan Offen**: Thanks for having awesome, perfectly honorable freshmen boys when I was writing this story. Your boys make up all the best that became my guy characters. You answered questions about hockey, the secret life of boys growing up, listened to pitches, rejection letters and years of babble while you gave me your constant friendship and support. And to those boys, who soon will be amazing, honorable men. Thanks for being in my life. Listen to your moms. They are as awesome as you are.

To **Sharon and Ana Rosa**, my only adult, non-writing pre-readers, and dearest friends. I could not breathe without you. **Deb W.** and **Susan B.** fearless mom-world-changers and activists. I hope this makes you proud. And to my scattered, too-busy-to-meet **book club**, and **Celtic Steps** friend-family, esp. **Cari Reha** who got me an amazing congrats-cookie once that I still think was magic. Everyone, too many to list. Thanks for seven years of your unconditional love. I love you right back. Sorry cant list you all.

Mrs. B. Reader, blogger, beautiful writer, fairy godmother. You say it was no big thing, just another day for you, but for me...I will never forget how your words & time so generously given made me feel. Thanks for spreading the *Joy* and being part of my dream come true. xo #ff **@joyousreads**

Tracie Schultz: Editor, reader, writer, amazingly patient mom of 4 boys and brave friend. Thanks for your courage, insights, time, hard work & absolute shining light through this whole long, strange process. I would not have had the courage to finish this without you. Have I said it yet, today? "I promise...it's gonna work out, and I am almost done with edits...are you?"

Cindi Madsen, Jodi Anderson, Milt Mays, Marty Banks, DeAnna Knippling, Michael Shepherd, and the beautiful friends I've met via fate and luck through **Pikes Peak Romance Writers of America**, **SCBWI**, and **PPW**: my world would have been very lonely indeed without your beacons of writing light. Especially **Cindi**, who gave me my very first author quote. #FF and read books by @CindiMadsen. #amazingwriter #girlrocksromance

A special shout-out to **Giovanna & Elmer Mercado**, my other parents. My sanity. My friends. Without you two, and your deep love, I would have no success, no prayers said for me at lunch and probably, no garden wars.

To the girls from **www.YAromance.com**. My readers. My confidants. My inspiration. And for many years, my only fans. You are all amazing people, writers, dreamers, artists, singers, photographers, tweeters, and poets. Thanks for reading my pages, terrifying me with your relentless critiques, and making my story ring true. **Kika, Jenna, Saoirse, Sydne, Keva, Kenzy, Kimmie & dear Masha**. Thanks for the fun, your feedback, and for helping me with this book, and the next one. xo

Geoff Foley: Friend. Technical editor, movie-maker, artist, co-dreamer, possible saint, and of course, world's best programmer. I could not have trusted anyone else. Thank you for giving me the gift of friendship and holding my e-hand when I cried (200 times). It's an honor know you.

Peter Freedman: Dreamer, gold miner, Renaissance man. Fine artist in hiding, patient teacher, friend and lover of all beauty. Thanks. #angelsAREreal #canNEVERrepayyou www.peterfreedman.com

Strider, our dear, sweetest dog. Thanks for sitting outside my office, every darn day. Your eyes never doubt me. **Best. Dog. Ever.** <3

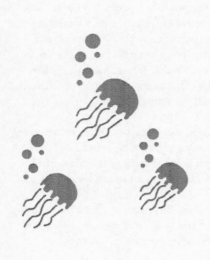

about the author

Anne Eliot lives, loves, and writes in Colorado.

For more information on her other work please visit her website:

www.anneeliot.com

2436465R00184

Printed in Great Britain
by Amazon.co.uk, Ltd.,
Marston Gate.